The Brigade

The Brigade

by Hanoch Bartov

Translated by David S. Segal

Holt, Rinehart and Winston
New York Chicago
San Francisco

Excerpts from "Don't Fence Me In" used by
permission of Music Publishers Holding Corporation,
copyright 1944 by Harms, Inc.
Designer: Ernst Reichl
8625154
Printed in the United States of America

to Yehudith

Not all incidents and characters contained herein are figments of the author's imagination. Nevertheless, actual events have been freely transformed in the process of literary narration. Consequently the author is answerable only to the characters he has created and only before them can he be called to account.

Contents

The Brigade

I Peace

We first heard of the Germans' surrender as we lay out of sight
on the far side of the slope, between the railroad tracks and
the Lamone River. There, every morning, we would loll in the
whispering shade of the olive trees unobserved, killing time till
noon when all danger was past. There we were, encamped,
though the front had long since moved far north, surging ahead,
with all motors roaring past Lake Comacchio, past the Po, on
toward Venice, with the war's end just around the corner. From
east and west, columns of tanks were rumbling into the heart
of Germany while we alone lay basking in the sun, the battle
reserve of the division, the corps, perhaps the entire Eighth
Army. Obviously, we told ourselves, even were we to race we
could no longer overtake the war. We no longer heard the can-

1

nons, not even in the still of night, and could no longer see the glow of flares and fires beyond the Apennines. The days were hot and quiet, and at night only the stars shone. The war was but a distant rumor reaching us via the walkie-talkie as though from another planet, then fleeing like a comet. In the heat of the major offensive we had been taken out of the lines, never to fight in this war again.

But military routine held its own. Every morning the commanding officers would drive the riflemen on, like Cypriotes their mules, racing them up the chalky mountain ranges, through overgrown plantations and the aftergrowth of abandoned fields. Every morning the scouting patrols would advance in front of the mobile units, while the machine-gun squads on the left covered the rifle squads flanking from the right. The troops would slither forward, spring to their feet, storm ahead, regroup, and drag themselves back the way they came, dusty, weak-kneed, soaked with sweat, as if they had just passed the final test before the real, impending battle.

It's enough to drive you crazy, the companies would grumble. It's all over now, and anyway, we were on the line, we know the score. In combat under the British you never have to hit one lousy hill twenty times a day. First the planes flatten it, then the artillery churns it up, then the tanks move in. Only after that do the riflemen enter the scene.

So the men maintained, but command of logic was not the commanders' forte. At any moment we can be thrown onto the line. As long as the war hasn't ended, it's still going on. And anyway, the commanders would add, anyway, all our battles lie before us. Onward.

So it went for those who had no choice. But we—we who were attached to headquarters, stretcher-bearers, signalmen, O.D.'s, anyone on sick call—we were free agents, so long as we didn't run into R.S.M. MacGregor or anyone else with stripes. Until noon no one could loaf; that is, no one could look as though he were loafing. So right after breakfast we would head for the shade of the olive trees in our hideout and wile the dangerous hours away.

Poker would set the wheels rolling and the others would follow his lead. From the moment he lifted himself out of the dugout beneath his pup tent and rolled up the flap, he would be busy rounding up hands for a game of poker. Generally, he could count on Brodsky, from the stretcher-bearers' unit, who played out of sheer boredom. Mushik the cook, even when he worked the morning shift, was a sure hand; if he had lost the night before, he would try to recoup his losses, and if he had won, Poker would force him to play. That morning Poker had managed to recruit Giladi from the second platoon. Giladi had sprained his leg on maneuvers, and the doctor had prescribed three days of rest for him.

As for me—I sprawled alongside, not playing or doing anything in particular. I was half listening to the voice of Bing Crosby gurgling out of Hershler's walkie-talkie, splattering on the mess-kit top that served as a crude amplifier, and bouncing back at us tinnily, and half abandoning myself to monotonous, snail-like introspection. I knew very well what I did not want to think about and whenever I did I pushed the thought away and turned to something else.

Giladi. What was such a strait-laced fellow doing playing poker in the morning? His glasses were thick and the skin beneath them folded, slack and pale. I had heard that he had been one of the leaders of the rebels, the men sent to the guardhouse for refusing to put our Palestinian insignia on their caps, an insignia that looked like a two-shilling piece. His quiet, softspoken manner just didn't fit in with sitting down to a card game.

But maybe I was fooling myself. Maybe I had no idea of right and wrong. Giladi looked like a bank teller to me; no, like a grammar teacher. According to what people said, though, he was the leader of the protesters who wound up in the guardhouse—and all of them were Sternists. But there he sat, weighing every card, his face giving no indication of winning or losing. Damn it all—how could he even sit down with Mushik the cook with his face like a peeled beet, eyes like jelly, short, stubby fingers. . . . But what did I know of Giladi if such people were his friends? Maybe stinking Poker who slept in his overalls, and Mushik, who had already been caught with a kit bag full of canned goods, were not as I had pictured them.

Ah, let them alone, I told myself, wondering how long I

3

would have to wait till the supply truck came back from Forlì and how long it would be before I knew whether I had received a letter. Forget about the letters, I warned myself, the ones waiting for me when I got back from the hospital and any others that might patch it all up again. Forget it. Forget it. Not everyone can be as methodical as Bubi Meinz and his girl, who numbered their letters and spared themselves all the doubts gnawing away at me.

My eyes turned toward Bubi, leaning against the trunk of an olive tree, the walkie-talkie separating him from Hershler. What a good-looking guy. It was enough to make a man jealous. If only I were like him, I thought again, aggravated; I would have very little to worry about. His long curly hair, his square, jutting chin, his eyes lighting up his face like sunshine. There must be something in what they said, that he was half German—even to his tightly closed mouth and his stubborn silence broken only by a daily letter to one girl. The hair rippling over his tranquil arms.

But let Bubi alone, too, I thought. Yesterday's letters weren't so bad if only I would unwind and stop reading between the lines, like Noga asked a thousand times. After all, hadn't the unit been shunted from place to place? And me, shipped from one hospital to another, with a damn case of German measles, and then finally to Pesaro, to a recuperation camp. Couldn't it be that my letters had not yet reached her? Sure, and most likely just because she was so worried about me she was wracked with doubts until she finally wrote that strange letter that I was still young and my life hadn't begun yet and why tie myself down and it would be better if I took advantage of what I came across and should consider myself free of all promises and obligations, etc., etc.

Something that felt like a rubber ball choked my throat and a wave of self-pity swept over me. Really now, who could believe such honey-coated altruism? As though I didn't know what the world was really like, how men and women alike hide behind polished phrases—anything so as not to appear as they really are. *It's very clear, dear girl, very clear: you're sick and tired of waiting; and maybe you might have waited, too, if it were for someone or something, if all that had passed between*

4

us had not been one huge mistake from the start, one of millions of wartime love affairs that start in a canteen of soldiers and nurses and pious seminarists, complete with pressed uniforms and a burning love of the homeland, and wind up in a letter like this, saying that you are still young, and I am not good enough for you, and good luck, and wet tears, and I will remember you forever and if you can, please do come to my wedding.

Let Noga alone, I thought, forcing myself back to the placid morning, to the murmuring shade of the olive trees, the sky spreading over with mist, and a pervading, pleasant odor like washday in our courtyard. The music of Glenn Miller's orchestra spilled out of the walkie-talkie. Everyone was wrapped up in himself, as though we were not in the same war. Hershler had brought his walkie-talkie with him for our sake. As for himself, he had no time for nonsense. His head resting on his palms, his elbows wedged against his raised knees, he was preparing, as ever, for his matriculation exams.

We had both enlisted on the same day; his serial number was one digit lower than mine. Since then we had gone through a great deal. We had stood guard over an explosives depot in Wadi Sarar, factories in Kurdenai, and the enormous camps of Tel-el-Kabir. Then we went to Italy where I became a stretcher-bearer and he a signalman. Rumors were flying that God only knew how many more years we were to serve, either in Europe or in the Far East, but he constantly dragged his kit bag full of books around, preparing for the university. And he knew exactly what he was going to study—geology.

He raised his eyes from the page for a moment, then let them fall back again. He was always pressed for time. He had been a top ranking student in the Classics Gymnasium of Budapest (or Prague, maybe) before he had emigrated to Palestine with Youth Aliyah.* I think he had been educated in a religious institution, or that he himself was somewhat religious. He ate no bacon or ham. He was such a stickler for neatness and cleanliness he could drive you crazy. And he was getting ready for matriculation. He knew by heart all the rules of Latin grammar

* Youth rescue and rehabilitation organization.

5

in verse, and Bialik.* It was a risky thing to exhibit the least sign of friendliness toward Hershler. Just suggest that he spend the evening in Rome with you and at once he would drop his books and drown you with gratitude until you didn't know where to turn to escape him.

It was his bad luck that had gotten him into our company, most of whom were seventeen-year-olds afraid they would miss the war if they didn't latch onto its tail end, Palmachniks who had grown sick and tired of the Palmach,† high school students fed up with their studies, *kibbutzniks* who excelled at basketball and *moshavniks‡* with arms like wagon shafts. Such was Hershler, who had joined us that morning, bringing his walkie-talkie along for us, even though he needed quiet for his studies. He had come over to me. I knew that he rubbed Bubi the wrong way, Bubi, leaning against the same olive tree, who had also been a ward of Youth Aliyah—but what a difference.

I felt carefree and relaxed, sunk in the dry warmth of the morning and all my surroundings, and that sweet sadness, without beginning or end, that was myself. Just then, at the very moment that Bing Crosby's voice was dripping into our ears— "I want to go where the West commences"—the song was cut off and an overwrought baritone voice announced in English, with an American accent, that a telegram had arrived that very moment: so many years and so many days after the outbreak of the Second World War—it had come to an end. "It's all over —over here!" *Here,* he repeated with emphasis, to let you know that there was still the Western front. And there were still the Japanese. Further details would be broadcast as soon as they came in, he said. Right now we ask Bing's apologies and return to where we left him: "Tra la la la, until I lose my senses, Don't fence me in . . ."

Just so—I still recall the moment vividly—the Second World War came to an end. Strange: a war should end on a field of slaughter, amid shattered bodies, smoking tanks, snorting

* Poet and prose writer; one of the giants of the renaissance of modern Hebrew literature.

† The Palmach was the commando division of Israel's pre-State, clandestine army.

‡ *Moshav*—a freeholders' settlement.

6

horses and a mammoth groan cleaving the world apart. But we lay in a tranquil field of early May on the northeast slopes of the Apennines, with no one to make us rejoice, or tell us that this was no simple moment in time's flow, one of many waiting for ages to appear, preceded and followed by a stream of other moments. No, this was the one, the only moment that we and our youth could never reclaim. We were all silent. Hershler raised his head from his book, as though ready to spring to his feet.

"It's over, guys! The war is over!"

"It's over, it's over," said Poker, without taking his cigarette from his mouth. "Hot shit."

Hershler sat down again and looked at Bubi. Bubi kept quiet. So did I. I felt the same as Hershler, but like him was afraid to look foolish. What were we so tight-lipped about, why didn't we know what to do with this moment we would never see again?

From the other side of the bivouac we heard voices, Tamari's above them all. He, too, it seemed, had not gone out to the field. Suddenly he burst into view from the other side of the slope, in his hand the clipboard he constantly carried with him so he could have something on which to rest the damn "War Journal of the Hebrew Soldier" he was writing every day. Maybe he had dashed up to the top of the hill so he could have a place to shout from. At any rate, as soon as he saw us he ran straight at us, waving the clipboard and the notebook, panting, cumbersome, white-haired; only his cries were childlike. "The war's ended, boys! . . . Hur-rah! . . . Get up, boys, peace has come, peace. . . ."

"Fine, now we can play in peace. Brodsky, deal!"

Strange as it seems, not one of us stirred. It all happened in the wink of an eye. Tamari, as suddenly as he had burst upon us, stopped dead in his tracks. His eyes—those young eyes ever burning with a black fire, the fiery knowledge of what is important, meaningful, necessary—clouded over with gloom. Two deep slits appeared between his thick, bushy eyebrows. Without saying another word he turned abruptly and went back down to the bivouac, dropping out of sight. I knew I wanted to get up and run with him.

7

But on the other hand, why all the fuss? I hadn't won the war. Besides, I was choked up with nostalgia, distressed that everything had already happened and that I had accomplished nothing.

Not so. In a split second everything flashed before my eyes: the outbreak of the war, just when I became *bar mitzvah,* then that night at the wedding when they filled me with wine and I roasted all the pikers who shirked service, and afterward, when I dashed off into uniform, to guard duty, to the wastelands and finally to the front, where I spent half the time in a hospital sick with the German measles. No, no, it all should have been different. I should have wailed in agony for those six childhood years that passed me by, wailed at taking leave from those years —if leave them I did. Why were we lying around like logs?

"Paralyzed or something, Brodsky? Deal!"

Only a few seconds had passed. The radio played on, the olives did not dance on the trees and though our brains were buzzing, no feelings burst out to the surface.

"Count me out."

Giladi threw down his cards, raised himself on his palms and stood up.

"What do you mean, count me out?" yelled Poker. He had a rasping, smoke-eaten voice. Whenever he was that worked up, you knew he had a great hand or that he was bluffing to the end. "You don't leave a game in the middle."

"Don't be a child. The war is over."

"So they tell me. You might think that till now you'd been shooting with cannons. Sit down and finish the game."

"I'm very sorry. Not now," he said, turning to go.

"What kind of man are you, Giladi? There's more peace in those lousy tents than here? When you play, play!"

"Maybe we really should go down," Mushik mumbled half-heartedly.

"What's down there, Mushik, you *schmuck?*" Now Poker vented his spleen on the cook. "You think they'll pin medals on us down there? They'll grab us to dig a new latrine. A man has to know how to lose decently, too, Giladi."

But Giladi no longer heard him. He had left for the bivouac

8

and had dropped out of view. Now we were all on our feet, Bubi, Hershler, Brodsky and I. Poker went on cursing out all that had ruined the game for him, just when he had a wild card, but he was only railing to banish the strange silence that could no longer be broken.

2

Below, among the low pup tents, alongside the farmhouse which served as battalion headquarters, in front of the kitchen, in the transport platoon—everywhere, soldiers were congregating. Nothing could trigger the cry of peace coiled tight inside us for years. The men stood around talking as in weeks past, each advancing his own pet theory. We'll be an occupation army in Germany five, ten, twenty years. No, that never. They'll send us to Burma. The British would like that, us rotting in the jungles. One thing's sure, peace or not, they'll be in no rush to ship us home. No milk and honey for us.

But all that was said was as nothing compared to that underlying gray sadness that stifled all rejoicing—a fear that the good news had cast over us, a fear that no one named yet existed nonetheless. This joy was not ours, peace was not ours. Not ours.

I took off for my tent. Brodsky went with Mushik to the kitchen to hustle a snack, but I wanted to be by myself for a while, to look over the airmail letters one more time. I slid into the pit we had dug beneath the tent flaps—two ledges for sleeping with a deeper section between for our legs. I sat down and pulled the letters out of the pocket of my fatigues, folded at the head of my bed. The dainty, confident script plunged me anew into depression. That delicate, beautiful Hebrew penmanship, etching an ever deepening estrangement; and even the English handwriting of the military address showed her maddening dual personality—rounded script, but pointed; fragile, but razor-sharp. What more was there to read? What could I hope to uncover if everything was crystal clear, clear as all that was changing there, so far away, constantly. All the

9

signs were there. The plural form. "All of us here worry about you." "The Yishuv* is proud of you all." "The papers are full of stories of your bravery." And there were more signs. Why, in both letters, did she simply sign off "Yours," instead of "With love," or "With kisses"? These things are never accidental. Something had happened. It had to happen. What difference what she wrote?

I stretched out on the blankets and closed my eyes. I had to take sick right on the line—as though it weren't enough that I had been made a stretcher-bearer, a porter protected by the Geneva Convention. I came down with German measles. I told them I was healthy, that the fever would pass. But the regimental doctor sent me in an ambulance to the field hospital in Faenza. There they took my temperature again and sent me to Forlì and from there to Ravenna. "Why do you take a man with a little fever and rush him from one place to another?" I asked the British nurse, but instead of answering she merely indicated I should undress. It was already late at night and only one electric bulb lit up the dark hall, crammed full of American field beds. It seemed to me that this, too, was simply another sorting room. Men came in and went out. The wounded and sick were carried on stretchers. Bandaged heads. Torn clothing. Everything reeked of hospital smells, salves and medication, and I was the only one there with a child's disease.

I sat on the field bed until the nurse passed by again and yelled at me. My whole body was on fire and my eyes closed of themselves. Without seeing anything I took off my clothes, crawled into the pajamas and lay down between the thick wool blankets, without a sheet and without a pillow. Maybe I really was sick, for at once I was floating in a black cave, in a dry, burning well. I was running with sweat, and nightmares seized me, one after the other, each suffused with the odors of war books I had read in my childhood. Remarque. *Hell. The Army Behind the Iron Thorns. Katherine Becomes a Soldier.* Lysol, carbolic acid, gangrene and shit. Shit. In my troubled sleep I sensed how the stench was surrounding me, saturating me, drowning me. I awoke with a start. It was still night. Everyone

* Jewish community of Israel (then Palestine).

10

was sleeping in the dark; only the scant light of the lone electric bulb shone from the hallway. My mind was clear and cool, but the smell, a strange smell, was still in the air all around me, in the bed, in the blankets, in the pajamas.

My pajamas had been fouled, I realized in a panic. I threw off my blankets and stepped out of bed, mortified. I did not call for the nurse, so as not to draw anyone's attention to me. With legs spread wide apart I waddled to the corridor, where the dim light was all but buried between the cracks and the dark walls. I saw only a few stretchers and notices warning against talking and venereal diseases. I stood by myself and examined the pajamas that had been taken off, so it seemed, by another soldier, perhaps a very short time prior to my arrival at the hospital; they had been mistakenly left on my bed. The shirt was completely fouled; it was filthy with dull streaks that had been absorbed by the gray cloth. Not me, another soldier, I reassured myself, but I immediately pictured in my mind what that other soldier must have looked like and a shudder of fear went through me like an electric shock. I shouted for the nurse, but my voice trailed off in the emptiness of the corridor. I was afraid to cry out a second time, for it seemed as though I were trapped in a lost, long forgotten moment, a baby who had made in his pants. I was even too ashamed to look for the washroom, but I could not stay there that way all night.

I went back to the room, silently got undressed, and lay down naked between the strange blankets—and who knew what was woven between their hairy threads—wide awake, waiting for the morning, without being able to know it when it finally came since the windows were sealed off with bricks and sandbags and blackout shades.

Even now, in the pit we had dug for ourselves beneath the pup tent, the burning shame coursed beneath my skin. Then, in the morning, I blurted out to the nurse what had happened; but her cold, British eyes did not conceal her thoughts. I had won her contempt, even though she brought me a change of pajamas and walked me to the washroom with professional solicitude. I myself experienced fresh doubts; I desperately sought to escape from the withering glances of the nurse and from all

11

the truly wounded lying about there. I was overjoyed when that afternoon I was moved to a different hospital.

I lay in Rimini for a few more days and read André Maurois' *Ariel*. The book had been sent to me many weeks before, at a time when Noga's letters arrived daily, but since it had made its journey by surface mail, it arrived only then, like a straying echo of voices vanished long ago. I knew why she had sent me precisely the biography of the young poet, even as I knew why she had previously sent me *Madame Curie*. The ludicrous situation into which I had been thrust now launched me into a world of fantasy. What a life of poetry and love, stormy emotions and self-sacrifice one can live. How I envied the life of Noga, slipping from between my fingers, when both of us could have been flying off together to a different life, to that of those rare souls who yearn to be consumed in the fire of great and mysterious deeds.

The low tarpaulin flaps blazed above my head, and I lacerated myself with all that might have been, with all the hopes gone awry, with these two letters that had been waiting for me upon my return to the regiment, stamped with all the postage marks of my long journey from the regiment and back again. Impatiently I had fled from the convalescent camp and, hitchhiking, hurried as fast as I could to get back in time for something, if only the last day of the war. But a different task awaited me—a trip to the military cemetery, to help bury two comrades shot by snipers of the German rearguard in that last assault I had missed by one day. The battalions occupied the tops of the conquered hills. Behind them lay the river and before them the broad plains reaching out to the Po, but the front no longer existed. There were only two airmail letters that made it quite clear that Noga, too, was gone forever. While I was still journeying back to Noga's room, hidden among the pines of Jerusalem, Brodsky returned, carrying under his shirt a tin of Bully Beef he had frightened out of Mushik. By now the din of the companies coming in from the field in honor of the great event was inundating headquarters. For a moment the noise seemed like a genuine celebration. We raised the tent flaps and sat down to eat Bully Beef and bread.

Only then, when all the soldiers had returned to their tents, was Freedberg found dead in his. He lay on his back in the pit, barefoot, his big toe caught in the trigger guard of his rifle, his head split open and drenched with blood.

After some time we all agreed that this peculiar coincidence did not signify what we thought it did at that first terrifying moment. How could Freedberg have known, the night that he shot himself, that at ten o'clock the next morning the war would come to an end?

After he died we all agreed that Freedberg had been destined for such an end. He was a very strange man, everyone recalled —even in his volunteering for the army and becoming one of us. He was tall and broad-shouldered, but nonetheless had nothing of the soldier about him. Though tall he was bent, though broad he was rounded, and his face was as pale as a stay-at-home's. Even his gray eyes seemed too heavy for him to bear, about to sink into their sockets. On parade the sergeants would yell at him to lift his head up and keep the rhythm, for somehow he would always be one half-step behind —in marching, turning, or presenting arms. All this was said in retrospect, as Freedberg had been one of the true volunteers. He always tried to be an exemplary soldier: before we entered the lines he posted on the battalion bulletin board a long poem, "The Army of Redeemers." It gave us all a laugh since we knew what kind of a soldier he was. Only after he committed suicide—and in such a way, out of the blue—did we begin to ask each other about Freedberg, for until then it was as though he had not existed. His death alone gave meaning to the story of his life, whose details were put together only then.

It seemed he had volunteered at the very outset of the war and had been among those Pioneers who managed to serve in France and then fled via Dunkirk. After a while, he was sent back to Egypt in a mixed commando unit that fought in Ethiopia and was disbanded after the return of the emperor to Addis Ababa. However, it happened that in his fourth year of service he found himself once again in a company of new recruits in Sarapand, marching again on the drilling field, lagging behind the young recruits by a half-step, painfully struggling to carry out every command. Only once did I hear him actually

13

speak, and then he gushed. It was in Rome, in the Vatican, on a Saturday. We—the youngsters—were walking about wide-eyed and open-mouthed at the sight of all the ivory and gold and frescoes and ancient books, stunned by the massive treasures stored up in these endless halls and corridors. But Freedberg (how had he come to be among us?) knew what he saw and with astonishing clarity explained all that he, too, was seeing for the first time. He knew everything from books. He had studied—so he told us—medieval history and had specialized in the history of the Roman Catholic Church.

On that Saturday in the Vatican, his surprising revelation only served to corroborate our view of him. But now that he had been found dead, all that had been known about him seemed very peculiar; surely these few superficial facts somehow had to contain some kind of explanation; why, in God's name, had it happened? Was it simply because his tentmate had spent that night in the guard tent that he seized his first opportunity alone in the dark pit, in utter loneliness, to put an end to his life? Why on that particular night? After a while we calmed ourselves and gradually wrote Freedberg's death off as an unhappy accident. But it was not so at that moment when the news spread through the battalion. Accident, fate or omen—we could not escape the thought that this was the morning after the war. And how was it no one heard that lone shot? That's what bothered us.

3

The troops began drifting onto the highway to Forlì as soon as dusk fell, without passes and with no questions asked. I did not know what to do. I was in no mood to be dragged to the city with the rest of the herd—how long could you stretch your legs in that godforsaken town, drink beer in the Naafi, stroll by the Fascist monument, see a movie, go back to the Naafi to take in the canteen review, drink beer, mill about on the desolate plaza? But then again, I was in no mood to stay behind in the empty bivouac. I was even afraid, you might say. Had others come to drag me off, I wouldn't have put up a struggle,

14

but where was I to find such buddies? During my two years in the army I had palled around with a few fellows but made no real friends. And not only in the army—from the day I had been wrenched from the circle I had grown up in I did not have a friend.

At fifteen I had become a worker. My head was awhirl with ideas hammered home in the movement: not everyone is cut out to be an egghead; workers are the salt of the earth. I would work and study both. I began making the rounds from one war project to another, my co-workers, laborers who had suddenly come up in the world after long years of crisis on the *moshava*, after longing daily to "get settled," after days or weeks of un-employment. My fellow workers were not at all as I had pictured them when I dropped out of high school; but I even lost my old friends, as soon as their matriculation tests drew near. Life is a raging sea, we had written one another in our class albums, and only he who rows with a will can reach shore safely. I rowed on alone, brazenly, stoically, but my boat filled with water and only went in circles.

Desperately trying to recapture what I had light-headedly cast aside, I cloistered myself behind the dusty windows of our narrow apartment and studied incessantly, utilizing every hour not spent in the factory; but in so doing I only drove away my friends more quickly. All of them won their diplomas, and I fled to the army to begin anew once more. I groped about in a barracks full of strangers, many wandering blindly like myself: thirty-year-old idealists, deserters from Anders' Army, drop-outs from the border patrol, *kibbutzniks*, rejects of the land who, until then, I had not known existed. No doubt it was my fault that here, too, I could forge no lasting links. No sooner would I strike up a fragile friendship with a few soldiers of my age and temperament than the units were reorganized. I began to feel more and more that I was fated to be constantly up-rooted. No sooner would I begin to strike roots than either I would rush off or someone else would send me packing. Now everyone was heading for Forli in the tumult of victory, but I was unable to suppress the tumult within myself. I had to do something, move out, spend the day somewhere else.

"*Yebyuhamut!*" Brodsky cried out heatedly as he stood before the tent, peeling off his work clothes as though they had caught fire. "Why should we stink up the camp? Come on, let's move."

I knew I would go with Brodsky from the start. We were so unlike each other that we made a good twosome. We occupied the same tent, helped each other and left each other alone.

"Not to Forlì," I said.

"Where else, then?"

"Once we went to Cesena. There's an opera there. We saw *Madame Butterfly* at a matinee."

"Opera? Do Uzbekis go to see *Madame Butterfly* in Tashkent? Opera . . ."

"Where to, then?"

"Maybe to Bologna."

Brodsky only mentioned the city by chance. But the prospect fired his imagination. "Come on, let's go to Bologna. It's open now, isn't it? To Bologna, Elisha. *Yebyuhamut!*"

"Okay."

Every suggestion was okay even though Brodsky's eyes were not lit up on my account. Bologna, at any rate, was fresh territory, the city that only yesterday lay behind enemy lines on Route 9. But now peace had come to Italy. One could go out onto Route 9 to thumb a lift anywhere. Imagine!

We walked along the graveled path of the railroad track. The bridges were still destroyed and the trains were not running. Ruined houses and abandoned farms lay on both sides of the track. But it seemed that day that we already heard the sound of the owners returning, that the trees were shaking off their dust and that the ruins looked different than they did before. In a skimpy garden, near the road, a farmer stood hoeing a patch of gray earth. He wore black pants, a faded striped shirt, and a black scarf. The black hoe struck between his bare feet, and his face and arms were as sooty and time-eaten as his clothes. Where had he been all this time—hiding nearby? Or had he returned that very morning from afar? His black clothes, ragged as they were, seemed festive. We stood at the crossroads, not taking our eyes off the man. Though he spied us at once, he waited a while until he could pretend to discover us. He straightened up, took off his scarf, smiled, and bowed low. When he saw we didn't intend to bite him, he moved toward us and asked for a cigarette. Brodsky put him off with a coarse gesture.

"*Grazie,*" said the farmer stepping back, ready for anything. "*Grazie signori!*"

I don't know what possessed me, but suddenly I shouted at him, "*Finita la guerra! . . . Basta. . . . Finita! . . .*"

The farmer was gaunt and his back was somewhat bent. Again he removed his scarf and scrutinized me for a long time, without altering the smile that flickered over his grooved, blackened face.

"*Guerra!*" I repeated. "*Finita! Ojee Tadeshkee kaput. Pace. Pace.*" Only then, to please me, did he nod his head up and down; but his smile turned strangely sad.

"*Bene. Justo!*" It seemed that he had done his duty by saying those two words. But suddenly he unleashed a torrent of speech we could not comprehend. Again he stepped toward us and now it was obvious that I had to offer him a cigarette— maybe a whole pack. But because I lacked the stomach to face Brodsky's ridicule and the farmer's gushing gratitude, I let him give up hope and go back to his work.

The afternoon was slipping by as we stood on the crossroad and the few cars that passed us did not stop. Just because of that I was determined to get to Bologna, come what may. I recalled that on my way back from the hospital, the week before, I had found there, alongside the road heading to the town, a flourishing cherry tree. We walked along the road looking for it.

"Here it is! Kirschenbaum!" cried Brodsky jubilantly. He was not tall, and generally he was very niggardly in his movements, but now he sprang onto the stone fence, grabbed hold of the tree, and began plucking away, filling his cap with cherries. "Do you know why I love *kirschen?* That's my name—Kirschenbaum!"

"How did Kirschenbaum become Brodsky?"

"They had an extra Brodsky in the Jewish Agency so they gave me his papers. When I fled from Anders."

17

"But didn't everybody get Hebrew names—Ben-Chaim, Amichai, names like that?"

"Right away they saw a Hebrew name would fit me like tight shoes. Anyway, what's the difference—Kirschenbaum's nothing and Brodsky's a bigger nothing. The main thing is to eat *kirschen*, Elisha . . . and you were always Elisha Kruk, hah?"

Those confusing questions. As though I were to blame. I nodded my head.

"Anyway, as far as I'm concerned my family was wiped out before they made me a Brodsky. What's the difference?"

I was happy when a staff car arrived and put an end to the conversation. You get used to a queer fellow and his name, it seems that you've really figured him out, and suddenly he's got a different name, a different genealogy. Brodsky, too, resumed his usual mask and slapped me on my knee. I already knew what he was going to say. "Today you're coming with me, my boy. We're throwing you a party—victory celebration."

"We have an agreement, Brodsky."

"No agreements, today—canceled. We're living it up, sonny boy."

"You go on ahead and I'll wait for you in the Naafi till you're finished."

"I'll grab you by the pants, Elisha. It's peace today."

And without a second's delay, to the delight of the Indian driver, he began to sing boisterously with the strange gaiety that had taken possession of him. "*Morze, nashe, morze . . .*"

I was drawn to Brodsky yet shrank from him, perhaps because I knew just what it was that drew me to him. In his company I could somehow be other than myself yet at the same time lord it over him, by staying purer and cleaner than him. All those Anders' Polacks were a strange lot, a filthy crew, the likes of whom I had never known until I came to Saratand. They were all foul-mouthed and knew every place by its whorehouses.

It wasn't simply that they were shameless and made a great show of everything. Brodsky, for example, when I first met him —in the stretcher-bearers' unit—looked like a sharpie you had to watch out for. He was only twenty-three or twenty-four, as I later learned, but a man's age is not only the total of his years.

18

There were no more than four or five years between us, and he was no shorter than me nor was he any weaker; but he was slightly stooped and his head was a bit too close to his shoulders. His face was lined with wrinkles, especially at the corners of his squinting eyes and alongside his jagged mustache, which drooped slightly to the left. Only when we had gone through a great deal together during months of training and the few weeks at the front did I discover his toughness, his adaptability, his cool courage, and the soldierly comradeship he would hide right up to the moment it was needed. Only then did I discover that he radiated a strange *joie de vivre* which sprang perhaps from the fact that he had already put a reality more bitter than death behind him.

He had hundreds of stories to tell, and he would toss them off as asides, each more horrible than the last, from the day he fled his parents' home until his desertion from Anders' Army in Rafiach. The fact that he needed me although we were absolutely different flattered me, for above all it pointed to a hidden stratum of his inner self. He would always belittle me and tease me with his sexual escapades. But even when he urged me to join him I somehow knew that the one day I should say, "I'm going with you," he would be surprised—perhaps even disappointed.

4

But not this time.

The road to Bologna, like all the other roads, passed through fields opening out onto a sprawling plain, ranges of trees, blazing carpets of poppies, Bailey bridges stretched alongside the debris of wrecked bridges, columns of civilians making their way north and south on carts, on trucks piled high with wood, and on foot. Gone forever was the mysterious Route 9 somewhere off in the Shangri La which the divisions were struggling to capture and all official bulletins spoke of. One of our scouting patrols reported, after penetrating deeply into enemy territory, that they had seen a tiny segment of the road, but now we were straining to see the yellow triangular signs hanging on the wires

19

alongside the route with one word on them—MINEN. German mines. Only those signs and the piles of bricks left over from wrecked bridges and houses showed that the war had been entrenched here for an entire winter. Now we were traveling in the heat of May beneath misty skies, with the earth sending up white dust. We were going to Bologna.

The staff car stopped for us at the end of the street that shot up between two rows of burnt-sienna houses fronted by colonnades. The sun beat down on the empty road and on the many domes of Bologna spared from the ravages of war. Afternoon silence. Few people. Closed stores. The ancient fragrance of the Renaissance, rather than the charred odor of our era, greeted our nostrils. There was no trace of destruction where we walked, only dark alleys and heavy pillars. At the top of the truncated hill the street led into a piazza framed by brick walls. The plaza shook beneath the vehicles of the British, the Americans, and the other nationalities of the Eighth Army. At the foot of the wall hung black curtains behind rows of photographs arranged like a formation. Wreaths of flowers wilted in the sun next to Red slogans. But it seemed that we alone were lingering here alongside the wall of executions. The piazza was abuzz with noisy soldiers, among them, of course, the Palestinians, jostling each other, querying: "What unit are you from? How are things going here? You met Jews already? There are Jews here, there are, really . . . And Germans—there are thousands of prisoners here streaming down from the north. There's no end to them, battalions, divisions; they're going to send them to Africa, to Australia, to Canada, they say. Come on, boys, let's spit in their eyes."

"First you're coning with me," said Brodsky, looking at me narrowly, white threads gleaming in his eyes.

"I'll wait for you here in the Naafi." I smiled. "I'm in no rush."

"Come with me. They won't rob you there—"

"Leave me alone, Brodsky."

"It doesn't scar you for life, *schvantz!* You'll go back to your girl friend as clean and pretty as you left her."

"Don't want to. Don't need it. I'm a child."

"You want to, but your head is holding you back. If you go

to a whorehouse, how can you stay innocent? You want to go home smelling of perfume!"

"I should go to a whorehouse just for the *mitzvah*?* No soap."

"Go tell that to the girl who sends you dried flowers. You can go; no one will know!

"What do you want from my life, Kirschenbaum?"

Taken aback, Brodsky laughed, but he flared up in an instant: "Because of that girl of yours you'll always be Elisha Kruk, but today be—let's say—Alyosha Karakel, afraid of nothing. When anyone is so scared of sinning once, it's a sign his insides are very dirty. A man needs women, that I can tell you. It's more natural than all your flowers and poems . . . and her, you think she lives only on perfume?"

Suddenly he grabbed my elbow and shoved me forward. "Come on, just keep me company so I won't be bored."

"Keep you company? How?" He had gotten to me with his last remark.

"Up to the door, Zionist . . . just up to the door. . . ."

As always when he was in a passionate, ecstatic mood Brodsky began singing one of the regimental Friday-night-gathering tunes, spicing it up with a half dozen Russian curse words, singing it over and over again—playing solitaire with epithets instead of cards. With his cap pushed back on his head and his hands stuck in his pockets, he dragged his nailed boots over the paving stones beneath the colonnades of Bologna, singing and striding forward like a man who knew where he was headed. I followed after; why I don't know.

Actually that's not so. Brodsky spoke the truth. I was possessed by black demons and even though I swatted at them like mosquitoes they never stopped buzzing inside me. What desire was, I didn't know; what lust was, I didn't know. But my thoughts gave me no rest; I could feel the blood pulsing in my eyes, clouding my vision. Not only Brodsky, but I, too, had not yet seen lovely Bologna, the city castle, the ducal palace, the lofty walls, the pair of towers leaning toward each other.

We walked along an empty street. Soldiers were not to be

* Prescribed religious act.

21

seen here and the civilians had not yet emerged from their hiding places. It felt as if we had slipped back five centuries. My thoughts buzzed on. I reread the letters I had received the day before. In a short while I was to be nineteen. I would return home to the dreary, restricting routine of the *moshava*. I had fled, fled, but had not escaped myself. I longed to take the forbidden plunge and take my punishment, thrust my hand out and get burnt just like when I scalded myself and scarred my face. Just once.

The air was humid and the only sound was that of our nailed boots raking across the pavement. Once again the execution wall: black strips of cloth, rows of photos of young Italians— round eyes, soft lips, oily hair combed back. Why had it always seemed to us that death stared out of those pictures, or that the young men seemed to be dying before our eyes? Childish, empty thoughts. There were the new slogans on the wall:

LONG LIVE COMMUNISM.
LONG LIVE PEACE.
DEATH TO FASCISM.

"Where are you dragging us to? Why this direction all of a sudden?"

"I don't know. But this is it. Count on Brodsky."

All at once the streets became narrower and we found ourselves walking through winding alleyways. Here and there an air raid had left its mark. At the corner of the street, at the entrance to a pizzeria, drunken soldiers were congregated, wrapped around each other like pretzels, roaring lustily:

"Roll me over, in the clover
Roll me over, lay me down and do it again."

Brodsky sniffed about and turned toward a narrow alleyway. The buildings with their moldy, jaundiced plaster seemed covered with boils. The houses had no balconies and the closed shutters were swallowed up by the high walls. The churches had black gates with words affixed to them with nails. Once again there were slogans everywhere: VIVA PACE. STALIN. Another turn and suddenly a long row of soldiers was stretched along the entire narrow alleyway as though lined up for a matinee.

Brodsky took off his hat and squinted with pleasure.

"Ah—*nu*, how do I know, hah? Tell me, how?"

Again he spoke the truth. Everyone was there, each man patiently standing behind the next—a Scotsman from the Eighth Indian Division, a Maori from New Zealand, Brazilians from the Fifth Army. Those damn Poles and, of course, the Italians themselves from the Cremona Brigade. Only our boys had not shown up yet. So much the better; at least there was that to be thankful for.

Brodsky took his place at the tail end of the line and I alongside him. All stood silently, eyes fixed on the wide gate framing a narrow door, half-open, where the fat, indispensable madam stood, with a face like a football, her hair in a black net. That was the set-up. No one crossed the threshold until another soldier left the house. All was patience and order until someone yelled, "Next please!" and then the obedient line would move a half-step up like a train beginning to inch forward in a railroad station. It required a good deal of imagination to connect the docile line with its goal. Don't get excited, gentlemen; don't push, there will be enough for everyone.

Astonished, I looked at myself, standing there with all the soldiers heading toward what lay beyond the gate. A half-step forward, then a halt; a half-step forward, then a halt. I was neither ashamed nor confused; even the devils inside me had vanished. I felt nothing, only a dark curiosity. No, that's not the right word. Perhaps it was like that Sabbath morning when I chanced into Pinik's room and ate a sandwich of sausage and butter; or like the time I first lit a match on the Sabbath. Something you can't stop yourself from doing, so you do it; and once you've done it there's no going back. Ham and farina for breakfast. I know why Brodsky had been able to push me toward committing the last forbidden act just that day. He didn't have to over-exert himself, for this lust had been with me for a long time, murmuring in my dreams.

When I would wander by myself, a stranger in foreign streets, it would suddenly seize me, whisper in my ear, tell me to take

23

the plunge, burst out once again from the humdrum—no, hateful—world of Father. And now Noga, too. Stand in this line. Don't budge. Just move a half-step forward with the rest until you are past the madam. After that there will no longer be a way out. Once and for all shuck this last foolish fear chaining you to all the *don'ts* rankling your flesh—just once, and they will vanish forever as though they had never been. "There's no funny business here," Brodsky said mockingly. "It's the same with all women, Uzbekis, Poles, and Italians. Exactly the same."

The first time with Noga came back to me, from the moment that we shamefacedly entered the strange hotel in Haifa. I had struggled to look very sophisticated although I'd never stepped foot in a hotel until then and it seemed that the entire city was looking at us. The whole affair was a handful of rooms on a second story above a store. The corridor was empty, the lower half of the walls was painted oily green, just like the green beneath a dripping faucet; the tiles, some of which were sunken, were reddish-brown, the color favored by butchershop owners. A mixed odor of clean laundry, decay and cookery from kitchens in the neighborhood filled the afternoon air. At the end of the corridor an old woman appeared, tying her dressing gown as she sloughed along in her slippers. She looked at us with weary eyes as though we had brought misfortune upon her, took a hairpin out of her mouth, and gathered her frizzled hair together. "Yes?" she said.

"Do you have empty rooms?" I had hoped she would refuse us at once and spare me the questions I already had read in her tired eyes, moving from me to Noga and back again.

"How many rooms do you need?" said the old woman as she went to the reception desk, behind which hung the panel of keys. "One room," I said in a loud voice, knowing I could no longer conceal my burning ears from her gaze.

"Then why do you ask for rooms?" said the old woman, not letting up. She continued to arrange her hair, one eye on us and the other on the keys. What is she imagining, what is she thinking about the tanned youth in uniform and the small girl in a blouse and sandals, a girl who looked even younger than she was? When would she start lecturing us? I tried bra-

24

vado to cover up my confusion. "I asked for rooms because I didn't want to take your last one."

"So," said the old woman, "you're a smart young fellow, soldier. You have a very smart boy friend," she said, turning to Noga, who all this time was trying to shrink out of sight.

"I'm not her boy friend, I'm her brother. Show us the room." I had thought up this ruse from the first moment we had started out on our trip. After all, they might ask for proof that we were married. But at that moment I threw the sentence out unthinkingly, needlessly. The old woman took a key, turned toward one of the rooms, opened it, and walked inside without turning her head. We went in after her. The shutters were closed and the darkness was cool. It was a spacious, high-ceilinged room with two narrow beds and a table in between. In a moment the door would close behind us and we would be alone for the first time in a room completely ours, without the Jerusalem stares of Noga's parents, without the tension of rendezvous in alleys and stairways.

"Okay," I said. The old woman said nothing, turned on her heels, and shuffled out of the room to the reception desk. Noga remained in the room while I followed. The old woman pointed to the open register and told me to write our names. She asked for no documents, only that I pay in advance. "You're both staying here tonight, too?" she asked. It was already obvious that I wasn't fooling her, and what she thought of us was also obvious. . . .

"I'm leaving," I said to Brodsky.

"Come here, Elisha." Brodsky grabbed my hand and tried to pull me back to the line, which had grown shorter in the meantime. We were already near the gate and the fat woman whose double chin rested on her black sweater. Snake-like the long line of soldiers stretched out behind us. This endless snake entered into the women beyond the gate who absorbed everything in an unbroken rhythm like machines.

"I can't."

"Don't be a *schmuck*, Elisha. It'll be good for you, take it from me."

"I'll wait for you in the pizzeria around the corner."

Suddenly I experienced a glorious feeling of victory, as

25

though I had foiled a wicked wizard. *Who is brave? He who conquers his desire.* No, that was not it. All that wonderful day with Noga and all that followed when we lay together in one bed, then moved to the other in order to fool the old woman, ourselves, our wild shyness—all of that rose before my eyes and I could not risk ruining it. I loved Noga and wanted to stay as I was, not wind up a link in this degrading chain. I wasn't interested in the letters and didn't want to think forbidden thoughts. *Ah, Noga, Noga, if you were only here to see how faithful I am, how I truly love you.*

"Wait, I tell you, *schvantz!*"

5

Half of the pizzeria lay below street level. The veil of glass beads covering the doorway tinkled and glittered at passers-by. I entered, and paused for a moment to accustom my eyes to the murky interior. I walked down three steps into the fragrance of wine and pastry and the dim light. The greenish-brown bricks of the walls and ceiling glowed dully. The small quarters exuded a soft heat, as of home and peace. That is, at first glance.

My eyes fell upon two tables at the far end of the pizzeria and the tumult of a group of American Negroes hit me in the face. Army whisky and the proprietor's steaming spaghetti. As I stood wavering on the bottom step, about to turn and leave, I was hailed in a booming voice by one of the seated assembly: "Come on over, George!"

He was the leader, leaning back slightly in his chair toward the doorway. I raised my hand in greeting and retreated one step. I'd better clear out, I thought, before I get mixed up in a drunken victory celebration. But it was too late. The man rose from his chair, stretched out to his full height like a black tree, extended two arms and ten hooks and took a giant step toward me. Though midway up the steps, with the strings of tinkling glass behind me, I felt like a dwarf. It wasn't just his height, but his proportions, too: a head like a jet-black, gleaming iron ball; eyes like phosphorous bowls; nostrils broad and

26

gaping as though all the air in the world could not fill his lungs. "Be thou blessed, our brother," the giant thundered. "Surely you would not slight a band of soldiers, fellow Christians breaking bread in this humble inn!" He came up one step and laid a heavy arm on my shoulder.

" 'Pass not away I pray thee from thy servant,' Abraham said to the angels. So the Holy Book tells us."

"Thanks, but I'm looking for a friend," I whispered. The group frightened me; but my sympathy had already gone out to the dark stranger.

"We will be your friends. We all lose friends and find friends. From now on I am your friend."

"Thanks a lot," I mumbled in confusion and came down a step.

"All of us here are soldiers, all friends, eating the first repast of peace. And I declared unto my brethren that the first man to enter this inn would be a bearer of tidings. Sit down with us, my lad."

He was drunk, he and all his friends who stood up to greet me, yet somehow that table laden high with food and drink seemed an altar prepared for an ancient rite. Later I realized where it had all come from, the roast meat, the spaghetti and tomato sauce, the relishes and chocolate, wines and whisky: the soldiers had tithed the consignment that their company, a transport unit, had moved from the port to the officers' mess. At first glance, though, that groaning board looked like something out of a fairy tale, especially when all you could expect in a pizzeria in those days was a little sour wine and brick-dry wafers. I was seated at the head of the table to the left of the leader. Plate and cup were placed before me.

"An Englishman," he said, pointing at my uniform with his bottle.

"No, I'm—"

"Wonderful." Overjoyed, he filled my cup. Now I saw that his curly hair was fringed with white and that his face was deeply pocked. He addressed the company around the table: "Brethren! I knew, I knew from the start that our Lord God would not place at the table we set, to praise and glorify His blessed name, an Englishman. God knows how to test his serv-

27

ants—ask me how well he knows—but not in this way. He
would not bring to our table, to this victory feast—an Englishman. Those sons of bitches battled mightily, ready to fight to
the last American—that's right—and to the last Pole . . . a
Pole, eh?" Now he addressed me again, clinking his glass
against mine and urging me to drain it dry. "Brothers, a toast
to the brave Polacks . . . they say the Devil, that big son-of-a-
bitch himself, would skirt your positions . . . these Polacks are
a tough bunch . . . to our young friend, the brave Polack!"

No sooner had I emptied my glass in honor of the Poles than
it was full of whisky again. I was ready to agree to everything
he said so long as he would let me leave. They spoke like
preachers, but their mad drinking was not for me. I wanted to
escape.

"Ask the Polack to say something in Polish. Something nice,"
someone called from the end of the table.

"Yes," said the leader. "It would be good to hear something
nice in Polish."

"But I'm not a Pole," I finally said.

"Then what are you?" asked the leader disappointedly, as the
protruding flesh glistening between his brows reddened.
"You're not a Chinaman, that's for sure."

"I'm from the Land of Israel," I said, showing them the insignia on my sleeve. "Palestine."

The leader's flashing eyes opened wide in amazement.

"What do you mean, Palestine?"

I explained over and over but my words fell on deaf ears.
They thought they had misunderstood me, since that place
was found only in the Holy Scriptures and had nothing to do
with armies in Italy. There had to be some other country in
the world with a similar name.

"Jerusalem!" I cried, slapping my fist against my chest. "I
come from Jerusalem. Nazareth. Bethlehem. All those places
are in my country, and my country is Palestine."

I removed the bronze insignia from my cap and showed the
leader the word Palestine in raised letters. He read the word
and passed the emblem on to his friends. They all felt it and
read it as though they were witnessing a miracle.

"Bethlehem . . ." The swollen flesh between the giant's

beaming eyes glistened with beads of sweat. His whisper was scarcely audible: "Did you really say the word that I thought I heard you say? Bethlehem . . ."

"Exactly. That is—Bethlehem is in my country. You asked where I come from. So, from—"

He erupted like a geyser, springing to his feet, smacking the table with his mighty hand so that all the dishes shook.

"Brethren, did you hear whence he came to us this day, the youth who sits at our table? Did you hear that he—bodily, even as we see him with our own eyes—comes from the birthplace of our Lord Jesus Christ?"

"Ah, our Lord Jesus Christ," whispered the black soldiers. "He comes from Bethlehem."

"A miracle!" thundered the giant, waving his hands.

"Either I'm stone drunk or this is really a miracle," whispered the soldier sitting next to me—who was really drunk.

"A miracle!" the giant thundered, laying his hands upon my head as my father did when he used to bless me on the eve of the Day of Atonement. "May our Lord Jesus Christ bless thee, our brother from Bethlehem."

"Hallelujah!" the assembly thundered in response.

"It is no simple coincidence, brethren. Someone—oh ye servants of God—someone sent to us this day this youth, this sweet Daniel, to sit with us at this holy feast, on this day when He smashed the skull of Satan, the Antichrist who said that Negroes are monkey's seed, that whoreson bastard Hitler. . . . Someone sent this youth from Bethlehem to us on a mission, that he might reveal to us something of great moment. . . . What have you come to reveal to us, our brother from Bethlehem? . . . No!" He lifted his glass and indicated to the others to do likewise. "First let us lift our glasses to our Lord Jesus Christ and to his messenger from Bethlehem who has honored us, downtrodden and wretched Negroes, on this day of victory!"

They were drunk, wondrously drunk; their eyes filled with tears. I could not destroy the joy they sought but could not take part in such a fraud. I kept quiet and drank.

"Tell us," the giant said, "did you see with your own eyes the cradle in which the Lamb of God first saw the light of the world?"

29

"How can he talk, if he hasn't drunk anything!" cried one of the assembly, and the leader again filled the glass I had just put down.

"You saw it with your own eyes!" the giant cried, nodding his head vigorously. How could I betray him now?

"I saw it."

"Hallelujah," he moaned with a shudder.

"Hallelujah," we all roared. We lifted our glasses and the black poet, pearls of sweat glistening in all the pits of his face, preached over the cup: "A red sun burst forth this morning from the womb of night and the light of peace has covered the earth, and now this sweet youth has come to us from Bethlehem. Let us lift up our glasses to peace, oh brethren. A toast of love to him that is near and to him that is far off, brethren. 'The Lord is my shepherd; I shall not want . . .' "

Now I only longed to feel the slightest fraction of Messianic fervor that swept through the pizzeria like black fire. I drank a great deal, quickly, and once more I felt like I did that night on the roof in Tel Aviv when my relatives filled me with wine and unleashed my tongue.

"Tell us of Christmas in Bethlehem!"

"Blessed be the glorious name of our Lord, the Saviour!"

"Say what you will, Daniel . . . you said that your name was Daniel?" The giant laid his hand on my shoulder.

"Daniel prayed to God in Bethlehem," one of the soldiers cried. "Tell us, Daniel."

Indeed I had been in Bethlehem at Christmas a year and a half before. In the bisected church of the Nativity, held by—which sections held it anyway? My Bethlehem was the trip that the two of us took, Noga and I, on a clear Jerusalem day from the Jaffa Gate. If they ask, I will tell them of the Sea of Galilee. About the company's work camp that summer, when I was no longer studying. I'll tell them of Capernaum, how we swam there alone, the two of us, after that night in Haifa in the hotel on the mountainside.

"Speak, Daniel!"

"Bethlehem," I began, "is a small village in the mountains of Judea. You can see it from Jerusalem. Its houses spill down the mountain slopes to the road and its hills are covered with

30

all manner of fruit—red figs, green olives, vines, wheat, barley. There is no fruit in the world that does not grow in Bethlehem." "The blessing of our Lord upon Bethlehem," echoed the leader. "And the stable, did you see that too?"

"I saw everything." And I told everything, what I had seen and whatever rolled off my tongue. My ears heard the words pouring crazily from my mouth. My mind told me to be still but my heart beat at the tip of my tongue. I had to talk, just like at the wedding on the roof, in Dizengoff Square. The eyes of the soldiers burned, and the more I spoke the fiercer blazed that fire.

"Certainly," I said. "There at the bottom of the hill, at the end of a paved courtyard you can see the stable in which Jesus was born. It has been miraculously preserved, just as it looked that day. It is overlain with fragrant straw and there a wooden cradle stands. The Church of the Nativity, built around the stable, is of white ivory inlaid with precious gems. The Church gates are made of pure gold just as the dome is, arching overhead, higher maybe than the dome of Saint Peter's. Before we left for the front I went there on Christmas Eve. The snow covered the mountains, a heavy snow, but all the clouds parted and the sky shone with millions of stars. A full moon stood in the heavens, aglow with blue lights as though reflecting all the snow covering the earth from the peaks of the mountains of Judea to the desert and the Dead Sea. Speechless I stood in the plain of Bethlehem watching the brightness shattering on the golden gates and the golden dome. Only the braying of a donkey broke the silence. Then—at that very moment—the air was filled with jubilant, glorious music. The stars, the moon, and the sea swayed like silver tongues and that harmonious sound filled the earth from Jerusalem and from Nazareth, from Mount Tabor and from the Sea of Galilee . . ."

Words gushed from me like a fountain and I drove them, like posts, into the mire of words that had gone before. I told myself I knew clearly that I was drunk, that this was only a mad game; but why was I pushing away all the other words tickling my throat, struggling to burst forth? That December moon was quite different.

Our company was guarding TNT in Wadi Sarar. I would take

31

off two or three times a week, slipping down the rear slope of the hill to the railroad station to go to Jerusalem. As I spoke, my nostrils filled with the acrid stench of urine on Jaffa Street and I saw puddles of water, shining like lepers' flesh on the slimy stones, heard the rustle of pine needles, which to me always meant a trip to a strange land. Our intoxicating night in the room of her Jerusalem home, a room the like of which I had never seen before; nights in open alleys where the wind wailed; nights on stairways, jacket to jacket, sweater to sweater; enchanted nights that never ended but were only cut short when there was no longer any choice, when I had to turn back in the bitter cold of two or three in the morning to catch the four-thirty train to make six o'clock formation at the camp's parade ground.

All this I spoke of, even though my tongue painted a Bethlehem that never existed. The eyes of my listeners flickered, blinked and closed; only my stories ignited a few last sparks in them. But even as they were going out like candles, a sense of freedom welled within me. I'm not drunk, I told myself, but I have to speak precisely to these men. When the steel band strangling me is uncoiled, when it becomes a long string of words outside me, I will rise and go. I will no longer think of what Noga must be doing this very moment in reveling Jerusalem.

"The stars," I said, "whoever has not heard how the stars of Bethlehem ring on Christmas Eve cannot understand what brought Jesus of Nazareth into the light of the world."

"Hallelujah!" grunted the giant. His head lolled on the table, resting on his right ear, and his gleaming eyes struggled to focus on me. The protuberance between his brows had turned into a huge tear. His pitted face ran with tears. His voice swathed me in black sheepskin. "Praised be our Lord, the babe of Bethlehem."

"Hallelujah!" answered the voices, drunk with revelation, from the ends of the table. How could I rob them of this vision, how could I rob myself?

"The stars," I said. "Only in Bethlehem are there such stars, whose melody is love. The stars of winter."

"The stars the Wise Men saw," whispered the giant.

32

"The star they saw in the East that led them to Bethlehem. There it stands." Why, I asked myself, why are the stars of Jerusalem lovelier than the stars of the coastal plain? That last night, before I was to return to Egypt, we sat together at the edge of the quarter. Ragged clouds stretched out from the wadi to the stars, and the turrets of the old city rose tall in the night. My hands roamed beneath her jacket, beneath her dress, seeking to memorize the curve of her narrow shoulders, the freshness of her small breasts. We swore eternal love. By the eternal city. By the stars. By the whisper of the pines. "That star, whose name is the star of Bethlehem, is seen nowhere else in the world. Only there . . ."

"*Meshugener,* what are you doing here preaching to *Shvartzes!*" *

Like a sword the voice cleaved through the cobwebs of my brain. I turned my head. In the doorway, in front of the curtain of colorful beads, stood Brodsky, his hat pushed back on his head, his face obscure. Next to him on the bottom step stood the proprietor, his hands folded across his belly, his fatty face shining with contentment. Brodsky had returned from the whorehouse, and there I was sitting and waiting for him. I wanted to vomit.

"That's not the guy I'm looking for," I said to the leader, but his head lay heavy on the table like a steel ball.

"Elisha, get up and get the hell outside. You're drunk."

"I'm not drunk."

At once I got up to show him he was wrong. I would go out to the street with head high and shoulders back and not have to tell him what I had said there.

At that instant the leader realized I had gotten up. "Daniel, our brother, do not leave us. Tell us more about Bethlehem." He stretched out his hand toward me, but I slipped out of his grasp and the hand fell feebly to his side.

"Where's your cap?" asked Brodsky. I touched my head. It was bare. I walked stiff-leggedly back to the table. It was a frightful scene. The soldiers were seated about the table with their eyes turned up; they made no sound, as though they were

* Negroes.

33

spirits of the dead. I had to get out before something terrible happened. But the cap. A soldier can't go about the streets without a cap. Through the swirling darkness I spied the beret. On the floor. I picked it up and hurried toward the door.

"Bethlehem, eh?" said Brodsky. "Can't leave you for half an hour . . ."

"Let me alone!" I fled outside to the sidewalk and began to run across the paved stones toward the colonnades, the Renaissance walls, the pure air. I only wanted one thing—not to vomit and make a fool of myself in front of Brodsky.

6

We walked apart from one another, two strangers only the army could have brought together. The whisky I'd drunk was going to work in reverse. I felt as though I had been pitched from a plane without a parachute. Down I sank as my sadness soared up to meet me, spiraling upward like thick columns of smoke. I was cold and sober, my mouth was bitter, my limbs felt heavy. If only I could find some dark nook, some secluded spot where I could stretch out flat on my face and lie motionless until the storm within me died down, until I was at peace once more, or until I faded into the darkness forever.

But Brodsky, calm and content, his hands in his pockets, walked at my side whistling softly. Brodsky was not one of those who would return at midnight from "after-duty hours" and broadcast to the whole platoon his exploits with the woman he'd spent the night with—how he handled her, how she responded and why, delivering every detail in a filthy, unbridled stream; only by sounding off, it seemed, did such men put the stamp of reality on their acts of fornication.

Brodsky was none such—but he was by no means pure-minded. Out of the blue, he would say without any equivocation, "Very sorry, going to get laid. Got to. I got the urge." He would make the announcement with a nonchalant shrug of his shoulders, unburdened by fears or doubts but with no display of passion. He had the urge, that was all. Afterward, he would walk about, hands in his pockets, whistling softly, munching cookies, drinking coffee. The woman he had just had no longer existed. And maybe she had never existed.

I tried to paint a picture of the inner Brodsky, a youth who saw his home destroyed in the war and then was forced to flee eastward, to Soviet Asia. But damn it all, why did that Brodsky have to hide behind the Brodsky walking by my side, who was only what he chose to reveal? A man who had an urge. Just as Mushik was only what he showed of himself, a pudgy son-of-a-bitch who stole his buddies' rations. What was I doing looking for hidden virtues when everything was so ridiculously obvious, simple, animalistic? Most likely I was only fleeing from my own desires, wrapping myself in high-sounding moralistic phrases to cover up those same wild fears chasing me ever since I left Father's house. I was forever straining to escape, cut all ties, change myself or my surroundings, but those damn rules and regulations were like thorns in my flesh, thorns I was afraid to yank out lest I suddenly discover I was only another kind of Mushik or Brodsky, and not—not who?

"Let's go eat," said Brodsky. "You'll feel better."

"I can't eat."

"Then come with me, I'm hungry." He said no more than that. He summed up his entire sexual escapade in two words: "I'm hungry."

We went back to the Renaissance plaza. The army traffic through the narrow streets in front of the chamber of commerce and the ducal palace was as heavy as before. Everything was one hodge-podge. A rowdy bunch of boys and girls wearing red kerchiefs came toward us, calling excitedly. *"Salud amigo!* Today we're all Reds. A new world. *Ciaou Regazza."* What's the difference, buxom girl, what you were ten days ago. Today we're all partisans who have had our fill of battles that never took place but will someday become a legend of resistance. *"Banera rosa, banera rosa!"*

Again we passed the leaning towers and the colonnades on the way to the Naafi. Why hadn't I gone in with Brodsky, instead of garbling nonsense and thinking about Noga, who was no longer mine, who never would be?

Was it just that I was squeamish, or afraid I didn't have what it takes? And what would I retain of this one day that would never come back to me again? What did I do that day? Ran to Bologna? "Why Bologna?" the boys would ask. Ha, Bologna! What do you know! There's a plaza there, like this, you see. Now there's this certain whorehouse there. And a pizzeria. And I sat in the pizzeria and waited for Brodsky, waited until he finished. And then . . .

"Come on Brodsky, let's go back."

"Already? I want to eat."

"It's beginning to get dark." I found an excuse. "And at night it's hard to get a lift."

Brodsky's narrow eyes looked puzzled, but also revealed that he, too, had had enough of the city.

"If you want to, we can go by way of Forlì. We'll eat dinner there and get a lift with a regimental truck."

"Let it be Forlì, then!" Brodsky's eyes flashed.

A misty May sunset danced on the burnt bricks of centuries past. Somewhere beyond the Apennines the sun was setting. In the morning the sun would shine from the sea, like at the rest camp in Pesaro. Brodsky was at home everywhere, ready for another round.

"Let's live it up, Elisha! Bologna's a dump!"

I didn't care where we went as long as we did not linger there or go back to camp. As long as we moved on, moved on to some other place.

"Forlì, then!"

On the wide plaza, across from the execution wall, stood military vehicles with soldiers milling about them. We wandered about the trucks. The Palestinians we had met when we first passed there had already gone and the rest of the vehicles had either headed north or were going nowhere. Suddenly we spotted the Star of David on the fender of a Dodge. Whenever we would find a Star of David it would send a shiver up our spines. Our cars, our roads—the fancied power of the weakling, the flaunted pomp of the flea. So it always was at such times, but I was doubly happy to see the insignia—a clock showing the number of the unit: 9:05. Pinik's company. Suddenly I felt as though the day's events had come full circle and that things I had never stopped imagining were now actually happening. Since the day we had arrived in Italy I had seen

36

Pinik only once, when he came to visit in Fiuggi. Before that I had not seen him since he enlisted, shortly after that unfortunate wedding.

We saw no one in or around the truck but decided not to stir from the spot. Better try our luck there than go out on the road and hope for miracles. I said nothing to Brodsky but secretly I hoped that was Pinik's truck. If only he were to appear, the hero of my long-lost childhood, I would bare my heart to him. With him you could talk, laugh and even cry—and that I understand only now, when I am no longer a child.

Brodsky and I sat facing each other on the runningboards of two trucks standing side by side. Shadows from the tall buildings darkened the entire plaza, while in the sky clouds glowed like red blossoms. Doves sailed through the bright air, sank into the darkness of the plaza, lighted on the floral wreaths, pecked and flew away. Across the way two children appeared who had stealthily crept between the wall and the rear section of the trucks. They stood alongside us, silent and patient.

Brodsky motioned to them to come near.

"Let them alone," I told him. I knew what he would do and was furious. Once, we had left the mess hall, our mess kits half full of food. Children with tin cans were rummaging around the garbage. They asked us to empty the potatoes and soup into their utensils so they wouldn't have to scoop the mush out of garbage cans. But Brodsky chased them away crudely and sent his slop splashing into the barrel. I remembered his stories of the winter of '39-'40 and could not understand his cruelty.

"Want a cigarette?" he asked the children in a gentle voice. But they were too much like him and could not be easily snared. They did not move.

Brodsky took an unopened pack of Lucky Strikes out of his pocket. He tore the wrapper and tapped the bottom with his middle finger. Two cigarettes jutted out.

"Beat it!" I was furious. I wanted to stop this sadistic game. "*Andare via! Presto!*"

The boys, experienced, did not move. Brodsky took out the cigarettes and held them out, from afar.

"*Andare via!*" I leaped from my place to chase them away, but they only backed off toward the wall waiting to see which

37

of us would win out. "What do you want from these kids, you shit?"

"To give them a present." He threw the two cigarettes out. While they were still in the air, the boys leaped to catch them. The cigarettes fell to the earth and the boys swooped down, grabbed them and turned to flee.

Brodsky took out a third cigarette and crushed it between his fingers until the tobacco scattered over the stones of the plaza. Sick bastard, I said to myself. I don't want to have anything to do with him, the pervert.

"From the day the war started I was like this. Worse, but like this. A hunk of shit."

"Kirschenbaum," I said mechanically.

"Yes, Kirschenbaum." At first he smiled wryly; then suddenly he laughed aloud, raspingly, like a creaking closet. "You say Kirschenbaum and I look around to see who you mean."

"How did you get to Anders'?"

"I was hungry. I was sick of going hungry. I'm a man of peace." His smile had leveled out, signaling the start of another abominable tale. "I'm a man of peace, but things worked out differently for me. Once—it was winter—the earth was hard as iron and the wind cut us like knives. We wanted to dig into the earth but our picks broke. That was the winter I spent with the partisans. Dead Germans we had killed were lying around. We laid them out in rows and built walls out of them with water and snow. We lived there. Two weeks."

"You lived there?"

"We lived there."

"Between those walls?"

"Between those walls. And I, my good fellow, am a man of peace. That's right."

He would have said more in that mad twilight hour were I only to have asked him. But I withdrew into a shell, frightened to peek into the tiny crack Brodsky had opened up for me. A man of peace.

Three soldiers came across the plaza heading toward the truck. No mistaking them, even in the dark, and even one hundred yards away. Most of all, the one on the left, whose likes could not be found in any other army. It looked as though he

38

had gotten his uniform together and put it on as he was walking—using whatever he found. His pants were tight and his belly pushed them up; the pants had already pulled free from the anklets and the anklets no longer met the shoes but clung to his legs like canvas bracelets. His hat was much the same; if not for his ears it would have fallen down to his chin. As he drew near we saw that he was a sergeant and he looked as though he had just returned from pioneering in Palestine. The sergeant saw us first. Looking us over he arched his eyebrows, two thatched huts above his eyes.

"Hitchhikers waiting here, eh, hitchhikers? . . . You got a lift to Bologna, eh, daredevils?"

This was no simple builder of the homeland. Arching his eyebrows, he displayed small keen eyes. Between them there descended a nose with a concave arch, narrow at the top and flattening out at the bottom as it approached his nostrils, a nose like a plow, and beneath it thin lips like a groove in dry earth. One of the true zealots, in whose presence you begin to take stock of yourself. I was ready to eat my hat if he did not ask immediately about Tamari.

Sure enough, no sooner had we mentioned what regiment we were from than we were met with the much-anticipated question: "And how's Tamari, eh, a good man, eh?"

No formality here. The sergeant's fingers, like Tamari's, were stubby. They were no doubt members of the same *kibbutz*.

"Luck's with you, boys, running into us now. And even though you don't have passes, climb on board. Hoop-la!"

"No, we're going to Forlì," Brodsky said, not giving up yet.

"What do you mean Forlì?" said the sergeant, wrinkling his eyebrows. "You're going with us. One-two. Jews, eh, did you meet any Jews here?"

"*Nein, nein!*" laughed one of the two other men, the driver, it seemed. "That's all they were looking for!"

"So they weren't looking for them, maybe they ran into them. By chance."

I shrugged my shoulders. What was there to say? I had decided to ask after my relative Pinik, partly to change the subject and partly to put myself in a better light.

"Pinik!" the sergeant flung his hands out as though he had

found a long-lost brother. "You're Pinik's nephew! Very nice. Very nice. There's a man with a soul, a big soul, very big indeed . . . so you're Pinik's nephew . . . *nu*, then jump on board young fellow and we won't tell Pinik where we found you and what you were busying yourself with . . ."

7

With the lights on high beam we traveled onward. The cold night air ripping into the open truck raised goose pimples all over us. Peace. Peace. But our hearts remained behind in that last night before we hit the front. . . .

Beyond Ancona, South African troops were riding ahead of us with their narrow-brimmed pith helmets, dusty white, their eyes opaque. They were leaning silently on their weapons while we were shouting with all our might so that the enemy might hear and tremble. In the dark we encamped in an abandoned summer resort and went down to the seashore to test our ammo. There we stood firing into the low waves until the bitter odor of burnt powder hovered in the sticky Adriatic darkness. After the firing, we cleaned our rifle barrels with boiling water and oil, cleaning and polishing them as if it were a holy task. Our headlights scarcely cut into the thick blue. In the nearby field a double row of yellow eyes flickered like a muster of scouts. In the dark and salt air of the seashore the airplane motors roared above those yellow eyes into the strange darkness, toward the war that we were fluttering to like butterflies.

Five years before—more—Mother had stood on the porch of our house. "And I wanted to visit them once," she had wept. "I'm telling you Mom," I had said to her, being all of thirteen years old, "it won't last more than half a year, you'll see." Now we were there in the wintry Adriatic dark with ground-level explosions thundering dully on the horizon. The roar of the cannons was swallowed up in the darkness like crashing breakers. It was an endless night. The new Dodges rumbled in the dark. Major Sanders personally supervised the loading of the ammunition.

Someone started a rumor that there was a movie in the town.

40

We were tired from the long journey, dusty, overwrought, and we knew we would be getting up at two or three in the morning to go out to the lines while it was still dark. Who'd want to sleep on such a night? We piled all our gear in one room, and went out to look for the movie. I asked Bubi Meinz to wait for me a minute, but by the time I'd gotten back to the road he'd already taken off with Leizi. I called after them but they had disappeared into the darkness. Hershler said that Bubi had gone with Leizi and a few other soldiers. "Come, the two of us will go," said Hershler.

Hershler talked the whole way, but I kept quiet. I could not stop thinking about Bubi, who had promised to wait for me, but had taken off with Leizi, that gawky, pimply-faced guy from Mikveh Israel. Hershler said, "From the day we set sail on the Danube in a rickety riverboat I dreamt only of this; that one day I would come back to Europe through the battle lines. My life's dream is being fulfilled."

It irked me to have to listen to such pathetic gabble, especially from Hershler, whose company I did not prize. By keeping silent while he bared his soul I was making a hypocrite of myself. "Beat it," I wanted to yell, "leave me alone, how can you say such things?"

But Hershler continued: "Kruk, I'd like to ask a favor; I know you'll do it." (Here he clasped my hand between two moist palms.) "I have a relative in Jerusalem, in the new Beth Israel. If anything should happen to me at the front, write her a letter and send her my personal belongings. The army will send them, but maybe you could keep an eye out—"

Powerful headlights rushed at us, lighting up the truck and the fields alongside the road. Bright lights followed right behind us, too, slicing off the miles like sheaves of wheat. *A Diaspora Jew, this Hershler: they make a spectacle out of everything—kisses, oaths, clasped hands.*

But everything was over and done with. Beyond the hills, flares soared like comets, tracer bullets silently pursued one another in thin red lines. Sounds of mortars and Bren guns assailed us: the troops were using up the left-over ammunition. Good times—but what a lousy feeling inside. It all turned out so differently from what I had imagined, from what I

41

had drunkenly said that night on the roof three years before. From the moment I had left the pizzeria, dizzy and pie-eyed, I was dying to tell Brodsky that story. No, not from that moment, but from the moment he had said, "I am a man of peace"; but somehow I could not bring myself to it, like a man running after a wagon but afraid to jump aboard. I would have told him while we were traveling if the youngest of the three soldiers hadn't been sitting with us. He was from Pinik's company and I couldn't have spilled out my guts in front of anyone except a perfect stranger. Brodsky was a stranger, but that soldier, a communal worker no doubt, maybe Pinik's friend, paralyzed my tongue.

The truck reached the crossroads and turned off the main highway. We rode parallel to the railway on a dusty track, bouncing from one ditch to the next. To the right, above the chalky hills of the front, batches of fireworks were exploding, cascading into rainbows, plunging into the night sky like waterfalls. The hills, the village, the tall square palace on the left, the fir trees, the ravaged spire of the church—all would glow and fade, glow and fade, as in a fairy tale.

The truck stopped in front of the farmhouse—staff headquarters—and we jumped out. Between the bivouac and the grove of olive trees a huge bonfire was blazing, bordered by the silhouettes of seated soldiers, singing. A little farther on, where we had hid that morning, I saw the source of the dazzling display of fireworks: two-inch mortars were hurling out smoke shells, the dynamiters were setting off flares, and the machine gunners were shooting off magazines of tracer bullets. Every time a flare floated slowly down, suspended from a parachute, we saw a veil of smoke hovering over the valley and caught the bitter smell of gunpowder. For the last time.

For a moment we stood there, the two of us, our heads tilted back, entranced. Such splendor I had seen only once before at the outbreak of the last offensive, before I was taken to the hospital: the bomber squadrons, the tank batteries and the canopy of flares crashing into the hills before us; the last German front, the fiery beauty of the furnace.

"I'm going to sleep," said Brodsky.

I didn't care. The hours I had spent with Brodsky seemed

ugly and shameful to me. Why hadn't I stayed behind with the rest? I had let Brodsky waste that long, irretrievable day.

"Okay," I said. "I'm going over to the fire."

From the distance it had seemed that the entire battalion had gathered there, but when I reached the circle of light I realized that the small group's huge shadows had deceived me. Tamari crouched by the fire, feeding it twigs and olive branches, boards and solar oil. A few steps behind him, careful not to get his handsome uniform dirty, stood our military chaplain, his hands spread out in front of him, singing in a sweet tenor cantorial voice, "Wait, oh wait, wait in heat, wait in cold . . ."

A few weak voices strung along with the rabbi. Tamari sang feelingly as he worked. On the ground near the fire sat Giladi and a few of his friends, singing too. Beyond the campfire other soldiers stood around a field table drinking coffee, their eyes on the bursting flares. My stomach began to rumble and whisky vapors filled my mouth. Amazed that I was not drunk, I walked over to the table to have some coffee. I spread some jam on a piece of bread, borrowed a cup, and looked for friends. From afar it had seemed that joy was ablaze in the bivouac, but at close quarters I saw how strained the celebration was.

"The army boys!" someone cried and the rabbi, without pausing for breath, sang at once: "The army boys, with their sharp bayonets, the army boys . . ."

But that, too, failed to spark the assembly. Standing by the table I saw Giladi across the bonfire talking softly to his friends, who leaned forward attentively. The shooting beyond the slope had died down and one last flare exploded suddenly, lighting up the entire valley, the bivouac, a group of soldiers next to battalion headquarters, then sank slowly downward like a weary star and faded out into the darkness. The party was over.

At that very moment beyond the circle of the campfire we heard the familiar rusty bark of Sergeant Major Isaacson; this time, however, he was not spitting out orders but fragments of a song, *"Un alts iz drek, alts iz drek, nur di heilike toira—"* ("All else is crap, all else is crap, only the holy Torah—").

In a flash he was standing by the chaplain, bareheaded, his uniform unbuttoned, his tie loosened, grunting fervently as he clapped his hands, *"Furt a yid kein eretz yisrael mit gegan-*

43

bete schoire—" ("A Jew heads for the Land of Israel with stolen goods—").

All conversation ceased; we were stunned by what we saw. Sergeant Major Isaacson was one of the most hated men in the regiment. He was a carbon copy of the professional British non-coms shipped to training camps after years in India or East Africa. True, he was not English, his skin was not tattooed like an Englishman's—from the waist to the Adam's apple, from the shoulder to the fingertips—and he did curse in all four unofficial Palestinian languages: Arabic, Russian, Yiddish, and a bit in Hebrew. But in every other respect he was worse than the worst bastard among them. His shoes were not shined but burnished like black steel; his clothes were not starched but sewn from tin khaki; his belt and anklets shone from white chalk and his buckles were gleaming brass. Encased in this uniform was a lean-faced visage with sunken cheeks, and lips stretching from ear to ear. His eyes were syphilitic. So we had summed up his personality when he was the sergeant in charge of drilling exercises and we had been recruits. He would plant himself at the edge of the parade ground, open a mouth wider than a bear's cave and race us back and forth over the length and breadth of the asphalt lot, his voice snapping at our heels like a pack of baying hounds: "Hup-Hup-Hup-Hup! Hup-Hup-Hup-Hup!"

Woe to anyone that Sergeant Major Isaacson's syphilitic eyes fell upon. Months after basic training our reflexes would jerk automatically at the sight of any three stripes approaching. After a while, when the regiments were reorganized in Egypt, Isaacson turned up again and became sergeant major of B Company. They said that he was afraid of getting a stray bullet in his starched back, but you would never know it from the way he continued to tyrannize everyone, nor would you know it from such a sudden display—a weak-kneed, tipsy wild man leaning heavily on the chaplain's shoulder and barking, "*Un alts iz drek, un alts iz drek* . . .*" The shock affected us all, as though it were at last proof that our army days were over. Voices from the circle of light and the darker surrounding regions joined in with a will, singing the verses and the refrain; even the rabbi with his sweet tenor joined in, and even Tamari

44

mumbled something, smiling faintly as he continued to feed the fire. A fresh air of abandon swept over us all.

But only for a second. As we were singing we saw the sergeant who had driven us in from Bologna draw near the campfire. Where had he been till now? Hadn't he come to see Tamari? How could I have jumped out of the truck, forgetting the sergeant entirely? And why had he lingered so long near headquarters? Now he stood waiting patiently until the song ran its course. But before Sergeant Major Isaacson could begin "Katyosha," the sergeant approached Tamari and tapped him on the shoulder. Tamari turned his head around and with one motion dropped the log from his hand, flung both his arms around the sergeant, yelled "Iziah!" and kissed him on both cheeks. Iziah, hunched over the somewhat shorter, thick-set Tamari, returned the embrace and the kisses, but in the process tickled Tamari under the armpits so that he sprang back with a guffaw.

There they stood, the two of them, in front of the entire battalion, two men as old as Father—no, older—palling it up, patting each other, barraging each other with questions, pressing hands time and again, serious but light-hearted, not pausing for a moment, all their feelings on the surface, far removed from all of us who willy-nilly were witness to this warm, powerful encounter. As the old fellows hugged each other, the sergeant leaned toward Tamari and whispered two words in his ear and the latter's brows knitted. Now, I thought, he's telling him what's brought him here in the thick of night. Tamari, whose close-cropped graying hair and muscular build lent him a handsome and solid appearance; Tamari the swarthy South Russian Jew was transformed by Iziah's whispered message into Tamari the communal worker, the emissary of the Yishuv. Suddenly a thick veil of secrecy cloaked the two. Tamari, bent as though burdened with a heavy yoke, linked arms with the sergeant and drew him into the darkness. We were left alone with the songs that would no longer be sung that evening, with the fire's glowing embers, with the mystery.

Suddenly everyone began saying what had scarcely been put into words that entire long day.

"That's Iziah Balaban."

45

"Don't tell me that you don't know who Iziah Balaban is!"

"From the agencies. *The* man."

"Boys, if Iziah Balaban dragged himself here this soon, it's a sure sign that big things are brewing."

"What?"

"What? They're going to ship us out."

"Fine, fine, but where to, that's the question."

"Germany, I say. As an occupation army."

"It should only be true, just for one month. After that they would never forget us."

"After that, they'd have good reason to hate us."

"You really know the English. Straight to Burma they'll ship us. To the jungles. Germany's out and so is home."

"Maybe that's what brought Iziah here—to organize opposition. We just won't move."

"Before we know what's happening, we'll be surrounded with Japs."

"We'll move into Germany. By ourselves. As deserters."

"A revolt, eh?"

"What do you want, better we should go to the jungles?"

"What are you talking about, jungles? They'll take our weapons and our equipment and send us home packing. One by one, as civilians."

"They sure as hell won't. That's all they need there—thirty thousand discharged soldiers!"

"So what will they do with us? Send us to Germany?"

"It should only happen. Just for one month."

"It wouldn't be much, only one Kishinev,* in round numbers: one thousand houses burned down, five hundred killed, one hundred raped."

"What do you mean one hundred? I have to kill one by myself. In cold blood. And rape one woman. In cold blood. After that I don't give a damn what happens."

"You would, I believe it. But Tamari—can you see Tamari storming into Germany like a Cossack?"

"Let him, goddamnit. That's what we're here for. Not for Roosevelt's freedoms or the British Empire or Stalin. We're

* The site of a famous pogrom in Russia, 1904.

46

here to take revenge. One wild Jewish vengeance. Just once to be like the Tartars. Like the Ukranians. Like the Germans. All of us—spoiled, sensitive, farmers, students, humanists, workers—all of us will move in on one city and burn it street by street, house by house, German by German. Why should we be the only ones to remember Auschwitz? Let them remember the one city that we'll raze. After that I'll be ready to leave for Burma."

"Hear, hear, Giladi—a regular Jack the Ripper!"

Everyone laughed. How could they do otherwise, picturing pale, spectacled Giladi, the spitting image of a bank teller, as a murderer and a rapist? Leizi, Bubi Meinz and some of their friends returning from Forlì had just seated themselves by the fire when Leizi sprang to his feet and sounded off in a similar vein. But Leizi was very tall, passionate, with long arms laced with young muscles; he spoke in a slow and sleepy nasal tone. Maybe he, calm and menacing, was fit for the job, but Giladi . . .

Giladi, too, was smiling, but his eyes burned behind his glasses flashing the reflected light of the embers. The conversation wandered off in many directions, but it still simmered with the sentiments that had just been expressed. It was no coincidence that Giladi said what he did; it was no idle turn of the conversation. He had just opened a window into the black fire eating at his guts.

The conversation died down. Someone heated up coffee.

Mushik brought out more bread and a tin of jelly in honor of Giladi, and we all drank, ate and went on talking. In his nasal, sleepy voice Leizi described what he had seen that day in Forlì.

"You can't imagine what was going on there. Prisoners were being moved in all the time with their vehicles, their officers, their three-wheeled motorcycles—they got off and went into the stadium. I felt like I was going crazy: what were they, prisoners, or guests at a convention for old party members? Thousands of them were packed in there. There was hardly a guard in sight. Here and there you saw someone with a rifle or Tommy gun.

"The German soldiers are healthy as horses. There were German Fords in good shape, Volkswagens. I saw them pushing

47

into the stadium and I thought that in one more minute the *Führer* would speak and then they'd race back to their vehicles and take care of us all, all of us standing around waiting like *schmucks*. It was a lousy feeling."

"You should've tossed a few hand grenades in," Poker volunteered.

"I'll tell you what you should've done, a few mortar shells, that's what you should've shoved up their asses," Mushik declared after he had spread out at Giladi's feet.

"Why waste bullets?" a voice piped up from the darkness. "I'd just have spilled benzine all around the stadium and burned it up."

"Why waste benzine?" a second voice demanded. "I'd lock them in there and let them eat one another up. Very slowly."

"Talk is cheap," Bubi Meinz said suddenly.

"What would you have done?" asked Leizi.

"I don't know. Something. Something that would frighten their children winter nights. 'Ah, what the Jews did to us!' Something that would take the place of Grimm's fairy tales. That would wake up children in the night five hundred years from now."

"Right," said Giladi, looking up, as though Bubi had taken the words out of his mouth.

Despite myself I could not take my eyes off Bubi's virile, very German features. I had faith in his beautiful, clear-cut hatred. He could do it. I would go with him. With him I would do anything. Suddenly I heard myself—there on the roof—yelling at the top of my lungs, reviling the entire family gathered for the wedding and most of all Pinik, who worked in the army camps and on his trips home came in with his pockets jingling and his hands full of the choicest goods from the Australian canteens; I stood there screaming. "Why don't you enlist, all of you, why don't you fight, all of you, Why aren't you at the front, all of you? What are you doing throwing weddings here on the roof with sandwiches, with sausages, with beer, with wine? How can you live it up like this, all of you?" As though in a dream I had returned in an instant to that evening after which I could no longer look the family in the face. I had spoiled the celebration and had set myself up as a judge and a preacher. And who was

48

I, after all?—a drunken sixteen-year-old. What right had I to have such gall, to set myself above them? How I had despised myself the next morning and the long days that followed. Even after I volunteered, I hated myself, all through the war, standing guard over empty warehouses, and even during those weeks in Italy. But when I saw the black fire in Giladi's eyes and heard the cruel judgment of Bubi it seemed to me that perhaps I had not spoken nonsense on the roof after all.

As I looked about, the conversation took a new tack. Leizi and Bubi had drawn their like about them—members of training farms, agricultural schools and farm settlements; Giladi rose and left, his friends following one by one. Shimaleh, the signalman, mentioned the name of some hero, uncorking a flood of stories—of the Max Fine School, of the Sachneh pool, the Valley of Jezreel train, the slowest on earth, the trip to Mt. Hermon, Bubi's first day in the draftees' training farm.

All these were tales whose tellers never wearied of reciting and whose listeners never wearied of hearing, not because they contained anything new but, to the contrary, were so sweetly familiar, like an old waltz, like a Morse transmitter whose secret code binds its listeners together. They were sprawled on the ground, lying on their backs, heads on thighs, or they sat back to back, this clique I yearned to be part of with all my heart. Why then was I sitting to the side, on the projecting end of a fallen tree, with them but not of them? Why did it seem to me that I was sitting behind them, that they were not aware of my existence and would not notice if I got up and left?

I rose and no one urged me to stay; the conversation flowed on, no one paused to take a breath. I went back to the bivouac. The men had already crawled into the dugouts beneath their pup tents. The fireworks had died down and the cloud of smoke had vanished. All that remained was the starry May sky. I walked past the narrow dugout a tent had once covered. Freedberg had committed suicide there the night before. His neighbor had been moved to another tent and the narrow pit stared from the ground like a gouged out eye. I went down into our dugout, stripped and stretched out between the thick wool blankets. The snoring of Brodsky and the raucous laughter of the clique outside echoed in the close darkness. An ocean of

49

sadness welled within me. Noga's letters lay beneath my head; there was no mistaking any longer what they contained. Even her sure hand showed it, the words racing onward, young and bubbly.

"It's spring in *Aretz*,* people are studying at the university. We're working. The gang got together Saturday night." Peace was a fact and the sentimentality of the war had gone forever.

How simple the letters were; there, a different kind of life was shaping up very quickly, but as for me, far away, what was to become of me now? Open-eyed I stared into the darkness and only two words buzzed toward me like mosquitoes: What now; now what?

* "The Land." Palestine (before 1948) and today Israel. Also *Eretz Yisrael*, the Land of Israel.

II   The Broken Sword

The night before we were to leave for Germany, the entire
battalion was summoned to a memorial parade. The trucks
quieted down after a hectic day of loading and formed a large
three-sided C on the paved area to the right of the bivouac; we
formed an inner rim by companies. Equidistant from the tips
of the inner C but beyond it, toward the railroad track, a pole
had been set up for the flag which, until then, had not been
allowed to fly within the bivouac area. The officers, standing
at ease, were clustered to the side waiting for R.S.M. Mac-
Gregor to give the signal.

The R.S.M., decked out in his Scottish regimental finery,
stood rigidly at attention, as if he had drunk plaster of Paris.
His black swagger stick clamped beneath his armpit, he barked

brusquely to his right and to his left—"Battalion!"—until not a head moved, until the clearing of one's throat sounded like a thunderclap.

All at once he tensed his body even more, pivoted on his right heel like a music-box dancer and strode with ringing steps toward the chalk square in front of the flagpole. He halted, about-faced sharply, lifted his knee to his belt, then stamped down on his heel, pressed his right fist even tighter into his tartan kilt and suddenly—as though a mine had been set off—his mouth gaped open from the collar of his uniform to his forehead, and a horrendous roar shook the valley. The battalion froze; at the second roar, all rifles slapped against hands and shoulders. The valley was suddenly still.

Heads immobile, only our eyes moved to take in the scene: hundreds of soldiers, the anti-tank guns, the big Dodge trucks, the pageantry of the journey we would begin before sunrise. This was a moment to remember, like that first breath-taking parade in the Egyptian desert exuding odors of the factory, spanking new tires, the bright colors of unfaded uniforms, American cigarettes. Regiment after regiment marched by then, kicking up dust, hundreds of trucks snorted in place like war horses; the flag was swallowed up in the clouded air. Power! Power! Power!

And now this parade before Germany. One announcement —"We are moving north"—and all past disappointments faded away as though they had never been. Ranks of armed soldiers, rows of trucks, jeeps and motorcycles, the folded flag tied to the pole, two corporals flanking it to the left and the right, and Shimaleh standing ready, bugle in hand. "Battalion!! Battalion —*attennnnn-hut!*"

Regimental Sergeant Major MacGregor was putting in his last appearance on the parade ground of the Empire: "Battalion!! Battalion—stand at ease!"

Stripped of individuality we melted into the battalion. For a split second R.S.M. MacGregor hesitated and only the badge quivering on his cap gave any indication that he was alive. Another roar: the battalion leaped to attention. The battalion shouldered arms. The R.S.M. executed an about-face and strode toward the group of officers and the adjutant, Captain What's-his-name, who strode out to meet him. Twenty-six years of service were bound up in this moment and every move bore the mark of a maestro. Captain What's-his-name tensed his muscles, too, snapped to attention after the R.S.M., returned a wishy-washy hand wave to a salute swift as an electric shock, turned and paced into the chalk square; but our eyes followed the shrunken Scot striding across the parade ground like a glorious old battle horse to stand behind us at the far end of the battalion.

From then on, all went according to the prescribed order. Captain What's-his-name shouted at the officers: "Gentlemen: *Posts!*" at which all the sergeants and master sergeants about-faced and walked to our rear as the group of officers opened up like a fan, each man striding toward his position in front of his company or platoon. Now the parade was to pass over to Major Kaplan, who was to replace Colonel Griffith that day. Major Kaplan had no feel for ceremony: a dwarfish man, every step he took marred the entire proceedings. Only his voice matched the dignity of the occasion. Three cries and we stood at ease. Three cries and we had shouldered arms. The battalion was handed over to the colonel for the last time.

With the brazen abandon of a combat soldier, Colonel Griffith had not taken off his riding boots or his parachutist's windbreaker. Except that he lacked his field glasses and his map case, he looked just as he did when dashing about among the companies during the months of training and at the front. He saluted brusquely, as though in a rush to leave for a new command, and before we knew what was happening, we were once again at "present arms," the officers with their fingertips raised to the brims of their caps and Shimaleh lifting the bugle to his lips, sounding the call to colors.

The haunting bugle blast trailed off in golden tones toward the sunset, caressed the valley, crossed the river, skimmed over the city, hovered over the turret of the castle, and sailed on to the chalky ridges to the northeast, to the front lines—where were those jagged lines, where?—which we had so yearned to reach just once, to meet hatred with hatred, death with death.

The polished rifle trembled in my hand, the rifle that had

53

been returned to me only that day. Struggling to suppress the stinging tears, I turned my eyes away from the slowly rising flag and stared at the thick neck of Lieutenant Freund Putzovski. Anyone who wanted to be reassured that the war had ended had only to look at Freund Putzovski who had returned to us from some meaningless assignment.

Putzovski had earned his name one day in the battalion mess hall in the Egyptian desert. The food was not ready and we all sat in the tent hiding from the sun, hundreds of us clanging away with knives and forks on our mess kits like a percussion orchestra gone mad. Lieutenant Freund, who even then was our mess officer, had tried in vain to distract us. But the louder he had bawled, the faster we had clanged. It was then that the poor wretch had come out with his prize statement: "Maybe I'm a putz, but you are *putzovskim* . . ." He said more at the time, but we only seized upon that one word and made it his second surname; the more fastidious among us took pains to refer to him as Von Freund Putzovski. Now he was to take charge of the platoon as we made the transition to peacetime.

It was funny: there I was, doing everything to remind myself how ludicrous he was, this man who became an officer, God only knows how, but I could not free my mind of the clarion call of the bugle. I could not tell whether the flaming veil of color in the sky was the sunset or a web of trumpet blasts. Think of something else, I thought, there's no need to exaggerate.

Was that laughter convulsing the ranks? Tamari—what was happening to Tamari? I stood in the middle rank and Tamari in the first rank, somewhat to the left. Then the polished tones of the bugle were accompanied by a loud chirping noise as though someone were hiccuping. I saw what was happening— Tamari's head was shaking. As he struggled to muffle his weeping, Leizi, standing behind him, was rocking with laughter at the sight of the old man. The laughter passed through the entire left flank of the platoon. And over all these noises, from the rear, rose the rumbling of Sergeant Major Isaacson.

The flag raising ceremony was over. The two corporals stood once more at both sides of the flagpole, and the bugle was

54

clasped firmly against the thigh of Shimaleh, the bugler. Now the chaplain entered the chalk square next to the colonel and read off the names of the battalion's fallen members who alone would remain there the next day beneath the gray hillocks.

Ah, desolate Romagna—no sooner had we come than we were to depart. Ah, water-drenched Emilia—the trenches running off the irrigation ditches; the shrieking shells arching slowly overhead, the canteens filled with Bianchi wine, the beds and closets that we sent up in smoke. the chickens from no-man's land. That was about it. We had faced an enemy we had never seen, not even once. We had fired into empty fields and were fired at from empty fields. The war had gone forever, the hour of vengeance would never be ours again. We would come home with unsoiled clothes and hands unstained with blood— we, the avengers.

The cantorial voice of the chaplain, chanting and enunciating every word as prescribed, strained to reach every corner of the regiment. " 'Oh Lord, who art full of compassion . . . they were swifter than eagles and braver than lions . . .' " But suddenly the smooth melody fell apart, the words took on flesh and stood before us, rebelling against the neat and orderly ritual. " 'And it is written, "for he that avengeth blood hath remembered them; he hath not forgotten the cry of the humble." And it is written, "He will judge among the nations; he filleth them with dead bodies, he crusheth the head over a wide land . . ." ' "

The chaplain mumbled the last sentences in a low voice, almost like Father had the first Rosh Hashana* of the war. Swiftly he stepped out of the chalk square.

Colonel Griffith remained alone. Grasping the two ends of his black swagger stick behind his back, he went straight to the point: "When I was given the task of training this battalion for battle, I knew very little about you. Today I thank fate for having given me this privilege. Better trained units fought in this theater of war and for a longer period of time; and they suffered incalculable losses. But I doubt very much if any regiment

* Jewish New Year.

55

in the army hungered for battle more than you. As commander of this battalion I came to realize that war can be a lofty moment in the life of a real man. I learned from you that the right to fight, to kill or be killed in battle—a right often denied so many of your people—at times constitutes the highest freedom given a man.

"I grieve that we were not able to do more, but for the few brief weeks that we spent on the front, I felt fortunate; and if a man whose task it is to send men to kill and be killed can feel that way, it is a sign that you led me to understand the real goal of this war—the salvation of man's image, for our fellow men and ourselves.

"Secondly: at dawn you will be on your way to a new assignment, one which will strain your ideals to the breaking point. You will be forced to prove the applicability of morality to men who butchered morality. My comrades in arms—" He cut short the sentence he was about to utter. Snapping to attention and thrusting the black swagger stick beneath his arm, he concluded with a smile, "I have said too much. God help you. Thank you all. Good-by."

Colonel Griffith turned, saluted the flag, motioned to Major Kaplan, and strode briskly toward battalion headquarters. This was a deviation from set procedure; it seemed that the colonel, overwrought, had mixed up the order of the ceremony. Not so, however. Major Kaplan waddled into the chalk square, threw out an indifferent "Attenhut!" and turned his head in the direction of Corporal Macover of the battalion headquarters staff who had helped raise the flag. The latter approached the chalk square, stopped at its outer fringe, and took a sheet of paper from his pocket. After mumbling a few words inaudibly he declaimed aloud, precisely and clearly, just like a Hebrew teacher, the "commandments for a Hebrew soldier on German soil":

"One. Hate the butchers of your people—unto all generations!

"Two. Remember: You are the emissaries of a people prepared for battle!

"Three. Remember: The Jewish Brigade in Nazi Germany is a Jewish army of occupation!

"Four. Remember: The fact that we come as a military unit with flag and emblem in sight of the German people, in its homeland—is vengeance!

"Five. Remember: Vengeance is a communal task. Any irresponsible act weakens the group.

"Six. Look like a Jew who is proud of his people and his flag!

"Seven. Pay them no mind—and do not come under their roofs!

"Eight. Let them be anathema—they, their wives, their children, their property and all that belongs to them—anathema for all generations!

"Nine. Remember your mission: The rescue of Jews, immigration to a free homeland.

"Ten. Your duty: Dedication, loyalty and love for the remnants of the sword and the camps."

His voice had grown progressively hoarse from one commandment to the next, rusty even, until it was difficult to hear him; but at that point he lifted his head from the paper, cleared his throat and cried aloud, sending a tremor through us all: "Cursed be he who fails to remember what they have done to us!"

The blood surged through our veins. Everything meshed into one tapestry—the armed companies, the vehicles at our backs, the flag before us, the passionate words, the feeling that was all ours, unlike the devious sentence with which the colonel had ended his speech. Morality, eh? "Let them take vengeance with disdain upon the destroyer." Eternal hatred. So we looked upon that moment.

Corporal Macover concluded and stepped back. Major Kaplan turned the parade over to Captain What's-his-name and left the parade ground. The captain dismissed the officers and waited for R.S.M. MacGregor, who once more crossed the field, stood before the adjutant, received the parade, turned on his heel, tensed his small frame a little bit more, and roared "Dismiss!" for the last time. He had volunteered for the Brit-

57

ish Army during the first year following World War I when he had just turned sixteen, and the next day he was to return to Scotland. We, at the next day's dawn, would be on our way to Germany.

2

The sky had begun to pale at the edges by the time we had piled up all our gear, stuffed all our personal belongings into our kit bags, duffel bags and ammo cases, taken down our tents, and loaded the truck for the long trip. The battalion tumult was overwhelming: the field stoves hissed beneath the cauldrons of tea, the command echelons rumbled in place like the generators of the dispatch riders' motorcycles. We went to sleep as well as we could in the empty, uncovered dugouts.

Just as I managed to stretch my legs out and cover my head with my stocking cap we were showered with the good-morning blessings of Sergeant Major Isaacson: "Get up, you carcasses!" Eyes closed we arose, leaving behind us the empty dugouts, even as the Israelites in the desert must have done morning after morning. We took our cups out of our kit bags and stood in line for tea, bread, and jam.

The last of the stars faded, the headlights of the trucks went out, and the wet mist wormed into our flesh. We crammed into the truck one on top of another, jammed our legs into every free space between the piles of duffel bags, personal equipment and rifles. Once again we pulled our stocking caps down to our chins and tried to sneak a little more of the night into the dawning day. Until we got started.

We still were not moving. The motorcycles were rocking, the jeeps were wheezing, the trucks were rumbling in place—and the battalion was asleep. Somebody in the know said that the convoy had started moving, but this time we were at its end. Who gave a damn? We wanted to sleep.

Even when we heard our driver, through the darkness of our stocking caps, press down on the gas pedal, grind the gearshift and jerk the truck forward with a mighty thrust not one of us shifted position. We knew how to roll with the punch. The truck was moving—let it move. It stopped suddenly, wheels screeching—let it stop. The entire platoon was cradled in sleep.

The heat was pleasant so long as the world was swathed in the morning mist, but very shortly our outer coats and woolen hats did not serve to guard our sleep. They were hot, itchy, and aggravating. We peeled our clothes off and opened our eyes. Clouds of dust filled the hot air. Bologna lay behind us, the mountains vanished in the distance. Green plains filled the horizons as far as the eye could see.

We went off the main road onto temporary roads leading to temporary bridges. We proceeded very slowly through the choking dust, thirty or twenty kilometers per hour, traveling fifty minutes and resting ten. We drank tea, traveled a little farther. Soon the entire convoy was spread out over a broad field, the M.P.'s directing every unit to its place.

The trucks halted and as we jumped out of them we saw the field kitchens had already been set up to greet us: canned beef in vats of boiling water, hardtack, the hubbub of setting up camp. But scarcely did the C rations—gobs of fat floating in sewer water—ooze into our bellies, than the convoy once more got ready to roll.

Slowly we moved out. Again we descended dusty roads and arrived at a gigantic pontoon bridge stretched across the Po, alongside the skeleton of the real bridge. Onward we went, northward, through an endless valley. Perhaps we were deceived, but it seemed that from all indications there had been far less destruction here than in the south. Houses stood on their foundations. Even the bridges were whole.

The long summer day was drawing to an end and the tang of the sea hit us in the face. "Venice!" someone cried, and in the distance, so it seemed, we could see the peaks of towers so familiar from picture postcards.

"If we camp here," Leizi said to Bubi, "anyone who doesn't take off for Venice is a *schmuck.*"

"I think we're setting up camp already," said Bubi. "Start running."

We discovered that the first trucks in the convoy had already gone off the road and that the men were scattered about the field pitching their tents. Our truck, too, crawled to its spot. We

59

leaped onto the field, finding it spongy as though after rain, anxious to hammer in our stakes. Venice was on everyone's mind, but by the time we prepared our quarters for the night, night fell upon us.

"I'm getting you a pass," Bubi said to Leizi, who stood in his shorts in the doorway of their tent, getting ready to go to bed. "I'm a man of my word."

Even Poker was not rounding up hands for poker. The night before we hadn't slept at all and we would be woken up the next day while it was still dark. The next day, we thought—the next day we would be entering Germany. "Not Germany," Tamari corrected us, "Austria." "Germany, Austria," said Brodsky, "they should both sink in the same hole."

By the next day, as lunchtime approached, we were beyond the Mediterranean area. Even though it was only past Udine, the dipping ridges of the Alps began to gather in around us. We sat beneath the canvas canopy looking at what we had put behind us.

Admiring the Alps was not our business, but who could not have been amazed at those awesome vistas suddenly thrust upon us. Certainly not us, from the lowlands of Palestine. The cool, clean air of the north displaced the fetid heat of the Adriatic plain, pure blue against the blackness of the forest pressing in upon us, stretching from the narrow valleys to the bald peaks of the mountains, piercing the heavens like stone swords. The trees were pressed tightly together, one looking over the other; at any moment, it seemed, they would spill onto the road cutting through the mountainside.

Suddenly, around a bend, the mountains on the right fell away like gates flung open, and below us, in a broad valley, translucent water coursed over a smooth-stoned riverbed, bubbling, gushing, leaping with abandon over the polished stones that seemed like the bottom layer of a mighty highway yet to be paved. That fierce stream was dashing wildly to its destination somewhere in the valley while our convoy crept along, climbing slowly upward. Again the ridges closed in like scissors upon the winding road.

Towering trees and a thick green carpet covered the earth. Not one field was burnt black by the sun and no thorns were

60

strewn in the dust. Only an endless forest. Parallel with the road ran the railroad track and telephone wires, and here and there we saw ripped out railroad ties, overturned cars and bent pillars. But the crystal clear air, the fragrance, the thick forest —it all seemed as though the stories that Mother had told of her distant childhood were coming true, as if we were in some dream world or a moving picture.

Who would have believed that such lands really existed and that I would see them with my own eyes? Slowly the convoy crawled up the towering mountains, each one taller than the next, and suddenly we were in the midst of a nightmare. Coming in the opposite direction, southward, military trucks rumbled toward us—one, three, five, an entire convoy. At first we did not realize what it was we saw, but then someone shouted, in fright or amazement: "Germans. They're German troops."

We leaped from our seats and squeezed to the back to see the incredible sight. A long convoy, trucks smaller than our Dodges, painted a different color of camouflage: ours were olive green and theirs, brown. Officers in uniform sat in open Volkswagens, signalers rode on three-wheeled motorcycles in calm and orderly procession—an army moving from one front to another.

For a moment I forgot that the war was over. I was seized with panic: we had chanced into these mountains by some horrible mistake and were trapped in the heart of enemy territory. There was no way out. The fantasy lasted only a split second, but the terror was all-encompassing: the pastoral had shattered. All at once.

How was it they were traveling here in their vehicles, under their own power, with such military precision, their organization unruffled, their spirits not crushed? Where were those officers in the Volkswagens leading their men? Who gave those motorcyclists permission to travel freely? What kind of war was this, if this was how the vanquished looked? No blood, no fire, no tears. A German convoy was rolling by us in peace.

I don't know that those were my exact thoughts at that moment. First came the shock. Someone cursed softly. Another man cursed aloud, shouting bitterly. But the Germans continued to stream down the mountainside. Suddenly we exploded.

61

"*Kurva sinah!*" yelled Brodsky, who stood in the center of the truck atop a pile of duffel bags. "They're laughing!"

"Give me something I can throw at them, the pigs!" yelled Poker, who had forced his way to the back of the truck.

"Move for a minute!" said little Ostreicher.

"Let me alone. I've got to open a head," Brodsky cried heatedly, looking around frantically for some kind of weapon. "*Yebyuhamut!*"

"Then move over a minute," said Ostreicher, bending over. "This piece of iron." Poker turned his head toward Ostreicher and without saying a word, pushed him aside, bent over and yanked two duffel bags away from the rear door.

When he got up he had a hooked stake in his hand. He clambered to the door, leaned out of the truck, holding onto the canvas framework with his left hand, and waited. We all were quiet. Another German truck appeared and slowly began to pass us. Poker raised his right hand and with a brief circular motion flung the stake into the opening of the truck crammed with men. A sharp cry shattered upon the steep mountain slope and at that moment our truck became a cage of wild men. The entire platoon roared in answer to the one cry that rose from the German truck as it disappeared behind us. We began searching for other implements, any kind of murderous tool. But what was there to find in a truck loaded with kit bags and duffel bags?

"Give me something," yelled Poker. "Let me open up another bastard's head."

"I've got something," cried Hershler as he leaped up, holding his kit bag in his hand. Quickly he began untying the bag. "Just one minute."

"Hurry!" cried Poker, slapping the canvas excitedly. "They're slipping through my fingers."

"I've got it! Let me through . . ." Bubi suddenly sprang to his feet in the corner and began to clamber over the gear, burrowing into the depths of the truck where the tents and boxes of battle rations were. He quickly dug into them and came up with one box. "Leizi, throw me a bayonet!"

"Corporal Meinz, what are you doing?"

It was Tamari: we had completely forgotten he was with us in the truck. That he addressed Bubi by his full military title indicated his displeasure with Bubi's scheme. But Leizi, who had also seized upon the idea, had already removed the German bayonet from his belt, the one he had taken from the corpse of a German killed in the famous ambush by Bubi's unit. He threw it to Bubi.

"That's no way to act, Bubi. And besides, what will you say to the major? He holds you responsible for all the combat rations."

Bubi did not answer. With lips pressed tightly together he wrenched asunder the steel bands binding the crate, then plunged the blade between the boards and ripped them apart. The entire truckload of men urged him on with their shouts, Poker above all: "Shake it up! They're getting away, the bastards!"

"Take this in the meantime," said Hershler. We had forgotten by that time that he, too, was rummaging through his duffel bag. As I was seated between him and Poker, Hershler handed me a statuette wrapped in a sock. "Pass it to him, Elisha."

I grasped the heavy statuette, about twice as big as a hand grenade, and in the process saw what it was—a cheap facsimile of Moses. I weighed the statuette in my hand, reluctant to hand it over as a missile.

"Give it here, already!" Poker yelled.

"Give it to him!" said Hershler.

Poker snatched the statuette, once again hung by his left hand from the truck's framework overhead, and waited for the next vehicle.

"You can't do this." Tamari could no longer contain himself. "Men, how can you wound defenseless prisoners? We're not—"

The roar of the entire platoon drowned out the rest of his sentence, as Poker hurled the statuette into the next truck that passed; the ensuing cry of pain was greeted by our jubilant roar. By now the carton of combat rations was open and Bubi had taken out shining tins of jelly and margarine. Brodsky had discovered, on the floor of the truck, a wooden mallet and a metal T square.

"Let's go!" yelled Poker.

"*Aleihum!*" yelled Ostreicher. "*Aleihum!*" we all yelled in response.

The craving to act like barbarians, shattering all rules, seized us like a fire grips thorns. *Let them remember that we passed them and that when soldiers from the Land of Israel approach they should quake in their boots!* They knew who we were by the yellow Stars of David on a blue and white background on the fenders of our vehicles, by the big flags waving over the drivers' cabs (where had they gotten all those flags from?), by the words written large in German on the sides of the truck and on the canvas: "*Die Juden kommen!*"—"*Kein Reich, kein Volk, kein Führer!*" We had the flags and the slogans: now we would put some muscle behind them.

"Let's go!" Poker stretched his hand out toward the preserves.

"Wait!" said Leizi. He had a gigantic hand; when Bubi threw a tin to him it was lost between his fingers. Unlike Poker, he was not one to rant and rave. He stood by the opening of the truck with his long hands somewhere above his head. Whenever a German truck would pass he would hurl a tin straight ahead, and it seemed to us that we could hear it strike home.

"Bull's-eye!" Poker yelled. "Another one."

Leizi was the marksman, Poker called the strikes, and we were beside ourselves with rage. *Let them remember who they met on the road.*

"It's not only us!" Poker announced. "They're giving it to them right down the line!"

It was true. The Germans were no longer placid tourists. They bunched together in their trucks trying to hide; their cries of agony were music to our ears. Right down the line.

Suddenly our truck stopped short and we were flung back inside. Poker informed us that the whole convoy had halted.

"Stones," said Brodsky, as he and Leizi leaped to the side of the road and began to gather stones suitable for throwing. "Hurry up before we start moving again."

But the convoy did not move. Officers and British sergeants from the escort of the prisoners' convoy dashed about on the road shaking their fists at us. They disappeared, then returned in the company of our Major Sanders, Lieutenant Freund Putzovski, and Sergeant Major Isaacson. Freund Putzovski delivered a short speech calling our attention to the articles of the Geneva Convention relating to prisoners. We jeered him silently. We had adopted the German interpretation of the Geneva Convention. When the officers passed on to another platoon, Brodsky and Leizi once more leaped to the ground to gather more stones.

Nonetheless the convoy stood still while the prisoners' convoy continued southward. The British and our officers kept their eyes on us while we waited for an opportunity. Poker dashed off to other trucks and returned with information for the distressed Tamari: "*Haver* Tamari, they hit those Germans good and hard. With chunks of iron, stakes, picks. Good and hard."

A Mercedes with German officers passed by, followed by a few jeeps with military police. The convoy came to an end and we were left alone in the mountains. The hatred subsided as suddenly as it had erupted and sank into the hundreds of vehicles, a snake whose head by now perhaps lay across the border. The truck jerked forward. We continued our journey. We all squeezed ourselves into our original places once again. Bubi was suddenly quiet and withdrawn and Leizi stretched his long legs out over the bags, on his face that habitual opaque and sleepy look. Unless he was very active—throwing grenades, stacking trunks, wrestling for fun—he would close his eyes and sleep. They were a great pair, Bubi and Leizi; neither took part in the debate Tamari opened.

He was shaken to the core. "It's not possible," he blurted, his black eyes flashing, "it's not possible! What's happening to us, men? To wound people just like that, for a thrill, people we don't even know, unarmed prisoners of war. . . . It's terrible I tell you . . ."

"Shu-ut up," we yelled, adding a few catcalls.

But undeterred he went on: "Don't forget that we have a mission."

"This is part of the mission."

"The British won't close their eyes if we—"

"Fuck the British."

"Men, we're at the mercy of the British. If we go wild like this in Germany—"

"You bet we will."

65

"They'll ship us out and then what will we do?"

"Oh, can it, Tamari. Enough of your sermons."

"The Jewish people—"

"Leave us alone. You don't have to shit in your pants because we opened a few heads. We'll open some more."

"You're impetuous. You don't understand the task that history has laid upon you."

"Shove it! Goddamnit, Tamari, you're giving me a headache."

It was Poker. He hated Tamari and insulted him at every opportunity. But then, sensing that for once he was speaking for everyone, he really lit into him: "Write it in your diary. Write that we murderers pounced on the poor Germans. How horrible, what will they think of us in Germany! What kind of youth do they raise in Palestine, wild men—"

"Shut your mouth, Poker!"

It was Bubi. With one sentence he silenced them all. God only knew where he got his power from, that Bubi who would write numbered letters to a girl in Youth Aliyah, who had apple-red cheeks and cold German eyes. You could love a guy like Bubi. He folded his arms across his chest and let his head drop. We all kept quiet, because our arguments didn't begin to match the intensity of our feelings at the sight of the enemy passing by.

Daylight began to fade from the agonizingly beautiful surroundings; every man withdrew into himself. The truck began to coast down a steep incline and a broad valley opened up behind us. The steep ridges divided and mounds of grass jutted up between them, hills carpeted with greenery and dashing brooks. In the distance patches of white, remnants of winter lay scattered on the mountain peaks. The sun still shone but the valley was already streaked with black shade. The shoulder of a mountain thrust onto the road, almost, with black-beamed huts affixed to it. We passed over an arched, stone bridge with the water roaring beneath us. We passed more and more houses with lower halves made of plaster and white lime and upper halves formed into sharp black wooden cones. A stream of water in a wooden trough ran from a spring at the foot of the mountain to a mill wheel. The houses began to form a village street. But even the Bailey bridge, even the group of wrecked houses did not detract from the pure, legendary beauty that

66

surrounded us. Little children stood in the doorways of the houses waving hesitantly at us. Their hair was flaxen, their eyes were like star thistles. A woman was shouting something in a courtyard but we didn't know in what language. Good God, why was everything so beautiful!

"Look at us!" cried little Ostreicher, who was dashing about at the rear of the truck. "Look how they paint us!"

On the outer wall of a two-story house, above the doorway of a store, a colorful, somewhat faded placard was affixed. It showed a hunchbacked Jew with a wispy beard, wearing a gaberdine gown, hauling Uncle Sam on a leash, bent beneath a sack of dollars.

"So it's true then, that's how they see us?" said Leizi, forcing open his sleepy eyes.

"What did you think, then?" cried Ostreicher. "See for yourself!"

What did we really think? A thought began to form in my brain, but before I could open my mouth we were all flung forward as the truck ground to a sudden halt.

3

The truck had halted within the town limits. Instantly we leaped to the ground, stretched and dashed about, sniffing out the area to find what sort of place we were in. Up and down the small street we roved, then went to a shallow stream beyond the single row of houses and swallowed some cold Alpine water. Returning to the road we took another path. We made a slight flanking movement and discovered a house built differently than the others—it was small, rectangular, and had a flat roof and large windows. We circled it until we came upon an unlocked door. Entering, we found a schoolroom. Desks, clothes hangers, children's paintings on the walls. A scribbled-on blackboard. Had the long vacation begun here or had the new conquerors disbanded the school?

I rummaged through the empty desks. Only in one did I find a book. In German. Bubi read it and deciphered it. It was a primer for the second grade. Exquisite paper, a few words on

67

every page printed in large, prominent letters with plenty of space; there were rhymes, illustrations, sharp photos. Unconsciously I began to think of the concepts I had picked up from Noga; I began to judge the book as an educator. More than that —since I could not really picture all we had heard during the previous few weeks, the book had the effect of strengthening the message that the voice of my childhood whispered incessantly within. In the end it would turn out that it had all been a terrible mistake, that actually man was only man—not an angel, but not a fiend either. This was a beautiful book whose authors, editors, and printers had taken pains to see that a child would take it in hand; they had aimed at his level of understanding, labored to make reading a pleasure for him, carefully balanced abstract words with concrete pictures, the amassing of knowledge with cultivation of feeling. A lovely book, I said to myself as I leafed through it.

There he was, the *Führer*, the picture I had anticipated from the first moment. He seemed just like the rest of the book— very civil, bareheaded, double-chinned, beaming at a little girl in a peasant's dress with shining, yellow hair. Already he, too, seemed human to me; had he leaned over me like that I would have been beguiled; no—I would have seen the world so familiar to me reflected in his eyes. That was the worst of it all: there was no "murder in the eyes." The truth did not float like oil on water. How could I hate this class, this beautiful book, things I could not grasp? Already we were with the *Volksdeutsche* and never in my life had I seen so enchanted an evening as that which greeted us as we left the school.

The trucks stood on the road and no one knew whether we were journeying on or staying there the night. We had not eaten dinner, night covered the mountain tops, and everything was still a mystery. Suddenly Freund Putzovski ordered us to take our personal gear off the trucks and set up sleeping quarters. We would eat when the cooks were ready.

"And tomorrow we move on?"

"On a *kibbutz* you ask questions, in the army you carry out orders," Freund Putzovski said angrily, and stalked off.

The classroom was occupied almost entirely by the men

from our truck. We used all our blankets and laid out common bunks. For weeks we had not slept on a level floor or in a room we could stand up in. We overslept and no one bothered us. Only when we began to worry that we might not be found did we get up and go out to the street. But the convoy had not moved. No one knew what came next.

As usual the rumors began to fly: the travel schedule had been fouled up; we don't stop in mid-journey just like that, a new order must have come: to stop until further orders were received. Because of what we did to the German prisoners, the rumors had it. And maybe, others maintained, maybe they deliberately deceived us and we were the only ones fooled by all those oaths before the flag.

"But didn't the colonel take part in the ceremony? He even went out of his way to mention the test that awaited us."

"That only proves he's a foxy Englishman and a rumormonger like the rest. He's not with the battalion any more, so what does he care?"

"Then why did they bring us right to the border?"

The politicians, strategists, and everyone well versed in rumors figured out the answers all that day. We heard their explanation from Giladi, an explanation consistent with the accusations Giladi constantly leveled at the English: "This area lies on three borders; it's part of the territory contested by Italy, Austria, and Yugoslavia. If any armed conflict breaks out over Trieste, it will spread here, too. In that event we'll be Britain's military arm, defending Italy's interests against Yugoslavia. We will thereby have the option of starting World War Three. For Albion's sake, we will not be still . . ."

Giladi was not a rumormonger. Definitely not. He maintained that even if the rumors were plucked from the air they only testified further to the truth of that amazing military phenomenon: a stubborn rumor begins to pass from unit to unit, and sometimes from one country to another, supplanting all other rumors and convincing everyone. Rumor makes it a reality long before it becomes a reality announced by the high command. "You'll see," laughed Giladi, "we're staying right here."

69

Right he was. Toward evening Sergeant Major Isaacson arrived and assembled the scattered members of the company for a parade. We lined up on the road and a moment later Major Sanders appeared, too, together with the platoon commanders. Completely disregarding the matter of Germany and as if nothing had ever been said about it, the major informed us in a few words that our company was setting up quarters on the spot. The sergeants would take their platoons to the quarters already assigned to them. The next morning a new daily schedule would be posted and the life of the company would revolve around it.

"I would like to conclude my remarks with one clear statement; you would do well to keep it constantly in mind," said Major Sanders. "The war is not over. There is still heavy fighting on the far eastern front. Peace has not yet come and we are still soldiers in the service of His Majesty. We are governed by the King's Regulations exactly as before and, at any rate, this company will conduct itself as a well-disciplined military unit. If we bear that in mind, we will be able to reap the maximum benefit from our stay here no matter how long it will be. That is all. Sergeant Major, take the company!"

And that was that.

The battalion spread out over the entire town. Our company was quartered in the railroad area, some in houses cleared of civilians; our platoon got the ground floor of an apartment house for railroad workers. Before we had a chance to realize what they had done to us, our days were filled with the same old routine—parades, drills, boot polishing, arranging our quarters with military precision, exercising, maneuvers. Every day was crammed with activities, the scenery was maddeningly beautiful, and letters from home reminded us of peace and our personal problems. During the few free hours we had, we climbed mountains, went to the movies, and began to get used to thinking about the future, about civilian life that suddenly seemed so close and frightening—even though everyone spoke of nothing else. Perhaps this was a way of not thinking of the degradation that was ours, at having been stopped in such a way, right on the border.

4

Take me for example.

All during those three days, from the moment that Corporal Macover, during the memorial parade, had read aloud the "commandments of the Hebrew soldier in Germany," and up to our halting at the border, I was in a state of exhilaration I had not known since my boyhood fantasies, since long before I actually experienced the devastation of military life. It seemed that once again I was no longer the captive of my imaginings, as I had been that winter night when I swore allegiance to the Haganah;* or when I attacked Pinik during the wedding on the roof; or when I could not smooth the ruffled waters of my youth, torn as I was between the sordid reality of the factory and my home, rent by tragedy and my high flown dreams so that I had to run off to the army. This time the fantasy was reality. Now I was one of the fighters in a glorious Jewish legion, in history's first Star of David conquest . . .

And as usual I plunged from the loftiest heights to the bottomless pit. And as usual, when the fantasy faded—the world turned black. Everything conspired against me: the procrastination on the border. Noga's betrayal. The letters from home crying for help. The fear of peace.

I was assigned permanently to one of the sections in Company B. I found myself in the same room with Tamari, little Ostreicher, Poker, Leizi, as well as Zunenshein, and two of the most disgusting characters in the company: Arusi, whom everyone called the Syrian; and Fleischtchik, whom even the Sergeant Major always addressed as "Shtickfleisch." † It would have been difficult to imagine a stranger octet than ours. Poker turned the room into the company card-room. Shtickfleisch, being a miser, played only rummy, but both he and the Syrian stood up for Poker just to irritate Tamari. They meant to provoke Zunenshein, too, but that lay beyond even the Syrian's power.

* Defense forces of the organized Jewish community in Palestine.
† Chunk of meat.

71

Before he was drafted, Arusi had been a barber's apprentice and in the army he served as his own tonsorial shop. Lovingly he would lavish attention on his soft hair, parted in the middle of his forehead and tumbling over his ears and down the back of his neck in oily curls. He would shampoo his head, smear it with cream oil until it shone like crows' wings, shape it with a net, comb it endlessly—all the while boasting of his conquests the night before and the pleasures awaiting him that coming night. He withheld no details in describing his exploits but shared the most secret techniques he employed with every woman. For example, the woman who took our shirts and underwear to wash, the one who lived not far off, at the bottom of the mountain. Her husband had served in the Italian Army and had never returned. "A cunt that couldn't be satisfied, like a horse. But with me she shrieks for joy. I finish her off. Last night I drove her so crazy she cried. She never had anything like it in her life, she said. Look, Tamari, look what she did to me, the crazy bitch." The Syrian lifted his shirt, drew near to Tamari who was sitting on his bed writing, winking at all of us the while. "Look how she sank her teeth there below, in my belly. Look, Tamari, look and tell me if your girls in the *kibbutz* do things like that to you. . . . Lift your head up, Tamari, let Arusi teach you how to warm a girl up so it drives her crazy. . . . You tell him, Leizi, you're from the *kibbutz*. . . . He should learn a little bit. . . ."

Tamari, utterly muddled, would get up and start gathering his things together. Arusi and the foursome playing cards between Poker's and Shtickfleisch's bed would burst out laughing. Leizi and Ostreicher would laugh, too. Tamari would dash outside.

Not so Zunenshein, whom Arusi had tried to provoke; everyone respected Zunenshein, who they said had been a famous journalist in Czechoslovakia, or something like that. Arusi gave up pretty quickly and it was no wonder. I had seen Zunenshein during the period I had been attached to the company as a stretcher-bearer, but only now that we were living in one room did I become close to him.

He was younger than Tamari, forty at most, which is to say, twice as old as I; but he, too, seemed to me to be one of the old

72

men. He smoked a pipe which, as far as I was concerned, already identified him as a man of distinction. The short pipe went well with his large head, which somehow looked like the head of a Russian chess player. His tangled locks were brushed back, yet every hair seemed to stick up individually like pointed, rusty wires. The same was true of his thick, bushy brows beneath which you expected to find shining, black, actor's eyes. However, his eyes were very calm, even somewhat opaque, like blueish, frosted glass. So it seemed those first few days. After a while I was amazed that I had not seen immediately the sad wisdom in those eyes. He would get a great many newspapers and books from England, and every free moment would find him lying on his bed, smoking and reading. But he never seemed too preoccupied and never showed any anger when interrupted. To the contrary, he knew how to hold a conversation with every one of his neighbors, even with Shtickfleisch, who spent all his energies feeding his ever-hungry body; even with the Syrian.

He was endowed with that rarest of qualities—to elevate the man he was speaking to without condescension. With the Syrian he would discuss women, with Shtickfleisch, various kinds of foods, but I took pride inwardly in the fact that he was especially affectionate toward me. He would tell me of pre-war Prague and of books he loved; and after I told him once how I would sit and study after work during blackouts, reading English novels with the aid of a dictionary, he began urging me to look into his newspapers and books, and guided me in the selection of subjects and authors. At that time a few courses were organized in the regiment, both as preparation and to distract and stir us out of the apathy that had settled in. Zunenshein did not leave me alone until I promised that I, too, would start studying.

Zunenshein's friendship during those weeks was something I was able to appreciate properly only much later. I was given to periodic attacks of apathy, deeper and more sustained than I had known till then. It would go like this: When my hopes and dreams "shattered on the rock of reality," as they say, I would fall on my bed, my face buried in my blankets, my back to the world, and doze. There was no anger, no tears, no turmoil; I just lay on the bed without moving, without speaking,

73

without eating, floating in darkness free of all thoughts or beginnings or endings, in a realm where everything was of equal worth—meaning everything was worthless—where it did not matter whether everything disappeared where it had come from or whether it would recur a thousand times. Worse, I was sunk in a total depression that had lasted since my return from the hospital, since those two letters I interpreted as Noga's breaking up with me.

I had foreseen this break from our first meeting and had never stopped warning myself of it. Nothing marred our relationship so much as my sure feeling that it was shaky to begin with; and out of a compulsion to put it to the test again and again, I took a sick delight in seizing upon any weak point, and by straining to prove that the crack was indeed a crack, I would distend it feverishly until what never was there to begin with did appear in the end. So Noga claimed. I hammered the idea into my head, she said, that since she was already a student in a teachers' seminary while I was only a soldier serving the homeland, and since she was the daughter of a slightly higher than average official in national institutions while I was, after all, only the son of a pioneer in a *moshava*, it was a sign we were separated by a cultural and economic chasm forever, like Lady Chatterley and the gamekeeper. . . .

"You don't have to be so literary. It's not because I'm serving the homeland. It's just the opposite—I'm serving the homeland because I wouldn't have continued my studies anyway."

"Oh, no. You volunteered."

"Because I was sick and tired of the factory. Because I wanted to get away from the *moshava*. That's all."

"You can't fool me. You're very sensitive even if you are a little neurotic . . ."

"A little!"

"I love you just the way you are—an ugly soul in a beautiful body."

"In a pressed uniform."

"Why do you make fun of me like this all the time?"

"If we had met in my factory when I was in blue overalls, instead of in the Menorah Club . . ."

74

"Then what? . . . You're a child, Elisha . . . a child . . . child . . . child."

"Why a child?"

"Because you don't understand anything. What do I care about your blue overalls? What difference does it make? If you like, go on with your studies, if you don't, don't go on. . . ."

I had only heard her last words. "If you don't, don't go on." Noga, I thought, why did you say, "If you don't, don't go on"? Surely you knew I wanted to, had to, but that I just lacked self-confidence and that on the other hand if I didn't continue my studies and simply returned to the factory and to the *moshava*, we would be cut off from each other. Or perhaps your true estimate of me and my capabilities crept into the casual, seemingly loving remark. Perhaps—precisely because you cared for me—you wanted to prepare me for the very likely prospect that I would not go on with my studies, that I could not, after five, six or more years, return to the students' bench to learn two hundred chapters of the Bible, physics, trigonometry, integrals and differentials, memorize all of Lachover* and Macbeth. . . .

Of course I could not. Only a maniac like Hershler could haul a kit bag half full of books around with him, bury his head in his hands, study endlessly, memorize all of Bialik from "To the Bird" to "Who Knows the City of Listina?" Not I. I knew full well my place in the world, where I came from, and where I would be able to get to, right to the tip of the chain around my leg. Only when you lay on a bed with your head buried in the covers in the darkness were there no chains or ties.

It was all determined from the start and had I had an ounce of brains in my head I would have broken it all off the moment I realized that my trip to Jerusalem was not simply a pleasant way to spend one evening a week, but that the entire week was one long wait for that evening. But I lacked that ounce of brains; I was moonstruck by that girl, the very opposite of all I had ever known. I had grown up in a barracks with all the family's affairs conducted in one room, one person bumping into the next. Noga's parents lived in an old stone house in

* Noted Hebrew literary critic.

75

Jerusalem full of high-ceilinged, shadowy rooms, dark furniture, books, pictures, threadbare rugs. Noga's older brother worked as a watchman while he studied at the Technion in Haifa, and she had a huge room all to herself. She left her mark on its every corner.

It was a long time before I got up enough courage to enter their house; we would usually make arrangements to meet in one of the coffee houses in the city. The first time she took me to her parents I swore to myself that my feet would never cross that threshold a second time. My tongue stuck to the roof of my mouth and no matter what they asked me I could only stammer confusedly in reply. Not only her father but her mother spoke a rich flowery Hebrew in loud, aggressive voices, with pronounced Russian accents. It seemed to me her mother was appraising me, deciding as she spoke that I was not worthy of her daughter. ("A precious girl, a wonderful student, too sensitive, like her father.")

She had no need to convince me; I knew very well I was not worthy. Nonetheless I continued to travel to Jerusalem. I did not have the strength to give up Noga, who showered me with endless tenderness, sweetness, and peace. I loved to sit in Noga's room and silently watch her work, paint, put her insect collection in order, prepare for a test; I loved to sit and listen to the rustle of the trees in front of the shuttered window, and the silence of that vast home; I loved to look at her slim, swift-moving fingers and that look of concentration in her intelligent eyes as she studied; I loved to see that impish look of hers when I would tell her about our adventures in camp; I loved to get her angry by drowning in self-pity—just so I could hear her say afterward in her warm, comforting voice: "You're a child, Elisha . . . a child . . . child . . . child."

I didn't have an ounce of brains. I loved Noga. I had had no girl before her and would never have another one like her. She was the one love of my life, unexpected, undeserved, and therefore sure to leave me one day and join all the fantasies that sooner or later shattered. Consciously and unconsciously I pushed our relationship to that brink.

When I came back from the hospital and found the two airmail letters clearly indicating that something had happened during my long absence from home: "Your whole life is before you, etc. . . . and who knows whether or not you will find me as you left me, etc." I answered her in a long, rather gruff letter that actually I was not at all surprised such thoughts should come to her mind. The two of us were changing and in which ways we both knew well: She would study, get a job, find her niche in society, and since she was no longer so young (unlike me, who was always young), she was naturally concerned about the purpose of our correspondence especially since the present situation might extend a long time—years maybe, if there was any truth to the rumors that we would be stationed in Germany as an occupation army or would be sent to the jungles of Burma. Really, there was no reason to keep it up. Farewell and all the best. "Thanks for the memories," I wrote, "thanks for the letters. Warmly."

Since then I had waited for a letter, a letter that would make light of my pomposity, banish all the doubts I had raised, declare anew, unmistakably, that all she meant to say was that it was I, perhaps, who no longer wanted her—not at all the twisted message I had construed through my sick imagination. But I got no letter. Not prior to our setting out and not upon our arrival at the border. I thought only of letters. At first postal communications fell into disorder because of our transfer to a different area, but then everyone began getting mail as usual. Bubi, who was now in the next room, proudly announced that his system of numbering letters had proved its worth once again: not a letter was missing. Now I knew it was all over. She was sick and tired of me and I had handed her an excuse to break off once and for all. I and no one else.

And as though everyone had conspired to drag me back to where I had started from, I suddenly got a letter from home: "Things aren't going well. Father's leg, which broke a few years ago when he fell off a scaffolding, is giving him trouble again. The doctors don't know what to say. Maybe it's not a fracture but a pained nerve. Mother's nerves, too, aren't as they should be. We read in the papers about the terrible cataclysm. We've heard nothing from our family and we pray our fears will prove false. Making ends meet is hard. Your sister Nehama will finish elementary school this year and wants to go on to high

77

school, but where will we get the money? Dear Elisha, all our pain, Mother's and mine, is not physical. We miss you and fear for your safety. Enough, the war has ended in victory, you've done your part, now come home. Our neighbor Kubalsky tells us his son is getting discharged for family reasons. We can forge doctors' letters saying you have to come home, Elisha. Do this, Elisha. We really need you, not so much to help us out financially but because we miss you so very much. Write us right away and let's hope we'll see each other soon and rejoice together."

Ah yes, full circle once again. Already they sensed I would soon be coming home so they wasted no time in spreading their net. They already had sat down and talked the matter over: Elisha must be taken in hand. He always had hair-brained schemes. He can't sit still in one place, if we don't get him back home on the sly who knows where he will wind up and what will become of him. Let him come home, get his job again, save up a little money, no, let him help us get on our feet a bit first, then let him get himself a good girl . . . Ah, there's a problem: he's a shy sort. We have to find him a good girl, but let him come already, so we can keep an eye on him. . . .

Oh no, not that, I thought, screwing up my face. They wanted to drag me back to where I had started from. But all their sly scheming and groaning wouldn't bring me back to them. I was all alone, all alone. The past lay behind me; I was a free man; free to do just as I pleased and let the world go fiddle. Brodsky was right. "All you need is to get laid with any girl; that'll clear your head and put some zap into you. Then you won't have to drag around with those love-sick eyes, *oy.* . . ." Why hadn't I been able to walk in with Brodsky? I had wanted to, wanted to try it out, to sink my teeth in the last prohibition binding me to the frightening *don'ts* of Father; and I still wanted to—simply, without any melodrama.

By this time my head felt lighter and my legs, too. How simple it all was. I was alone. Without any passionate, nonsensical oaths of undying love, with no broken hearts. I was alone as I had always wanted to be; now I was being helped simultaneously from two sides. Suddenly I was hovering in empty space, attached to nothing. Who gave a damn about museums, operas, Jews, the Renaissance or the whole damn cultural pose

I had tied on like a strait-jacket? I was in Austria to stand on my head, jump off the roof, see if I could just go to a woman like Brodsky or the Syrian did, stray just once beyond the pale of my childhood in all its innocence, fear and utter boredom.

When I heard Arusi say he was heading for Venice in a truck driven by his friend, that he was taking off on a forged pass, I asked if I could join him and at once was swept away with a feeling of joyous abandon such as I had never known. "Sure thing," said Arusi poking his thumb between my ribs. "Come with me for once and see how they jump all over dark boys like you and me. . . ."

"Sure thing," I said.

5

We didn't go to Venice the next day because the company (with the exception of one platoon) was moved to another town twenty kilometers to the south for guard duty and to accompany some trains. The whole area was a strange conglomeration. We saw many partisans with red ties but were unable to understand their connection with Tito's Yugoslavia, two mountain ridges away; maybe they were *Werwulf* * in disguise. We heard that that region, which contained a large number of *Volksdeutsche*, also contained some of the most rabid Nazis. Sure, now they tried to pass as Italians to hide their past. But according to our neighbor, an Italian coachman transferred from the south, it was an open secret who they had been a month or two ago, an open secret where they were, the husbands of those women, the sons of those old women, the fathers of those young girls. If they weren't wandering around in the mountains and if they hadn't stolen back to their homes and put on civilian dress (those were the very men we saw all about us), then they were in the prisoner-of-war camps.

* A division of the Nazi youth movement called into being toward the end of the war and supposedly made up of below draft-age youths and soldiers who would continue to fight even after an area had been captured by the Allies. Few incidents involved them.

The people's faces there were no different than faces anywhere in the world; no matter how hard we tried we could not make out the features of the devil's henchmen in those townspeople living on the slopes of the mountains. Our town seemed innocent enough. Above it the dark forest clambered up to sharp peaks bracketing plumed, downy clouds; and below the town beyond the bridge ran a river zippering together the feet of our mountain and the mountain opposite.

There were two coffee houses facing one another, in the town square and from which one could see everything—the main highway, the two alleys, groups of *regazzas* passing by at twilight. They were not like the girls of the south, tan with eyes like black olives, Mediterranean, almost Jewish; instead they were like the Christian maidens in romances, poems, movies—fairskinned as though they had grown in the shade, flaxen-haired, plump and full-breasted, red-cheeked, the kind of girls you tumble on a threshing floor, the same Christian girls that terrified so many pious Jewish men. Ah, what a crazy mess. We knew from six years of warfare, from all we had read, from our dead relatives, that Europe was covered with blood; but here all was a pastoral.

And then there was the railroad.

Our two platoons were quartered in an abandoned barracks on a hill at the outskirts of the town—a group of structures surrounding a courtyard, the enlisted men's quarters set apart, the officers' apart and the animals' too. (Previously they had all been barracks for the horsemen of *Il Duce.*) On the very first day that we quartered there, everyone who had not been sent to guard the storehouses skewered out of the mountains, or had not been grabbed for guard duty, went down before evening to wander about the town.

Very quickly we found ourselves on the street leading to the railroad station. To the side of the road stood a modest building of a seemingly insignificant station. To the south the railroad tracks were being repaired, but trains were still coming in from the north. All the time. From Klagenfurt, from Vienna, even from Budapest. From Warsaw, too? "Maybe from Warsaw, too," said the stationmaster. "Why not? In a little while a train from Klagenfurt will come in," he told us.

80

Not only the main track itself but the side tracks, too, seemed to be a cemetery for railroad cars—each car with the stamp of its home station imprinted on its side, from Breslau to Zagreb. Among them were cars damaged by aerial explosions that left invisible wounds, rendering them useless: wild grasses sprang up around their rusting wheels. Ploesti. Warsaw. Kiel. Amsterdam. If only a few voices had stuck to their sides we would have heard the moans of the Great War.

As we stood on the platform we heard the whistle of an incoming train. Smoke mushroomed up from beneath the train, blotting out the mountains. The cars crept alongside the platform, holding their breath, jam-packed freight cars with men sticking out of open doors, narrow windows, in between the cars. Theirs was a mass of mixed uniforms, neither civilian nor military, burning eyes, wide-open mouths, national songs, numberless small flags pouring onto the platform, every man holding a little flag in his hand, waving it vigorously, as though that would distinguish him from all the other returning soldiers, so the world might know it was indeed he who had returned home in peace.

Except for two or three railroad workers and ourselves there was no one waiting in the station. The jubilant shouting and the national anthems and the red, white and green flags all descended upon us. And as for us, we stood there as a delegation of sorts—not for the main body of men returning to their homelands, but for those few souls who were perhaps scattered throughout the cars, no flags in hand, no joy in their hearts. They, upon seeing us and the insignias on our uniforms, would surely leap at us, hang on our necks and whisper in trembling voices, "You are here, too? You waited for us? Us? *Shma Yisrael . . .*" *

Nothing of the sort happened. Bubi suddenly snapped, "What are we standing here like *schmucks* for? Who the hell are we waving at?"

"Why not?" said Leizi. "These guys suffered, too."

"Suffered, yeah. Half of them are Fascists and pricks."

* "Hear O Israel . . ." (the Lord our God, the Lord is One): the Jewish declaration of faith.

81

"Look at their faces," said Brodsky. "They ate German bread —the whole war."
We spoke no more of them, but quickly set ourselves off from the arrivees. No one approached us.

6

The next day we returned to the station to accompany a train leaving for Klagenfurt. I would have been happy for the opportunity to go on that first trip had it not been for Corporal Kuperberg. He was a red-headed pasty-faced fellow into whose hands I had fallen in Saratand. Before he had enlisted he had served two years as a *gaffir** on the border patrol in *Aretz* and came equipped with everything that made an impression on sergeants of new recruits: He was an expert in drilling and the manual of arms, the tip of his bayonet flashed like black steel, he would spend hours scraping his belt and polishing it with limewater; he would not leave a buckle or brass button until it shone like a tiny windowpane. Because of all these traits and the English phrases he had at the tip of his tongue he was given the great honor of serving the base commander. For one day. As a consequence, he was given one stripe, which ushered him into the inner councils of the officers of the British Empire. At the closing parade the colonel said every soldier had a commander's baton in his kit bag and Kuperberg was sure that was a reference to him. Now he was another stripe nearer his precious goal.

He was intolerable—he never smiled, and forced us to make the tables and benches on the base shine by scrubbing them with bricks. Before the Sabbath parade he would drive the squad crazy and at times it even seemed that he polished his red face with Brasso, and scraped and polished the white peach fuzz covering his pink arms with limewater. I was happy when I was transferred to headquarters company and didn't see him again. Now once more we were in the same company and had to travel together to Klagenfurt. It was a good thing Zunen-

* Auxiliary policeman.

82

shein, Leizi and Poker were coming along, too. We would have to maneuver carefully in order to outwit Kuperberg.

We pulled out at night. The car we had been assigned was loaded mostly with crates of battle rations. We spread our bedding out on the floor and made ready for the night. Poker, prepared for all emergencies, fished his candle-fueled card-playing lamp out of his kit bag and tried to get a game going. This was not to Corporal Kuperberg's liking, for: one, there should never be an open fire in a railroad car full of wooden crates; two, His Majesty's ordinances forbade card playing for money; three, we had to go to sleep. It didn't matter that not a one of us four actually wanted to be a partner to Poker—he and Kuperberg were up half the night debating the principle of the thing.

When I opened my eyes, thick, misty daylight was seeping through the cracks of the car door. I slid the door slightly open and saw a new landscape. To our right a lake stretched as far as the eye could see. Through the chill shower, clouds of smoke spiraled up into a pale, sunless sky. The horizon was opaque.

The earth swelled thick and green in the rainy dawn. Cows stood behind wooden fences chewing their cud in the mist. A house thrust sharp turrets upward like a fairy castle. Someone was riding a bicycle with thick tires down a graveled path, very slowly, in a black raincoat and a black casquette, its visor glistening in the wet. We had crossed the border.

The freight train crept slowly forward while the engine gingerly sniffed out the way. It was June, when everything lay still back home in the *moshava*, even the dust; then the wagoners would gather in the garage, beneath the eucalyptus trees; and in my factory the tin roof would be burning while the welders, their eyes shielded with goggles, would be lighting the carbide burners, grumbling, "Eight in the morning and already we're dying from the *hamsin*.* " But there in the railroad car the cold pierced us to the bone, while on the horizon, pressed tight against the lake, rose legends. We passed a beer house. There was a barrel hanging on the wall, large Gothic letters painted in a wide arc in red, black, and gold.

My grandfather—so my father often told me—came from

* Heat wave.

83

Germany. "Many Germans," my mother would tell me "lived near us." "The Germans are very educated people," my father would say.

We had an album full of picture postcards and in the wintertime I would sit all alone and leaf through the album, journeying to all the places painted on the cards—a moonlit lake, a maiden lying at the foot of a tall tree reading a letter with teary eyes, a horse and rider dying in a green field—just like these green fields.

Mother would say, "Once more I want to visit there, just once more. I'll take you to our village," she would say. "I'll show you what forests we had there, what a river we had, and in the summer, how green it was there in the summer."

Around the rim of the lake and in the suburbs of the city stood many houses ornamented like fairy tale sugar houses, with roofs intact and walls unbroken. Only when the train plunged into the city itself, into the neighborhood of the railroad station, did we see ruins—overturned railroad cars, the bones of houses. Railroad men stood among the ties signaling with their flags. The train slowed to a halt. A British sergeant from the military railroad service received the train. We were to stay within the station area, he told us, so we could go back on a train leaving early in the afternoon. We should find ourselves some corner of the station and set up, he said, and left.

We stood on the platform with our kit bags, our blankets, and a case of food. No one so much as bothered to look at us, to notice that we were Jewish soldiers and to tremble. The dreary platforms swarmed with refugees, thousands out of Europe's millions. Here, too, we saw the pennants, the national colors on coat lapels, all the nations of Europe: Frenchmen, Dutch, Greeks, Italians, Belgians. All of them were jammed into the trains taking them home. Men took leave of one another. Some wept, some laughed. All were pushing and squeezing into the cars. Now that the trains were heading in the opposite direction they were impatient to leave.

We stood in the press, shoved against the wall, unsure of what we ought to do. Corporal Kuperberg said we had to find ourselves a corner, get organized, sit down and eat, and wait for orders. By that time we had distinguished between the trav-

84

elers and permanent residents. The station workers wore almost military uniforms; the large Reich insignia had been
ripped off their caps, off their sleeves and from above their vest
pockets, leaving shreds of thread. They hadn't even changed
their outfits. They had ripped off the insignias and gone on
working at the same jobs, on the same line.

"First we get a room for ourselves," said Poker as he strode
into the office of the stationmaster. "Hey, *Du!* A room. We
want a room."

The short roundish man, who seemed to swim in his uniform, said that he did not understand.

"You damn well understand, you prick. *Scheisse!*" As he
spoke he turned his head to Zunenshein. "How's my German,
Zunenshein?"

"The important words you know," smiled Zunenshein, obviously pleased. Poker had already looked over the office and had
peered into the inner room, which he found to his liking. Without asking our advice he walked over to the short man and
whispered into his mustache in a thick Yiddish.

"*Dem zimmer, ya kalb, das mir nemen, herr kakman!*" *

We laughed, delighted at this display of our conquerors'
status. We gathered our belongings together and entered the
room confiscated by Poker. The stationmaster ran after us, crying aloud in the deep bass of a man accustomed to running
stations from birth, but Poker leisurely and politely arranged
his belongings, remarking at intervals:

"You should roast alive . . . *platzen sollst du†* . . . very
true . . . *Herr Schveinhundt.*"

The man stalked out, outraged and very sure of himself, and
returned shortly with another man like him, who now seemed
to be the true stationmaster. The man greeted us politely and
even bowed slightly, but before he could open his mouth, Leizi
grabbed the submachine gun, jerked a magazine out of his belt
and said, "Zunenshein, tell him that I'll fill him full of lead if
he doesn't clear out pronto."

"Idiots," yelled Kuperberg, "do you want to wind up in
jail?"

* "The room, you dog, we're taking it, prick."
† "You should drop dead."

85

"Tell him," Leizi continued, "that I'm not responsible for my actions." It was then I learned why I had suspected Zunenshein of being an actor. He cleared his throat, cocked his head, and said in elegant German, "My good railroad clerk! This young man will shoot you if you do not take your leave at once. He is a very nervous soldier from the Jewish Army, as indeed we all are. Would you care to be shot? Tell me, if you would be so kind—"

The two clerks stumbled upon our identity as upon a mine. They shrank, their faces stony with fear as though they had suddenly seen the ghosts of the people who had passed by endlessly in sealed boxcars, people whom they were sure of never seeing again. But there we were in that room in uniform, armed, different in all but our eyes, eyes like the eyes that stared through the slatted cars. Stiff-leggedly they backed out, their frozen faces on Leizi's Tommy gun, until they disappeared beyond the doorway.

We piled our belongings in the corner, took our weapons, and turned to leave for the city. We, not Corporal Kuperberg.

"Where are you going, fellas?" There was something pathetic in that word "fellas" coming from Kuperberg, an admission that he was losing his grip as officer in charge. Things were slipping through his fingers and politeness was his last refuge.

"To the city," said Poker.

"We have orders, fellas. . . . The train, it could pull out any minute."

"Let her pull out. We're in no rush to get back."

"It certainly won't leave before noon," said Zunenshein politely. "Let's have a short visit to the city, corporal, and then come back to the station, eh? Let's all go, eh?"

From the start we knew we were not going to coop ourselves up in the station, not on our first trip to a city across the border, but Kuperberg was subject to His Majesty's commands.

"For a half-hour" he said, looking for an honorable way out for us and for himself.

When we passed through the front room again we saw the tubby clerk sitting at his heavy desk, his eyes beads of glass in his round cheeks. This is not fear, a voice whispered inside me

86

as I saw how he was seated, his puffy hands grasping the table-
top; this is stunned hatred. He hadn't gotten used to our new
relationship yet, to our reincarnation, to Zunenshein's cold German, to the precise syntax of the murderous sentence he translated for them. Those gray eyes, sunken deep in his cheeks,
were crystals of hatred.

Leizi pushed his Tommy gun forward and with the end of
the short barrel knocked the rim of the clerk's hat upward,
sending it flying. The man did not move. Leizi slid the barrel
across the man's forehead down his cheek to his neck.

"Convincing, eh?" Leizi said to him in Hebrew. Poker
laughed.

"No, Leizi," said Zunenshein, as he held his arm. "Not that."

7

We strained to walk fully erect, we marched in step, striving to look like an official patrol. Civilians passed by us. Refugees streamed all about the station, men of all nationalities
hurrying home. No one noticed any difference between us and
the other British soldiers who were also walking about armed in
accordance with the general orders. In a courtyard, in the entrance to a bombed-out house, sat a few women in long dresses,
wearing kerchiefs tied beneath their chins, crouched over a
stove they had put together from broken bricks. Cooking vapors
rose from an inverted helmet placed over the fire. They looked
like Jewish women out of storybooks. We tried to get them to
talk to us, but they answered in a Slavic dialect. Gentile features looked up at us—broad cheekbones, eyes like smoked
glass, pinched lips.

To our amazement Kuperberg bent over and addressed them
in their language, to which they replied in amazed laughter.
But after one moment of astonishment they became very cau-
tious and confined every answer to a word or a shrug of a shoulder. Zunenshein whispered to us that he, too, who spoke Czech,
understood them and went on to translate their conversation
with Kuperberg.

87

They were from the Ukraine, they said. The Germans had stolen them from their homes and had sent them to Klagenfurt to perform various tasks. Now they were living there waiting for a train to take them westward to the Americans.

But didn't they want to go home?

"No," they replied, looking at each other as they stirred the bubbling stew in the steel helmet, "they won't ship us east."

"Why? Why?" laughed the eldest. "Because our hearts go out to pretty boys like you. . . ."

"Witches," Poker rumbled. "Tell them that we're Jews, corporal. Let's see how they'll look then."

"First ask if there are any Jews here, too, waiting for a train," said Zunenshein.

When Kuperberg told them we were Jews, I no longer needed any translation. They held their cheeks with their pasty hands and laughed until their large breasts shook. What fun, meeting such a bunch of clowns before breakfast, when the fire hadn't even warmed their chilly bones. Jews! Some joke!

Without any translation I got the gist of the conversation, linking the sentences together like a Hebrew translation of a Russian story.

"But we are Jews, dear ladies," Kuperberg said.

"Get out, you abortion! You want to make fun of a tortured old lady, my image-of-Christ . . ."

"Jews, as God lives. We're from the Jewish Army . . ."

Poking each other vigorously with their elbows, they laughed as though they would burst.

"You're a cute one, carrot-top. We saw the Jewish Army. They rode into the sky in trains of fire, in pillars of smoke. You want to play tricks on me, you tramp?" As she spoke the old woman grasped Leizi's leg. "And this one, this pretty one, is he one of your smoked Jew-boys, too?"

Kuperberg straightened up. Neither he nor Zunenshein continued to translate, but we all understood very well what was being said there, by the open fire, and the women, too, began to read their error in our faces, an error they could not comprehend. Terror stared from their filthy gray eyes. They froze in their crouched position like foxes suddenly caught at night

88

in the headlights of a speeding truck. Gripped by the same nausea we all silently turned and walked on down the road alongside the ruins fenced in by wooden scaffolding. We were treading scorched earth.

We walked through the streets and passed by a company of prisoners marching amid the scaffolding, tools on their shoulders, dragging their feet in the rhythm of defeat. At the sides of the road stood civilians accompanying them with pitying eyes. Us they did not see. Even if their eyes lit upon the insignia on our sleeves they made no connection between those insignias and us. We marched from street to street but no one fled before us screaming, "The Jews are coming!"

On one street corner we found a Naafi canteen where white-skinned girls in starched jackets walked among empty tables. We sat down and ordered coffee and sandwiches. The girls had nothing to do and we saw that we—Leizi and I—impressed them. One of them approached our table and smiled at us a bit forcedly. Poker, as was his habit everywhere and always, made a lewd suggestion to her, in Hebrew of course. The girl opened wide, curious eyes and leaned her body between me and Leizi, asking what Poker had said and in what language. The law of non-fraternization was still in effect, but she had already managed to learn English.

She beckoned to another waitress to come over. Two fair-skinned, beautiful girls who had become our friends in a moment. "This isn't English," said the first girl to the second, in German. "What country are these handsome boys from?" My eye began to wink involuntarily, but in the process the picture of the Ukrainian women we had just seen rose before me. I pointed to my sleeve and said, "Here's what we are."

"How lovely," laughed the girl standing between Leizi and me as she stroked the brigade's insignia.

"That's a Star of David," I told her. Her white face, the very image of a bonbon, wrinkled as she giggled. "What could that be? Canadians?"

Sure enough, we could have predicted the outcome. "You rascals, trying to pull our leg. There aren't any Jews except in horror stories, people with horns and hunchbacks. Don't make us laugh. They don't exist." No one would believe that we were Jews, that we were marching through this city in the names of our dead, as their avengers.

We returned to the street, by this time inclined to submit to the urgings of Corporal Kuperberg who was afraid of trouble and wanted us to go back to the railroad station. Better to lock ourselves up in our room until the train left rather than walk about the rain-washed plaza, in front of the towering gate, and know that no one had fearfully awaited our coming, that once we had arrived we frightened no one. What were we doing there if we could not shake that city to its foundations?

We stood in the paved plaza, centuries of unbroken settlement engraved in its stones, the trees, the people whose lives had not been disrupted for a moment.

We had had neighbors in the *moshava*, Jewish farmers from upper Austria, from Kärnten—a father and mother and two grown sons. They would sit for hours in the "Vienna" café speaking a kind of thick German just like we were hearing now. "Come on, let's get out of this madhouse."

Then we saw a tall girl stop. A bright raincoat clung to her body and a black beret covered one ear. As she passed, her eyes opened wide at the sight of the insignia on our sleeves. She knows, I thought, my heart pounding like a child's. But she continued to walk on swiftly, only when she neared the gate at the other end of the plaza, her back to us, did she stop.

"She's Jewish," I said.

The five of us stood looking at her silently. Her back was still to us, but she turned her head with the slight movements of a secret agent. By now we all knew who she was, but fearing disillusionment we did not stir. She would have to make the first move. She walked on slowly in a wide arc that became a circle until she returned to us. She looked like a photo of Greta Garbo in her raincoat, black beret, her clear northern face.

"Is it you?" she whispered in German, as though the entire city were looking at us.

"Yes," Zunenshein answered warmly, in German. He seemed to embrace the girl although his body did not budge. "And you?"

"You're from the Jewish Army?"

"You've heard of us?" We exchanged questions like spies in enemy territory.

"They said you weren't far off, but now I see soldiers who are really ours for the first time . . ."

"You're a Jewess?" said Kuperberg, voicing what we had all wanted to say.

"With Aryan papers," whispered the young woman, her eyes flitting over the plaza looking for someone who might spring up at any moment and find her out. "I'm a nurse in an army hospital. I'm alone, I daren't tell who I am."

"The war is over," smiled Zunenshein. "We won, young lady."

"I know, of course, I know," she said, but did not return the smile. She was afraid to stand with us in the plaza. "Are you staying in Klagenfurt?"

"No," said Kuperberg. "In a little while we're going back over the border. . . . Fellows, we have to move on!"

"You see," said the girl, "I'm here all by myself . . . although there are a few Hungarians. Tailors. . . ."

"Jews?" Poker revealed unaccustomed emotion.

"You a Magyar?" asked Leizi, looking him up and down.

"Jackass, me? My family. Who knows?—my great-grandfather maybe."

"Do you know where they're living?" Zunenshein asked.

"Certainly, I've visited them a few times. They were very lucky. They were on their way to be killed, marching on foot."

She took longer strides to put more distance between us. We walked slightly behind her as though we, too, agreed it really still made sense to be afraid, to beware of the searching eyes of the enemy. A strange procession: five armed soldiers trailing a lovely girl who knew there was no longer any need of Aryan papers, but still did not dare to leave her hospital. She went on working at her same job, went on living among those same people—the wounded, the doctors—being someone other than herself, refusing to believe in the freedom her true identity would afford her. Stealthily she now walked through the city where she had lived, who knows how long, the same city in which she had probably been to the station to welcome the wounded, seeing in the process the sealed boxcars heading east. Silently we walked after her. I had the strange feeling this moment was out of our time: we had fallen into another era.

Once again we were not far from the railroad station in the bombed-out district. We drew near a large house, one of whose sides had collapsed. From the courtyard we walked down a wooden staircase into a large cellar, a storeroom of sorts, its ceiling supported by two columns of pillars. While we were still on the steps I heard a band of men singing full-throatedly and fervently, "Yo ribon olam v'olmayo, ant hu malko melekh malkhayo." ("Oh, God, Master of the Universe, Thou art King, King of Kings.") In the center of the cellar stood a long, low chest which somewhat resembled a packing crate for eggs. It was surrounded by crude benches, wooden boards resting on boxes and bricks. Around the table sat a group of men singing, not noticing that we had entered. ". . . ant hu malko melekh malkhayo."

As my eyes got used to the cellar, making out the divisions between living quarters (blankets and sacks stretched from pillars to walls), and as I made out the small band surrounding the wooden chest—at that moment my only thought was that it was the Sabbath day; until then we had forgotten. Despite myself I saw my father seated at his table, singing the same Sabbath hymns, accompanying himself by tapping the bread-knife against a fork or on the white tablecloth. "Tsur mishehlo okhalnu bor'khu emunoy, Sovanu v'hosarnu, kidvar adonoy." ("Rock of whose bounty we have eaten, bless Him, O ye faithful ones; we have eaten and left over in accordance with God's word.") Wine stains from many Sabbaths. Gnawed-on fish bones. Crumbs of the khalah crust and poppy seeds Father would push together with his knife. Candlesticks not touched since the night before. "Yo ribon olam v'olmayo . . ." How far I had traveled in the short time since I had fled my father's table. Like a planed board, shellacked and polished, like a stone smoothed by water, I had left all behind me. It was as if the Sabbath had never existed, as though my sister Nehama and I had never sat down and sung so loudly, as though it was not I who had descended those cellar steps, there to discover the Sabbath day.

What had that assembly been doing one moment before we

92

entered? How had their table been set? I cannot remember, for suddenly they looked up and saw the nurse in her raincoat and black beret coming down the steps with us. Years later, when I began reading in books about Hassidim and pious Jews welcoming the Sabbath or delaying its departure, singing on and on, hoping that at any moment the Messiah would come—I would see before me those Hungarian tailors in that cellar near the Klagenfurt railroad station.

They did not doubt for a moment we were the Jewish Army; they adjusted to the fact instantaneously. We all spoke at once —they, an upper Hungarian Yiddish; Kuperberg, a thick East Galician variety; Poker, the Palestinian Yiddish of a man educated in South Tel Aviv; and Leizi and I blurted the few scattered phrases that we knew, he even less than I. They caressed us, took our caps, inspected the quality of the cloth of our uniforms, read our insignias, toyed delightedly with our rifles and Tommy guns and asked us to take them with us at once—they, their tools, their belongings; they were ready to leave. That very Sabbath. *Nu, rabosai,** no sooner said than done.

Kuperberg began to get nervous. "It's not possible," he explained to them. "We're in the British Army, we have a job to do; we'd be investigated. It's not possible. We'll go back to our company right away and tell whoever must be told we've found Jews and in a few days—depend on *Eretz Yisrael*—people will come and take care of you. . . . No, now we would only ruin everything. . . ."

At first we all pounced on the corporal. "What's the difference, we'll take them with us. How many are they—twelve, sixteen? We can squeeze them into our railroad car, bring them back to the barracks and then we'll see. The train's ours. The border's ours. We'll take them."

Zunenshein changed his mind almost at once and made joint cause with Kuperberg. "You can't do such things on the spur of the moment, without official permission. They must have a plan for helping Jews—what to do, where to assemble them. We think we're the first, but others must have preceded us, others who are working under orders of the agencies."

* Gentlemen.

93

"Oh, shove your agencies!" Poker snorted. "They'll do whatever the English want them to."

Leizi and I both sided with Poker. The idea of doing something concrete, tangible, of bringing a carload of Jews with us back over the border on our first trip—that captivated us. We had to act. The agencies, what did they know of these Jews who were ready to be led away on the Sabbath itself? What did they know of this girl?

As we argued among ourselves, with Kuperberg urging us to go back to the station, the Hungarians' enthusiasm began to cool. At first they had surrounded us, patted us, clung to us, ready to follow us without batting an eyelash. But now they began to raise difficulties.

"Why dash off on the Sabbath day on a freight train, when maybe no one's waiting for us there, maybe they won't even know what to do with us? Maybe it would be better to wait here a few more days and see how things turn out. And what about our families? We can't abandon them. Maybe we ought to head back to Hungary, find them, and then come back. Anyway, here we have the privileges of war refugees—what would become of them if we left for Italy on our own for some isolated village where we wouldn't be able to make a living? And who knows if we could reach *Eretz Yisrael* from there? We should simply dash off, just like that? Where would we go?" All at once everything fell apart; the whole affair had become tasteless.

Their stories ate into us like acid, stories told to us later again and again, so I need not spell out in detail what we heard from the tailors for the first time. Since they had been craftsmen they had been kept in work camps and only when the Red Army entered Hungary had they been handed over to the S.S. to be moved west. There, in upper Austria, they had been liberated. We sat facing each other: they, wretched tailors in clothes given them after the liberation, the surging fire we had kindled in their eyes fading away; and we, unable to bear that encounter.

"Let's at least take Esther," said Poker. In the short while she had spent with us she had told us she was from Lodz and

94

that she and a friend were equipped with *Volksdeutsche* papers which had gotten them to that town two years before.

"Let's take Esther, Corporal Kuperberg," Zunenshein said. He, too, felt guilty about having disappointed the Hungarians.

"I'll wait a few more days," said Esther. "I want to go with my friend."

"And in the meantime? Will you go back to the German hospital?" asked Zunenshein.

"What else can I do? I have a room there, food, protection."

We did not know what to advise her. We gave her all the cigarettes we had with us. We talked her into walking us to the railroad station, where Poker slipped her a sealed tin of twenty-four chocolate bars from a crate of battle rations. Once more we urged her to come with us. But she was still gripped by some incomprehensible fear. Almost in a panic she kissed us good-by and fled, disappearing among the ruined houses.

A few short hours after we had arrived, we stood on the platform of the railroad station, disheartened, disillusioned, exhausted. The sergeant from the railroad unit stalked toward us, scowling. Not knowing where we had disappeared to, he had already phoned the M.P.'s. The train was to leave in another hour, if not sooner. We had best climb aboard our car at once.

"Never fear, Sarge, we wouldn't stay here," piped Poker, friend to every man.

We passed by the unseeing eyes of the stationmaster and his companion: they were patiently waiting for us to leave, to go back where we had come from. They would stay, the bastards. We entered the room we had appropriated and examined our belongings and the chest of rations. Nothing was missing. They'd made sure we would have no grounds for complaint. We spread our blankets out on the boxcar floor and lay down, having no desire to see the city, the railroad clerks, or the refugees packing the train we were on from one end to the other. None of that interested us any longer. Silently we had come and silently we would go, bearing with us only the memory of the Hungarian Jews seated about the Sabbath table and the one girl on the plaza whom we had left behind us. We would close our eyes and be still.

95

III Judgment

Slowly the train staggered up into the mountains, creaking, its
wheels straining as though it were out of breath, as though at
any instant it would slide back, with all that mass of humanity
crammed into the cars in front of us. But we didn't care
whether we moved or stood still. We were sealed off from the
darkness outside and had sealed ourselves off from the car as
well, burrowing beneath our blankets. Sporadically, we would
wake up at the sound of cars banging into one another, the
clanking of chains, the shouts of railroad men—then sink again
into a half-sleep. God, how many stations were there on that
milk route? Or maybe the train had broken down. Or maybe
we were switching tracks. Since the day before we had not
changed our clothes and we were dizzy with the smell of soot,

the sudden stops, and the din. Nonetheless, we did not move a limb. When we got there we would know what was what.

We were standing still for longer than usual and outside there was more than the expected tumult of shouting and cars jostling back and forth. I heard the door slide back on its runners. Through my stocking cap, through my closed eyelids, daylight broke.

"It's the border, guys," thundered Leizi.

I peeled my cap off and raised myself on my elbow, wrapped like a mummy in the blankets I had wrapped around me. A bright blue day filled the doorway and looking sidewise, I saw the peak which by then I knew so well. While we had been closeted in darkness the sun had climbed to the mountain's height and had sprung beyond it. Damn them, those mornings were enough to drive you crazy!

Down at the foot of the car we heard angry shouts in Italian as Leizi choked with laughter. He was leaning against the corner of the car facing outward and only then did I see what he was doing.

"So what were you coming around here for without an invitation?" he yelled at the spluttering railroad man. "Did you think we were giving out tea?"

Even Kuperberg laughed and raised himself on his elbow; only Poker stayed stretched out on the floor cursing and demanding that Leizi close the boxcar door. Finally, he too gave in and got up to view the morning.

The train jerked forward and crawled out of the station. Songs erupted from the railroad cars and the station workers waved their hats, shouting in welcome. The wheels picked up speed, clouds of smoke mushroomed behind us, and the men's voices were drowned in the roar of the train.

The valley narrowed as we approached the side of the mountain. The smoke lay thick upon the forest as if snagged by bayonets. Wrecked telephone poles and wires ran alongside us. Once again the brakes shrieked, the cars clanked against each other, then slowly we glided into the rows of stationary boxcars. With our gear bundled up and our weapons in hand we prepared to jump off, hoping the truck would be waiting for us at the station.

97

But of course it was not. We decided to go to the town's one plaza, where the main highway crossed the road leading to our barracks. By that time we no longer cared if we had to stay there all day. We sat down on rickety chairs in the entrance of the empty café. Before us, in the center of the plaza, a fountain played. The road heading north lay to our right and the one heading to Udine to our left.

Opposite us in the Poste Café a bunch of teen-age boys whistled at two girls who dashed across the plaza to disappear in the doorway of a store. Leizi, his long legs stretched out in front of him, read all the signs on the walls, syllable by syllable: "*Typographica Belina Cartoleria—Liberaria. Banca del Veneto.*" Time crept by. Bitter and despondent we sipped some kind of black soup. What were we accomplishing by sitting around there, and what was waiting for us at camp? They would flock around us, ask about our exploits across the border—and what could we say?

At about eleven the supply truck passed by on its way back from the regimental quartermaster's. We flagged it down and piled our gear on board. Mushik the cook was seated beside the driver, and Poker didn't let him alone until he let him examine all the mail. Zunenshein, as usual, had received a roll of newspapers from England. Leizi had been sent a mimeographed pamphlet from his *kibbutz*. Kuperberg and Poker were left out in the cold, but I got a letter from Father. And that was all.

Every day I reminded myself to forget about Noga and her letters and every day I would whisper to myself, "They'll come today." I waited in vain. How could I get them when they were no longer being written? We climbed aboard the truck. I cleared a space for myself among the gear and cartons of supplies and began to open Father's letter. But I already knew it by heart even while it was still in the envelope: *Greeting and consolations. And how were things with me? Things were thus and thus with them. And the whole country was turning handsprings for pride over "our precious, beloved children who risked their lives and redeemed Israel's honor in the sight of the nations." And so forth. And so forth.*

Up to the paragraph enumerating all their woes, on the other

98

side of the sheet: *Alack. And alas. We're suffering, we long for you. What of the future? You've done your share. When will you look to your family's needs? And our health—don't ask. In short, what are you waiting for, our dear Elisha, why aren't you looking into a discharge on family grounds at once? And as for the Nazis, may their name be blotted out, now we have wreaked vengeance . . ."*

I stuffed the envelope into a pocket of my field jacket and stared at the green earth and blue sky. Noga would never write again. It was over and done with; why should I have been surprised? Hadn't I myself suggested we no longer keep in touch with each other? Hadn't I written just that to her?

No, just the opposite. "There's no sense in a rote correspondence," I had written, "better to hear the truth than get charity mail. If you're fed up, I won't be angry. If you found yourself a boy friend more attractive than a good-for-nothing rambler like me, I'll be the first to congratulate you. That would only be natural, we know a little of what comes of war romances. To love long distance, on the strength of a memory, passionately —only an unusual girl could do that; and if anyone is guilty it's me for having naïvely thought that you, Noga, you were that unusual girl. My mistake. Forgive me . . ."

So I wrote her then, slyly confident that in the return mail all kinks would be ironed out and Noga would write in her clear, neat script that only a telephone that was out-of-order had gotten everything mixed up and that she was still just like the girl in the poem by Goethe she had enclosed with one of her first letters. The poem had been carefully copied in her own hand, a poem that softly sang itself:

I am with thee
And though you go ever so far,
You are near;
The sun sets,
The stars of heaven rise,
Ah, would that you might appear.

Sure, I thought, the anger swelling within me, mixing with everything else that was suffocating and wrecking my life—"I am with thee!" *If you are really with me, why don't you can*

99

your damn pride and write one word, anything to give me an
opening, to let me write you, to pour out what I can tell only
you, you witch. Why don't you write me that it's a lie, that
all my suspicions were the product of jealousy? But you, your
pride is more important; well then if your pride is stronger
than your love, if you can cork up your love so easily, what do
I need it for? I, too, could lock my love up I decided, enraged.
But through my weary brain ran the lines I had read again
and again:

> I will remember thee,
> When the beams of the sun
> Shine from the sea;
> When the face of the moon sails
> On the lake
> I will remember thee

2

When we jumped off the truck onto the gravel courtyard, we
saw the company gathered around the entrance to the granary
that lay at the foot of the artillery unit. They couldn't have all
come there by coincidence—it must have meant an assembly.

Yet they couldn't have been summoned to a parade; they
were all dressed come-as-you-are: one man in fatigues, another
in overalls, one man in high boots and another in sneakers without a belt or weapons. Silently they pressed together. Something big was brewing. I gathered my belongings and started
to head for the granary just as Hershler crossed my path on the
way from our quarters.

"What's up, Hershler?"

He stopped, but seemed distracted, as he was when suddenly
called away from his reading. Even if he had heard me he did
not understand. I repeated the question.

"A meeting," he said. "A company meeting."

"Why all of a sudden?"

"I should know?"

"What's it about?"

"What's it about?" He was still elsewhere. The sun danced on his glasses as on mirrors. "I don't know what it's about. Tamari, he called the meeting. It's a big secret."

"Tamari, what kind of meeting you pulling on us?"

It was Poker, who by that time was at my side listening to Hershler. He had spotted Tamari leaving the company office for the granary.

Thick-set Tamari hustled across the gravel like a bag of cement in pants, his head thrust forward, his cap askew, the emblem in the middle of his forehead between his eyes. Without slowing down he urged us on from a distance: "Hurry, men, hurry."

"Either you tell us what the meeting's about or we go to sleep," yelled Poker.

"What meeting?" asked Leizi, finally conscious of the stir about him. He was bent beneath his gear, facing our barracks.

Tamari, who had already passed by, suddenly changed directions without breaking step, as if he were drilling, and thrust his hands out toward Zunenshein.

"You just came back from Austria, now, didn't you? I'm all mixed up." As Zunenshein's hands were full, he grabbed his elbow. "Did you find any Jews?"

"What's going on here?"

"*Oy v'avoy.*" * Tamari let out a long sigh and immediately repeated his question. "*Nu,* tell me did you at least find someone?"

"We did. We'll tell you the details later."

"What? Jews? Really?" Tamari was in a rush to get to the granary, his whole body strained in that direction, but his eyes, set in a face that showed twenty years of work in the sun of the Jordan Valley, stared at us, wide and wet, like the eyes of the tailors in the cellar. "*Nu,* Zunenshein, say something. How many? Where? One, two, *nu?*"

Unwillingly and in clipped, dry sentences Zunenshein told what had happened in Klagenfurt. The company moved from the threshold of the granary to surround us. The gravel burned beneath Tamari's shoes, but nonetheless he insisted upon hear-

* "Ah, woe is me."

101

ing every detail. When we asked him once again what was the topic of the meeting he had called, we did not get an answer. Excitedly and moving in every direction at once he squeezed all our elbows, turned, and made a way for himself toward the storeroom.

"Get inside, men, get inside. Everybody. . . . You, too, leave your gear and come on in with us."

He stood in the doorway and started pushing everyone past him. Suddenly he spotted Leizi, his bags piled on his shoulder, heading toward the barracks.

"Leizi, where are you going?"

"The boys will fill me in," said Leizi, lengthening his stride.

"Leizi!"

The thunder boomed from an unexpected source, the throat of Sergeant Major Isaacson. Only then did we first see him standing on the concrete stoop of the company office—he, Major Sanders, and Lieutenant Putzovski. Leizi halted and wordlessly turned about. The company, suddenly dwarfed, began pushing into the storeroom.

"Something stinks here!" Poker muttered. "But really stinks!"

On the way in we tried to find out what had happened in our absence. No one knew. Some shrugged their shoulders, others conjectured. Perhaps new orders had been given and opposition was being organized. News of Trieste had come over the radio. Maybe it had something to do with the underground effort against the English in *Aretz*. Who the hell knew? What was really amazing was that everything was going on in full view of the major, with his consent. Tamari had met with him for over an hour. What then could it all be about?

Even though we did not know, I felt the affair could not be all that secret. The air was electric: submissively, obediently, every man found a place for himself on stalks of hay or the bare, concrete floor; some faces were tense and grim, others' feelings were veiled; a solemn clearing-of-the-air was in the offing. Even if we didn't know what was what, we knew, as sure as a rheumatic can predict rain, that a storm was about to break.

Soon not a man remained in the courtyard. Tamari, however, kept popping in and out promising repeatedly that he would begin in a moment, but it seemed that someone was still missing and we could not start until he knew everyone was present. Finally satisfied, he entered the granary and announced, "Duty Sergeant, please."

Bubi—Corporal Meinz—who had been leaning against the granary's iron gate, advanced one step toward Tamari, but not beyond the lighted rectangle of the doorway. He raised the sheet of paper he held in his hand and his eyes lingered there for a moment. His face was shadowed and his eyes, usually bright and shining, seemed as dull as the dismal, concrete granary walls. The walls' chill stiffness cast a pall of silence over us. Inwardly I wagered that Bubi knew and even had some part in what was taking place; he as well as the officers standing in the courtyard. Obviously Bubi was not pleased with what was going on.

"I'm going to call the roll; answer 'Here' to your name," said Bubi quickly and half-heartedly, and began at once. All the members of the company had been summoned, including the quartermaster, the cook, the hospital orderly, the clerk, the drivers—everybody with the exception of the platoon that had been sent to Villa Alta. Little Ostreicher was squatting on his heels. Brodsky was leaning against the wall with one shoulder, facing the door, as though debating whether to stay or leave. Giladi was sitting on a pile of hay in the left sector of the semi-circular threshing floor; his glasses glowed in the dim room like owl's eyes and he chewed mechanically on a stalk of straw.

There was Hershler. There was Zunenshein, reflective as ever, completely preoccupied, it seemed, with chewing his pipe. No doubt Leizi was silently cursing out Isaacson, but he pretended to be sleeping as his fingers glided over the pimples on his forehead. Mushik spread out in front of him, and took care not to lean his head against anything. All, all were there, and every name called out by Bubi, every "Here" shouted in reply from the granary, magnified the silence, sucking us deeper into the mystery in which we were all enmeshed for good or ill.

Still holding the paper before him, Bubi turned his head slightly toward Tamari and his thin lips, which always reminded me of his alleged German ancestry, showed the trace of a smile.

103

"Tamari," he added as an afterthought, a last gesture toward protocol.

"Here!" Tamari answered in a loud voice, as if to say, "I am present, gentlemen, and I am included in this list of individuals. Like everyone else." It was a rather exhibitionistic self-diminution: I am just like Brodsky now—Brodsky, who could not stand Tamari ever since he'd tried to talk him into joining a *kibbutz*, in the process describing how guys like Brodsky were turned from "potsherds" into tall, proud men. We know you're here, Tamari; talk already.

"I'm finished," said Bubi, stepping back to his place beside the doorway.

"*Haverim!*"

Tamari's eyes were on the granary floor. As he spoke he did not lift them but, to the contrary, lowered his voice, as though addressing the spot before him. Even though he looked entirely different, his whispering sounded to me like Father's praying devoutly before the ark on the eve of the Day of Atonement.

"*Haverim*, last night, here in this neighborhood, a certain . . . something . . . happened. Really, I can't understand how such . . . a terrible thing . . . could have happened. And I hope . . . I pray . . . that no one from our company had a hand in the matter. Believe me, men—"

He stopped speaking. Deep furrows creased his forehead, as if he were struggling to decipher a message engraved at his feet. The company waited in silence.

"Well, then—we are not holding this meeting to discuss what a Jewish soldier must do and must not do under any circumstances; no, we're not here to discuss that . . . even though, *haverim*, I, personally—and, if I may say so, I cannot hide my feelings from you on this point—I have my own personal position, a position independent of this particular place and this particular time, rooted deep within me, in fact, I would say in the very depths of our Jewishness, the heritage of every one of us, and woe befall us if we desecrate this—"

"Goddamnit, Tamari, what are you talking about? The guys don't know what you're driving at."

It was Poker, of course, who had spoken out. Flowery language always got him nervous, especially when he was anxious to know what was going on. Thin laughter rose from the edges of the granary.

"One minute . . . one minute . . ." Tamari lifted his head, but his eyes were shut tight. He held his clenched fists tightly against his chest, as though in pain, and breathed in deeply. "It's hard for me, men, you can't realize how hard and I don't know how . . . how . . . to begin . . ."

"Maybe you ought to begin with the affair itself!" Leizi suggested in his nasal tone, as though half asleep. The laughter swelled.

"This is the affair!" Tamari opened eyes swimming in black ink and turned to Leizi. "This is the heart of the matter, Leizi —how to avoid peripheral nonsense that can wreck our real mission, how to teach the company to act . . . in such a way . . . as to further . . . our best, our noblest interests.

"Men, I intentionally prefaced my remarks by saying that we have not come together to discuss ethics, even though I know . . . I know, believe me, I know and I feel how it pains comrades whose position differs from mine, who believe that the beautiful standards of our normal world have no relevance here, comrades who would prefer that we—"

"You're driving us crazy, Tamari. Can the philosophy and tell us what this crap is all about."

"Poker, shut up!" Corporal Kuperberg had spoken. Even though at that moment he was one of us, he could not stand any breach of military procedure.

"All right then," said Tamari, sighing deeply. He proceeded. "Two hours ago I was called to company headquarters, to Major Sanders. The British M.P.'s phoned him this morning. Two women, a mother and her daughter, came to the station this morning claiming soldiers broke into their house outside the town last night, attacked them . . ."

Once again his voice began to fade into a whisper. "They tried to molest them, physically; they claimed there was even an attempt to rape them and . . . to kill them. They fought back, yelled, so they told the M.P.'s, and managed to frighten off their attackers. According to what they said the soldiers took some money, watches, and other valuables."

Tamari's voice, which had grown progressively weaker, was

swallowed up in the silence of the granary so that we did not realize he had finished speaking. For a moment a pall of silence thick as a fog descended upon us. Our thoughts groped about in all directions seeking to link what had been said and hinted at, to our own guesses.

But then Zunenshein asked calmly and quietly, "How did the women know their attackers were soldiers?"

"They were dressed in British uniforms and wore our insignia on their sleeves—a yellow Jewish star on a background of blue-white-blue. So the women claim."

"They didn't wear overcoats?" asked Zunenshein.

"It would seem not, from what they said," Tamari answered in a feeble voice.

"How many were they?" asked Leizi, his curiosity suddenly aroused.

"Two went into the house. But it seemed there were more outside."

"I don't see why they had to wear insignias if robbery's what they had in mind," said Arusi.

"That's just what I wanted to say," cried Mushik, rising and turning toward Giladi. "They must have been Italians who disguised themselves on purpose to confuse the police."

"One of them spoke German and the mother says he let her know he was a Jewish soldier."

"Maybe they were from the *Werwulf*—they want to make trouble for us."

"So the major told the M.P.'s, but they're very doubtful."

"What's there to doubt? A Jewish soldier would force his way into an Italian home to rob the owners, decking himself out with our insignia and going out of his way to speak German? It's ridiculous!" So Poker swiftly summed up the case.

"The two women aren't Italians."

Giladi had spoken. As though drawn by a magnet, all eyes turned to the left sector of the threshing floor. He sat quietly, hardly moving, chewing on a piece of straw he held lightly between two fingers. His yellowish face was hard to distinguish in the gloom of the granary. The rims of his glasses shone as though he had just lifted his head from a ledger.

Never was the difference between him and Tamari as pronounced as at that moment. Giladi's thin skin was pulled taut over a face of beaten steel while every muscle in Tamari's face, dark and wrinkled like a cluster of figs, was aquiver. Tamari was annoyed by Giladi's interruption and his lips began to frame a reply, but at that moment, little Ostreicher flung out his own question: "How do you know that they aren't Italians?"

"I know it from the M.P.'s."

"How do you know what the M.P.'s said?" Tamari seemed confused, unable to fully grasp Giladi's intent. In addition he was obviously irked with Giladi for distracting the group from the matter at hand.

"And you, Tamari, did you ask who the women were?"

"What's the point, Giladi? What are you getting at?" Tamari cried, his anger surfacing. "Two women were attacked last night. They claim soldiers robbed them and tried to rape and murder them, and the M.P.'s suspect us!" Suddenly Tamari cut himself short and resumed what he had started to say in the beginning.

"We're not a bunch of riff-raff thrown together under the British flag. . . . Listen to me, men, I beg of you. . . . We're not a gang of thugs, like those thugs of . . . of Sienkiewicz . . . where everyone settles his own score, fights a private war . . . over some point of honor . . ."

"What point of honor, Tamari?" cried Giladi, who usually spoke so restrainedly, forcing his words out slowly and distinctly from between tight lips. Now his words sprang out turning midway into a shrill soprano: "The honor of the Jewish people! That's—a mere point?"

"Honor and life, too, Giladi," said Tamari. "We can't wage private wars here. We're entrusted with a mission only we can fulfill, and woe is us, woe is us, men, if we botch this one chance. No man here has the right to wage personal wars."

"You already said that!" shouted Poker, rushing to Giladi's aid.

"What?" Tamari's train of thought had been broken.

"You already said that!"

"All of us here are emissaries—an army of rescue for those who've been spared, *haverim*. We have a job to do. And pre-

107

cisely because no one can really control us, and everyone can do as he likes, we must dedicate ourselves to this one job—and that's the great effort, the noblest effort—all others must be subordinated to—the rescue of Jews. Zunenshein will tell you. They're waiting for us like for the Messiah—the Messiah. In the camps. On the borders. In railroad stations. We've got to reach them."

"What are you working so hard to convince us for, as if anyone here disagreed?" Leizi shouted angrily.

"And besides, Tamari, for God's sake have a heart. The boys' afternoon'll be shot soon," said Mushik, rising to his feet. " 'Scuse me, I gotta go to the kitchen . . ."

"Mushik, SIDDOWN!" Sergeant Major Isaacson was standing in the doorway next to Bubi. Something must have really been rotten if he was there. We couldn't have gotten down to brass tacks yet. Without a word Mushik slipped back into his seat.

"Tamari, may I?" Zunenshein raised his pipe but did not wait for permission. "This discussion is taking a very strange turn and I'm afraid we still don't understand what you're driving at. Now, there's a specific matter under discussion—two women, the soldiers, and so forth. Let's focus on this incident."

"Alright," said Tamari. "Fine. Well then, what is the incident? Just this: the M.P.'s think the two soldiers are to be found among us, all of us sitting here. And we—don't interrupt! —and I, I, too, fear, *haverim* . . . that the police will conduct an investigation. So, I've brought you together now quickly in order to ask—in order to insist—that the two men stand up and identify themselves. Now. At once."

Bedlam broke loose. Actually it should have happened the moment Tamari described the episode, but somehow his words didn't sink in. We had been busy clarifying details, unable to grasp the total picture. But now that Tamari had baldly stated that he, too, was sure our men had done this deed and, in addition, demanded that the two would-be rapists identify themselves, all the bitterness choked up in us from the day we were halted on the border gushed out.

"What the hell you saying, Tamari?"

"Why our men all of a sudden? That's all they got to do, rape Italian women?"

"Suppose they did, what then? Last night they were rapists and murderers, today they'll get up and beat their breasts?"

"Why's this company business anyway? Let the police knock their heads against the wall."

"It's the English cooked it all up, if you ask me . . ."

"Sure, that'd suit 'em just fine!"

"Like they poisoned what's-his-name—*nu*, the Greek premier—"

"Where do they get the balls to dream up a story like that?"

"Actually, it all happened different: two whores the boys didn't want to pay . . ."

"Bet you're right."

"They ran to tell the police they hadn't been raped."

"The old one must've foamed at the mouth—they snatched her cherry."

"The whole thing's too funny. . . . Come on guys, let's eat!"

"Just tell me one thing: if they were out to rape those two bitches, why didn't they rape 'em, huh?"

"Right you are: they oughtta be raped."

"Why don't they hang 'em up by the . . ."

"Tamari, Tamari, why'd you get so worked up for?"

"An army's not a *kibbutz*. Whoever's guilty—let the police find him."

"Come on, let's eat!"

4

"SHUDDUP!"

In an instant silence reigned. The company, which was already streaming toward the door of the granary, froze out of years of habit. The voice of Sergeant Major Isaacson, whom we had forgotten about for the moment, rooted us to the spot. Once again we were no longer just a group of guys at a meeting but an army company whose every move was governed by orders.

"Everyone back to their seats, one—two. Siddown! You

there, want to wind up in the company office? Sit down, I said. If you don't shut your mouths, all of you, we'll carry on outside, at attention. Ostreicher, you paralyzed or something? Sit down. For Christ's sake act like soldiers for once!"

"We will proceed, Sergeant Major," Tamari said slowly, obviously displeased with the latter's intervention.

"Okay."

The silence continued for another moment. We had all returned to our places and sat down but Tamari did not go on. His eyes were upon the sergeant major, who finally realized he was being asked to deprive us of his company, as had been agreed, apparently, from the start. Only when he had turned and left did Tamari continue.

"This discussion is strictly confidential, men. We'll go on from where we stopped. We'll go on until we finish. I heard some of the remarks you were tossing around and I wish—I must tell you, you still don't realize what happened here last night and what lies ahead of us today. The two men mixed up in this affair must reveal themselves and at once."

"I'd like to know," Zunenshein interrupted, "why they have to identify themselves and what will be done to them if they refuse."

"First you owe me an answer to my question," Giladi called out from his corner of the room.

"Which question?" asked Tamari.

"Have you found out yet who the two complainants are?"

"I told you I don't know. Two local people, a mother and daughter."

"Well then I'll tell you: they're two Germans. Nazis." He fairly screeched as he leaped to his feet. For the first time we saw him without any mask of reserve, just as his friends had described him.

"I ask you to sit down!" Tamari cried. "How have you decided they're Nazis or even Germans?"

"I'll tell you how I know—from the M.P.'s. The attackers couldn't have been *Werwulf* men: that family is known in this area as a Nazi family. Why were there no men in that house?"

"I don't know. That's none of our affair. We have to concern ourselves with what we have to do—and quickly."

"But as far as I'm concerned, this is the crucial question. You come preaching about robbery, rape, murder. You lecture us on riff-raff, tell us we're not dealing with affairs of honor here. But you haven't answered the real questions: doesn't it make any difference if these soldiers—even if we assume they're really our boys—tried to rape and murder two peaceful citizens or tried to take revenge on the Nazis? Is there or isn't there a difference?"

"Giladi, please," said Zunenshein in a soothing tone. "Of course that's the crucial question. Nevertheless, it seems to me that first we must get an answer to what I've just asked. Tamari, you assembled the company, described the affair, and you insist that the two men reveal themselves. Why? Why do you think this meeting will be of any help? And what will be done to the men if they refuse to identify themselves? What will happen then?"

Tamari took a large handkerchief out of his pocket and wiped his short neck. The silence grew. Now we would get down to business.

"I'll tell you," said Tamari, stuffing the handkerchief back into his pocket, thrusting his fingers beneath his belt and hiking his pants up, all to gain time. "I'm not one hundred percent sure the two men are sitting here now, even though I fear very much—but if they are among us, here—

"The major called me this morning. All of you know the major's our friend. I felt this today, not only from what he said but from his understanding of all that concerns us. Such things shouldn't be said aloud, but I don't know if many of us would be willing to do what Major Sanders is doing, even though he knows the dangers involved. But I'm only telling you this to let you know what a spot we're in, a spot we can get out of only if we all pull together, on the double. Well, then, the major told me the local M.P.'s have already handed in their report of the incident to the regional command, and there's every reason to believe that the military government in charge of civil affairs in occupied territory has been informed. There's no chance of fudging it over or of letting local authorities take care of the matter. The army's called for an investigation."

111

"Who's afraid of their investigations?" Mushik cried aggressively, lifting his head as he looked at Giladi.

"Spoken by a man with experience," yelled Arusi, at which we all burst out laughing, not only to ease the tension but because we all recalled the many shakedown inspections Mushik had to stand for suspected pilfering of mess rations.

"What's so funny, boys!" bellowed Tamari, as though someone had pricked him with a dart. "Can't you understand the matter at hand? Or what lies ahead if it turns out these men are ours? I want you to know in less than three hours an identification parade will take place in the courtyard. The M.P.'s will arrive and we'll all have to present ourselves."

"What did you say?" Giladi asked in disbelief.

"At three-thirty the company will parade, Giladi."

"And the women will pass through the ranks and seek out the rapists and murderers among us?"

"If you'll let me finish, Giladi, you'll understand the parade is our one way out. It will enable us to satisfy the M.P.'s and free us of this whole affair—clear us of all suspicion quickly and openly."

"And suppose Tamari, just suppose we don't turn out for this parade?"

"We must," said Tamari, shaking his head from side to side. "You will. That's for sure. What the British boss says, you'll do."

Again, Giladi leaped to his feet and with determination strode through the group toward the door. This was quite a different man from the introverted, well-mannered fellow we knew who played poker and spun fascinating tales. As he neared the door I saw that his face was paler than the light bulb. But Zunenshein, who had sprung up from his seat like a cat, seized him by the arm.

"No, not this Giladi. I beg of you. We're so few. It's beyond us to fight this. We're alone, time is short, we have no one to turn to for advice, no one we can shift this responsibility to. Tamari, you listen, too—in this affair all of us, to the last man, must be convinced, for anyone here can cast a veto simply by refusing to take part in this parade."

"I'll have no part in this abomination!" cried Giladi, his body straining toward the door as Zunenshein clutched his arm. "Seventy men, seventy Jewish soldiers should turn out and line up for two Nazis whose husbands, brothers, sons. . . . How can you even imagine such a thing? It's enough to think of my old father standing in their line-ups while the real murderers walked by him—maybe the same men not to be found in those Nazi women's home because now they're—"

He broke off the sentence as he broke Zunenshein's grip and stalked back into the granary, toward Tamari. For a minute we thought Giladi would slug him. But he only stood very close to the old man, looming above him, and said brokenly, "Now I understand the prayer for a life free of shame and disgrace! What a disgrace. What a disgrace."

"Giladi, I want you to listen to me for a minute, too," Zunenshein called.

There they stood, the three of them, Zunenshein in the doorway and Tamari and Giladi next to each other. "I say that when this debate is over, even if it goes on until the M.P.'s come, everyone can cast his own veto by refusing to parade. But for anyone not involved in last night's incident it's only a question of principle with no practical relevance. The M.P.'s can arrest us all and investigate us one by one."

"Only by force," screamed Giladi, "but not of our own free will, on parade, with such enthusiasm. They would have to drag us out—and that they wouldn't do."

"That's the question, Giladi. And we have to be sure of the answer before we reach a decision. But as for the two men who would be identified by this parade—if the two are here at all—they'll be found out whether we have a parade or whether we're investigated one by one."

"That's just why I asked for a parade. If you would only let me finish—"

"You *asked* for the parade?" Giladi gasped.

"Yes. And the major talked the M.P.'s into it."

"You're ready to throw two of our boys to the police just like that?" cried Poker, springing to his feet, joining forces with Giladi.

"The two men will not be in the parade. So I ask them, I beg them to identify themselves now so we can still—"

113

"Am I dumb or plain crazy?" yelled a voice from the rear. "There'll have to be a roll call. The two men will obviously be missing."

"No one will be missing," Tamari said quietly, his eyes darting from side to side, as though fearful of being overheard. "Two men from another company are being sent to us. Maybe they've arrived already."

"Do you think the major's a jackass?" cried the voice from the rear. "He won't see that two men have suddenly been switched on him?"

Tamari kept quiet. As the silence enveloped us the whole scheme unfolded: the two men would not be discovered because they'd be missing from the parade. That would prove our company had no hand in the affair; the case would be closed, and the company would be whitewashed.

A murmur of amazement and admiration filled the granary. Well then, what had all the shouting been about? What was the big problem? If they want us to, we'll line up for them for two minutes. Let them send the German women through the ranks, they won't find anyone—and "peace upon Israel." Would that be the first time we had pulled such a stunt? That's what we always did with the British—with the illegal immigration, forged identification papers, the loyalty oaths we swore as *gaffirs* to undergo training with arms. *Yalla,** boys, time's a-wasting. They could have told us from the start what they wanted without getting our balls in an uproar. They want a parade—let them have it.

As swiftly as the words poured out we heaved a collective sigh of relief. We all seized at the simple solution to the practical problem confronting us. Not only would it clear us of this seamy affair, not only were we tired of sitting in the granary with our stomachs rumbling from hunger; it was Major Sanders' sly collusion that gave the stamp of legality and an attractive front to the whole affair. Would we pull the wool over the M.P.'s eyes and trip up those two damn Nazis! We'd fix them, all right!

Above the rising din one voice suddenly sounded clearly:

* Come on.

114

"So if we're finished, let's break it up. No need to rot here all day."

"Finished? Finished what? We haven't begun yet!"

It was Giladi. As before, he stood near Tamari, his back against the wall, his pale face tilted downward as though he were ready to gore someone.

"So you're finished already! One—two! You've already swallowed the mush they cooked up for you—a handful of Jewish sentimentality, a sprinkling of national responsibility, and a pot full of bootlicking every Britisher."

"Giladi, I object to your language—" said Tamari.

"You don't object to anything now! Before we reach any decision on such a parade—and I still think there'll be men here who understand the terrible implications of the out that Tamari's come up with—'a practical solution' as he so elegantly puts it—a solution whose purpose is clear as day. We all know there's a routine police procedure which the M.P.'s—as we were finally told—considered: a man-by-man search. The M.P.'s examine the I.D. card and gear of every member of the company. But such a procedure would rob them of the opportunity to resort to their old tactics. The two soldiers would be discovered, arrested, and news of the affair would take wing, infuse a new spirit into thousands of our men, goad them on to more, many, many more acts of vengeance that would redeem the honor of the Hebrew flag we dropped right here as soon as we arrived at this cursed border."

"Giladi, this is no time for speeches. Time's running out."

"But we're not," Leizi drawled through his nose. "We want to hear him."

"The decision we come to isn't a private affair, men: all of us, not only Tamari and his friends, all of us want to reach the Jews, but he thinks this goal allows us to forget about Jewish vengeance and to stain our military honor . . ."

"What does attacking two women in the middle of the night for loot and God knows what else have to do with military honor?" yelled Tamari, but even as his words left his lips, he regretted them. Giladi, though, would not desist.

"'Looting and God knows what else.' How lovely. So it's not only the British M.P.'s, but you, too, who think the two

115

men who tried—only tried—to wreak vengeance on such a small scale are rapists and murderers, and have nothing to do with our sullied honor. Fine, let these two men stand up if they're here, stand up and identify themselves . . ."

As his cry filled the storeroom I fully grasped for the first time that we were really talking about two of our own men, that it had already been agreed they were the ones who had broken into the German women's house the night before.

Giladi stopped speaking, as if he actually expected the two men to get up and show themselves on the spot. Not a man moved, only confused smiles flickered on the faces of the seated assembly. "Fine, let them get up so we can see who they are. Let them get up and tell us what led them to that Nazi home, let them show us the acid eating away at every man's guts here: thousands of brave young men, all volunteers sworn to avenge the blood of our slaughtered brothers, to wreak vengeance in war or in peace on the butchers and their henchmen, on the people who applauded them, who strewed their path with roses, who welcomed the slaughter and grew fat on the spoil—all of them, every man, woman, and child. We don't believe in turning the other cheek, Tamari, and even if we did, we couldn't turn it because it no longer exists. They destroyed everything in their furnaces and Jews didn't give themselves willingly to them—because they didn't even leave us our will power. They destroyed everything. Only one hand was saved, only one small fist. Us. Here. What should this clenched fist do Tamari, what do you suggest it do?

"We got into the war much too late. Sure, they'll tell all kinds of stories of how brave we were to dupe us a little and make sure we can sit at the victors' table, too. But can we ever forget the truth? Can we ever forget how the Jewish people were crushed in this war, our troops never having faced enemy forces? Sure, we'll speak of the million Jewish soldiers in the Allied armies, but not one Jewish corps will go back with one Cassino* on its torn flag, not one squadron will return with broken wings leaving a smoking German city behind. This we

* Mt. Cassino, one of the bloodiest battles of the Italian campaign.

116

can't forget: we left the war unavenged. The one small fist is still clenched, in a spasm. It will never open up, this fist. It will stay clenched, its fingernails piercing its own flesh, its blood frozen, the memory of vengeance never unleashed blackening it with gangrene.

"Years will pass, the world will be at peace again, and even this war will sink into the pages of history. Already we see how allies are becoming enemies and enemies, allies. Right here on this very border the armies pass by each other. But even when this war fades into history's dream, even then: when the British children, descendants of the Blitz, ask how that massacre was avenged, they'll hear—even then—of Dresden and Hamburg, of that great vengeance. And when the children of Leningrad ask how the siege and the starvation and the epidemics were avenged, they'll be told—even then—of Stalingrad, of the Red soldiers, red from the blood and fire of their foray into Germany.

"Only yesterday I heard, from a man who returned from that area, of an unwritten law of the Soviet Army—and God bless them for that law! Wherever they go, free reign is given the soldiers for a full twenty-four hours. They murder, yes, they murder innocent victims. They rape, ah yes, they rape young virgins who've done no wrong. They burn, pillage, destroy all morality—a full twenty-four hours. When the Germans try to describe the terror of these twenty-four hours they'll find no parallel except in their own deeds. When those twenty-four hours are over the conquerors impose an iron discipline upon their troops and anyone who is a law unto himself is punished severely. Only then can the world return from chaos. That's how I see it. Not the principle of the other cheek, but a God of vengeance. You can free yourself from the horror of bestial crimes only through bestial retaliation.

"But what's to become of us? Shall we go on carrying inside us, in our sick hearts, this nightmare of Amalek, pass on our hatred in whispers from one generation to the next? We want one day of wild revenge. Murder for its own sake, just as they did to us. Rape for rape. Looting for looting. Innocent victims for innocent victims. Only then, only after we cleanse ourselves of this canker, this rot, this nightmare of helplessness—

117

only then, clean and at peace with ourselves can we take our place in human society once more. Then we can forget.

"We're going to have our own state, we'll have to seek out allies just as surely as we'll have no lack of enemies. How can we live as free men, and sanely choose friends and allies without first being healed by this hour of vengeance? Tell me, you tell me, Tamari, when our children—the people for whose sake you ask us to stand in this identification parade today— when they come and ask us how was it possible we lived here without taking vengeance, what will you answer them? What? What will you have to say to them?"

Giladi's torrent of words held us in a trance; our flesh ran with goose pimples. We could not withstand his argument nor did we wish to. Giladi had thrown fear into us all, a sweet, dizzying, endless fear. The veil had been ripped off, the moment confronted us. How true his horrible words: that was our mission, nothing else mattered. How could we have thought, just a moment before, that we had freed ourselves of this affair?

Giladi no longer spoke but stood pale and silent, his back against the wall. All were silent: Tamari, too, as if he were alone. It seemed he had no choice but to leave the granary and report his failure to Major Sanders.

But that did not happen. Without looking at Giladi, he said hesitantly: "What will I tell our children? I don't know. I don't know if they'll accept the answers I give myself now. But I've answered myself. I think—I think I have answers—"

"Not answers. Just one. One answer to the one question they'll ask: How was it possible we lived here peaceably without taking revenge?"

"I do have one answer, a very practical one."

"They'll want another kind, a moral one."

"I have a moral answer, too, a very personal one—but we don't have the time now. Men, we have less than two hours left and we have to come to a decision. My answer—"

"Doesn't interest us."

"GIL-A-DI!" Tamari's cry was indescribable. It was as though a lifetime of toil and self-sacrifice, of serving as an example for everyone, shattered in that one shout. His forehead and neck became a grillwork of swollen veins.

118

"You it doesn't interest! But for all those who've survived, from Bergen-Belsen to Auschwitz, that answer is everything. Right now it's everything. They're waiting for us and we must get to them. We'll find them wherever they're wandering, wherever one man still breathes. We'll reach every camp and monastery. We'll reach the farthest of places. There will be no barrier we shall not break, no border we shall not cross.

"Maybe you don't know, men, but even today our boys are traveling from country to country, stopping at nothing to reach Jews. If need be we'll not only stand this parade— we'll forge visas, bribe, lie, steal, break every law in the Torah to save every Jew left alive. For now, that answer's enough for me.

"You ask me what I'll tell our children. And what will you tell our children if after a few murders, rapes, robberies, and burnings they take our weapons away, ship us out of here, disband us? What will you say when they ask you how was it possible we were here, thousands of young men, hundreds of trucks and didn't find a way to take the one chance history gave us, but . . . but instead spent our time in theatrics!"

"You have no right to say that, Tamari." It was Zunenshein, whom we had quite forgotten about. Could he have agreed with Giladi?

"But that's how I feel, deep down. A man wanders through a forest and bands of murderers slaughter his mother and father; what should he do, endanger the members of his family who survived by hunting down the wife or daughter of one of the murderers, or should he rescue his own family first? First comes rescue."

"But that's no analogy, Tamari, we can't reach a decision in that way." He took his pipe out of his mouth and approached Tamari. Unlike the two others, his face was not contorted with emotion, his words were somewhat more convincing.

"You can't label a man's cry 'theatrics'; especially any one of ours, when we're so powerless. A man wanders through a forest, you say. True. But can a man who's suffered so much and been forced to flee, he and all his family who've managed to survive —can he escape without being tormented the rest of his life by the agonizing realization that he's helpless, impotent? How can you agree to such a thing, Tamari?"

119

"Then what do you suggest?" Tamari yelled in a broken voice. "Come on, now, what do you suggest? Time's flying. What do you suggest? That we shouldn't be impotent, that we should suddenly become an empire so we, too, might enjoy the conquerors' glory, so we, too, might enjoy an hour of vengeance? Fine, let's decide right here we're an empire.

"Impotent, you say. That's what Giladi wants, to put our impotence to the test. I can't accept that. Under any circumstance. You'll see what vitality we still have. Persecuted—yes; weak—yes; forced to wade up to our necks in death all our lives—true. But what are you trying to prove here today? Go be a Russian, Zunenshein, be an American, then you'll have your victories and your vengeance, and no more fear of impotence . . ."

His quavering voice shattered like an earthen jug. Tamari no longer addressed the two men, but all of us, in a choked and sobbing voice: "Men, don't you realize what's at stake here, what depends upon everyone here? Men, get up and tell us who you are, get up and let me speak to you, let me convince you. It can't end this way, it can't . . ."

We were gripped by a silence as terrifying as a hand grenade that has not gone off. No one spoke and no one moved. What was everyone yelling about if the two men would not reveal themselves, but by their silence had decided the issue? What did they want—that we should all go out to the parade so they should be identified by the women? Then again, maybe they wanted to force us to resist the police.

"Men, how dare you be silent? You have no right. . . . Get up and stamp on me, spit in my face, I don't care. But don't sit here without saying anything."

"Goddamn it, Tamari, something's sick here!" Leizi burst out.

"Most certainly." Kagan, the company clerk who, amazingly, had restrained himself thus far, rose from his seat. "Alarming things have been said here, things none of us will forget, things we might not have thought of until now. But this meeting is based on the supposition that the two suspects are seated in this granary. Maybe they aren't stubbornly keeping quiet—maybe they're simply not here."

"Exactly," shouted Ostreicher. "From the first moment I said they were gangsters from the *Werwulf*."

120

"Let me tell you, Tamari," insisted Leizi, who even in his anger sounded half asleep, "it's sick, this debating about something that might never have happened. Just like Jews, arguing whether or not to open the window when there isn't even a window."

"*Yalla*, let's go out to the parade and have done with it," said Arusi, rising. "I'm glued to the cement already."

"The only parade we'll give those whores," yelled Poker, "is in bed!"

"What the hell's the difference? Let's get it over with . . ."

"We're abnormal," cried an unknown voice from the rear.

"Sure we're abnormal." For the first time Brodsky spoke out. He was still standing by the wall facing outside as though disgusted with everything that had been said. But now he snatched his cap off his head and pushed himself into the group of men at his feet. "Abnormal if we do, and abnormal if we don't. What kind of revenge are you whimpering about here? This is revenge, to steal a few pennies? You speak about Russians—you, too, Giladi! I'll tell you what the Russians would have done: that's how they would have handled them," he said, drawing his fingers across his throat.

"Then there would've been no one to run to the police, no witnesses, and we wouldn't have had to sweat here three hours yammering about revenge. *Yebyuhamut!* But that's Jews for you—gabbers. It's all the same: Poland, Palestine, army or no army—talk, talk, talk. Here!" He plunged his hand into his pocket, yanked out his wallet, grabbed a fistful of Italian bills, and threw them at Tamari. "Here, take these lira and give them to the whores and let's have done with it. Enough of your vengeance!"

Before he even finished speaking he turned to leave.

"You're not leaving, Brodsky. No one's leaving. No one's leaving until we finish." Tamari's muffled sobbing had become an unashamed wail. Like a madman he dashed for the door, blocking Brodsky's path.

"Men," cried Tamari, his words bubbling up between saliva and tears, "we're here for only one purpose, only one purpose —to save Jews . . . to save Jews."

We could not look at him, but at the same time could not

take our eyes away from him. He was beating his chest with his fists, lacerating his face and shrieking: "You two, you have no right . . . Who are you? Who are you to stop these Jews from being rescued? Who are you? You two, you have no right . . ."

5

We had reached an impasse, not knowing what would come next. One hour remained until the parade, we had not eaten lunch and we were not of one mind. Tamari's stance—"Pass over my dead body"—was ludicrous, but nonetheless no one dared push him away from the door and leave. His wild outburst had shaken us all. What were we before the massive truth to which he clung? Were the two men to rise, then, identify themselves and make room for the two others who had been sent from another company, all of us would have gone out to the parade, unable to withstand Tamari.

We stayed inside, confused and silent at the spectacle of the old man howling in the doorway. Seventy men in one granary eyeing each other, every man suspected of what had been done the night before. Except for the five of us who had returned that morning from Klagenfurt.

Except Tamari. Except Zunenshein. Except Giladi.

Wait a minute, why take Giladi off the suspect list? He was the one who had broached the idea of attacking innocent victims so convincingly, so feelingly. Maybe he had done it.

No, if he had, he wouldn't have spoken out that way.

Then someone who had kept quiet had done it. Who? Hershler? Sitting behind me without opening his mouth? It was funny imagining Hershler in such a spot, flinging a woman to the ground, yanking her skirt up.

Maybe Kagan, the company clerk, a former Jerusalem teacher who had been released from marches and field training and other "heavy duty" because of his flat feet.

Maybe Bar-Yohai, Berele, son of the famous Bar-Yohai, one of the founders of the Hazhomer.* Now he could have done

* The first organized Jewish watchmen in Palestine.

122

it. He reminded me of the stories they told about his father. Rather bony, but when he dressed in shorts and showed off his stomach muscles it was something to see. And the way he never spoke was enough to frighten anyone. Then there was that night that he ran Anshel "Sausage" around the headquarters with his hands up, to give the boys a laugh. He had a bayonet on his rifle, too. Berele could have done it.

Or Anshel Sausage. I would have liked to have seen him with those two women. He got the name Anshel Sausage because he never ate cooked rations during his whole period of service with His Majesty's Forces. He would get a huge kosher sausage once a week and every day he would lop off a few slices. He's the man, I smiled inwardly.

Shtickfleisch—that fat animal was capable of anything, although had he found a ham hock in the Nazis' kitchen he would have chosen that over the thighs of both mother and daughter.

Maybe he and Arusi were the two. What the first lacked in lust the second made up for. But neither of them spoke fluent German.

Suddenly I caught myself. What was I doing? I was listing the suspects, but not according to the motives outlined by Giladi. To the contrary, I was splitting the company down the middle, those whom I respected and the dregs. I had faith in my suspicions of that last group.

Little Ostreicher, for instance: nervous, weak, something of a con man, a war case—him, certainly.

But Bubi, for instance, good-looking Bubi standing in the doorway all the while, not moving, not saying a word: could you picture him pouncing on a mother and her daughter?

But wasn't it just the opposite? Because the action would be so foreign, so unnatural for most of us, we could get what we were after by a one-time act of vengeance, rather than—

Rather than what?

I didn't want to think about it, I just wanted that terrible meeting in the granary to end. My thoughts tumbled about as Tamari stood pleading in the doorway with Sergeant Major Isaacson reappearing and disappearing. Time was flying; soon it would be too late to convince the two culprits. The tight lips would win out.

123

"You have no right," Tamari wailed brokenly, as though mourning the dead.

"No one here's royalty, to put himself before everyone else's . . . Our people are dying . . ."

"One minute," cried Zunenshein, lifting his pipe.

"Don't start all over again, now," rumbled Poker, standing up. "We know it all, already."

"Still, I feel I have to, that is—listen to me a minute, Poker. . . . I have to take part in this, I'm as responsible as anyone for whatever we'll decide." He spoke slowly, in a low voice, as though addressing Poker alone, but from one sentence to the next his audience grew. "It seems to me the question before us was clouded over at the start, for me too, so that many of us have not been able to decide one way or another. Look now, some of us think the question is: Will we come out of this as winners or losers? That's a bad mistake. It seems to me—no, I'll say I'm convinced, even—we come out losers either way. The choice is no choice at all, Giladi!"

He turned his head toward the wall Giladi was leaning against. Since he had concluded his tirade, he had stayed in that same position except for bending down occasionally to snatch a piece of straw to chew on.

"The picture is even blacker than you paint it," Zunenshein continued, "there's no way out of this tragedy—none at all. Tamari, in discussing the practical problem confronting us—our responsibility to the surviving Jews—brought in his ethical position on the general question of vengeance; but these two issues shouldn't be confused. From the practical standpoint I share his feeling—because we're the dream of a nation, the last hope of all who have been saved from the furnaces. If I had doubts before, meeting those Jewish tailors from Hungary yesterday removed them. Anyone who's read the stories about David Hareuveni,* for example, knows what I'm talking about. Our Jews are pinning all their hopes on the Jewish Army coming north from Italy, and if Tamari's fears come true, and this incident—and others—will wind up in our being shipped out of

* Sixteenth-century Messianic visionary who sought to establish a Jewish Kingdom and acquired many followers.

124

here, who knows what will happen? But that's no choice. The fact that Tamari is right in no way detracts from the terrible truth of your remarks, Giladi."

Now he turned toward the doorway where Tamari stood wiping his face and close-cropped hair with a huge khaki handkerchief. "Do you hear me, Tamari? At first glance it seems you're right in that 'moral position' you didn't want to talk about because, God help us, if we can take revenge only by reducing ourselves to thinking and acting like Nazis. That would be more than ironic: it would be history's curse.

"But all that's just on the surface. Here's what I say: Were we to suddenly adopt the teachings of Jesus of Nazareth and proclaim our weakness as our strength—that would truly make us strong. At the same time, of course, we would still be history's victims.

"But can we be such men? Don't we base our lives—including our volunteering for the brigade—on just the opposite premise: that we're sick and tired of being weak and persecuted, that our strength is our only salvation? We'd be lying to ourselves, Tamari, if we suddenly were to assume a Christian attitude. And living such a lie, we would not be able to endure the trial that lies ahead. Tragedy we can accept, but not a lie. We restrain ourselves from taking vengeance only because we know too well we're here as victims, not as victors. Therefore, and only therefore, we'd best not prate about principles but do whatever we can under the circumstances. And we'll do it, Tamari, with open eyes—knowing we'll never be able to forget how we couldn't take vengeance, knowing we'll never have peace of mind.

"Here you're right, Giladi; but you're wrong, as I see it, in thinking we have a choice. We have no choice. That's the tragedy . . . Myself—I can't comprehend how murder can lay the groundwork for life, how corruption can serve purity. That's the ethical code I grew up with and it's guided me all my life. But what I say now is just the opposite: Now raw might has become the God of an entire world—and I agree it was crushed not because it lacked the right but because it lacked sufficient might. Yesterday in Klagenfurt a man who thought I was British told me that was their big mistake, not teaming up with us to wipe out Russia; that's all they're sorry for. All this shows that the time has come for raw might to serve the right. You were correct, Giladi, in what you said about the Russians: after they prove to these people—and, more important, to themselves—that their right is also might, they'll be able to lay down their arms, forget everything.

"But for us, Tamari, we're doomed to walk on with this memory, because we could not take revenge. That's the tragedy —you understand, *haverim?* That's the tragedy, because God help us if we forego vengeance, but God help us seventy times more if we don't reach the Jews, for we are the last dream they have. We can't escape this fate, not now nor in the years ahead. Our children will ask us and we'll lower our eyes. Just so, just so will we live."

We were exhausted, hungry, we no longer had any strength for this endless debate. Nonetheless we went on listening in silence, hoping that all the words would help bring the matter to an end, whatever that might be.

"We have no choice, *haverim.* We must go out to the parade. But we must realize the lesson of this trial. And even those who can't understand now, in time they will grasp the meaning of the destiny we now take upon ourselves anew. We will never reap the blessings of forgetfulness, never know peace. The vengeance we never took, the hatred we never extinguished will eat at us forever. There you're right, Giladi. But we have no choice."

"Out to the parade ground!"

Sergeant Major Isaacson's voice was hoarse as though he had just woken up and was clearing his throat, but we all heard and a tremor passed through the company. Three twenty-five. Four hours had passed—and nothing had been gained: all in vain the speeches whose like we had never heard and would never hear again, in vain the rending of hearts. Now we were back at the beginning—we didn't know whether to obey or disobey and would soon know who the two men were regardless.

"Out to the parade ground! Shake it up there, one! two!"

6

As the Sergeant Major raised his voice we hunched over in our seats. The order to go outside had been given; our legs began to move of themselves. We heard the order to fall in, but we hesitated, dragging our feet, looking at one another but somehow moving toward the graveled area in front of company headquarters. Had Giladi yelled not to go out to the parade, had he himself refused, had some contrary impulse suddenly seized one of us—but Giladi moved with all the men, jostling one another like a long line of railroad cars tugged by a locomotive.

"Faster—you there, waiting for private orders or what? Move your ass! Move it! Schiffer, stop walking in circles like a whore with the clap. Everybody out, hup—hup! Hershler, double time!"

Isaacson's rasping voice now blasted at us through a clear throat, leaving no room for our own thoughts even were we to have them, even if those four hours in the granary hadn't drained us to the point where nothing mattered any more. We only wanted to have done with it quickly, to forget everything that was said.

"Hershler—stop! For Christ sake c'mere or your mother'll rue the day she bore you, Hershler!"

Everyone collided, ground to a halt, and turned toward the object of Isaacson's tirade. We saw Hershler, his hands covering his face, staggering toward the barracks. At the same time out of the corner of our eyes we saw Tamari dash over to Isaacson to whisper something, saw Isaacson thrust his hat forward like an M.P.'s, covering his forehead, his eyes, and half of his nose. His silence and the fact that Hershler kept running, disappearing into the barracks, told all.

"Hershler?" Like lightning the word swept through the ranks. "That Czecho-Hungarian prick? Him?" For a moment the company hesitated. Our astonishment bubbled out in sighs of relief at the prospective happy ending. Hershler! Yes, Hershler, who had sat still four hours without breathing a word. But he was only the first. There were two men: who was the second?

Before we could digest this incredible revelation we were all snared in Isaacson's net, trotting forward like circus animals beneath the whiplash of his voice: "B Company . . . B Company fall in! Quiet! You've talked enough today. From here on in you better act like an army. Not a sound. You've said enough today. B Company. Zunenshein, I'm talking to you too . . . an army's not a synagogue . . . fall in! Corporal Kuperberg, get these men into line! Jump to it now, jump to it! Hup! Hup! Hup!"

Many years have passed since then, but that day has stuck to me. For long stretches of time it fades from my mind as if it had never been. Then suddenly, without any warning, it swamps me as if it had not yet ended, as though I were still standing there in the barracks square on the slope of the mountain with the Alpine peaks looming overhead, the sky washed clean and a frail north wind pushing a black cloud over the tree-covered hill before us, blanketing the ground, the forest, the courtyard with shade while the company stood on parade. And when that day bursts to the surface I feel the shame burning beneath my skin.

How was it that in spite of everything we went out on parade? How was it that that long chain of events and that grueling debate we heard more than took part in had no effect on us? How did we make the leap, in one fell swoop, from soul-searching to blind, soldiers' obedience? So often I try to reconstruct that leap but never can figure it out. At times it seems to me we knew full well what the decision meant and that the itching under my skin began at that very moment; and at times I'm convinced we didn't understand what was said—by Zunenshein, for example—and that only over the years did that identification parade become what is now a searing shame within me.

Well beyond that leap to discipline, we had formed three ranks and snapped to attention, stood at ease, snapped to attention. "Dress–right–dress. Ready–front!" The parade had begun: there was no turning back.

The M.P.'s had not yet arrived. Major Sanders and Lieutenant Freund Putzovski were standing on the concrete stoop in front of the office while we stood at ease. Our eyes traveled from right to left, seeking out Hershler's stand-in, trying to discover whether anyone else was missing and if there was another strange face in the ranks.

"Bubi." My ear heard the whispered word again and again. Heads turned in search. Slightly to my left I spied Klitchovsky, from battalion headquarters. He was to be one of the two. And Bubi—true, he could not be seen in the ranks. I was gripped with joy, as though I'd heard that I myself had done the deed. What a lovely resolution: manly, handsome Bubi. Even now he had quietly slipped away without our realizing it, without any declarations or confessions. How could we have guessed that Bubi's head would have been full of such thoughts, and who could say what those thoughts were? None of us. As always he would keep silent: no one would ever know what drove him to that particular house one day after we arrived in the town.

What had suddenly burst loose inside him? And the two women's story, however true it was—what had he wanted to do when he broke into their home, and why had he stolen money and valuables? We would never know, even as we would never know why he had chosen to drag Hershler along. I hadn't the slightest doubt Bubi had worked out the whole scheme and Hershler had only been brought into it. It was more than surprising: it was downright insulting. Not that he should have chosen me—why me all of a sudden?—but Leizi, how had he skipped over Leizi? And who was Hershler anyway, that softy, that *yeshiva bucher,** a guy you never noticed. Why should Bubi choose him, of all people?

Our thoughts were cut short. Two M.P. jeeps roared through the gate to the courtyard, throwing up white dust as they ground to a shrieking halt in front of company headquarters. A captain and two lance corporals jumped out of the first jeep and a sergeant and the two women stepped down from the second. The M.P.'s looked like they always do—flagpoles in battle uniforms with seams where creases usually are, wearing white belts with burnished brass. We all looked at the women who, as soon as

* Student at an Orthodox religious seminary.

129

they stepped out of the jeep, shrank back against the wall of headquarters. The mother, tall and bony, wore a black skirt and black stockings and a kerchief that almost covered her head. The daughter was not quite so tall as her mother and somewhat fuller. When she stood up there was something very captivating and feminine about her. Her hair was chestnut-colored and somewhat flaxen. Her dress clung to her ripe body, her full thighs and breasts. The two of them stood motionless, their faces turned slightly to the wall, as if they were the ones to be identified.

In the meantime the beanpole captain had drawn near Major Sanders and snapped to a brisk salute à la R.S.M. MacGregor. The major lifted two fingers chin high as if to say, "No need to get excited and just remember who's the major here." The captain bent down to the major and said something. The major turned to Freund Putzovski, who stood slightly to his rear, and passed the quiet message on. Freund Putzovski, his fat behind jiggling, hurried over to the sergeant major.

"Very good, sir!" Isaacson barked, in response to the whispering of the lieutenant. He turned on his heel, thrust two fingers into the pocket of his field jacket, took out a sheet of paper— maybe the same sheet from which Bubi had called the roll— carefully rebuttoned the pocket, thrust his chin out and, to make an impression on our military guests, thundered, "Attenhut!"

Unlike Bubi, Isaacson pronounced each and every syllable loud and clear. Whoever's name was called sprang to attention, cried, "Here, sir!" and snapped to parade rest. "What's this horseshit for?" whispered Poker behind me. "All for those two whores." But he and all of us answered to our names, obedient, well-disciplined, ready for the inspection to begin. Inwardly we smiled at our private joke.

"Hershler!"

"Here, sir!" Klitchovsky sprang to attention, then stood at parade rest.

"Corporal Robert Meinz!"

"Here, sir!" cried a razor sharp voice at the head of one of the ranks. I turned my head to look. It was Uziel from the regimental transport platoon. One of the faithful. That Tamari

130

—he had cried, rolled on the ground, but he had thought out every detail and had forced his will upon us. We were standing there, after all.

"B Company—open ranks—open ranks, march!"

The M.P. captain turned toward the women and signaled them to join him. They approached the head of the first rank and from there began passing before us, the women and the captain first, followed by Freund Putzovski, Isaacson, and the M.P. sergeant. Major Sanders stood in his place completely detached.

There we stood in three long rows while the women slowly walked by, stopping in front of every soldier, looking him up and down, straining to identify the two men. Very slowly. It was four o'clock. A slight breeze blew from the right as we stood facing the sun. The black cloud rising from behind the mountain trailed shadow over the entire courtyard. The bitter cold sent goose pimples up our flesh. The women walked slowly onward, from one soldier to the next. And we stood there, all of us, for identification, silent, disciplined, staring at the mountain pass to the west, at the towering peaks, at the two women.

Now they were standing in front of me. The mother had a hard rectangular, bony, face. Her skin, which must have been very white once, now was stretched taut across her bones. As she passed by me I forgot the color of her eyes, remembering only that they showed no fear but rather an iron resolve to find the guilty parties. The company didn't frighten her: she was intent on spotting the two faces imprinted on her memory.

The daughter was frightened, though. At close range she was not so pretty—her limbs were too flabby and her huge breasts sagged toward her belly. Her face was too full, and whenever she lowered her head she formed a double chin. She did not look at us at all; only when her mother stared at her and yanked her skirt angrily would she lift her head and look in our direction. She had northern eyes, like Alpine lakes.

Slowly they passed through the first two ranks and were approaching the end of the third. A slight stir was heard to the rear and I turned my head to see. The woman had gone back to the head of the third rank and was standing in front of Leizi.

131

She looked at him for a long time, then finally shook her head and opened her hands as if to say, "Sorry, but he's not the man," and left the formation.

She remained standing to the side, tall, aggressive, waiting for the M.P. captain to tell her what to do. He approached her and apparently suggested that she go through the formation a second time to see if she might remember. For a moment she stood there, looking at us with a fascinated expression. Suddenly she decided. With a brusque motion of her head she summoned her daughter to come with her and strode toward the jeep without looking back once. She had guessed, I thought, that the two men she had seen the night before were not standing in the formation and she was trying to end the ceremony with a show of pride. The sum of it all was she was playing a game of face. The bitch! We had outfoxed her and now she was denigrating the whole parade.

Without waiting for the M.P.'s she climbed into the back seat of the jeep followed by her daughter. The captain approached Major Sanders, who had not moved from his spot all that while, exchanged remarks in a whisper, pressed his hand and Freund Putzovski's, saluted briskly, and turned toward the jeep. The engines were already coughing, the corporals and the sergeants were already in their seats. The captain bent over and slipped into his seat, one foot resting on the jeep's running board. Gravel was flung back and white dust rose as the vehicle jerked forward. They turned around, their gears grating, and zipped out of the courtyard. The whole affair had taken only twenty minutes.

When the jeeps were only a faint roar in the distance, we saw that the major was smiling at us. Sergeant Major Isaacson looked at him and the major indicated with a mischievous wave of his fingers that he should turn us loose. He turned around and quickly disappeared into the company office.

His reaction had an immediate effect upon the sergeant major. With his middle finger he flipped his hat back on his head, smiled at us with his lizard-skin lips and said with finality: "Okay, boys—the bullshit's over. Hold it!" he yelled suddenly as the ranks began to move. "Chow in one hour. Double rations. *Yalla*, to the barracks!"

7

That's all that happened that day. For all our talk we had grown no wiser. That same evening Bubi and Hershler were sent on leave to Milan. Tamari was called for illegal immigration duty. Only a week later another company came to take our place. And all of us, every man, tried to forget what had happened.

When I look back on my actions in the days that followed, it seems I simply did not consider and perhaps did not even understand—as Zunenshein had said—that I would not be able to forget that parade, no matter how hard I tried.

IV Growing Pains

Once again we were quartered in the railroad workers' building on the same floor above the cellar. This time, though, Poker moved quickly and with foresight: He darted into the building first, took possession of the largest room for himself and the other "hands" in the platoon, then scouted about the area until he discovered a real table in one of the abandoned houses. He flipped it upside down onto his head and brought it back to the room. Before nightfall he had gotten hold of a light bulb from one of the offices and sat down to his first "service." "Things have to be organized," he said. "We're going to be stuck here a long time so we might as well be comfortable when we play."

We all shared his feelings. We knew that henceforth our days would be long and empty. We began to do everything lethargically, as though wading through water, struggling to stretch our few activities over as many hours as possible. We would leave for meals early, plod over to the kitchen, wait patiently, dawdle over the food, chat leisurely, wait for each other, and trudge off in a weary caravan for the return journey. But it all availed nothing.

The long June days were endless. We did not stand guard duty, nor did we train, as we had not yet been incorporated into the courses organized for the division. We poked about the courtyard like clucking hens, we sat by the roadside watching the convoys go by or the train coming from the border, we played dodge ball, observed our neighbor saw trees and pile them up in his cellar for the far off winter, watched the nights' slow descent. When at last darkness had us completely surrounded we would take refuge from depression in Poker's room where there was light, the chatter of card players, a chance to sit on the window sill, hold a book, look at the cards or at the stars that shone brighter as the darkness deepened, or listen to time whirl on in a vacuum.

The third day after we got back, I sat down on the window sill, my back against one frame and my foot against the other, trying to read one of Zunenshein's English journals. Occasionally I glanced at Poker, laughing in advance at his fellow players' ill fortune or cursing the wretched hand he had been dealt. Shtickfleisch had brought back from the kitchen a mess kit loaded with bread and jelly, which he was stuffing into his gaping mouth one slice at a time. I looked at Brodsky, humming softly, tossing out curse words like rings of smoke; at Arusi, fretting and fuming to see his beautifully starched clothes and wavy hair going to waste, all because his laundress had been replaced by another girl in our absence. There I sat, steeped in that dreary existence from which there was no escape, resolved that that night—definitely that night—I would frame my request-for-discharge-for-family-reasons and attach it to the doctor's letter that arrived with the last letter from home. But I decided once and for all I would first write Noga demanding she send me a straight-from-the-shoulder letter explaining everything, mercilessly, anything to put an end to the sudden silence caused by God only knew what. Yes, I would write her. Definitely. That very night.

How can you do such a thing—a full month and not a sign of life. More than that—two months. Let's say, even, my last letter was a slap in the face: I still deserve an answer. Be angry, insulted, but have the guts to get everything out into the open instead of taking advantage of the fact I can't reach you, like a coward. Yes, like a coward: How else can you explain this break-off out of the blue as if I were a snowflake that melted on your coat. No, no, you sneak, I won't let you do it. I'm going to write you, Noga: Tonight. I'll force the truth out of you.

Let me tell you, I can't believe you would have been so offended if I hadn't somehow touched on the truth. Yes, I made it easy for you, I helped you get rid of me; and you're not entirely wrong, Noga, in thinking I was moving toward this break-off, frightened of being tied down forever. There's some truth in that, in my hunger for the outside world, my need to be like one of the citrus trees in the nursery in our yard. No sooner does it shape up as a slender young plant than spades are thrust into the sandy soil on all four sides, slicing the thousands of frizzled threads linking it to the earth, cutting through its roots. Then it's lifted out by itself, clutching a clump of sandy soil in its roots, wrapped around with a wet sack, and carried to some far off place to a new life, to bear undreamed of fruit.

Yes, I want to escape—but not from you. I'm not strong enough for that, Noga. Like a yo-yo, the farther I go the more I'm pulled back. I love you because I love myself. You're the only girl who loved what no one else found in me. With you I can dare to dream of mountain peaks. Without you I'm just like the thorn—what do you call it, nu, you know what I'm talking about, that plant that always overran our yard so Father and I always had to burn it after every summer: thorn, thistle, bramble, briar, thorn bush, zilla? Or maybe just a bitter apple tree. . . . Oh, what's the difference anyway, what damn thorn I'm like! With you I feel like our winter, like the summertime here, green with hope.

136

How can I convince you you're not the home I'm running away from, the home I'll never go back to no matter how they lure me, even if I have to rot in this damn army five more years. No diseases, no doctor's certificates, no tricks. I left to make a new life for myself. But I'd fly home to you, you sweet devil, like one of those fuzzy thorn seeds, right now; this very night, now that you must have finished all your exams and gotten all your high grades, I'd come to your room, sit down and look at you, take your cold hand and walk with you among the warm stones of the city, maybe through the Valley of the Cross or stand above it, at the head of the road, looking past the bald, leprous rocks, past the stony olive trees, at the distant wall, always so strange to me, like from some distant, enchanted time.

Do what you will Noga, I'm going to write you. Now. And say all these things. No more military censorship now: the letters aren't opened any more, I don't have to be afraid of some busybody poking around in my mind; and I won't be embarrassed any more. You always used to ask why my letters were so dry and factual. All right, today I'll let loose everything I locked up for fear of your knowing eyes. You won't get away from me so easily, and even if you want to shrug me off, you'll always suffer knowing no one will ever love you like I did; no one will ever need you as I do. I'll sink into your flesh like a burn, Noga. . . .

Thoroughly worked up I swung my feet into the room, when I heard from the courtyard, directly below me, a voice: *"Haver! Shalom!"*

Before I even stuck my head out the window to see who had called, those two simple words sent a chill down my spine. I looked outside. All was darkness; only a bare patch of light spilled out from our window onto the yard. In this square stood the man, his head tilted back, his face toward me. My first glance confirmed what I had immediately guessed when my back was turned: he was not one of our soldiers.

He was a civilian in a black military tunic, with a thick head of hair bunched up like a busby over a wizened, fox-like face. I saw everything all at once as if I had met a ghost—the dim but

137

prominent eyes, the shadows resting on concave temples, his sunken cheeks, his nose jutting out of his gaunt face like a crooked finger. A man who had come from afar.

"*Shalom*," I whispered in amazement.

"Tell me please, *haver*, how can I reach the headquarters of the Jewish Brigade?"

His question was straightforward and matter-of-fact, as though his standing there was an ordinary event, both for him and for us. He awaited no joyous outburst on our part, only that we should direct him to his destination.

"Excuse me," I said, "but who are you? How did you get here all of a sudden in the night?"

"From far off, from far off." It seemed to me he was answering my thoughts, but his voice, a deep baritone, was as dry as before.

"How many kilometers is it from here to headquarters?"

By this time everyone in the room had pushed to the window, shaken like myself at the sight of the man standing below in the square of light. His clothing, his appearance, his Hebrew—not only his use of the word for headquarters but stating our exact title, "the Jewish Brigade"—all gave evidence of his having come from "there." That is, really from far off, from regions no one had yet reached. But how had he suddenly turned up here alone, at such an hour, right by our barracks? We all showered him with questions, rushed out to the courtyard, but he didn't answer. He only asked repeatedly how he could quickly reach "headquarters."

"Headquarters is a long way off," Zunenshein told him. "And how will you get there at night?"

"How?" said the stranger. His question was an answer.

"We'll get him a lift," said Arusi. "I'll hop over to Rahmani. He'll take him there without any trouble."

That promise, which did not take into consideration the route, suddenly calmed the man; we prevailed upon him to come with us into the room and wait until Arusi returned with the vehicle.

It seemed unbelievable—all of us squeezed into the room, surrounding the stranger as he sat down at the table between the mess kits and the cards. The man was of average height. Though he wore a heavy coat, the color long since faded, he seemed very frail, but his was not the leanness of a starved man or an ascetic. His eyes protruding from his sockets seemed to stare at some distant point; his entire body seemed to nourish the black fever burning in those eyes. He sat silently where he had been seated and covered his disheveled hair with his hands, not speaking unless spoken to and even then answering with veiled and measured phrases.

"So tell us something," said little Ostreicher, unable to contain himself. "How did you get here all of a sudden?"

"Not all of a sudden. I was sent to you."

"But where from?"

"From the Remnants' Brigade."

"What's that?" said Poker.

"The remnants, *haverim*, the partisans, the forest bands; the rescued embers, the remnants of the holocaust."

"How do you know Hebrew so well?" Leizi asked from the side; I, too, was dying to know the answer to that. Actually it was not hard to guess where—no doubt he was a Tarbut school graduate*—but only now did our naked knowledge take on flesh, flesh that we wanted to touch with our fingers. This stranger, who had come to us from out of the darkness, awesome in his appearance, was actually one of us, speaking our language, coming to us straight from the forest, directing his feet to this spot on the border as though to a star.

The man's lips formed a smile, and only then did I see that they were full, turned slightly outward; they retained a faint pinkness on the inside. How old was he? When he smiled he was, for a moment, almost a child, but once again he withdrew into his burning eyes, into his hands pressing his cheeks together. Abruptly he sprang from the box he had been sitting on.

"I can't stay here, *haverim*. I must reach headquarters as swiftly as possible."

"It's a shame Tamari isn't here," said Zunenshein.

"Who's Tamari?" the man asked, his curiosity aroused.

"One of the communal workers. He'd join you and help you find the men you're after."

* Hebrew school system in East European lands in the twenties and thirties.

"I'll find them. It's best I be on my way."

"You won't go on foot!" cried little Ostreicher.

"In Russia you learn to walk," Brodsky said suddenly.

"Yes," said the stranger, looking at him, "we know how to walk."

"Here you'll go on wheels," said Zunenshein. He grasped the man's coat in a movement typical of him. It was evident he wanted to hug the stranger, but was holding himself back. "Here you're at home. Dear *haver*, we are so moved by your being here that we haven't asked and you haven't told us anything about who you are, what the Remnants' Brigade is, what country you come from, how many of you there are. Tell us something."

"Tell you something?" the man said. "To tell you something I'd have to stay here all night and all day and all of the next night . . ." Only then did his husky voice begin to quiver. He spoke slowly, every word shattering on the floor. He stretched one hand toward Poker, who was tapping a cigarette out of his pack of Luckies. Quickly Poker gave him the whole pack. Only then did I see the man's fingers sticking out of a hand, narrow as his wrist. His fingers were very slender and his bones showed through paper-thin skin. How could such a delicate, lovely hand go with such a furrowed face? He drew the cigarette to his lips, and as he sucked in the smoke, his hand trembled. Quickly he thrust it back into his coat pocket. But we all had seen that tremor.

"Young man," said Zunenshein, "when did you last eat?"

"I'll eat when I reach headquarters. I'm afraid they haven't found a car . . ." He moved toward the door.

"How long you on the road?" grunted Shtickfleisch, who had remained seated by the table all that while with the mess kit full of bread in front of him. "It'll take another half-hour. Please, first have a little bread."

The man lowered his eyes for a moment to the bread and it seemed his whole body was leaning toward the mess kit. But in reality he had not moved. From the road we heard the honking of the truck.

"That's it!" cried Leizi, standing by the window. "Here they are."

"*Shalom, haverim*," said the man, taking the cigarette between his fingers once again. He hesitated for a moment and whispered, "My brothers, be blessed." Then, after another pause, as though his ears were not listening to what his mouth was uttering, "Even if the rumble of your wheels comes too late."

Sharply he turned toward the door and did not turn his head back. We all pressed through the doorway after him. Arusi was already on his way to the barracks and the driver, Rahmani, stood before the hood of the Dodge.

"You the one?" Rahmani asked. "Do you speak Hebrew?"

"I think in Hebrew, too," said the man.

"Great. Then *yalla*, up you go. We have a good stretch of road to cover."

The man turned to the cab of the truck, but Shtickfleisch restrained him and thrust into his hands the bread, which he had wrapped in newspaper.

"Take it. Take it, I tell you. It won't hurt you to eat something, *mensch*."

Rahmani had already turned on the motor, but the man still stood among us, the cigarette glowing between his lips and the bread in his hand, as though deciding what to do next.

"Actually, I don't know," he said, his voice competing with the whir of the motor, "whether there's any need for me to go to headquarters. I was sent to ask you what we, the survivors, must do now. Now I know your answer. We'll start out on our journey. To you. Our brothers are waiting for us on the border. I'll take this bread back with me as a memento of this first meeting. *L'hitraot.** We will arrive."

2

And one day, they began crossing the border just as Tamari had said they would in the granary, and just as the stranger had foretold. Suddenly the border was rent asunder; we hadn't known convoys were already rolling toward the border, and only when we heard the singing coming from the road, familiar

* *Au revoir.*

141

songs but nonetheless eerily different, did we realize they had already arrived.

There was rain that afternoon, and the hut was filled with the stinging freshness of winter and its sadness, too. In the summer all is open and dry, and in the winter everything is closed, the air silky and gray, the water spattering on the roofs' shingles and streaming down to form pools around the hut. And I am standing by the streaked window, looking at the earth swamped with water, frightening myself with wild fantasies hovering in the downpour. But over there the afternoon rain was gone as quickly as it came. The clouds lost themselves beyond the mountain, leaving the greenery greener and the washed earth cleaner and again it was late June. In Poker's room the white bulb shone, the players were shuffling their cards and Leizi and I were sitting on the window sill, our feet hanging outside, while below, at the entrance to the house, Arusi was trying his luck with a young Italian partisan who had come to live with her aunt on the third floor.

We didn't bother to look at any old convoy. Day and night they would rumble by, wearing out their tires, from south to north and back again. The trucks were of the 78th Division, to which we were attached, and the 10th Corps, which included the division. And there were the German prisoners who kept streaming south, who the hell knew where to. One morning a special convoy passed by—Russian prisoners being sent back home, all of them dressed in new American summer uniforms, stretched out on the padded American benches of G.M.C.'s, but with red flags flying over the drivers' cabs. We weren't impressed with convoys.

But that day we suddenly heard the broken singing borne on the wind as though from some distant time and place. A convoy of Dodges passed by very slowly, switching on to high beams as they entered the town. The drivers honked, and from inside the sealed, canopied trucks we heard the singing, every truck emitting its own fragments of sentences: "*Artza, Alinu, Artza Alinu . . . Heveinu Shalom Aleichem . . . Zug Nit Keinmal Az Du Gehst . . .*" "We have come to the Land . . . We greet you . . . Never say that this is your last journey . . ."

Slowly the trucks and the songs rolled by, the singers unseen.

Leizi and I jumped into the courtyard and ran out to the road. It seemed they had been allowed to show themselves after safely crossing the border, for the canvases of some vehicles had been flung back revealing the faces of the passengers squeezed in the rear door. Though they were illuminated by the headlights of the trucks behind them, I couldn't make out individual faces. Refugees. Patchwork clothing. Turned-up collars, heads wrapped in scarves, blank faces. But their hands stretched out toward us as they cried: "*Shalom, shalom, shalom, shalom* . . ."

And that was all. We counted more than twenty trucks, all of them belonging to the Brigade, while others who ran out to the road that night said they'd counted thirty or more. Where they came from we did not know. Where they were taking them to we could only guess. Southward, as near as possible to *Aretz*.

The next day we learned a little more. Not far from our camp, near Malborghetto, a way-station had been set up for the smuggled refugees, where everyone was given a hot meal as well as emergency medical treatment. Afterward they would climb aboard trucks of another unit and continue their journey south. We told each other we'd have to go there sometime and see what went on, but it was very hard finding the time. Major Sanders organized anew the daily schedule of the company and Sergeant Major Isaacson made sure it was carried out. Corporal Kuperberg would drill us every morning on the railroad platform and Lieutenant Freund Putzovski began the manual of arms all over again. Whoever wasn't training was assigned K.P. duty and whoever wasn't peeling potatoes was sent to guard the camp at night. Afternoons we'd be deluged with general education courses and only four days after we returned to the barracks, men began to get three-day passes to Milan and Venice. Most of the secret convoys traveled the main highway and we were only asked not to get in the way.

We knew our rations were being cut, but we were content. We were told we had willingly given up our weekly portion of chocolate, but we were content. We were asked to donate one blanket each as well as every extra article of clothing we had, and we did it gladly. No more was asked of us. Not of me nor of anyone else in the company, with the exception of Ta-

143

mari, who, to no one's surprise, turned out to be one of the heads of the way-station.

Bubi Meinz and Hershler were missing, too; they'd never returned from their leave in Milan. Only after a few days did we learn that Bubi had temporarily been assigned to another unit and that Hershler had disappeared in Milan. Rumor had it he'd gone to seek out his parents in Budapest.

Zunenshein, too, stayed with us, but he had lost his calm. He no longer sat in his corner puffing on his pipe, scanning his journals. Afternoons, as soon as exercises were over, he would take off, to return only late at night. Our beds were adjacent, so when he came into the dark room and pulled back his blanket I asked him where he had been.

"There," he said.

"And how is it?"

Zunenshein was a well-mannered person. More than that, he believed deeply in the power of conversation; he was never one to scorn any person or shun any topic. Every one of us found himself speaking very politely to Zunenshein, maybe because that was the way he always acted with us, but not now. He avoided my question, got undressed and lay down. I was afraid to repeat myself lest he burden me with something he had carried away from his hours among the refugees smuggled in daily from the north. We were all afraid of getting too involved.

Nonetheless, the next day, when he came back from the way-station and all of us were still sitting in Poker's room, I followed him into our room and repeated my question.

Zunenshein said nothing. Only after he had made his bed while I still sat on mine did he light his pipe and say, "Elisha, did you ever read a story called 'A Prince of Judah'?"

"No, why?"

"Too bad. It's worth reading. I can't stop thinking about it these last few days." Without my asking he began to tell me the story, describing in detail the meeting between Pontius Pilate and his friend, how the two proud old Romans reminisced, going over all their noteworthy deeds, right up to the heart of the story: Jesus of Nazareth . . . Pontius Pilate had no recollection whatever of ever having had anything to do with a man from Nazareth . . .

144

"What's the point of the story, Zunenshein? Who's Pilate here?"

"That's not the point. The point is, when I think of myself and the period in which I find myself, the moral of the story strikes home. Only today I stood there and said to myself, over, and over, 'Never forget this place. Here is history.'"

The next day I went there myself—only by chance. That afternoon we were eating by the side of the road and the supply truck came up alongside us. Suddenly I heard the quartermaster say he was going to the refugees. I suggested to Brodsky that we take advantage of the opportunity, but he just shrugged his shoulders. I left my mess kit with him and jumped aboard the truck.

I don't know what that place at the foot of the mountain could have been used for before they made it a way-station. Maybe it had been a lumber mill or a small work camp. One two-story building stood there, together with a number of long black barracks, German style. Between the building and the barracks stretched a yard of sorts that was bustling with people.

At first my eyes took in the soldiers, a cross section from all the units. A few of them were from the corps; you could spot them by what they were doing. At the entrance to the building they were dishing out lunch to a long line of people. A sergeant taking down names was the focus of a second group, a huddled mass of refugees. Other soldiers were running around the barracks, shouting to one another, calling to the people who filled the yard, but they were obviously getting nowhere with their efforts at organization. The other soldiers were a nuisance as far as they were concerned, since fresh circles of people kept forming around them. Everyone asked about everything, about names, places: "Perhaps . . . Maybe . . . It seems to me . . ." and "Maybe we ought to go back to the bulletin board and look over the list of new arrivals." Persons in charge kept asking the curious not to interfere, but no one listened to them. All the soldiers were trying their luck: after all, wasn't this their first encounter with men who had returned from that world?

I stood to the side so as not to get in the way, already sorry I had rushed to a place where I had nothing to do. I had no one to search out, no one to rejoice over me.

And that was not all. I began to look closely at the survivors. Not at the mass of tattered refugees, but at one tall man, at one living head; I couldn't tear my eyes away from him—maybe because he loomed over all the others. Though he was unshaven, his hair consisted only of scattered clumps, as though he had just emerged from the fire. What a bald pate, what ears! And his lips: they were covered with rusty scales rather than flesh. From the distance I saw no fresh wounds, no flies circling above them. His fingers were not scraping his flesh to gouge out the pain. His skin was dry, but he was as unaware of that as he was of the striped prisoner's uniform he had not changed. His gigantic fingers, which seemed nourished by the very sores they bore, gripped a cold bowl of soup that from time to time, he drew to his scaled lips, before circulating among the soldiers once again. He would ask everyone the same question and when they started in horror at his appearance he would walk on to repeat that question, which I couldn't make out. Only his fingers curled about the bowl of soup showed that the man was alive.

I was terror-stricken at the thought of his coming over to me and ashamed of that terror. Goddamnit, why was he allowed to walk around like that, why wasn't he being taken care off, hospitalized, given clothing fit for a human being, I thought. I forcibly tore my eyes away from his scab-covered body and quickly looked for someone else to focus upon.

A woman, young it would seem, although you could only guess at her age and her figure too. Rooted to one spot, she seemed to be sleeping amid the jostling crowd. Back and forth she drifted unconsciously with the tide of bodies. She was swollen and ugly. Her puffed feet scarcely squeezed into the army boots without shoelaces. A black satin dress was stretched over her distended belly and the seams were split open the length of her thigh. Over her dress she wore an American fatigue jacket, the insignia and buttons ripped off, and her head was completely covered by an American workcap, an olive sailor hat of sorts whose wide brim fell over her forehead and her ears. The woman—or girl, perhaps—stood in one spot, sleeping. Her cheeks, puffed up like dough, all but covered the slits of her eyes.

146

Suddenly, for no reason whatever, that frozen face broke into a smile. Had she seen someone or was that smile but a remnant of the body she once had? She lifted her hand to her hat, and her sleeve, which no longer had a button, slid down to her elbow. Her fingers stroked the hat as if it were a hair-do. I wanted to run away. I was afraid of bursting out in tears or crumpling at her swollen feet. Ah, she was only a girl, a little girl at that! Should I crush her to my chest with her innocent smile, that coquettish hand movement? I couldn't bear looking at such faces.Why didn't they take her somewhere, find a bed for her in some quiet spot so she wouldn't have to stand there on her swollen feet? I'll take her place in the afternoon line, I thought, find her something to wear instead of that tight party dress somebody got her during the long journey.

I did not stir from the spot. Revulsion stopped me from approaching her and shame would not let me turn and flee. Finally, when I resolved to tear myself away, I saw who she was smiling at—Zunenshein, drawing near with plates of food and slices of white bread in his hands. Suddenly her smile lit up her whole face. I was worried that Zunenshein might find out I was there, but I was anxious to learn what would happen next. Weaving through the crowd, I trailed his voice. He was speaking Czech.

Her arm linked with his, the girl walked forward heavily, as though on stilts. They turned into the nearest barracks and I followed after, wanting to be sure the girl was really alive. She was slightly taller than Zunenshein and twice as broad, but he supported her entirely. Then clear sharp laughter, like xylophone music, burst out above them. She clung to him like his child or his mistress. They reached the wooden stoop of the barracks and slowly walked up together, he first and she leaning on him.

I drew near the door. From the side I could see into the barracks. There was a row of wooden double-decker bunks set tightly together with straw for mattresses and covered with our blankets. Dull faces stared from every bed—here the shrunken head of an old man, coal black; there a boy lying on his side, his face round and soft, unscarred: with two fingers he was picking away at the white army bread loaf, flicking off tiny crumbs

147

and putting them into his mouth, as if he were eating a bun. Above him, on the upper bunk, sat a woman, her dress rolled up above her knees, her blouse unbuttoned, exposing her chest; she scratched her breasts mechanically, oblivious of all the confusion about her.

I went back to the spot where I had first stood, apart from the crowd. I kept telling myself that these were the people we had spoken of for so many years—but I was so far removed from them that electric wire might have separated us. There were young men from Eastern Europe who looked just like the folks back home. They spoke the same kind of Yiddish I had heard in our house, and Hebrew words, too. They were helping to bring order out of chaos. But still they were different, and even our own soldiers seemed other than their usual selves. The refugees freely hugged them, squeezed them, poured out their feelings in a stream of Yiddish: "*Haveyrim! Haveyrim! Mir veynen mit glickliche oygen! Am Yisrael chai! Lum'n dich kush'n, Yiddisher soldat! . . . Mir vellen boyen un kempfen!*" "Comrades! Comrades! We're crying for joy! Israel lives! Let us kiss you, Jewish soldiers! . . . We want to build and fight!"

These men came equipped with American whisky they'd gotten in one of the camps they'd been brought from. One ran to get a bottle, and it was passed from mouth to mouth, each swig accompanied with cries of "*l'Chayim!*" hugs, and prophetic orations, the men kissing each other and squeezing hands in Russian fashion. I, too, drifted into that group, took a swig from the wet neck of the whisky bottle and sang with them all the songs their predecessors had sung upon arriving in the covered trucks. I strained to be part of that scene, to plunge into that sea of emotion, but the feeling of alienation was not washed away by the whisky or the songs.

Suddenly I saw Tamari, whose absence till then had astounded me. Angrily he broke up the group: "*Haverim*, we do not drink alcoholic beverages here. Time and again I've asked you not to; we will not tolerate this behavior . . ."

"O-o-o-oh," answered the young men from the east. "We're free men . . . *Zazdravayeh!*"

"Free, but smart. And anyway, get ready to move. In two hours the trucks will be here and everyone who's not sick goes south . . . Kruk!" He turned on me. "What are you doing here?"

"I came to see—"

"There's nothing to see. It only holds things up. Everyone with nothing to do here please clear the area."

Tamari was working like a dynamo. He had found his true calling. Sleeves rolled up, his shirt was drenched with sweat under the armpits and down the back; his forehead, too, glistened as though he were plowing in the Jordan Valley. His flashing eyes seemed to be racing ahead of his thick-set body. There wasn't a man or a problem that Tamari did not take in hand or straighten out. When the sergeant who had been writing down names finished his job, Tamari told him to run off the list at once and hang a copy on the bulletin board. That was most important. Every day people were discovering relatives or fellow townsmen. The mess steward who had been borrowed from one of the regiments approached Tamari and told him there wasn't enough bread and most likely never would be. People were stuffing their clothes with bread constantly.

"We caught one," the mess steward said, "stuffing two whole loaves into the straw of his bed."

"What do you mean, 'you caught one'?" snapped Tamari.

"We saw him pushing his way back in line again to grab some more bread, so we put the finger on him."

"What do you mean, 'put the finger on him'?" Tamari cried, his face flushing. "What did you do to him?"

"What did we do to him? We didn't do anything to him, we told him to stop stealing."

"I asked you not to use the word 'steal.' They still can't believe that tomorrow there will be more bread."

"Well, there won't be," said the mess steward, "if they keep this up. A whole division doesn't eat this much."

"But don't say they steal," Tamari insisted.

"Fine, so they don't steal, they take."

Tamari shrugged his shoulders and dashed off. He would be able to say he had done something there—he would not want to say more. And whoever was not doing anything was not to disturb him.

I didn't leave, but kept walking about the yard trying to close the gap between myself and those who had returned from the dead. I thought of how I would write Father and tell him I had come there and had seen them; I would describe the convoys and the first hot meal they got and the warm reception given them, but Father—I knew very well—would quickly write back: "And what of the family, did you find anyone from the family?"

I stood in front of the wall on which hung the list of persons passing through the camp from the first day; the list showed their names and the communities they'd come from before the war. Jeeps and trucks kept bringing in soldiers from our units, all of whom raced to this bulletin board. I, too, pressed among them, doggedly scanning every name, every sheet, struggling to fish up the names of all the relatives ever mentioned back home. That's all I had brought with me, names and fragments of stories. I never knew the family itself. Grandfather and Grandmother had long since become faded photographs. They were lucky enough—so Father often said—to have died in time. The other grandparents I didn't even know that well since, being so religious, they left no pictures behind. Then there were the brothers and sisters on both sides.

But all I could remember was my own family name, Kruk, and in spite of myself, I couldn't remember my mother's maiden name. I didn't know the last names of all my aunts after they married, since at home they were only mentioned by their first names. Besides, I had always made myself scarce every time Mother or Father's friends would drop in to rehash the endless stories of a land I had never seen and people I had never known. They always boasted of how they had come from the tiniest villages that had one street at most. If I came across the name of one of these places that kept cropping up in their stories, I said to myself, I'd be able to tell if all those refugees included one of our kinsmen.

I found no one and became very depressed. A strange feeling gripped me. Even though I mocked myself, told myself I was nothing but a Motel ben Peisi* in reverse, I felt like an

* Literally a "ne'er do well" (character in a Sholom Aleichem work).

150

orphan standing there to the side while others frantically and vainly struggled to salvage one person from all they had lost. I found no one because I had lost no one; and I had lost no one because I had never had a family.

I was already turning to leave the immigrants' way-station when I spied a bunch of boys behind the building. At that spot where the narrow valley ended and the tree-covered mountain arose, work had begun long ago on some huge structure, some project or other, but only the concrete foundation had been laid. On that foundation, among the iron rods sticking up from the concrete like black antennas, the boys had gathered. Unclear as to what drew me to them, I approached as they crouched on the ground in a tight circle.

There were six or eight of them, the youngest looking ten or so and the eldest maybe fifteen. They were tossing coins just like the Australians used to on the promenade in Tel Aviv; we called the game Tree or Palestine.* Every toss was a big event, accompanied by shouts of victory or groans of disappointment. All the boys held coins and currency, and tossed in or swept out money with the facility of experienced gamblers; only their feelings were childlike. The littlest one turned to me and asked in Yiddish if I wanted to play. I winked at him and said I was afraid of losing my grandmother's inheritance. My fractured Yiddish tickled them. They said I should play with the cigarettes I no doubt had in my pocket.

"I don't smoke," I said.

"And what else don't you do?" jibed the pipsqueak, sweeping in his winnings. The innuendo set everyone laughing, myself included. Since he was completely bent over, all his weight resting on the tips of his shoes, I grabbed him by his pants and swept him into the air, supporting him under his knees with my left hand.

"I don't let babies get fresh. That's one thing I don't do."

The little fellow kicked and struggled furiously, while his friends doubled over with laughter. I lowered the boy to the ground and let go of him. He clenched his tiny fists and cursed me bitterly in Polish. This, too, amused his friends, who were curious to see what I would do next.

* Heads or tails.

151

"I don't curse, either." I smiled at the little fellow and extended my hand in peace.

He gestured coarsely in response: "All the soldiers here are sweeter than honey," he said. "Bet the war with the Germans got you all upset. Nuns in pants."

"Oh no, nuns'd know stuff he don't," said one of the older boys.

"You're telling me!" said the little fellow.

He seemed smaller than a ten-year-old. His head was wide, even flattened somewhat, and his black eyes, slanting, were a good distance away from his pug nose. But his thin lips had the bitter twitch of a much older person. He wore a new shirt and pants of the *Hitler-jugend*,* and the buckle of his leather belt had the German inscription, "God is with us."

The other boys, too, wore new clothes that had been creased and dirtied during the last leg of their trip. Looking at them, the laughter that began to rise in my throat at the sound of "You're telling me!" stopped dead. Suddenly I realized what had drawn me to them: There hadn't been a youngster in the yard—not one infant, toddler or child. Their laughter had drawn me behind the house; a small mischievous gang having themselves some fun. I was nineteen and only ten weeks before I had held the body of a man whose life gushed from between my fingers. For the first time in my life I had wound field bandages around the spreading blotches of blood on a man's chest, without realizing he was already dead.

"Children don't go to funerals," Father would tell me, and "Aaron's descendants can't go near graveyards," he once said with an enigmatic smile, "but unfortunately we're near-descendants." In my childhood this "near status" infuriated me; I was vexed that we had lost our priestly station. In the course of time I came to realize it had been said in jest, but cemeteries always made me uneasy. I kept my distance from the cemetery in the *moshava*. But, then I arrive in that courtyard to hear people with lifeless faces tell what they had gone through. Should I repeat what I overheard those first survivors say that June of '45? All has been told so often that our hearts have grown scales. I have no intention of rehashing those sto-

* Hitler youth, the junior branch of the Nazi Party (1926-1945).

ries, of describing the deathly terror that gripped me as my eyes fled from smoking faces to dead faces, as my ears first absorbed the names of the camps and the forests and the pits: "They took us . . . We stood there . . . I lay that way from time to time . . . What did we have to lose? We ran. You see with your own eyes, here I am . . ."

Suddenly that small band in back of the house. Their eyes dancing, notes of the occupying powers rustling between their tiny fingers. They were laughing. By themselves. Just as the cells of their bodies kept multiplying by themselves. Children.

I sat down on the concrete foundation and said, "Try and ask. Maybe there's something I do know."

"What will they do with us now?" asked the eldest.

"They'll take you to *Eretz Yisrael*," I answered, smiling.

"Look at this hero," said the little one, "he's brought us to *Aretz* just like that. And you've fixed it up with the English already?"

"Fix up"—they never stopped using that term.

"Fixing up" was the standard by which everything was measured; that is, take, grab, rob, lie, use any means to reach your one goal, to leave death behind you. They could never be deceived, even in their dreams, I thought, so I answered their questions as though I were talking to myself.

They were very curious and were never satisfied with any answer I gave. But when it suddenly dawned on them that I had been born in *Aretz* and could tell them stories of when I was a little boy, stories of the *moshava* and my adventures in school and in the orchards and the fig orchards and the horse races that ended the harvest season and how I pulled the wool over British eyes and became a *gaffir* when I was fourteen and how I fooled the whole world, forging documents to get into the British Army before I was even seventeen. When I told them anything like that I saw the embers of their childhood glow as if fanned by the wind. They, too, began to tell stories, all of them, very quickly, any stories. They pressed against me like tots, touched me, tried on my hat, tried my belt for size, and told more and more tales . . .

I will not retell today, after so many years, what those laughing children revealed to me that green sunny day in the Italian

153

Alps. They laughed as they spoke while I felt myself shrinking, felt the words scraping my flesh like rusty nails. I heard of their lives and all the while I saw my own life. Where had I been for nineteen years—loving, hating, striving, rebuffed, sad, happy? What was I, in the end, but a bag of wind. *Let me kiss your wounds, children. Let me flee from you, children, and forget you quickly, at once, and heal the gashes from your rusty nails. Take some chocolate. Take all the money in my pocket. Take my belt. Only let me get out of here.*

"I have to go, children."

"She'll wait for you," the little fellow said, winking. "Sit with us a little while longer. Get your money out and we'll play."

"I have to run. I'll come back and see you tomorrow."

"Tomorrow we'll be someplace else already," said one of the older boys who, physically, was one of the smallest; the *Hitlerjugend* uniform was bunched up around his broad leather belt like an empty sack. "Gee, it'd be nice if we could meet you in *Aretz.*"

"There's a lot of fellows like me there," I laughed. "Nicer, too."

"But we know you already."

I did not have the strength to take leave of them. We flipped coins. We laughed, we roared, and they cleaned me out of my last lira. Again they were in high spirits. The eldest ran to the barracks and returned one moment later, pulling a bottle of whisky out of his shirt.

"Where did you all get whisky from?" I asked in amazement.

"Don't ask questions," said the little fellow. "Drink!"

From the yard I heard the beeping of truck horns and voices louder than usual.

"I think your trucks are here."

"They'll wait for us, *haver.* Drink *l'Chayim.* Drink! What kind of a soldier are you?"

I swallowed first and then every one of the boys from the fifteen-year-old to the little ten-year-old devil suckled from the bottle. The sergeant who had taken names that afternoon yelled from the distance. The eldest stuffed the bottle into his shirt. They hugged me one by one and kissed me on both cheeks. I could not hold back my tears.

154

"Come on now, let's go. I'll walk you to the truck."

The large Dodges formed two long lines in the field facing the road. The people who were to travel on were already standing nearby with their few bags in hand—Tyrolese packs, kit bags, here a new suitcase made of pigskin, there a deerskin traveling bag. Within a matter of minutes they were all on the trucks, with the exception of the weak and the sick whom the directors of the camp were detaining for a time. Tamari was still dashing about as though his body were plugged into a generator. The sergeant organized everything quietly, inspecting the lists of those moving on and those remaining, passing among the trucks and giving instructions to the men in charge of the convoy. I saw the tall leprous-looking fellow; the boisterous young men who had arrived from the east; the bloated girl still accompanied by Zunenshein, who led her to one of the trucks and sat her next to the driver; and my boys, too. They kept saying good-by even as they clambered aboard the truck, but many others followed close behind them, so they quickly disappeared. They had fixed up a spot for themselves on the floor of the truck and were probably afraid they would lose it.

Only then did I make out the insignia of the unit painted on the tailgate of every vehicle: Pinik's company once again. There it was, the clock whose hands pointed to 9:05. I bubbled over with childish hope, just as I had the day Brodsky and I visited Bologna. To come across Pinik at that moment. How had I not noticed the 9:05 before?

"Pinik isn't with the convoy," one of the drivers told me. "He's working in the company garage now in a town near Venice."

"Any way of getting hold of him?"

"If you come during working hours. After that he's very busy," the driver volunteered, his lewd smile buttoning my lips. I wasn't interested in hearing scandal about Pinik.

"Send him your regards or did you change your mind already?" asked the driver. He looked like he belonged to a foreign detachment: all the drivers did. He wore a silk jacket like the American pilots, a patched officer's hat, gym shoes, long sideburns, and a moustache à la Don Ameche.

"Send him regards from Elisha Kruk, his nephew."

155

"Ah, that's a different story. Very nice. Pinik's a fine chap and don't you go listening to any gossip."

"Who gossips about him?" I asked innocently.

"Don't kid me. You heard alright, my boy. Pinik's a fine chap, take it from me. You go and visit him sometime . . . he'll get you a *regazza*, too . . . they're all stocked up, him and his buddies, ha, ha . . ." He grabbed my wrist with his left hand and slapped his palm against mine. "Say, why did you enlist after the war?"

"I enlisted two years ago," I answered angrily.

"At fourteen?" he guffawed, exposing two rows of perfectly matched teeth which he seemed as proud of as his thin moustache.

"Take care of yourself," I said, and left.

The engines were already rumbling and the jeep began to bounce across the field toward the dirt road. One by one all the Dodges pulled out to the main highway. The shadows from the mountains elongated, filling the entire valley. In the paved yard between the building and the black barracks stood the soldiers and the few refugees who had been left behind, their eyes on the trucks turning black in the distance just like the forest spilling down onto the road.

A hand rested on my shoulder and I sniffed the odor of Zunenshein's tobacco. Thinking he wanted to speak to me, I turned my head in the direction of his hand, but he silently followed the convoy with his eyes until it disappeared around the bend in the mountain. I didn't move my shoulder away even though I felt uncomfortable at his taking up our conversation of the night before. I still picture Zunenshein as an actor, like Walter Pidgeon in *Mrs. Miniver*: the quiet laying on of hands, the sweet tobacco, the quiet Alpine twilight. But I knew he was spinning out his life in silence, behind doors closed to strangers' eyes.

"*Nu!*" cried Tamari, who came upon us from the rear. "There go the convoys. We're waiting for another one tonight."

"It's written somewhere in the Bible—" said Zunenshein, regarding me. "Maybe Kruk remembers, he studied in a religious school."

"You studied in a religious school?" Tamari looked at me as though for the first time.

"Somewhere it says 'worm of Jacob,'" Zunenshein began again.

"Yes, there is a line like that," said Tamari. "In the prayer book, too, I think."

"I'm not well versed in either. But the convoy brought that phrase to mind: 'worm of Jacob.'"

The entire sentence leaped before my eyes. "'Fear not, thou worm, Jacob, and ye men of Israel.' I think that's the way it goes."

"Bravo, Kruk," Tamari bellowed, slapping me on the shoulder. "I didn't know you were such a scholar."

"That's the sentence," Zunenshein exclaimed happily. "Exactly."

"That's really very nice. Well, men, must get on with the work." In an instant Tamari had turned and walked back to the house.

Zunenshein stretched his arm out and pointed with his pipe stem at the mountains to the west. They were black as the massed clouds above them, but a thread of shining sky divided them.

"Lovely," he said, "this place, this hour." Without pausing for breath he added, "If you wait here a little longer, you'll get a lift back to the battalion. I'm going too."

The detail had all returned to their duties. The visiting soldiers had already gone. A bare bulb cast a pale light over the entrance to the house. The cooks had already begun dishing out the delayed evening meal. I stood by the bulletin board and saw a new list of names had been hung up; I began going over it, name by name. A few of the people who remained in the way-station gathered in the pale yellow circle of light. All of them were going back to the names, both the first list and the one that had just been put up before nightfall, hoping against hope they would not be disappointed again. The light and the names engendered fragmented conversations and I soon found myself within that circle, asking questions of others and being addressed myself. Then one of those rare events took place, the last hope of many.

157

Among that group bathed in light stood a young fellow who caught my eye with his sharp, jerky movements, as though his limbs were being yanked about by some hidden puppeteer. Standing with his gaunt head cocked toward one conversation, the very next moment he pulled away and plunged into the midst of another group, fearful of missing a word that was said, even as his eyes sought out what was going on in still a third group. He was truly a strange looking fellow: small, every exposed limb of his body gaunt and dry as a matchstick. A new wool suit hung from him, the sleeves rolled up, exposing the white lining. When not otherwise occupied he would pull up his pants, which received no support from his hips. At the mention of any name he would rise slightly on his toes and stretch his lips—a ludicrous but pitiable sight and amazing in his indefatigable pursuit. I asked him where he came from and instantly he pulled himself up to face me and answered with a smile,

"From Poland. You, too?"

"My father and mother. And what city are you from?"

"Near Piotrkow. You, too?"

Already I was confused. I had heard that place mentioned often. We had relatives or acquaintances there, but the immediate families of both my father and my mother were from different towns. I went over everything my memory could dredge up.

"No, those aren't ours." He nodded his head sadly but at once sought another opening. "And the others, from Piotrkow, maybe you remember their names?"

His face was narrow and in the light of the one bulb in the yard the shadows flitted over its many hollows. His eyes, distant from one another, darted about in their deep sockets ready at any instant for news from afar. I brought up every name that had any possible connection with that town.

"No, they aren't ours. But we do have family there, in Palestine."

"And what's your name?" I asked, as I should have at the start.

"Krochmal. Which Krochmal do you know?"

158

Certainly. I smiled in spite of myself. That name had always tickled me ever since a relative of mine, one of the pioneers who had come to the country before the war, had married a fellow from Jerusalem with a hat and tie by the name of Krochmal. Every time Krochmal was mentioned in our home I pictured Mother boiling a thick brew of starch, pouring it into the washtub and throwing in the bag of blueing.

"Oy!" The youth shot up on his toes and touched me. "I think that's it!"

I began to dig into the recesses of my memory, hauling out every chance recollection I had preserved of this husband of my distant relative. One by one the details meshed while the Krochmal in front of me examined them eagerly like a man who has unearthed a treasure, until there was no more room for doubt: it was plain as day that the two Krochmals were really relatives, even though the youth had not been thinking of that specific Krochmal when he said he had family in Palestine.

It was an eerie moment. The youth's joy was contagious: it seemed as though he, indeed, was the man I had been seeking. Suddenly I was no longer an uninvited guest at a stranger's celebration, for I, too, had a relative there, one who had turned up through one of those incredible freak occurrences which were, actually, all that one could still hope for. I opened my heart to him wholly, ready to serve him in any way in my power. I began to probe into the details of his life during the war. Where had he been? In the camps, really? What exactly did they do with the prisoners? And those who survived—how, how did they do it?

He spoke willingly and at length, as if he had been waiting for the opportunity. While speaking he linked his arm with mine and pressed against me, as if seeking refuge. The physical proximity left me somewhat uneasy, but at the same time I felt a wonderful sense of satisfaction at being able to offer protection to this youth who no longer was an anonymous person but Krochmal, a blood relative of the Jerusalemite Krochmal, husband of my own relative. I told him I would write home that very night and inform them of his having survived. I asked him to tell me if he needed anything I could get for him, if he wanted me to bring him something the next day.

159

"Nothing, nothing," he said nestling against me. "Enough that I found someone of ours."

Again I found myself urging him to tell me everything that happened to him during that period.

"Auschwitz," he said, pulling up the wide sleeve of his new jacket to show me the number tattooed on his forearm.

That word has long since broken into human vocabulary and today is used regularly like other unfathomable terms such as Sheol, Tophet, Gehenna, Inferno, Styx, the Flood, the Day of the Lord and many others whose terror is so far removed that a man lives with them tranquilly. But this was in June 1945. And I, who had looked upon myself as a seasoned veteran, was only a boy who had fled from the home of simple, God-fearing people in a *moshava* that contained two drunkards, one an eastern and one a western Jew; a likable thief who went off to the war like me and was taken prisoner by the Germans; and two policemen. And there had been one terrible incident there, so the people said: a wagoner locked his old father in a chicken coop. But now I was standing in front of this shrunken boy who was telling me, as he rocked from right to left in a mocking motion: "Sure I was there. They didn't send us to a resort."

I barraged him with insistent and foolish questions and he answered with facts, episodes, anecdotes, supplementing his weak voice with the sharp Pinocchio-like movements of his body. "How was it possible?" I asked. And he explained. Very matter of factly and obligingly. He was eager to share everything with his new-found relative. As he spoke I struggled vainly to picture him—he was twenty-three years old, so he said— stooped, thin, in the midst of all the events he was describing.

"But still, how did you manage to survive? What kind of work did they give you?"

"In the crematorium," he said, nodding his head.

"What!"

He thought I didn't know what the word meant.

"In the crematorium," he said again, accompanying the word with the gesture of a man removing bread from an oven. "You know, they burned the people in an oven after they gassed them. If it weren't for that job—and look at me, I'm no hero

160

—if it weren't for that job you wouldn't see me alive today."

How I have struggled to rid my mind of that memory. But all the years have not dimmed it or in any way changed its grotesqueness—except for this one difference: now I'm strong enough to admit what I was trying to hide from myself then. But even today, in the still silence of my soul, I am not free of the terror, confusion and shame that gripped me when I heard that relative, whom I had just adopted, say so plainly and matter-of-factly,

"In the crematorium."

More than anything else I was filled with revulsion at the thought of being connected with him. That feeling was more powerful than the terror and the nausea. If only I could get out of there quickly, not remember that jumpy puppet. Not look into his eyes. Not breathe the air around him. And he had even said, "You wouldn't see me here today." Who wants to see you, goddamnit! Not me, that's for sure. Enough searching for family. I didn't want to ask questions or get answers, didn't want to be there at all, not see, not hear, not remember, not judge. I was looking for relatives—I found a relative . . .

Krochmal didn't stop talking and weaving plans. If I would write home, when would I write? How many days would it take before their answer would arrive? And if he wouldn't be there any more, how would they know where to find him? And maybe he ought to sit down right away and dash off a short letter I could enclose with my letter? Or maybe he ought to take my address and, upon arriving at a permanent camp, send me a letter? But then, we could easily be sent elsewhere so mightn't it be better if I gave him my parents' address so he could write them directly? Ah, who could have believed such a miracle would happen to him! But he believed it. He had been confident. To tell the truth, he had not stopped believing for a moment . . .

On and on he rambled, asking and answering, while I only nodded my head, wanting to disappear, melt out of existence. Finally Zunenshein and the sergeant emerged from the barracks. I hurried toward them.

"We're pulling out, Kruk," said Zunenshein, as they headed toward the command car parked alongside the building.

161

"And the letter?" Krochmal ran after me holding onto my sleeve, rising on his toes. "Just a few words . . . it'll only take a second . . ."

"They won't wait for me, Krochmal," I told him and continued walking toward the pick-up truck. "It'll be okay. Count on me."

"Maybe you'll come tomorrow?"

"Sure, sure I'll come," I lied.

"*Shalom!*" Krochmal stroked my palm with the fingers of his two cold hands. After I sat myself down in the truck he called after me, "Tomorrow, then! Don't forget me!"

"I won't forget," I said, and it seemed that the shame engulfing me was visible even in the darkness.

3

My letter to Noga vanished into the abyss, as if it had been written in smoke. I wormed around my vow not to write her another word until she resumed the correspondence by rationalizing that I needed three or four books. "We're dying of boredom here," I wrote her. "Who knows when we'll be discharged and how much more we'll have to go through till then. Just these last few days a timetable of army discharges was actually made public, based on each soldier's age and length of service. But if we're put on the general waiting list of the Empire, you can just picture the scene: a line of hundreds of thousands of soldiers headed by the old men who served five or six years, with the tail end brought up by squirts like me with just two years of service. Well, while I'm standing in line I might as well learn a little bit.

"They've organized courses here to prepare us for the matriculation exams. I don't need them, really, since I learned so much already I'll never use, but on the other hand, what have I got to lose? I'll read a little and pass the time. Anyway, don't forget to send Lachover. He's just as boring as the books he explains, but at least he condenses them. And by the way, Noga," I snuck in a line, "it's been about six weeks since I've gotten a letter from you. I know the mails are all fouled up, but still—is everything all right? How did your final exams go? Are you in good health? Write something. Did your letters get lost or maybe . . ."

A wretched ruse that left me doubly shamed. Still I could not make peace with the idea that I had lost Noga. To the contrary, every day I would grimace and come up with new explanations for her prolonged silence. I would wait for the letter which was surely en route, which would arrive the next day or the day after, stubbornly push myself into the swirl of men jostling about the company clerk and wait until he put the last envelope into someone else's hand. Only then would I turn around, hurt and helpless. *One sound, Noga, a cry, a curse, a sign that you're still alive and not a fantasy I invented in my loneliness.*

It seemed to me I could recall her only hazily, could only remember a memory. It got to the point where at night I would lie frustrated buried beneath the blanket, compulsively straining to picture her; that is, really conjure her up. If I had been asked by the police to describe her in detail I would know enough to say that she had delicate limbs and that even if she wound her hair up like a turret, and even put on high-heeled shoes (the last few months before we left she suddenly began putting on airs, I don't know why)—still her head would fit comfortably beneath my chin. And I could say this, too: her hands were cold. Her eyes were warm and she had a certain kind of laugh, unique . . . What kind? Well, you see, I'd say, she's not one to laugh much, in fact it's just the opposite, but when she does laugh suddenly, for two seconds an evening, it's like polished crystal, like a stream in the Alps racing over a pebbly bed here below, like—

Like another simile. I couldn't see a damn thing.

I would bring all my senses to bear in the dark, but I could not hear her laugh, could not smell her hair. My fingers had forgotten the tautness of her shy breasts. If I were cross-examined, I'd be able to mention a mark on her body, a scar acquired in her childhood over her knee (which one?), but she herself, in her entirety, I couldn't picture. Noga would not emerge from the dark. More than I resented being the prisoner of love, I was tortured by her rejection of me. That alone—that she tossed me aside—that alone I was unable to forget. I would exploit every hour the barracks were empty to take the bundle of letters out of my kit bag and leaf through them. For more than six months I had gotten her letters and at times two letters would even bear the same date. I would begin reading and her voice would caress my face. Until I met Noga I had never heard such a voice, I would tell myself joyfully, and immediately she was before me, her feet gathered up on the bed, her narrow shoulders visible through her white silk blouse as she whispered the words she had written:

"Today was a rough day for us. It's been a week that the Yishuv has mourned our dead. Today was declared a general fast day. Normal life has ceased—traffic has come to a halt and stores, factories and places of amusement have all closed down.

"In the streets all is deathly quiet.

"It seems everyone is carrying a stone on his heart. From morning until night I've lain on my bed. Of course, I fasted. And not because of any announcement, but because I just felt I had to. I had the feeling that my conscience wasn't too clean. My soft life, the studies, the comfortable house. And against all this—there. . . .

"Today I strived to be one with many dead and those who have remained alive. . . . Horrible pictures drifted through my mind. And they weren't all just the products of my imagination. I've heard a lot, I've read a lot and today I read more . . ."

My eyes raced from one line to the next, but I was no longer reading. My throat tightened painfully at the thought that Noga, that dear girl, was no longer mine, nor ever could be. Where was I and where was she? I pictured her taking the packet of my letters, if she still kept them, trying to find me somewhere in that ugly handwriting, those broken words, twisted lines, that clumsy, halting style. This is Elisha, she would tell herself. Now he's a soldier and I'm a student, but tomorrow when he returns to his blue overalls—not tomorrow, but maybe in a few years—where will he be then, with "all his life before him?"

Nu, the end of the affair could have been forecast from the

164

first moment, I told myself, and at once went back to deceiving myself: if she would answer my last letter, if she had sent the books I had asked for by regular mail, I would finally learn the truth and grind my teeth. *I have a lot going for me, Noga, believe me, I only need a little support and someone to believe in me. Just write one word. . . .*

"I took stock of myself today. In the final analysis, what have I been doing during this period? Have I, by burying myself in my books, freed myself from all other obligations? At times I think I'm right, that a person who wants to act effectively has to be ready and I'm not ready yet . . . I'm not ready yet. But at times I think it's not that way at all. What preparation do I need? Give what you can, I tell myself, look around you and you'll find things to do that are within your power . . ."

My throat nearly closed. If she wasn't ready, my fate was decided. What would become of me? When would I recoup the years I had wasted in a factory and the army, when could I overtake—but what, actually, did I want to overtake? What did I want to prepare myself for? What goal? Even that trivial detail I couldn't clarify for myself. "I'm not ready yet," I repeated, and almost felt hatred for Noga, who was only a moment's fantasy a person like myself would never enjoy a second time. But nevertheless, if only. . . .

A letter never came, but I did get regards of a different kind.

A new group of draftees arrived from *Aretz*. With the establishment of the Jewish Brigade during the preceding autumn, the draft, which had all but ended during the last two years, was suddenly revived, but even then, despite all the bugles and drums and shining miracles, there was no overflow of volunteers. All of them had been gathered into a few new units and trained in Egypt. The first ones reached us as we left the front, and when the last group arrived we were already on the border. Before embarking they had spent a short leave in *Aretz*, so we all rushed to greet the platoon assigned to our regiment, hoping for news from home.

They were seated on their gear on the platform of the railroad station opposite regimental headquarters. In previous years the drafted soldiers had been of all kinds, while here one

165

glance sufficed to identify only two distinct groups: young lads whose eyes were afire with volunteering and the lust for adventure; and men drafted for the work of "the organized Yishuv" —mature young men, well disciplined, keeping to themselves and displaying more than a little snobbishness by their knowing silence. *We're not "recruits" like these high school kids running around our legs. We're a team of buddies with a mission, let's not make any mistake about it.*

"What's going on in *Aretz?*"

"Everything's fine."

"What have you got to say?"

"Nothing."

"What made you enlist all of a sudden?"

"We enlisted."

"Where are you from?"

Silence.

One of the young recruits, a city boy, approached me. A tall fellow, pale, upper class. "I know you."

He knew me? Where from? Such a fragile fellow, with blond hair, maybe he even played the violin. I had no such friends in *Aretz*. Maybe he was from Tel Aviv? Perhaps he had studied in high school with relatives of mine?

"No, I'm from Jerusalem. We met at a party."

Birds began whirring inside me. I knew where—at a party of university students and seminarists. I remembered exactly— even then he had been in uniform, the uniform of the settlements' police force. He was a second-year student in the humanities. He had gone to high school with Noga's brother, which meant he was older than I. He knew that Noga and I . . .

"If I'm not mistaken you came to the party with Nehemiah," he said.

I didn't deny it. We spoke of Nehemiah, the link binding my schooldays with this young man, with Noga. I wanted to ask him about her, but I patiently held back. Any question would give me away and I didn't know how much he knew and what relationship he then had with Noga's brother. I would wait. They had begun organizing the new arrivals into groups to be moved out to different companies and he still had not opened

166

up. He knew nothing. Casually I asked him if he knew a girl who was also at that party by the name of Noga.

"Reznick?" he said. "Lovely girl. I was in the same class with her brother. You're going together?"

"No, we just met—"

"Through Nehemiah?"

"Yes, that's about it. What's she doing nowadays?"

"Doing very well, I understand. Finished her studies, with honors of course . . . Now I remember—the three of you were together at that party . . ."

"Right. Have you seen her recently?"

"As a matter of fact I did. During my leave. She looked more like a poet than ever, trailing clouds of mystery. Do you know the elder Reznick?"

"No," I lied, sensing that whether he went on talking depended on me.

"Ah, a wonderful man—a lot of soul. A lot. Tell me"—he suddenly looked at me suspiciously—"rumor had it Noga had a boy friend somewhere, a soldier. That wouldn't be you by any chance?"

"Me?" I laughed. "I should be so lucky. To tell you the truth, though, she did impress me. But I didn't get very far. We met once or twice and that was it. And with Nehemiah. A smart gal."

"Not ugly, either, even if she isn't pretty. Maybe that's because I know her since she was twelve. We're neighbors, and she and her brother and I were good friends once. A lot of soul and such a little body. And so serious—she got excellent grades on all her compositions. Boys were scared of her. And even though everyone admitted she had a good personality she was pretty neglected. When you get down to it, it's all a matter of taste. A wonderful girl."

"You're building her up as if I was ready to marry her. I was only interested, that's all."

"Even if you wanted to, it's too late for that. True, Noga's very poetical but only up to a certain point. She's just like her father with his practical Zionism. Lofty ideals—but in a plush, roomy house. When I met her she was with her bridegroom Rivkin. Count on mysterious Noga."

167

"Well then, you sure do have news," I said, twisting my face into a smile, anxious to hear everything to the bitter end. *"Mazel tov.* Which Rivkin is that?"

"I see you're not from Jerusalem. There's only one Rivkin. The office of Rivkin and Associates. Lawyers. A member of the London Bar. K.C. Real Estate. Trials that go on forever. 'You will legally redeem the land' and all that sort of stuff. One thing's sure, you don't have to worry about Noga Reznick. She's fixed for life. Well, see you. . . ."

4

Our platoon was to spend the day in Venice, shuttled via truck transport. Our pants and shirts were pressed.

It was just as hot there as in Tel Aviv, we were told. We were to leave early in the morning so we could spend four hours getting there and five coming back, all for the pleasure of running around from the piazza of San Marco to the Rialto, dashing through vendors' alleys to buy "souvenirs," floating down the Grand Canal in a vaporetto to the Lido, and returning out of breath to the railroad station. At 10 P.M. we were to head back to camp. On the dot.

I had decided at the start not to go. That wasn't for me. I was sick of the whole crew, like sticky underwear. I was in no mood for Duchies or gondolas, silk scarves or Morano glass and had no intention of trotting around all day shoulder to shoulder with the herd, gulping everything down like an idiot. Let them go, all of them, let there be peace in the barracks, so I could lie by myself on the bed or climb a mountain, go wherever my legs would take me. I didn't give a damn for Venice. I only wanted a little peace and quiet. So I had decided the night before when we went to sleep.

Leizi turned on his side, facing my bunk, and said in his faint, nasal tone: "So we're heading for Venice, huh?"

At once I sensed he was continuing the conversation that had taken place between him and Bubi when we had stopped to camp for the night on the outskirts of Venice. "Start running," Bubi had called to him. "I'm getting you a pass."

When Leizi lay in bed, swathed in blankets up to his chin, you couldn't see how tall and muscular he was, so that suddenly he was, after all, only a young fellow. Like all blonds he didn't shave regularly, and hairs spotted his cheeks, between his pimples, like clusters of red thorns on a ripe *sabra*. For a moment I thought his narrow eyes were laughing, but with Leizi you could never tell whether he was up to some trick or whether sleep was closing his eyes. Reminded of Bubi, it was highly unlikely he was smiling. Since that identification parade Leizi had remained without a friend in the platoon, and I knew he had never forgiven Bubi for having slighted him.

"I'm not going," I told him, though I didn't know why.

"Not going, just like that? Don't be a *schmuck!* Everybody's going."

"I don't feel like it."

"What do you mean, you don't feel like it, you jackass!" interjected Arusi, who was also in bed. "You have any idea what goes on in Venice? You don't see blondes like that anywhere else in Italy."

"How do you know?" said Leizi.

"I'm interested, that's how. My buddy, Rahmani, told me that before you turn off the ignition and get out of the jeep they're all over you. It's the sea gives 'em the appetite. And Kruk doesn't feel like it!"

"It's a once-in-a-lifetime town, Venice," Leizi said, winking at me as though we were the only two going. "All to gain, nothing to lose this round."

"No, I'm not going," I repeated stubbornly, even though Leizi's prodding had already weakened my resolve. Ever since Bubi had been transferred to another unit Leizi had sought out my friendship, and I couldn't have been more pleased.

"Ah, let him alone," said Arusi, disgusted. "He's crazy, that Kruk. When will you ever get another chance in your life to make a girl in Venice, intellectual!"

"He'll come, he'll come, don't worry." Leizi's eyes flashed mischievously. "Kruk, in the morning I'm turning your bed over if you don't get up with the rest of us."

In the morning I did wake up, very aware of the feverish preparations even though I lay buried beneath my blanket.

Leizi shook me two or three times and when I didn't move, he ripped my blanket off me.

"Go to hell, Leizi," I grumbled, pulling the blanket back over me.

Without saying a word Leizi bent over my bed, took hold of the wooden frame and turned it over.

"Stop coddling yourself, Kruk. Either you get dressed or we throw you into the truck in your drawers."

Leizi was a wild man who backed up his sense of humor with his muscles. And this time there was something very warm and friendly in his insisting I not stay by myself. When was the last time, before that, anyone had given a damn what I did with myself or whether I was happy or depressed? And out of the entire platoon Leizi was the one I secretly sought most to be like, but always in vain. Now he was looking after me like a kid brother. Even though I kept griping, he had won from the start. Leizi and I are going to Venice, a voice inside me sang. I got dressed, put cigarettes, a sweater, a bathing suit, and a towel in my kit bag and joined the platoon.

My mood changed from one extreme to the other. Why in the world shouldn't I go? What was I doing punishing myself again for sins I hadn't committed? Would Noga really be upset to learn I deprived myself of Venice?

Goddamnit all, Noga no longer existed. I was free of all obligations, unrestricted, unburdened by all the agonies of young Werther. Look here, I told myself, everyone's off for Venice, you're nineteen years old, healthy as a horse and raring to go, your kit bag's full of English cigarettes, the mountains are rushing away behind you, the sky is shining. Snap it, that damn last string tying you to your father's wretched world, to fear of sin, pure-mindedness, novelistic romance. Snap that string and float away like a balloon.

Enough blubbering and sensitivity, enough of bearing the world's pain on our shoulders, of "What act would most benefit society?" and "What does the Homeland need most at this moment?" and "What have I done?" and Constantin Simonov. How did the song go?—"Wait, oh wait, wait in cold, wait in heat . . ."

At last I was as I had always wanted to be, right where I'd

wanted to be ever since I was smacked with a ruler in the *moshava's* Hebrew school when I was seven, ever since I got fed up with my *keppela** and *tzitzis†* when I was ten, ever since I fled the factory and my home, fled the web of duty and boredom that held me bound in an invisible cage. Now I was alone, racing like a ball down a mountain slope on the way to Udine, approaching Venice. Let Noga marry the son of Rivkin and Associates; I would follow my destiny, by myself, in the summer heat, in Venice.

By myself, with Leizi.

Arusi gabbed the whole trip, letting us in on how he would handle the girls of Venice, willingly answering every one of Poker's questions, detailing how he won back the widowed laundress by his stunning charms, unparalleled in the entire regiment, as we would readily acknowledge when we heard with our own ears what that same laundress said to him during the act, sentence by sentence. We sat at ease in the truck beneath the canvas canopy, all dressed up this time, grinning over the dialogue between Poker and Arusi, though a bit repelled by the flow of vile stories that were supplemented from time to time by others' contributions. But we were all tense as well. Not Giladi, though, or Zunenshein either. It was funny to imagine them acting like Brodsky in Bologna. Brodsky, sitting deep in the truck, with his cap shielding his eyes, was whistling softly, as though exhaling. But why only him? There was pimply-faced Leizi, for example, I was sure he was as restless as I was. I wanted to try myself with a woman once, just once without restraint, free of fear, without any pleading or *mea culpas*, without poetry or sin, just body to body in a foreign land, wrapped in darkness, without any of my father's sick Puritanism.

I would have gone with Leizi without giving it a second thought. He was no Brodsky, he was different—different from me, too. No doubt about that. First of all, I came from a religious household, and already that counted for a lot. He'd been born without a *keppela* or *tzitzis*. He had gone to co-ed schools. He wasn't afraid to touch girls and they weren't afraid of being

---

* Skullcap, worn by Orthodox Jews.
† Fringed ritual undergarment.

171

touched by him. That sturdy body, those rippling muscles, his enthusiasm and gracefulness in lobbing a hand grenade or cradling a Tommy gun. I was sure he was the same way with women, grabbing and enjoying without any foolish talk. Not like me. To this day I don't know—and that's the honest truth —what passed between me and Noga, how it all happened, or if it ever really did happen. . . .

Sure enough, Venice was steaming hot just like Tel Aviv and we did everything I knew we would: we scurried over the bridges, alongside the canals, across the piazzas in small groups, frenziedly trying to take everything in as quickly as possible. First we had to take pictures of ourselves with the pigeons alongside the bronze pillars in San Marco, no, first we had to buy a silk scarf, no, silk socks, no, sheaves of wheat fashioned exquisitely in glass, objects that would prove, when we returned to *Aretz*, that beyond any doubt our feet had tread upon the isles of Venice. Leizi and I decided as soon as we got off the truck we would break away from the others and take in the city alone, but every alley we slipped into was jam-packed with frantic soldiers. We had less than ten hours to spend in Venice and how could that suffice for all that Venice held out to its visitors? Could we miss floating in a gondola? Not visit the Rialto? Not lick ice cream, not cruise down to the Lido? And the girls, when would we have time for the girls we kept bumping into at every step?

Finally we were alone, wandering in circles through the winding city. We crossed bridges, took in the slender boats gliding down the waterways, inhaled the stench of the narrow canals squeezed between the clustered buildings, stumbled into the noisy food market, and soon found ourselves, with burning feet, across the Rialto bridge, alongside the anchorage of San Marco. It was almost three o'clock and the trip to the Lido on the snail-paced vaporetto took about an hour, we had been told. Nevertheless, we pushed into the crowd going up the gangplank, so as not to miss anything, so as not to stand in one place, so we could travel and rest at the same time.

But that wasn't the only reason, I thought.

Since that morning I had waited for an opportunity to be

172

alone with Leizi. And Leizi, whom I had always envied for his ability to make friends so easily—Leizi, too, was lonely. Maybe by spending the day together we would draw closer, laughing, talking, revealing something of our true selves to each other. For despite two years in the same company, often the same tent, we were still strangers.

Time and again I had stubbornly insisted to myself that a man is more than what meets the eye. Take Leizi. Nature had gotten him off to a good start, with that superb body, tailor-made for sports and farm work, for everything and anything. In the close-knit circle of his group—farmers, graduates of agricultural schools, boys who had grown up in workers' quarters—he was talkative, spouting jokes; but apart from them he was always tight-lipped, stand-offish, sleepy, and maybe a little mixed-up. I couldn't figure him out.

As soon as he began to cultivate my friendship I began looking for profundities in Leizi. I was glad he had dragged me off to Venice with him, and all day I was hoping for something to happen. But no veils were lifted, no secrets disclosed. When he spoke, it was only of what he saw: "Golly, they really went to town here!" or, "They're kind of nice, these palaces, but just for a visit; I wouldn't like to live here. Everything's so old it's falling apart or dead. And it stinks. How can they live in the middle of these open sewers?"

All the dashing about began to get to him. I could see his face clouding over with boredom.

"Look, let's say we've seen all the palaces already. Let's get a good meal and rest a little."

Our conversation had never wandered far beyond such topics. We had been told that in the Lido, in the Churchill-Roosevelt Restaurant, we could get a great meal dirt cheap, so we boarded the vaporetto with a huge crowd of civilians and soldiers and floated down to the famous casino. We stuffed ourselves with cream puffs, Venetian ice cream and cold beer and sank into two soft arm-chairs in the drawing room, overpowering with its ivory and its crystal chandelier. We were out of the broiling sun, our clothes were drying off from our sweat, and our feet were stretched out on the soft carpet like royalty.

"Maybe we ought to take off our boots," joked Leizi, looking at the chandelier. "Bread they haven't got, but ivory—up to the ears. Let's stay here till the sun goes down."

I hadn't come with Leizi for that. What was there to the fellow, if anything at all? And Bubi, was he just another Leizi, too? And if he was, why had he chosen Hershler, instead of taking Leizi with him? Many a time I found myself on the verge of asking Leizi directly, but I could never bring myself to it. Everything that had happened that day—the long debate, the parade —I couldn't forget. Had I been asked to define what it was that would not be forgotten, I could not have said; but that something I wouldn't get over had happened—that I knew.

"Did you ever run into Bubi?"

"Yes, once." His eyes were half closed, but he answered straight off as though he'd been waiting for the question.

"Did—did he say anything to you?"

"What about?"

"How does he explain what he did? Why? Why in the world did he go to the Germans' house?"

"He didn't explain." His voice was dry, almost hostile. But I had to go on asking.

"Still, it's very strange—"

"What's so strange?"

"How did he know that house? When could he have learned they were Nazis, the mother and daughter?"

"He must have heard something."

"He didn't tell you?"

"I never asked him."

"But just to take off all of a sudden and do such a thing? Was he really out for revenge?"

"What do you think?"

"I'm just asking. After all he had done, why did Bubi go and—"

Again the silence rose like a wall between us. Leizi did not reply, but I was still out for an answer.

"Leizi!"

"Huh . . ." He sprawled out in the armchair, leaned his cheek on one arm and looked at me.

"Did he ever talk to you—about it?"

"Yeah, but not the last time." He yawned cavernously, his eyes lost in his face. "Bubi's not a talkative guy. When we both decided to leave the Palmach and join the army and people were arguing themselves blue in the face, he sounded a little like Giladi, said we had to take vengeance on the Germans. There was a book he kept quoting them, a Russian book, I think, you know, like on Radio Moscow—*A Death for a Death*. It was very personal, the way he hated Germans. That's about it."

"What bothers me is, he seemed to have had one thing in mind and at the last minute pulled back."

"Goddamnit, why does it bother you so much? Go ask him if it matters that much to you." And when I thought our conversation had ended and he had fallen asleep, he suddenly added, "I know exactly what happened: that *schmuck* Hershler went in his pants."

"Still, that doesn't explain—"

"That explains everything. Goddamn Jews." For the first time Leizi showed how strong was the grudge he held against Bubi. But immediately he lowered his voice. "Why are you thinking about that all of a sudden, Kruk? I'm dead tired. Come on, let's hit the hay . . ."

Even as he spoke his chin dropped onto his collar bone and his arms flopped across his belly. The one conversation I had attempted with Leizi ended where it had begun. Once again I was left alone.

5

"Elisha! Elisha!"

The voice rose out of a hundred memories. It was unknown, insistent, and I shrank beneath its whiplash, as if I had been caught by the sergeant major. But it was warm and familiar, too, and it stroked me like the west wind at twilight. I seemed to be stretched out beneath the wide double bed in our room, between the chilly cement floor and the springs that held untold strength in their tight corkscrew coils. One of the springs

175

was about to pop, I thought, right into my face; I pushed the spring up making it even tauter, but it was only mocking me, even if it didn't squeak like it did when Father and Mother turned over in their sleep. I was lying on my back, my fingers thrust into the springs, alert to the sounds floating down from space (in the dark beneath the beds every sound was distinct, just as at night): the ice wagon's bell, the wheezing cough of the old man in the adjacent courtyard, the sound of the milk can, the brown *email* can that mother tilted over the kerosene cooking stove, the barking of the dog that belonged to the German Jews who had come to live in Seligman's courtyard. Even the darkness beneath the bed was not complete, so I closed my eyes. Only then did I hear the voices. They had a life of their own, like souls or angels. They hovered, in darkness, on the face of the void.

"Elisha! Elisha!"

The voice was not unfamiliar nor did it belong to just any acquaintance. It was a voice I wanted to escape. I closed my eyes tight so not a ray of light could force its way through and my fingers closed around the bedsprings. Even if I were hooked, my captor would not be able to pull me in. So long as my eyes remained shut, all my fantasies meshed like knit-work and I didn't have to identify the owner of that voice—even though I knew full well by that time who he was. Somebody had grabbed my shoulder and was shaking me. I was sitting in an easy chair, my limbs heavy as lead, my mind fuzzy. Neither asleep nor awake, I knew Pinik was standing over me.

Maybe it was the voice that came through first, like when you tune in on a radio wave and disregard all the other waves humming around it; or maybe his face first came into focus when the haze clouding my eyes lifted for a moment. But that wasn't important. Even though I knew for a certainty it was Pinik standing above me, I didn't leap to my feet, overjoyed, but went through all the motions of getting up, as if it were a military maneuver: I rubbed my eyes, stretched my arms, mumbled a few indistinct words, doing all I could to put off this meeting with Pinik, this meeting I had so long prepared myself for.

I opened my eyes.

176

"Pinik!" I yelled, leaping to my feet. "What are you doing here?"

"Bless the Lido. Otherwise you would have come to Venice and left without even trying to find me, I suppose. What are you so tired for, rascal?"

"I hadn't realized I'd fallen asleep." Leizi was still dozing on the other easy chair, his head hanging in the air, drooped toward his knees. "I'm sure glad to see you."

"So glad, you went to the Lido to sleep."

"I know where to go to sleep." I heard myself making excuses, just as I had done many years before when I was a little boy and Pinik's favorite. "Just imagine, I get off the boat at Mestre and here you are . . ."

"It's a good thing you didn't think about it too much." Pinik laid his hand on my shoulders and looked at me close up, warmly. Strange, I thought sadly, Pinik's shorter than me.

"How many days are you here for?"

"Hours, not days." Outside, the sunset was scattering horizontal shafts. Windows, tin shingles, people in front of the building—all were afire in the day's last glow as it dissolved between sea and sky. "At ten we leave."

"Tonight?" White sparks flashed in Pinik's eyes, too. "Already?"

"I'm still in the service of His Majesty."

"If that's the case, I'm extending your leave. Scandalous: you're in Italy how long—eight months already—and we haven't had a chance to really get together once. Tonight you stay with me, Elisha."

"And go straight to the stockade when I get back."

"They won't do anything to you. We'll make up some excuse. It's worth your while to stay, my boy. We'll live it up good and proper, and tomorrow you can go with me. We're heading north. Nu!" Pinik was alongside me, warm and effusive, enveloping me with his joy. "I can't believe my eyes: is this tiny Elisha who sat barefoot next to the laundry tub, grimy, in black trunks, pulling potatoes out of the fire?"

"You remember?"

That morning, the day before Passover, marked the beginning of a revolution in my life. How clearly I remember the

177

moment—down the paved path separating the wild winter grass from the vegetable plots Father had just hoed, strode a tall beanpole of a man carrying two gigantic suitcases. He wore a short leather jacket and a casquette was pushed back on his bushy head of hair. At once I recognized him as Uncle Pinik from Poland. "Mommy!" I yelled, and Mother, who was fishing a steaming sheet out of the kettle with a broom handle, froze on the spot as though holding a mock flag. "*Tshotsha!*" cried Pinik. He dropped the suitcases, grabbed my mother, kissed her on both flaming cheeks, then turned to me, grasped my elbows, and swung me into the air. He was strong, outgoing, flowing with affection, not like the other immigrants who always turned up at our house for Passover. From the first moment I loved him with all my heart.

"Do I remember?" Pinik thrust his fingers into my biceps and lifted his chin up toward me. "You were small and tubby like a black olive and your eyes were blacker, a little scared and a little mischievous. Now it's just the opposite: I'm growing down and you're growing up."

He stretched up, straining to reach me. Actually I wasn't that much taller than him, but something had happened to Pinik—not a trace remained of the tall, slender youth of my earliest years. He had put on weight, started a pot belly, his face was swollen and pale, and his fleshy nose—everyone in mother's family had one—was pocked with holes as if pricked with a needle. And this was the god of your childhood, a voice within whispered bitterly.

Before me stood a different man from the driver's company, aging, balding, lusterless, clumsy in his every movement; but ten years before he had ushered into our yard all that was joyous, daring, and reckless. Very quickly, without any complaint, he had found himself quarters among the veteran construction workers. He moved from the porch of our barracks to the pioneers' quarters on the outskirts of the *moshava*. His wool pants and casquette disappeared; he would come to visit us evenings in short khaki pants, bareheaded, his socks rolled down below his ankles. He would speak excitedly of things I had never heard of in our home before, and only due to him did I start thinking about them. Every conversation between

178

him and Father ended in an argument, and I never doubted but that Pinik was in the right. "Fascism is clutching the world by the throat," he would say.

" 'I have not tended my own vineyard,' " my father would answer, quoting the Bible, and Pinik would laugh and start singing a Russian song to restore the peace. At times he would bring one of his friends and father's camp would be joined by one of the neighbors. Then the shouting would swamp the entire yard.

"A popular front," Pinik would insist.

"Don't tell me who the Bolsheviks are," my father would shout back. "I saw them in Twenty-two. They can keep their honey and their sting too. I was in Minsk. God help a revolution dreamed up by Jews and Gypsies."

"You, you only know one story, Minsk," Pinik would answer impatiently. "The world's on fire. Only an anti-Fascist front—"

"You're getting me angry, Pinik." Father would fume as he rose and stormed into the house. Pinik would guffaw and sing another Russian ditty.

He was good-looking and good-natured, so he had to be right. I loved to visit him evenings or on the Sabbath, sit to the side and listen to him talk or leaf through the books that kept piling up in his room, books with dark covers and fresh with the smell of ink, published by Mitzpeh and Davar. It came back to me, that morning I left the synagogue during the Torah reading and went to see Pinik because I knew some guests had come from Tel Aviv. They were sitting on his porch barefoot, in undershirts, smoking cigarettes, cutting up sausages and putting them between slices of bread spread with butter. Too late I learned I had eaten sausage and butter, but I was not struck down by lightning.

"What's that smile?" asked Pinik.

"I smiled?" I said confusedly.

"Maybe your Krukish eyes laughed by themselves. Grab your kit bag and let's go, Elisha."

"Sorry, but—"

"You'll be sorry if you don't. Believe me, you'll have a good time." He winked at me and laughed open-mouthed, revealing

179

his upper teeth. They were big and sharp just as I remembered them, when he would rip off orange peels, crack open almonds, sink them into the leg of a chair, turn it over, and lift it up without any hands to the consternation of mother and father. His laughter rang in my head like an alarm clock. What did he mean, "You'll have a good time"? That driver I had met in Malborghetto: what had he talked about? Hadn't it been about Pinik and the *regazzas*? I felt slightly queasy. But I would stay with Pinik. Who would have believed that he and I, together, wearing the same uniform in Venice. . . .

"I do want to, but—" To justify my refusal I pointed to Leizi, who slept on as if drugged.

"Let him alone." Pinik picked up my kit bag and began walking toward the door. "He won't get lost."

"No, I have to tell him I'm going with you." Now I had acknowledged my decision to give in to Pinik.

"Just like your father, Elisha—respectable to the end, come hell or high water."

I swallowed the answer that was on my tongue. To the contrary, I almost said, I wanted to be just like you. When I grow up, I used to tell myself, I'll be like Pinik. The exact opposite of Father.

We stood there in that glass and ivory drawing room, two soldiers in a foreign city, looking out on the intoxicating Adriatic evening, apparently standing on the fringe of that day ten years before, but in reality we were two people who had never met, heading out into the unknown.

I woke up Leizi and told him I had met my uncle and was going with him. I would try to get back to the railroad station on time, but if I came late they should try to cover up for me. I'd make it back to the base somehow. I couldn't tell from Leizi's sleepy face whether he'd been offended or not, but as soon as I was alone with Pinik and had left him behind I felt wonderful.

I have no idea what that island looks like under normal circumstances. In fact, I can only picture it as part of the map of Venice. Streaks of red tinting the sky like Titian robes turned ashen gray. We walked along a wide thoroughfare down to the very seashore. Soldiers walking abreast meandered down the empty street. Lazy waves crept among the pillars of an abandoned café. A few street lamps flickered faintly on their rationed current. The vaporetto that had just started back to the city puttered in the distance. Only that afternoon, when we had arrived in Venice, its deck had been crowded with civilians, but now the street was empty. Where had everyone gone?

Pinik bore right, into a dark street canopied by tall trees. Was it lined only with small houses with courtyards and gardens? Or were there two-story, three-story buildings, too, deluxe pensions, cafes spilling out onto the sidewalks, music, tourists, innkeepers? Maybe I remember so little because of my frame of mind at the time. Having seen that street at the beginning and end of one night, I only recall the two of us groping our way into it like lost wanderers in an abandoned city.

It seemed as though Pinik never would stop talking, but not about what lay ahead. Only as he opened up, did he begin to peel off the superficial and the obvious from our chance meeting, to return to those early years. Everything he mentioned called up a memory I had locked deep within me.

"You're just a kid," he repeated. "Why on earth did you run off to the army? What were you looking for in the army? what did you find? I remember when you learned to chant the *Haftara** for your Bar Mitzvah. You'd be singing away in a beautiful soprano and I'd be standing behind the blinds, listening. As soon as I would come in you would get all mixed up and begin to curse. . . . You don't remember that, now, do you? You do. . . . Well, then, I'll tell you something else: When you announced you were going off to become a worker, I raised the roof with your mother and father, you know that?"

"Yes," I smiled.

Pinik stopped on the spot, taken aback. "They told you?"

"No, but I had long ears."

"That I found out a long time ago. I was careful whenever you were around."

"Not careful enough, Pinik." I laughed. "Not at all . . ."

"What do you mean?" He sounded defensive; I knew what he was hinting at. My decision to drop out of high school had

* Portion of the prophets read every Sabbath in the synagogue.

181

shocked my parents and they blamed it on Pinik's bad influence. Father said baldly that I fell like "Katrinka" for Pinik's proletarian claptrap. "Talk is cheap. Even in *Aretz,*" he argued angrily, "even in *Aretz* a man has to get an education, learn a profession, get a diploma if he wants to be somebody and not a crumb blowing in the wind, like me. I fell off a scaffold, broke my leg and what's become of me? And Pinik, Mr. Smarty, look at him: first the construction layoff, then the trouble in the orange groves—wasn't he out of work half the time for more than two years? And now, wonder of wonders, he bums around from one camp to another. And I don't even want to talk about other things." (Here mother would glare at father to keep his mouth shut, but I knew what he was hinting at—about Pinik and Haviva.)

Mother was not as definite because Pinik was her relative, for one thing, and she had to defend him; for another, she wasn't sold on high school being so important if there were so many jobs to go around right then. After all, I might help get them out of the mud a little. . . . She wouldn't come right out with it though. "What's all this nonsense?" she'd say. "All of a sudden Pinik's a Bolshevik. He's a nice boy."

"So who filled his head with all of these ideas?"

"Not everyone has to be a professor!"

"So what does *Aretz* need, a ditch digger with broken legs like me, huh?"

To the ever-growing argument between Father and Pinik I added fragmented conversations and chance remarks and I knew that Pinik, even though he claimed he was not to blame, felt ill at ease because he knew what a big influence he had on me. Not only did he try to make me change my mind, but—so I concluded from what happened later—he confronted my parents with another facet of the truth: that they had actually forced me to go to work by always moaning about their financial straits. He was even ready, he said—at this Father was ready to toss him through the window—to contribute toward my education. The controversy raged furiously and only my decision, which soon became an incontrovertible fact, brought the argument to an end. Since that time I had regretted that rash,

irreversible step more than once and inwardly blamed both Pinik and my parents. If only they had pressured me more, perhaps I wouldn't have wound up where I did. Almost involuntarily I blurted out, "Not enough Pinik!"

"What do you mean?" But he knew very well what I meant.

"Nothing in particular. But I had long ears and I heard even
what people tried to hide from me."

"In general you were a somewhat strange child . . ."

"Somewhat?"

We both laughed. We walked down the darkening street as
the rustle of the trees blended with the whisper of the sea. At
that moment I looked upon Pinik as I had when I was a child,
and inwardly I thanked him for not bringing up what I had
done to him at the wedding on the roof, when I reviled him in
front of our entire family and friends.

"You know what gets me mad, Elisha?"

"What?"

"That when I came to you I was a boy, just as old as you are
today."

"No, Pinik, you were different, different . . ."

"Different? How?"

"You really want to pull it out of me?"

"Let's hear it!"

By then we stood in the gateway to the courtyard. The gravel
crunched beneath our feet. Light and dance music flowed from
an open window. Pinik pulled on a cord and a clapper hit a bell
on the other side of the door. Again and again he pulled and
the bell answered back as from a church. The music stopped
and the loud voice of a woman running toward us poured out
a stream of words against a background of light laughter. All
at once the door swung wide open. The laughter spilled out
over the threshold followed by a tall, vivacious beauty. She
bounced up and down shrieking endearments in Italian, then
flung herself around Pinik's neck. Her naked joy astonished me
and enlightened me, too. She saw me, a strange soldier, standing right behind him, but that didn't inhibit her at all.

Pinik reacted differently. He kissed her restrainedly and
placed his hands on her thighs, not to embrace her but to push

183

her away and in a voice that was rather too loud he announced he had brought a guest with him, a young relative. He spoke Italian rapidly, as though he had long been fluent in it.

The woman freed his neck and turned to me. Her expression changed very quickly. She swallowed her laughter and somehow seemed to contract. Even the scant light of the doorway revealed her lush, dark beauty. A wealth of hair was coiled up behind her ears like a snail. She bowed slightly and motioned me to enter.

"Come," said Pinik, walking in before me. The woman waited for me to pass by her, then, looking at me in wonderment—or was she smiling?—she closed the door behind her.

We stood in a room crammed with enough dark, antique heavy furniture for an entire home. The center of the room was taken up by a long table surrounded as though by a fence with high-backed, elegant chairs. Against one wall stood a cupboard sporting doors with many-cornered, polished glass. I would have expected to see fine silverware displayed there, but the half-empty shelves bore only army-ration fruit. Two arm chairs sat by the window like two fat matrons. The welter of possessions seemed ill-matched to the room itself, but maybe that was the typical interior of a well-furnished Italian home.

I had never been invited into a real home. In Rome sometimes at night I would find myself in some poor dwelling, sleeping in a room taken up entirely by a pair of gigantic beds with an icon hanging over them. Near the front we had been quartered in abandoned, ravaged buildings, but never had I seen a house such as this, in a garden, with heavy furniture and a plump young woman named Felicia.

I didn't know how old Felicia was, since at that time a woman of twenty-five seemed almost middle-aged to me. In the full light of the room she no longer looked so huge. She spun around before my eyes, her supple, ripe body churning up my passions like a shook bottle. I retreated to the easy chairs by the window while Pinik tossed his kit bag—like everyone else, he did not move without that magic kit bag—onto the table and emptied it of its contents: a complete black market. Every packet called forth a stream of words, hugs, and laughter.

Felicia's thighs were packed snugly into a narrow skirt and her breasts billowed from a buttoned satin blouse. Her every movement stretched her thighs taut, accentuated her hips, and set her breasts bouncing. I couldn't take my eyes off her, couldn't stop imagining her body clinging to Pinik's. Whatever had possessed me to follow him there, what did he want me to do for the two of them? Did he want to prove that this was the new Pinik, lining up a woman in every city like the driver at the refugees' way-station had hinted? I wasn't interested. What did he need me for in this lovey-dovey family nest—to eat dinner with them? To write home that Pinik had thoroughly recovered from what Haviva had done to him while he was roaming around the camps in the Negev? Had he no shame? Wasn't I Elisha, the child who looked upon him as an idol, as a god? It's not too late, I told myself, it's still not too late to clear out, to say I had changed my mind, that I didn't want to look for trouble and had to catch the regimental trucks before it was too late.

I could have gotten up and left—had I really wanted to. But I was trying to talk myself into leaving precisely because I wanted to stay so much. I feared where it all would lead to. But there I was, caught between my fear and a burning desire to trespass onto forbidden ground. I didn't stir.

And I didn't have time to, for everything was set in motion at once.

Felicia gathered the preserves, cigarettes and cream cakes Pinik had brought and left the room, with Pinik behind her. I looked around me: a bare bulb hung from the ceiling, there was no curtain on the window, in the corner behind the second easy chair trunks were piled up one on top of another. This was not Felicia's home.

Pinik returned promptly to tell me a warm bath awaited us. We would be able to bathe and put on fresh clothes while Felicia set the table.

"Fresh clothes?" I laughed. "Where?"

"Don't worry, Elisha. Nothing second rate about this house: our guests get the royal treatment." From a distant wing I heard the bubbly laughter of Felicia mingling with the muffled, gentle laughter of another woman.

"You'll put on clean clothes and you'll feel like a new man.

What are you looking at me like that for, Elisha? I'm not a magician and I'm not a criminal. Our company is quartered near here so we decided we had it coming to us, a bourgeois summer in Venice, in the Lido. We got hold of this house and turned it into a regular *dacha*—get it?"

Felicia returned with pressed and neatly folded clothing piled against her bosom. She motioned to me to get up and thrust the clothes into my arms, showering me with a long, laughing Italian sentence. She laughed all the time.

"Understand what Felicia said to you?" Pinik asked.

"I don't understand anything here."

" 'This is for you, my lovely Moor,' she said. Do you know who the Moor of Venice was?"

Felicia pressed the back of her hand to my forehead as though taking my temperature. She said somethig to Pinik and the two of them laughed. He less than she.

"Go take a bath, Elisha," he said, and I thought I heard an angry strain in his voice. If he felt possessive, so much the better.

The house was still an enigma to me. It was dark and gave off an odor of abandonment. But the bathroom indicated who its former owners might have been. The walls, the sink, the bathtub as well as the douche were made of lilac-colored porcelain. A mixed odor of women's perfume and soldiers' sweat filled the room. In the corner stood two pairs of army shoes, and the greasy work uniforms of men from the transport companies were hanging from hooks. What had Pinik meant, "We got hold of a house and turned it into a *dacha*"? I was embarrassed to think such thoughts. I told myself everything I was suspecting Pinik of was all in my own mind. Why not accept what he said at face value, the words and the women both? That there was at least one more woman there I knew from the laughter I had heard previously.

I filled the tub with hot water and slipped into it; I stayed there as long as possible. This was a rare opportunity, to luxuriate in a bath. During my early childhood mother would bring the small tin tub into our kitchen. She would place her largest pots on the Primus and the kerosene cooking stove and would bend over me, scrubbing my body mercilessly. There was a tiny hole in the tub no larger than a nail's head and mother would plug it up with a strip of linen. During my bath I would make a game of yanking out this cloth so a thin stream of soapy water would bubble out of the tub. Mother would yell at me and threaten to spank my bare behind even though the kitchen floor had long since become one huge puddle. When I began to get self-conscious I stopped bathing in a tub but washed in the shower room in the courtyard under a cold faucet. Only when I would visit our relatives in Tel Aviv in the wintertime —which happened maybe three or four times a year—was I able to enjoy this elegance of city living. As the years went by, to tell the truth, I stayed away from any kind of bathing that didn't involve flowing water—pools, bath houses, sinks or bowls were not for me.

But there in that all-porcelain room suffused with perfume I stretched out naked in the steaming water and felt myself— as Pinik had said—turning into another man. Thick vapors filled the air and a sweet torpor flowed through my limbs. I added more and more hot water until my skin was nearly scalded. I scrubbed myself with Palmolive soap and rubbed my tangled hair until the lather covered the water. Only then did I lay back, my eyes closed, listening to the blood pounding in my veins and the voices of the people beyond the door growing ever dimmer.

Evidently I fell asleep in the water or else blacked out for a moment, for suddenly I awoke from a long, complex sexual fantasy involving Felicia, Noga, the young partisan girl from the railroad workers' building, and all sorts of women I had and hadn't seen. I stood up. Outside the bathroom I could hear the noise of men and women talking and laughing. I pulled out the plug and rinsed myself with luke-warm, then cold water. I wrapped myself in the huge turkish towel Felicia had given me and rubbed myself dry until I was as red and fresh as the day I left the convalescent camp in Pesaro.

Only then did I see what Felicia had laid out for me—brown pants made of some synthetic material like American summer clothes and a yellow silk shirt. I dressed and looked myself over in the steam-covered mirror: not Othello, like Felicia said, but a young gigolo. Who owned these clothes that fit me so well?

187

When I returned to the large room everything there had changed. The table was covered with a white cloth piled high with plates, bowls, bottles of wine, and glasses. The company was completely engrossed in what lay before them, eating and chattering away. There was Pinik. How and when had he managed to shave and put on civilian clothes? He spotted me first and welcomed me with a shout: "*Pronto, pronto, signore y signori*, our cousin has come out of the water."

Making circles in the air with his left hand he called to me to come to the table, while with his right he tapped his knife against a glass. All faces turned to me. There were two other girls besides Felicia as well as two of our boys, one in a silk, reddish-gold smoking jacket colored just like the inside of a ripe *sabra*, and the second in an American short-sleeved shirt with a regular menagerie printed on it. They all clanged their silverware against the dishes, crying: "Cheerio, Elisha! . . . *Che bello!* . . . *Bei mir bist du shein!* . . . He lost half his weight in the water. Where did you pick up such a cute relative, Pinik? . . . *Buona sera, bambino!*"

"Quiet! Quiet everyone. . . . *Basta!*" Pinik silenced the group in a loud voice and, as I had remained standing in the doorway confused, he got up, walked over and led me to the table. Once again he was different, different from my Pinik and different from the one I had met at the restaurant. He, too, was wrapped in a silk smoking jacket, colored deep red like cherry wine. His sparse hair was wet and combed back and he looked like a gangster at a banquet in a Hollywood movie. (Despite myself I was reminded of the family fable of Elyakum, Father's uncle, who had gone to Chicago and became the head of a famous gang. Father would tell that story every time he wanted to warn us against going to America.) Or maybe he looked like a refugee from the opera in Rome. What kind of house had Pinik dragged me to?

He sat me down in a chair reserved for me, to the right of Felicia, then took his seat again, to her left. Maybe I really had fallen asleep in the bathtub, for everyone's face was aflame and the table looked like the aftermath of a riot. The cups were red with wine, but the eyes of the assemblage were even redder. Fishbones and strands of spaghetti dripping red sauce were

188

scattered over the white tablecloth. The bowls arranged in the middle of the table and the plates, too, were full of meatballs in rice and tomato paste, lettuce salad with oil and vinegar, potato chips and fried onion rings, slices of American cheese, Bully Beef, and green peas, split peaches (Australian preserves) —all of which had been utterly ravaged, as if sixty, not six, had sat there, and as if they had swilled and gorged themselves for a full twenty-four hours.

While Felicia was still loading my plate with whatever remained of the table's rich spread, Pinik took a bottle of whisky —yes, he had whisky, too—from beneath his chair and filled my thin-stemmed liqueur glass, as well as the glasses of all the others. He urged me to lift mine first.

"Let's drink l'Chayim, just as if we were starting this very minute. He'll forgive us for not having waited for him and we won't ask him what he was looking for in the bathtub for over an hour," said Pinik.

"But we'd very much like to know," said the owner of the shirt covered with animals. He looked like one of the soccer players in our moshava—small ears; his hair almost all clipped off, American Navy style; his angular lower jaw jutting out, narrowing toward the chin, as if he had a trowel in his mouth; two cold eyes, one squinting slightly while the eyebrow above the other arched up, like Clark Gable's. I was wearing his clothes if I wasn't mistaken.

"So he was in the bathtub!" the chap in the silk smoking jacket declared. Older than Pinik, he obviously liked to take the sun, for his pate, creased prominently along the rim of bald spot, shone like a Rosh Hashana twisted loaf. "That's the infantry, my good fellow. They don't get a chance to wash every year . . ."

"Cut it out," said Pinik, who had already lifted his glass. "Lift your glass, Elisha."

"I'm not drinking, Pinik." I had made my decision when I first saw the table, but as soon as I opened my mouth I knew what his reaction would be.

"Since when don't you drink, Elisha?" Now he addressed the others. "As a matter of fact, on some occasions he's quite a drinker."

189

"No, I'm not: I still have a bad taste in my mouth from the last time." With one sentence I had refused again, apologized for what I had said at the wedding on the roof, and skipped over the pizzeria in Bologna.

"Then have a glass to get rid of that bitter taste," Pinik insisted. "Now we're all soldiers. You're not a boy and I'm not a draft dodger. *Nu!*"

"What kind of a fighting man are you," cried the fellow in the *sabra*-colored coat. "One glass! *Avanti!*"

Felicia and the other two girls chided me, too, with words I couldn't make out.

"He'll drink," said Pinik, and at that point began to speak a mixture of Italian and Hebrew to his buddies and the girls. "This kid really put it away when he was fourteen years old. That was a night to remember. Spouted like a poet, like a prophet . . . Were you fifteen already that night?"

"Almost sixteen. Pinik—" I pleaded.

"He was almost sixteen. A shy boy who couldn't even count to ten. But when the wine went down him—he went off. Shook up old folks and stopped a whole wedding celebration . . ."

"Pinik, that's enough!"

"So don't tell us you don't drink. It's not a bad idea for you to drink every once in a while—once in three years. Why shouldn't we enjoy the poetry you lock up in the dark?"

Now he was addressing the three girls who had turned their soft eyes from the food and drink to look at Pinik and me. The soccer player's girl looked very much like Felicia, her younger sister, maybe, but she was slimmer and pale. And whether she giggled or called out, her face had a simple, lacquered look to it. The one sitting opposite me, next to Old Baldy in the *sabra* coat, was glorious; that is, I began to realize it very gradually. She, too, must have sunbathed a good deal: her skin was pure and translucent like glowing honey. Her eyes shone bright—later I realized they were Bubi's eyes—but their blue was mixed with strands of honey. When she wasn't eating or adding her voice to the general confusion I wondered what she was doing there, in that room. But all that came later.

Pinik was speaking Italian and they were laughing in protest. "This young fellow's a black cave. Words drip there in the

190

dark. Drip-drop. Drip-drop. Stalagmites. One drop falls onto another and turns into Morano glass. Into crystals. But it's all dark in the cave and no one can see *che bella poesia* no, *muzitsi* . . . Only when light gets in, floods it, only when you fill him with wine does he begin to recite and prophesize, the words turn into a carnival of colors. . . . One glass, Elisha!"

"Damn it, drink already and get it over with," grumbled the soccer player. "But don't sing anything. Words make me nervous."

"But he loves songs!" Pinik cried, as if he had struck oil. "Very much! There was one song you always begged me to sing you, from 'Vassily Rebyata.' They made up beautiful words for it in Hebrew, remember?" Without waiting for my answer he sang, glass held high, as though he were on stage:

"I don't care if I live in a mansion,
I don't care if I live in a sty;
There are plenty of crumbs in the world, boys,
But it's not all that crumby, say I . . .'"

They all cheered Pinik and cried out for an encore, but my eyes were swimming with tears. Pinik had called forth a vanished world in an instant, singing with youthful gusto as he had those magical summer evenings when I'd sit on the steps listening to him and Haviva and their friends sing on and on, while I said to myself, "Beautiful, beautiful. Yes, yes. Like all of you, Pinik." Why did he have to choose just that song, at that moment? To wring the tears out of me? To mock me? To mock himself?

"And this, too! You loved this one, too." Pinik was swept away by his own enthusiasm. "He was a little bastard, that Elisha.

The wind wails deep in the cellar:
No windows there, no light.
But there a man weeps like a baby
And dreams dreams all the night . . .'"

"I'll drink!" I cried. "Just don't sing, Pinik!"

I downed my drink at a gulp. All six cheered and, highly amused at the joke, drank after me. Even as the liquor slid down and began trickling into my flesh I felt its prickly sting, in my palate, the roots of my hair; felt a sweet, warm languor spreading through my body. Like the first glass in the cellar in Bologna. There a man dreamed dreams. Wasn't that just what I had wanted to do, wasn't that just what I had been hungering for ever since daybreak, when we came down from the mountains?

"Eat something, *haver!*" said Old Baldy, facing me, as Felicia leaned over to pour me red wine. I inhaled the ripe fragrance of her body through her green satin blouse.

"Watch out for that red wine!" laughed Pinik. "The first time, at the wedding, he got drunk just on red wine."

"Don't worry about me too much, Pinik. I've learned how to take care of myself since then," I said, taking hold of the glass. "To the *signore*, Felicia and—"

"Marcella," said the pale girl who looked like Felicia's younger sister.

"And—" I pointed to the honey-colored beauty.

"Anna Maria," she said. Hers was the sweet, muffled voice I had heard before.

"To Felicia, Marcella and Anna Maria," I cried, and drank the wine. It was chill and refreshing.

"He sure changes quick!" said the soccer player, with pursed lips, as though the change did not please him.

"I told you. Elisha's a poet. But his father—"

"Leave my father out of this!"

"Your father's a man I respect. But he never did anything forbidden. And that's very bad."

"Leave my father alone." Suddenly I was furious; and even though I well knew that it was childish of me to spring to my father's defense, I had to speak. "Does he have to do what's forbidden because it's forbidden or just the opposite, because nothing's forbidden?"

"Philosopher!" said Pinik. "Because it's forbidden, of course. Otherwise we'd have no rules to break!"

"Pino, let the poor boy eat something," said Felicia. "The plate is cold. A big sin."

I ate. Not because I was hungry but to stifle the liquor spreading through my limbs. My vision was not blurred, my hands were steady, but what had happened at Bologna was beginning to happen again. Balls of cotton seemed to blossom inside my head, throughout my body, I felt fuzzy and loose all over. Felicia drew near me and I wanted to touch her, drown in her ripe flesh. Anna Maria sat across from me, singing some Italian song in a delicate whisper. From the guffaws of the other two I guessed it was off-color. But she looked like a perfect virgin: I couldn't take my eyes off her. Her shining eyes, tinted with honey, peered at me through the empty crystal glass she held in her fingers. At another time, another place, I would have knitted my fingers with hers, would have taken her down to the sea, sat down to listen to that sweet voice, held her, undone the buttons of that linen summer blouse one by one. Although her coloring was entirely different, she was like Noga. Naked with only the two of us on the floury sand, Anna Maria would be like Noga.

The liqueur glass in Anna Maria's fingers was filled once again, as was mine. Her eyes smiled at me and she held out her hand so we could clink glasses. Don't drink any more, Elisha, I warned myself. But I drank. Pinik stood behind me, his hands resting on my shoulders, like a big uncle. They all chattered away and only Pinik's words floated down to me from above. How could I have ever thought so much of him, believed there was no one handsomer, stronger or more fascinating than he? He was disgusting.

He and his buddies must have stolen benzine and sold it on the black market. They must have hired out their trucks for private runs. They were tithing everything, setting up a private harem for themselves in the Lido. Pinik and these two guys and their three whores, and me right in the middle giving them a good laugh.

I got up to free my shoulders from Pinik's hands.

"Where are you going?" asked Pinik.

I hadn't thought of going anywhere, but the question put the idea into my head.

"I've got to go. I want to catch our train and go back with the others."

"What's going on, Elisha? You out of your mind all of a sudden? You're not going back tonight."

"I've got to." I despised myself in the yellow silk shirt, in the

193

tight pants. I turned to go to the bathroom to change my clothes.

"You can turn your back on me, but not on the clock."

"What time is it?" I didn't have a watch. Never did.

"Even if the ferry were to leave right now and even if you jumped on board the minute it pulled out you'd reach the railroad station at ten-thirty." He hummed a verse from a popular tango:

> "Do not despair, my dearest
> We shall meet there, my dearest,
> Somewhere between two worlds . . ."

"What time is it, anyway?" I stuck to my guns, unwilling to retreat. We stood there in the wide doorway, the two of us. All the others were on their feet, swirling before my eyes. Suddenly the voice of Tino Rossi dominated the scene—the beautiful furniture, the groaning table, the swaying figures. He sang from a worn record, as if through a comb, and all five melted into his song: "*Ho, Maria Magdalena* . . ."

"Nine thirty," said Pinik, laying his hands on my shoulders once again and drawing his face close to mine. His mustache was thick and drooping, and long hairs spurted out of his pitted shin. His eyes, eyes I had remembered as black, flashing and audacious, were clouded, resting between wrinkled lids and balding eyebrows like an abandoned nest. I lowered my gaze and tried to free my shoulders, but Pinik would not let me.

"Don't be a fool, Elisha. Days like these you'll never see again. You're nineteen years old. And here—ripe fruits, you don't even have to pluck them, they fall down by themselves. The sweet smell of rot is covering Europe. Eat, Elisha. Quiet! Don't talk! I've forgotten all about that night. You were a child, you couldn't have known what there was between Haviva and me, then. . . . Now you know, eh? They told you, eh? Fine, then. We've forgotten everything. Come on, Elisha, I won't corrupt you, and if I do—"

"I don't know how to drink, but I'm drinking. I'm drunk already, Pinik, and you know it."

"I'll take care of you. Finished!"

194

"Just like then. You were the one who got me drunk then, too. Made fun of me. I want to go."

Tino Rossi was rasping away, cutting into all corners of the house, when suddenly Felicia came between us. Her long arms hugged Pinik and me both. Her swelling breast pressed against my arm and her breath caressed my face.

"You're worse than the Italians. Talk, talk, talk all day . . . Does he know how to dance, the sad boy?"

"Go dance with Felicia, Elisha."

"I don't know how to dance," I protested, letting Felicia's strong arm pull me back into the room.

"Couples, ready!" Pinik commanded. "One, one-two. One, one-two."

Felicia did her best to make me dance, but her proximity left my legs in such confusion, I couldn't keep time with the music. We stumbled in and out of the furniture, holding one another. The smooth soccer player was dancing with Anna Maria. It was easy to see he must have grown up with a social-dance crowd in some *moshava*. His steps were well measured and polished; his lower jaw jutted out and one eyebrow was raised; one hand was holding hers and the other clasping her back like a waiter carrying a steaming tray. The bald guy was dancing with Marcella very purposefully, his steps small and regular as though he were on a track. Felicia passed by Pinik, took his glass, sipped and pressed it to my lips, like a mother giving a drink to her child. I drank. I was a prisoner in that room, held against my will, longing to unwind, not think about myself, but just float, dance, dissolve in the magic of the moment. I drank.

Anna Maria took me from Felicia and said she would teach me from the beginning. She was an expert with beginners. She filled me with confidence, like you fill a balloon. I grew lighter, felt myself rising. Anna Maria's body was slender and cool. My fingers pushed against her ribs. Like Noga. Different, damn it! I was dancing. Carefree and gay, I drank without thinking. Light-hearted, silent, I pressed her body to mine. Everything was so simple, I was so happy.

The alcohol in my body was turning to hydrogen. The record

195

player croaked on. My head whirled. They were all laughing. I was dancing with Marcella. With Felicia. With Anna Maria. Someone had dimmed the lights. We drifted into different rooms and back again. Felicia was kissing me. Or maybe I was kissing her. My arms gripped her tightly and she responded, pressing against me, whispering. I leaned toward her ear and kissed her neck. She laughed and pinched my thigh. How simple it all was. Simple. Simple. Drink a little more. Dance a little more. Dare a little more. . . .

The night was very long and disjointed, like colored beads that will not hang on one strand. Time whirled in circles, like a ring of ponies in a circus; the whip cracks and they go forward; cracks again and they go back; cracks again and they all stand on their hind legs. Then a fireman's band plays a waltz and every pony dances by himself. I was drunk and reveled in my stupor. At one point I ran over to Pinik and begged his forgiveness. "Forget it," he told me, "none of that's important any more."

"No, it's very important," I said, absolutely clear-headed, not stammering in the least. "I had no right to stand there on the roof and jabber away as though I were better than you."

"Who remembers what you said then?" said Pinik, shoving me away from him. "Go dance with Anna Maria."

"Don't tell me you don't remember, Pinik," I told him. "If I can remember what I said when I was drunk then, when I'm drunk now, don't tell me you forgot. 'How can you throw weddings on the roof this summer, with tables piled high with food, with music, when the Germans are moving on Alexandria, when they're waving the swastika over Mt. Alberus and heading for the Caspian Sea?'

"I remember what day the wedding fell on, Pinik. I'd been drafted together with the paratroopers' unit I was attached to. We all slept in the high school at the end of the summer vacation—the high school I wasn't studying at any more, the school we thought no one would ever study in again. Rommel was close to the Nile, in Southern Russia they'd gotten as far as Stalingrad. It seemed that any minute the paratroopers would drop from the skies, just like they did on Crete. I got permission to take one night off to come to the wedding. The city was blacked out and light bulbs painted blue were hanging on the roof. There wasn't any unemployment any more. And you, Pinik, you'd come back from Rafiach, tan, bubbling over, handing out presents left and right. . . ."

"Forget it, Elisha."

"I can't. I want to explain why I exploded like that. I couldn't understand how on a night like that at the end of August when the world was about to be destroyed—"

"Let me alone, Elisha. What do you want from me?"

"I didn't have any right to attack you, but you've got to understand how I felt. You filled me full of wine. The roof was spinning in circles. The papers were reporting on what had happened to the Jews in the occupied zones. And there—waltzes, Carmel wine, just like tonight, in the Lido."

"What don't you like tonight, Elisha?"

"You, Pinik. What's all this again, the last days of Pompeii? I didn't have a chance to tell you, Pinik. On the border, up north, I met a relative of ours. His job was to push bodies into the crematorium. Our relative."

"Go to hell, Elisha! Beat it! G'by!"

That moment stands out in sharp detail against the blurred background of that night. Pinik was sitting in one of the easy chairs and I was sprawled at his feet, begging forgiveness for that other night, but as I spoke, my apology became a fresh bitter cry. I clutched at his thighs, as if I could restore to that face, that plucked chicken flesh, its former beauty.

"Don't send me away in that tone of voice, Pinik. Let me ask you about the people who come to us in the convoys. I . . . believe me, I want to love their burnt faces, but I can't. I walk among them and I don't recognize a one. They're all strangers to me. But you, Pinik, you taught me all the answers, you sang me the songs of the new world that would rise on the ruins of this one, you taught me word for word, 'Yesterday—nothing; tomorrow—everything.' What are you sitting here for, today. Why? Why?"

"Get away, you stupid brat!" Pinik pushed me aside, rose to his feet and was gone.

That moment stands out clearest in my memory. I lay on the ground, dead tired, dying to sleep. Felicia was bending

over me, I felt her cheek glide over my face like a feather, felt
her breasts press against my chest. I seized her. Hands tried to
lift me up but I wanted to sleep right there on the spot, without
moving. That was all. More than that I remember only in fragments and all out of order. I hugged Felicia, drew her to me
with all my might so no one could take her away from me. And
so I fell asleep.

6

When I awoke, I was in a dream.

The two of us were in the same, dingy Jerusalem hotel we
had sneaked into that last night. Now, more than that first
time in Haifa, I feared the moment we would be left alone.
In my dream (I was wide awake in my dream), we lay locked
together in a strange room with thick walls and iron shutters.
Water flowed from a faucet on the other side of the wall. A
woman was laughing softly and a man answered with a yawn.
I was clutching Noga with all my might, but her body was cold.
"Elisha, hug me, don't sleep," whispered Noga in the dream.
(I swiftly differentiated between reality and my dream.)
"Come to me Elisha, come." But I was growing colder and
colder, like years before when I was a little child, when I would
stay alone in my room and the jackals would enter the court-
yard, stand beneath the window, and yowl. "Hug me, Elisha,"
Noga whispered, but as I pressed her body against me I felt
myself go limp all over.

"Tomorrow you're leaving, Elisha," said Noga. I knew very
well what she was saying. Fear chained me to that strange bed.
I would leave the next day and Noga would no longer be mine.
In vain did she whisper my name, in vain did I press her to me.
"Come to me," whispered Noga (in the dream, in the dream)
and tears for the heartbreak I knew would be mine, long hence,
streamed from my eyes. "Stalagmites," Pinik had shouted, "stalagmites . . ."

"*Caro mio*, tears!"

Felicia's clear voice tore away the veil of my dream, even
though my conscious mind was already viewing it from the side.

I opened my eyes. I was in a huge bed in a strange room. Thin horizontal rays of white light pushed through the slats of the shutters to the left; through my half-closed eyes they seemed to be pulling shining parchment sheets into the room. Felicia was to my right.

No, it was just the opposite. When that voice spoke, the woman I held in my arms became flesh and blood. I sprang back in fear, sat up, turned to the left, and saw the day. To my left Felicia laughed, rose on her elbow, moved closer to me, and with her long finger touched the corner of my eye.

"Why are you crying, pretty boy?"

The span to the dream was bridged again. I touched my eyes. They were moist and sticky. What had happened since the preceding night? Then I remembered: I had been lying on the floor holding tight to Felicia. Then what? Someone had undressed me, had sprinkled cold water on my face and on my hair (I was leaning over the toilet, vomiting) and had put me to bed. But what happened after that. How was it Felicia, in a silk or satin gown, was in that wide bed with me?

"*Dove tutti?* Where's everybody?"

Felicia looked at me from close up and laughed: "I frighten you?" She spoke Italian, so I didn't understand what she said. That is, everything was all too clear.

"*Dove tutti? Dove* Pinik."

"They left. All left this morning. To work. Oh, why do you cry?"

We lay in a wide bed as though that was what I did every night, as though I woke up every morning with a woman beside me. Felicia leaned on her elbow, her face toward me, one leg bent and her breasts spilling out of her gown. She looked at me with curiosity, without any of that wild passion we all had read about in dirty books. She wiped the corners of my eyes and kept smiling. Nothing evil had been done.

"Baby Othello," she laughed.

"What time is it?"

That was my only out: I hadn't returned to my unit, I was absent without leave, and now I had missed the train Pinik had promised he would put me on that morning. Was I in trouble!

"Time is all ours. Pino won't be back today."

199

Just like that. She had no shame, no dread of sin. Her body filled my eyes and now my hands were full of what I had just held in my dream. Not the dream, but a thought that had tortured me all that time: why had Noga left me for another? That stayed with me, the harvest of parched earth in time of drought. A throttled desire, a fear of some inner beast that paralyzed me, crushed me even when all other barriers fell. But why keep walking in a daze, I asked myself. Now I knew what was what. Everything was forbidden, forbidden, forbidden . . . the cold sterility of my home, the frightening fantasies . . . *Kivrot hata'ava*, "the tombs of lust." * What did that mean exactly, *Kivrot hata'ava*? I held Felicia tight, pressed against her as she laughed, eager for me to remove my hand and possess her.

Even before my fingertips traced her smooth flesh she drew close, hungry for me. "Simple, simple, simple," chanted a voice inside, but in the background, "Holy, holy, holy." †

Simple, simple, simple. I removed her gown and she arched her back making it easier for me. She didn't stop looking at me for a minute. By the light of the parchment scrolls behind her head I saw her eyes photograph every movement of my face. Her lips were thick, too crude, and something flickered there, no sooner seen than gone. She raised her bronzed arms and linked them behind my neck. The bridges were lifted. The beleaguered city was mine and mine alone. My every nerve drank in her rippling flesh. How funny: Simple, simple, simple.

"You won't cry again, pretty Moor?"

The thick walls of glass had been made of nothing, like a column of dust that refracts the sunlight. All my fears were dissolving like cardboard mansions. At home in the wintertime, the ravine on the edge of the neighborhood would overflow its banks. From the south, black waters would sweep in, bearing boards, cardboard shoe-boxes, empty oil tins. When the rain would die down we would float rafts and paper boats on the subsiding flood. The water would lick at the paper from below

* Numbers 11:34: "And the name of that place was called *Kivrot-hata'ava*, because there they buried the people that lusted."
† "Holy, holy, holy is the Lord God of hosts, the earth is full of His glory." From the eighteen benedictions in each of the three daily Hebrew services.

200

and seep into it. The sides would soften, the masts would collapse, all the folds would flatten out on the water into soggy notebook covers sinking in pinkish foam. I won't cry, Felicia. Everything is simple, simple, simple.

My face was buried in the pillow. Whisky vapors from the night before rose in my nostrils and the sweet scent of Felicia's perfume, the heat, the prickly sweat. Once again I was drunk or sad or weak. What was I so depressed for all of a sudden?

"Why don't you say something, Moor, why don't you lift your head up? I want to see you, pretty boy."

She raised my head with two strong hands and pushed between me and the pillow. Her flesh was warm and sweaty. I sat up and hung my legs over the bed, my back to her. What in the world was I doing in Pinik's bed, with his woman? How had I wound up in so naked an afternoon?

"Holy madonna, again you are crying!"

Behind my back I heard the bed creak heavily as Felicia rolled over to get nearer to me. I didn't want to touch her; I had to get away, flee back in time somewhere before this encounter. "Simple, simple, simple," my body whispered in dying cadence, while far off a second voice chanted dully, "Broken, broken, broken."

Felicia grasped my head like a nutcracker and turned me around to face her. Her hair, which had been gathered into a bun the night before, spilled over her shoulders like a silk scarf, shining jet black in the sparse white sunlight. A strange script seemed to glow and fade on her full lips like demon-writing. The waters began to well up within me again; I was seized with the desire to set sail on the surging foam. How simple and sweet the conquest—simple, simple. Her legs were folded beneath her as she leaned forward unashamed, as if our nakedness meant nothing at all. Her huge breasts swelled toward me. As through a magnifying glass I saw every vein, every fold in the abundant flesh rubbing against my body. But my desire had fled, I only wanted to turn away, not see. I didn't want an end to all shame, I had no desire for that glaring riot of nakedness. How had I gotten into Pinik's bed with this woman? Hadn't Pinik known what he was doing leaving me there alone? Hadn't he known?

"I've got to go," I said and tried to get up.

"Why?" Felicia laughed. "Pino won't come. Nobody will.

They went to Germany. For four days. Four days you'll stay here, Othello."

My eyes swept over the room, but my clothes were nowhere in sight. I was too ashamed to dash out of bed naked.

"If I don't get back today, they'll put me in the kalaboosh, in jail." Ever since we'd arrived in Italy we had begun using the few Arabic words we knew. A foreign language is a foreign language.

"For Felicia you wouldn't want to go to jail?" She teased, pushing her body closer to mine. I knew I ought to flatter her, say something nice, show my gratitude, but my tongue would not move. My eyes strained for something to cover myself with.

"You want to go, go! Don't waste your time, then! Go!" Her voice rose from the back of her throat, suddenly dry, foreign, contemptuous. All the better. On the floor, alongside the bureau, lay the civilian pants I had worn the night before. I jumped out of bed, dressed quickly, and left the room.

When I was in my uniform and hobnailed boots once more, standing in the dim and silent foyer, my hand on the door knob, I had second thoughts. How could I end things in such a way? Felicia was no Potiphar's wife nor was I a Joseph. Or a Jonathan either. I had tasted of the honeyed forest and knew I had done wrong. I stood before the large room where we had caroused the night before and surveyed the havoc—the table piled high with dirty dishes, overturned chairs, women's shoes, the shirt covered with animals.

A deathly silence held the house; not a sound was to be heard. Anna Maria and Marcella were still sleeping no doubt, and Felicia was weeping into her pillow. I couldn't run away like that, as if I were the righteous one. I had to go back and take leave of her, thank her. A moment of freedom, without fluttering heartbeats, arias, *amore*; wasn't that what I had been seeking all along?

I was afraid to enter the room, afraid to touch the black waters. Felicia, I don't want to leave, I still hunger for that faceless meeting of man and woman. Just don't cry when I come in.

She did not cry. Covered by the sheet up to her chin, her back to the sun, her hair over her cheek, she lay asleep. Her body was at peace, she lay soft as rolling sand dunes smoothed by the wind. My shoes rang out against the floor and I was afraid she would wake up. Nonetheless I approached the bed and bent over her. The springs creaked. She breathed open-mouthed, wisps of hair fluttering before her lips. I brushed her hair aside and touched her cheek. She did not cry, did not hold me, did not wake up. I turned to leave, pained at the thought I would never see her again.

I left the room. I left the house. No one ran after me. No one called me back. I was alone.

V   Enemy Territory

Twice I was in luck. I reached Verona in two lifts, but found myself stuck there on the road to Milan. I sat in the dark, my pockets empty and my kit bag full of cigarettes I hadn't sold in Venice, cigarettes that gave me the crazy idea of extending the leave I had taken. There was no escaping the punishment that awaited me anyway, so at least I'd see Milan. And who was scared of fourteen days confinement in our godforsaken Alpine village? As for the withholding of pay, we never drew it anyway. One week's pay equaled a pack of twenty cigarettes. I would go to Milan.

This I decided by the roadside, enveloped by the night, half-frozen with no lift in sight. Every once in a while a truck passed, but headed in the opposite direction, to Venice. And the voice of temptation, taunting me ever since I had left Felicia, whispered into my chilled ear: "Cross the road and get back there. A bed's waiting for you, Felicia's waiting. Just one more night. What's the difference?"

"It never happened. I've forgotten all about Felicia," I answered the devil.

"Smell your fingertips. You're full of her perfume, full of the smell of that luscious body. Don't be a child. It's just like Brodsky said: 'She didn't steal anything from you.' "

"I'm not interested. Pinik, Goddamn him, he took my last fears away, my last *don't,* the bastard. He left me alone with Felicia on purpose, maybe he even told her what to do with me."

"Stop playing the innocent. You can't deny it: it was simple, simple, simple."

"I wasn't there, it wasn't me. . . . Ah, Noga, how I've struggled to stay pure . . ."

"*Nu, nu.*"

"That's the whole truth. I—"

"—I'm dying to go back to Felicia."

"I'm going to Milan."

"What's there?"

"I'm free now. I'm all by myself, no strings attached and the world can go fly a kite. That's how I always wanted to travel— free as the breeze."

"A breeze stuck by the road. Without a lift."

"I'm not going back to Felicia."

"Fine, fine. Just go where all the cars are going."

"Not to Venice."

"We'll see about that later. First cross the road."

I tried to stop every vehicle going either way. A jeep whizzed by heading east. After it had gone about thirty or forty meters beyond me it stopped. Racing for the jeep as it backed up in my direction, I saw the blue and white insignia of the brigade on its rear. In the front, next to the driver sat a captain. My heart pounding, I saluted: now I was in for it. They had seen the patch on my sleeve, that's why they had screeched to a halt. On the captain's hat I saw the brass snake of the medics.

"Where are you headed?" asked the captain. His voice was warm; he wouldn't turn me in.

"To the brigade," I said. "As near to it as you can drop me, sir."

"For a minute I thought you were headed for Milan." He smiled.

"Oh, no, sir. Why Milan?"

"Milan's very lovely. I only wanted to tell you the brigade's moving."

"Moving!" My knees trembled.

"In forty eight hours. And if you don't have a pass—and you don't—you'd better come with us!"

"Thank you, sir! I—"

"Don't talk. Jump aboard."

My luck had held out again. We made the long journey nonstop at breakneck speed. That very night I was sleeping in my own bed as though the entire episode had been a dream. Milan had never existed.

In the morning Leizi told me there had been no need for deception. No roll call had been taken and that day everybody was feverishly preparing for the trip. I hadn't even been missed.

Where were we headed?

No one knew. Maybe to France, maybe to the Lowlands. We would be traveling through Germany, it seemed, but we certainly wouldn't be staying there. The British just wanted to get us away from the border, to put an end to the flow of Jews southward. They'd find some hole for us where we wouldn't be able to do anything.

This time we weren't as worked up as we'd been when we left Brisighella. The memorial parade, the oath before the flag, our guts on fire leaving for enemy territory—we had all buried that deep within as if beneath stones. This was no resumption of our discontinued journey to the border. They were moving us—fine; they would have us set up camp—fine. Hundreds of vehicles formed long lines across the green field, sluicing muddy ruts into the crushed grass. The dispatch riders set their motorcycles rumbling. On our last day we vacated the buildings and spent the night in the field in pup tents. Everyone buddied up quickly and Broadsky suggested we tent together. Since Bologna we had steered clear of each other. Now I was glad he had put that behind us and was extending the olive branch. I did alright with Brodsky as a friend. We complemented each other and he never lied to himself.

Brodsky found a good spot for us on the truck and helped me put my gear in order. As ill luck would have it, the very day before I got the books I had asked Noga to send me, books I had despaired of ever receiving. So go find room for them!

All the weeks we had gone out of our minds with nothing to do I hadn't had a single book of my own, but the day I was to leave I was setting out with a library—Hebrew literature, Greek history, mathematics, English grammar. She even went so far as to include the chemistry textbook from the British Institute I had loaned her.

Why had she gone out of her way to send everything—to placate me or to make sure I couldn't complain? Or to rid her room of all thoughts of me? Her room—as though she hadn't married that Rivkin or Belkin or whatever his name was . . .

But still, why did she have to return herself to me with those books just at that moment, the day after Felicia? *I love you Noga, I need you. Why didn't you add one line of your own to all these pages, besides your thin pencil marks and notes in the margins. Why did you suddenly wake up? Who needs this agony all over? Why?*

We left.

Once again the snake-like convoy slithered along the mountain slopes, resting frequently. Steep ridges opened wide, plunging us into the bosom of soft valleys. Italian script was replaced by picturesque Gothic letters. It was just like that trip to Klagenfurt, only this time we were traveling on a highway, heading west. We were no longer racked by emotions—we knew neither pride nor pain, consolation nor vengeance. We were being taken through enemy territory.

As night fell we pulled into a green field that looked like an irrigated stretch of alfalfa. The advance party had already designated parking areas for the companies: small signs had been thrust into the grass and the regimental M.P.'s guided us into our places. The Primus stoves hissed away. The energetic among us weeded out plots for their bedding. Brodsky and I pitched our tent, tossed our gear beneath the flaps, took our mess kits and walked over to the cauldrons. The company was already there, waiting patiently for tea, bread, jam, meat, and vegetables. We were old, old hands by now. We ate, left over a little luke-warm tea to wash off the grease, wiped our hands on the stained dish towel, and stood around in the unfamiliar darkness. As the field turned black and the mountains, too, we tried to convince one another that this was Austria.

In the dark someone came running to announce jubilantly he had just heard over the radio that Labor had won the elections. "Good news for us," someone said.

"That's ingratitude for you," said another. "Churchill wins the war for them and they throw him to the dogs already."

"They've got healthy instincts," a third added.

"What the hell's the difference to us? They're both of them whores. If anything doesn't bother them it's the Jews."

"*Yalla*, let's go to bed, boys. We'll see what's what tomorrow."

The six weeks we had spent in houses with mattresses beneath us and high ceilings above had softened us. Even after we had smoothed the ground and covered it with grass and rubber ground-sheets, and blankets, it was hard to fall asleep. Mounds of earth thrust into my back, my face rubbed against the tent flap, the air was close, stale, baleful. I turned from side to side, aggravated by Brodsky's loud snoring and my recurring thoughts of the Lido, the books that had suddenly arrived, Father's letters begging me to return to *Aretz*. The day we got to our next permanent camp, I decided, I would do everything to get my discharge. I had to go home. Things were not so simple, not so simple after all.

In my sleep I heard a booming as of tanks, as though we'd been thrust back into the war. It was hot, but I burrowed into my blankets. Something was crashing against the tent in a steady stream, like machine-gun fire. Blue lightning rent the sky and thunder crashed all around us. My face rubbed against the canvas: it was wet as a washrag. I woke up in the midst of a summer downpour. The rain was barraging the tent like a waterfall and our tiny triangular plot seemed like a trap. I reached beneath

208

the tent flap and my fingers sank in the mud. I turned to Brodsky. "You asleep?"

"How can I sleep?" he answered.

"Maybe we ought to run for the trucks?"

"Anyone who budges is crazy. It's just a summer storm. It'll pass soon."

We lay beneath the sagging tent and the rain while the water kept gushing down. It was stifling, dense, and the tent poles began sagging toward each other. The roof of the tent rested on my head.

"The tent's collapsing, Brodsky!" I yelled into the darkness.

"Screw it, man, let it fall! The main thing's to lie down and not move. We've got rubber below us and tarp on top. We'll lie in the mud like a mailsack and we'll come out dry."

But at that moment I sat up. A slimy bug had slipped into my blankets and down my back. I slapped out behind me to crush it but found it was water. From underneath the ground-cloth or who the hell knows where, water had trickled down my back. I shuddered, cold, almost terrified, as if thrust back in time beneath another rubbery sheet, the smell of talcum powder in my nostrils, afraid of the moment my eyes would close and I could no longer control myself. It seemed as if I were back in the infirmary where I had been dressed in those fouled pajamas.

It would still be best to get to some truck, I told myself. Outside, all around, I could hear laughter and shouting. Goddamn them, they had to put us in a valley that was a ready-made reservoir. I raised myself on all fours and moved toward the door.

"Come on, let's do something, Brodsky!"

"Don't move!" he shouted.

Too late. As I rose to my knees, in that pitch dark, my rear brought the tent down. The stakes pulled out, the poles buckled, and the tent fell on my back.

"That's even better," roared Brodsky. "Now we'll be covered on all sides."

"I don't intend to stay on my knees holding the tent up till morning."

"Course not, let it fall on top of us. We'll be warm and dry."

So we lay swathed in water, smothering and roaring like Indians with the rest of the company swimming in the field. I kept dozing off and waking up, praying for the morning and struggling to escape the wet. Finally the rain stopped. We lifted the flap of our tent, like Noah on Ararat, and looked out: the earth was bright and green and the skies were clear above. Brodsky pulled his rifle out from beneath his blankets and the two of us thrust up against the water-laden roof. Slowly we rose to our knees, with all our gear. Finally we found ourselves upright on our exposed bedding with the tent stretched around us. We flung it off with a swift thrust and stood standing on our relatively dry plot, taking in the mad scene.

The sun had not yet risen: a milk-blue light, neither of day nor night, prevailed. Not a cloud was to be seen in the sky, as if it hadn't been the source of the night's downpour. Scores of soldiers were sloughing through the muck, half naked, wrapped in blankets, loaded down with gear, groping their way to the trucks and the road. Almost all the tents were down and those who had not yet extricated themselves were poking about frantically under the tarps like trapped animals. Roars of laughter raced from one end of the field to the other as everyone took comfort in the ludicrous appearance of his neighbor. So did we.

Leizi came toward us wearing only mud-stained long-johns, his blankets bundled on his back, his kit bag under his arm and his shoelaces between his teeth. Stepping high in his bare feet he ran toward the road like a baby camel, sinking again and again into the slimy puddles hidden like mines through the field. Hah, a morning like this made the whole night worthwhile!

Brodsky and I began to go through our belongings right where we stood, separating the wet from the dry. Not only were the bottoms of our duffel bags and kit bags soaked, but half the contents of each kit bag—the half nearest the ground—as well. The books I had gotten from Noga only two days before were ruined. I felt a pang in my heart, as if this were an ill omen. If we had been able to camp there a day or two more I might have been able to save them, but they would just rot if I bundled them up. I had to spread them out in the field, but how could I?

During one of the hikes we had taken up the mountains we had come upon an abandoned inn full of German newspapers, remnants of food and other signs that it was a Nazi hideaway. There I had found a sheet and had slept in it ever since. I bundled up my books in the sheet to keep them separate from my wet clothes.

We dressed as well as we could and trundled across the road. The field kitchen had been damaged and a few trucks had sunk in the mud, so our departure was delayed. Taking advantage of the change in schedule we went back and spread out our wet clothes on ropes we tied to trucks and stood around warming ourselves in the rising sun and drinking the late tea.

Suddenly I saw a group of soldiers milling about nearby. From the way they were huddling together, intensely concentrated, I sensed this was no usual matter but some rumor or exciting news. I rushed over and to my surprise found Giladi in the center of the crowded circle.

I asked what was up and was told: Hershler had been murdered.

I pieced together the story from the questions asked Giladi and from his answers. Giladi had taken part in a mission that circulated in various locales, seeking out Jewish survivors. The night before he had come back from Vienna to rejoin the convoy. So preoccupied had I been with my own affairs that only upon his return did I learn he had been gone at all. He told how Hershler, who had disappeared in Milan, had left, as rumor then had it, to search out his family in Budapest. In Vienna, Giladi learned, he had linked up with some of our boys smuggling out Jews. They got him money and some forged documents and let him in on their undercover work. About two weeks later he reappeared in Vienna, reported he had found his mother and father and was heading back to Budapest to bring them across the border.

The men who told all this to Giladi had been astounded by Hershler, who wouldn't tell them everything. Maybe his parents had doubts about going with him, maybe they had even had a falling out. Hershler turned down their offer of help and said he would report back to them. He never did. Just as he appeared, he dropped out of sight. Everyone was occupied with a thousand other things, so they simply forgot about Hershler. Only by chance one of them heard that a Palestinian soldier had been killed in a traffic accident in the city. His papers showed him to be our Hershler.

"They claimed he'd been killed in an accident," Giladi said, and the tight circle pressed even closer about him. "They said he slipped and fell from the steps of a trolley car. Right away that sounded fishy to me. We know Hershler and our men in Vienna said everything he did was well planned and carefully executed. He was completely preoccupied with rescuing his parents. A man like that doesn't fall out of a trolley car. I decided to investigate on my own. I went over the police report, read testimonies—"

"And they let you?" asked Poker in admiration.

A thin smile spread across Giladi's delicate face, the face of a bank clerk: "Don't forget I'm a major—sent to Vienna especially to conduct the investigation . . ."

"You crafty bastard!" Poker exclaimed, looking at all of us. "So what did you find out?"

"He was murdered. One night he'd boarded a half-empty trolley car and a bunch of Nazis began insulting him. A fight broke out. Hershler was no weakling, but there were too many for him. The few passengers who witnessed it all disappeared. The Nazis beat him unconscious and then threw him—threw him beneath the wheels of a trolley coming from the opposite direction."

We were dumbstruck. We couldn't believe it. How could a soldier be murdered, just like that in a garrisoned city full of occupation troops?

"You sure? How could you know all those details? Did they rob him? Maybe something had happened beforehand?"

Giladi stood silent before the questions. His velvet-smooth face was a blank, but it no longer deceived us. Beaten steel lay below the velvet. His lips a pencil line, he said, almost contemptuously: "You still have questions, after all that's happened? You want to know why they killed a lone Jew at night, at the edge of town? That's all? After he was murdered was there any real investigation? Did they try to uncover the killers? Nothing. They took down the conductor's testimony. He said Hershler had jumped aboard the trolley while it was moving, slipped and fell beneath the wheels of a car coming in the opposite direction. The police wrote it all down and closed the case. The M.P.'s didn't even raise their eyebrows."

"But still, how did you get to the truth?" someone insisted.

"We found the conductor. We loosened his tongue, don't worry," said Giladi, his face a blank. "But Hershler—that came too late to help him any."

2

Our convoy was a sight the day we were to cross into Germany. Ropes and belts stretched from one truck to the next, loaded down with clothes hung out to dry while we wore or held onto everything rescued from the downpour. We looked like a camp of gypsies.

But only on the surface. We had not wandered carefree like gypsies from place to place; all our thoughts were bound up with every locale we had stopped in. And after four days, when we left via the other border, west of the Rhine, we were no longer as lighthearted as before.

We traveled through the Tyrol, glued to the border. The road wound through mountain passes, climbed from one peak to another and crossed into Italy once again near the Brenner Pass. There, we left Italy for the last time and found ourselves in the heart of the Tyrol.

Setting out upon this second journey we no longer were a boisterous band of conquerors. For six weeks we had been held up at the border and now we were obviously being booted out so the last gate open to us would be closed. That stifled any victory cries within us. I don't know what went on in all the hundreds of trucks rumbling through the mountain passes, but I know what went on in ours.

Why the whole truck? Just me. My entire childhood was spent in a radius of twenty kilometers: orchards, the seashore, the slopes of the hills of Ephraim. The first time I went up to Jerusalem in a train I felt like I was climbing onto the rooftop of the world; when I first went down by truck from Beth Shean to the Jordan Valley I plunged into paradise on earth. Who had ever seen such a river, who had ever seen such a sea? Now we were crossing towering mountains, rolling through thick forests stretching out endlessly above chasms. All about us mountains plunged down into abysses encompassing lakes whose lucid waters mixed the thick green of the forest with the patchwork blue of the sky. The land of make-believe, night elves, yodels, leather pants, straw hats. God almighty, there they were—Hansel and Gretel, the old men planted in the doorways of their cottages, puffing smoke from their long-stemmed pipes, and there, in the entrances to the beer-halls stood men thick as tree trunks. Not one shell had scarred any of those gleaming walls, not one bullet had shattered those polished windows. Here God had set aside a reservation, here the war had not confounded the year's seasons.

After we were inside Germany, with Innsbruck behind us, our wounds re-opened all along the convoy. Unorganized, not by command, once again the folded flags unfurled above the hoods of the trucks and the chalk inscriptions reappeared on the dull green canvases:

DEUTSCHLAND KAPUT!
KEIN REICH, KEIN VOLK, KEIN FÜHRER!
DIE JUDEN KOMMEN!

Everything looked the way it did on our first trip from the front to the border, only this time we did not sing or go wild. We sat silently, with eyes closed, inner voices whispering hypnotically, "Hate them, hate them, hate them . . ."

How do you hate the soaring sky, majestic mountains, fragrant forests, singing Alpine streams? What could we peg our hate on? The mountains spilled downward, valleys opened up, broad harvested fields emerged from the thick forests. Like pointed caps, sheaves of wheat stood in the fields tied to stakes.

We had come a great distance that day, even though we had started late in the morning. The commanders, it seemed, were determined to reach our original destination. A gentle day was fading into a lush evening, the dark under-growth whispered in the forest, church steeples thrust heavenward like spears, a veil of thin smoke hovered over distant villages. Where, where had the iron claw of war scraped this land? Where were the pools of bubbling blood? What agony: all the ruin we had seen from Taranto northward and this earth had to be spared.

I sat next to Brodsky and opposite us, near the tailgate, sat Zunenshein. From the moment we had entered Germany a change had come over him. His pipe never left his mouth and the minute it went out he would quickly relight it. He sucked in the smoke in short breaths, nervously, and his eyes never left the scenery. That wise calm that had won my heart had left his eyes, which now seemed almost black. From time to time his face tensed in expectation. Unlike himself, he talked a great deal, describing in advance the places we were nearing. "I know Bavaria well," he said. "In my youth I traveled about a great deal in this region. I studied a bit in Freiburg—that's much farther west—and then I lived in Munich. Here," he cried feelingly, "we're coming to a fork. Just a little ways on. The road to the right goes to Munich."

We took the left fork and Zunenshein swiftly announced that nearby lay Oberammergau. There was something strange in his quickness, in his zest at discovering his memory hadn't deceived him, that every place and every road were fixed in his mind so firmly even though, he told us, sixteen or eighteen years had passed since he had been there. It wasn't only that he remembered, I thought. He must have been a young man then, my age, so now he was reliving the stormy days of his youth. He pronounced every place name with a precise German accent, for he had been educated, so he had told me, in German. The Jewish community of Prague had been a great center of German culture.

"What's Oberammergau?" I asked, imitating his pronunciation, rolling the r's and elongating the long vowels.

I saw from Zunenshein's expression he had caught and understood the mockery. His face dropped and he leveled his eyes at me.

"It's a small village—no, a large hamlet—where they've been staging the Passion Play for three centuries or more now. It's a religious pageant in which only the residents of Oberammergau take part. It's not theater, but a mystery: both the players and the audience identify with the suffering Jesus, whom the Jews put on the cross. I was there. Once. A fantastic pageant, with hundreds of ecstatic villagers in it. It shook me to the core."

Zunenshein kept looking at me, but addressed us all. "Thousands of people, students like me, connoisseurs of folk art, just decent citizens, sat there identifying with the play. And I, as the pageant stretched on for hours, I began to realize how ashamed I was—of being a Jew. And terribly afraid. Any minute the sign of Cain would appear on my forehead and they would drag me off to Golgotha, overlooking the incredible scenery of Oberammergau. Only years later did I realize what it all meant. . . . People say that Nazism began in the beer-halls of Munich. Maybe so. But the deep roots of the slaughter of the Jews are here, on the border of the Tyrol and Bavaria, in Oberammergau . . ." His finger hung motionless, pointing at the scenery.

We traveled on, scarcely stopping. The sun began to sink toward the forest, but the long shadows of twilight stretched on endlessly. Night would not fall and the convoy would not halt. Zunenshein had set me thinking and had confused me even more. God, if only hatred could rip into my body like nails, lacerate my flesh so I would have to shriek aloud. . . .

Suddenly we stopped.

"A concentration camp!" yelled Ostreicher. We all leaped from our seats and pressed to the back of the truck.

The green summer licked at the roadside and in the distance the forest turned black. But right there, alongside the road, rose high fences of barbed wire and black wooden towers. Beyond the wire fence stood two-story structures that seemed like huge metal blocks in the shadows. Maybe there were barracks there, too. I couldn't tell. The convoy didn't stop but hardly moved either. The drivers in front of us had automatically slowed down, even while the officers yelled at them to keep going. Our scores of trucks crept by, as though struggling against the wind, while the people fanned out along the road, waving their hands, hats, scarves, shouting broken phrases.

216

They had materialized in an instant and only when our truck passed by the camp gate did we see how many they were. The gate was open and more and more of them kept streaming out. The same cry swept over them and over us. They sang, they yelled, but out of the welter of shouts and songs, two words rang loud and clear—"*Shalom*" and "*Aretz*"—in a long continuous cry from the moment we saw the first of them standing by the road until their voices and faces faded in the distance.

Maybe it was different. Who can remember exactly how it happened? Our emotions gushed out like cataracts at the gate of that camp. We shouted like madmen. Suddenly someone remembered the empty tool crates. Piles of candy we had grown sick of lay up in those emptied cartons. Everyone pressed forward to fling his own handful at the group of Jews so suddenly revealed to us and as quickly drifting away. For two days we had traveled through enemy territory with stony faces. Now at last we could smile, look on men who loved us, youths whose eyes yearned for us, women weeping for joy. *Here children, take our candy. Here men, take our cigarettes. You there, haver, have a pack. Here's one for you, too, yes, catch. Take everything we can give you before this moment passes.*

The convoy moved slowly on, as though linked to the fence, but our truck had already gone beyond the last boy waving with all his might at the truck behind us. We hadn't even managed to throw out all our candy. We all went back and stretched out on our damp gear as though a sword had severed us from that scene. A strange silence blanketed the truck.

On we journeyed, the darkness almost total. We headed into the suburbs of a city and sensed that we were about to make camp. The long, frequent pauses and the way we crept forward meant that the first vehicles were already heading into the parking area. Everything went according to the old army-on-wheels routine; no thinking was necessary. As our truck bounced down into an open field, everyone groped for his bags, then jumped onto the wet grass. Rain had fallen that day and from the look of the clouds on the horizon we could see another flood was on the way. Sergeant Major Isaacson roared in the dark and Corporal Kuperberg led us to a corner of the field.

217

"Here's where our tents go. We're setting up and heading for chow."

We emptied the truck of personal gear and tossed out the folded tents. Every pair of buddies grabbed a wet, muddy tarp and looked for a plot of ground. It was no picnic. And what a sweet, late July night surrounded us: the fragrance of wet fields, the forest on one side and, on the other, rows of two-story houses with pointed roofs. Lights shone from the small windows in the attics. Men rode by on bicycle paths, in the doorways women stood with their hands across their chests, their eyes on the field. Were we all crazy, hammering stakes into the soft earth, getting ready to sleep there? In the distance we could see a large granary: maybe we'd be able to find a dry spot there.

"Here we're not sleeping, that much I can tell you," Brodsky asserted. "They should sleep in houses and we should get fucking rheumatism on the ground?"

Something began to flutter inside me. I knew exactly what he was hinting at and knew I would go with him. Yes, damnit, that night was ours, maybe our only night spitting distance away from a German town. There were no more excuses. We were there in a wet field and that damn pastoral all around, and I had the books Noga had sent me, books I couldn't leave in a field like that, and there was Hershler's death and what Pinik had said in Venice. . . . When had I been there? Only three days before?

Red-headed Kuperberg ran about in the dark urging us to finish with our tents, grab our mess kits and get a hot meal. In half an hour there would be a company parade. No one was to leave the area.

"We're not leaving the area, huh!" rasped Brodsky. "In Russian they call a guy like that—" He said something in Russian.

"Translate, Kirschenbaum!" His name rolled off my tongue of itself, as I recalled how we had stood by the cherry tree.

"You still remember?" he asked, surprised. "It doesn't matter what I said in Russian. Let's grab our stuff and move out." We took our rifles and kit bags, closed the tent flap, and turned toward the houses. Suddenly, out of the darkness emerged Tamari.

"*Nu!*" He embraced us both warmly, his eyes darting back and forth between us. I wasn't sure whether he had chanced upon us in the dark, thinking we were someone else, or whether he was suspicious because of the weapons in our hands and where we were headed. "Did you see the Jews?"

"Where?"

"In Landsberg. What a pleasure!"

"Sure we saw 'em, why not?" said Brodsky. "We see the Germans, too."

Tamari was aware of Brodsky's hatred even as he patted him on the shoulder, smiling like a teacher. "It'll turn out okay, Brodsky, you listen to me, everything will be just great. They announced on the radio that Labor won by a landslide. That's cause for hope . . . We've got good reason to be happy today, boys . . ."

"I'm a man of peace, Tamari, and when *goyim* are happy I'm scared."

"They're workers, my good fellow. Our friends."

"My mother used to say, 'When a *goy* is sad, don't go near him, and when he's happy, run.' "

"*Nu*, fine." Tamari hugged us again, looked into our eyes, and was lost in the thickening darkness.

"Did you hear that?" laughed Brodsky, belching as loud as a detonator as we walked toward the houses. "The workers won in England!"

Now we walked on in silence, tensed for what lay ahead. Though we had not spoken of it outright, it had to happen. I knew Brodsky. Whenever he said, "I'm a man of peace," it was a sign that horrible memories were battering him and that soon he would tell me a story I had not yet heard.

We were at the edge of the field. The road led between two rows of houses. The street lamps shed little light. Low clouds covered the sky and we couldn't tell how far we had gone into the night. At the end of the path a villager leaned against his bicycle, his face toward our bivouac area. As we drew near him he bowed two or three times either to greet us or get our attention. He was dressed in a ragged German army jacket whose shoulder patches had been ripped off and baggy civilian pants. We walked by him sternly so he would know we had no friendly intentions. He hurried after us, wheeling his bicycle.

219

"Excuse me, please, gentlemen. One moment, please."
We stopped. Despite myself I was swept with a feeling of at-homeness I had to suppress. His German was so recognizable, so clear to me, as if I were in the *moshava*. It wasn't only the words: it was the man himself, in his fifties, stout, a bit fat, even, with a heavy face like the German Jews who had suddenly filled our *moshava*. Not like one of them, but Hollander himself, the fellow who introduced a startling innovation by opening a school for swimming in one of the orchards. Hollander to the letter. God, what a resemblance! The man leaned toward us and whispered, pointing, with his hand held tight against his body, at the third house down the road, on the right.

"There, that's an S.S. house." Brodsky and I looked at the man and at each other in amazement. "Yes, yes, there in the third house, that's where they live, the damn whores. The husband's vanished. He was a high officer in the S.S., the swine!"

As soon as he stopped talking the man put his leather casquette on his head, mounted his bike and was off. His heavy mountain shoes, his ease in riding the thick-wheeled bicycle, all that was surprisingly familiar in those hostile surroundings. Why had he stood there at the end of the road? How was it he had come straight out with what we hadn't yet dared to say to one another? Did he know who we were? What did he expect us to do? He turned a corner and disappeared, leaving us with our questions unanswered.

3

We turned from the road and followed the path leading to the house, Brodsky first and I behind him. The gravel crunched beneath our hobnailed boots. It seemed as I walked that I was not really there, that I was looking from the side at a fantasy scene. Our boots rang out in step, like in the movies, like in stories, like Gestapo boots. Brodsky stopped in front of the light green door, unslung his rifle, and pounded the butt against the wood. The hollow banging raised a loud echo. Again and again Brodsky slammed into the door, but the lattice alongside it stayed dark and we heard no sound from within. Again I had

220

that crazy feeling that all this just wasn't possible: we weren't in Germany and that house had nothing to do with the S.S. The man had lied to us; there wasn't a living soul behind that door. I, too, took off my rifle and began pounding. Hell with it, if they wouldn't open up we'd break in. We weren't turning back.

"Wait," said Brodsky, "someone's coming."

We heard footsteps behind the door. Someone was coming down wooden stairs. An electric lamp was lit in the window. My knees shook from emotion and God knows why, all the while I couldn't stop thinking of Felicia, of the rich body that was mine for the taking, of Pinik keeping her in that house in the Lido, Pinik, my childhood hero. When Zunenshein told us about Oberammergau, I had suddenly remembered sharp and clear, what else Pinik said to me when he picked me off the floor and lay me down in his bed. "Everything's gutted," he said. "The world's one black market and Europe's on her back with her legs wide open. So why not me? Why shouldn't I have a house in the Lido, why shouldn't a woman warm my bed, why shouldn't I have money in my pocket? Don't tell me what I used to preach to you, Elisha. I told you what others told me. Forget it all, Elisha, forget it. Forget it."

A key turned in the keyhole and the door opened slightly. A woman's head appeared in the crack. In the scant light cast by the street lamp I saw blond hair, a white collar, and a dress. Brodsky banged the door open with his rifle. The woman jumped back in terror and stood in the foyer, her fingers clutching the muslin apron she wore over her dress. Her mouth was shut, her eyes were frozen with fear. What now, I said to myself, what do we do now?

Brodsky stalked inside and looked around. An elegant home —a shiny waxed floor, an embroidered picture on the kitchen wall to the right, a slanting wooden staircase leading to the second floor, ornate rugs colored green, red, and sandy brown. The blond, heavy, smartly dressed woman who lavished such attention on this house was the wife of an S.S. officer, the anonymous informant had said. What would we do to her, what would we do to the house, why had we broken in there? Oh, why hadn't I stayed in the field?

221

"A room, we want a room," said Brodsky in a Yiddish that made no attempt to resemble German. The woman understood. She swept her arm inside, pointing to the steps, as if to say, "The room is upstairs, pick any one you choose." There was no question of refusal.

"Okay," said Brodsky, and began walking up the wooden steps. His eyes burned eerily, fixed on some distant point. His boots clomped on the stairs and so did mine, as though we wanted to drown out all other sounds. We were armed invaders in a foreign house. Below stood the woman in the entrance to the kitchen, strangely silent. Let her go to hell, what did she matter? What was I doing clomping away in my nailed boots, pounding with my rifle butt and knitting my brows? That was the question. What atrocity was I about to commit? There I was walking up the stairs, hovering outside myself as if I were playing at being someone else.

Brodsky opened the door to the attic and we both went in. The room resembled a trapezoid with the two long walls pointing in, following the slant of the roof. There was a window in the vertical wall covered with a colorful curtain. Two linen spreads with floral designs lay on the two beds. Above them hung a sampler of a snow-clad mountain scene, framed, with something written in Gothic letters. We smelled the odor of clean furniture, of a girls' room. I opened the window on the darkness, the fragrance of the wet field and the distant forest, the smell of the fresh rain that was just beginning to fall. From the street rose the voices of members of the regiment. More guys were looking for rooms.

"We should've brought our kit bags and spread our clothes out to dry," said Brodsky.

"Let's go. We haven't eaten either."

But Brodsky hesitated and so did I. If we began running back and forth hauling kit bags we would draw other men after us and there were only two beds there.

"Maybe a little later," said Brodsky.

We were tired and filthy. For two days we hadn't shaved and our shoes and pants were coated with mud. I was about to lie down on the bed but couldn't bring myself to it. Brodsky, too, sat on the edge of the second bed, closed-mouthed. A door squeaked below. We heard a girl's high voice, then muffled whispering.

"It's a girls' room, this room," said Brodsky.

"Uh-huh."

Again we were silent. The night was still young. We couldn't sleep, couldn't go out, and just to chat as if we were not in Germany, not in that house, was out of the question. Below us the women were no doubt quaking with fear. Hah! A girls' room. And the woman's not old.

"Kruk, did I ever tell you how we lived in an ice house, once?"

He had. That day, in Bologna when we tried to get a lift back to camp. But I said, "No. What do you mean, 'ice house'?"

"It happened that winter I spent with the partisans. I was almost a kid but I'd been hiding out in one place after another for two years. We were roaming around the forest. It wasn't what we see now, a little stretch of village, a town, a little bit of forest. There, a forest's a forest. And it was winter. Snow everywhere. The ground was like iron. We got an order to ambush a German convoy. That's a story all by itself, how we knew where they were coming from, how we lay in the snow on both sides of the road and suddenly opened fire with everything we had. Not one of them got away alive. Not a one. Know what we did then? We piled them one on top of the other, like walls . . ."

Suddenly he fell quiet, looked at me and began laughing. "You bastard, I told you that one already."

"When?" I asked innocently.

"In Bologna. While we were waiting for a lift. You remember damn well. There were kids there."

"I remembered," I said, "but I like to hear you tell stories. I like to hear you say, 'I'm not a man of war.' "

"That's right, I'm a man of peace. I wish I didn't remember what I do remember."

The steps creaked. Someone was walking up gingerly. While Brodsky had been telling me about the corpses that turned into walls of ice, I decided to tell him about my conversation with Hershler the night we arrived at the front. He didn't think he would come out alive and had asked me to have his belongings sent to some woman in Beth Israel, a relative. But before I

223

could open my mouth we heard the light footsteps on the stairs. A hand tapped timidly at the door.

"Yes!" I yelled.

The door didn't open. "Who's there?" I shouted, raising my voice. No answer. I rose from the bed, drew near the door, and flung it open dramatically. A young girl stood in the doorway. She shrank back, but she still was very close. Her face looked like it came right off a toffee tin—plump, thick lips like mulberries, a white, fleshy neck. She was a little shorter than I, but full-bodied. Her breasts bulged like melons within her blouse. A ruffled peasant's dress covered her fleshy thighs. Her pale eyes were deathly afraid.

"What is it?" I yelled right in her face. She was milk white and virginal. Suddenly I was dizzy with the odor of Felicia, my fingertips felt her nakedness. Only three days before. She's a lousy German, cried a voice within. A Nazi. Daughter of an S.S. man. You hate her.

"What do you want?"

"Tell her to bring her sister, too," said Brodsky

"What do you want?" I yelled in her face in Hebrew, but I knew I was feigning the emotion.

"Mother wants to know if you want to wash up or maybe drink something hot . . ."

She spoke German in a strangulated whisper. Somehow the German had no connection with our surroundings. I understood every word. I heard our neighbor, Hollander, in the moshava, heard his daughter calling at twilight, "Mooti . . ."

"No!" I yelled. "Get out of here! One-two!"

The terrified girl had already retreated to the top of the stairs. She didn't have to know Hebrew to understand me. She raced down the steps. Below, in the doorway to the kitchen, stood the mother and another girl, younger than her sister. I re-entered the room and slammed the door behind me.

"Ah, Jewish vengeance!" laughed Brodsky. "You won't rape her even if she cries for it. And you won't drink tea, either."

"Kiss my ass, man of peace."

"Hurts to hear the truth, eh, Kruk? After all those speeches we heard about vengeance . . ."

224

"So what about you, Brodsky? Why are you sitting there on the bed scared to move? Afraid of getting the room dirty?"

Brodsky didn't answer. His narrow eyes stared out the open window, indescribably sad, and I was all but ready to burst out weeping over my disgraceful impotence. We hadn't stormed into that house just for a lark, with our bayonets, our rifles, our hobnailed boots. Ever since that morning, ever since Giladi had told us of Hershler's death, that day on the border confronted me once again, with the identification parade, Bubi and Hershler's failure, the way we had to stand there in front of the two women. Wasn't that why we had come there, Brodsky and I, to do what Bubi and Hershler failed to do as soon as they crossed the threshold? And there we were, the two of us, two lousy men of peace. . . .

"Come on, let's go get our kit bags." Brodsky got up and approached the door. His drooping mustache cast a shadow over his lips and there was no longer any of the dashing vagabond about him. Unknowingly I had hit him where it hurt. "I'd say something to you, but . . ."

We tramped down the stairs. The door to the kitchen was half open and out of the corner of my eye I saw a heavy table with women sitting around it, not only the mother and the daughter. They sat there as though petrified, listening to our footsteps. I almost called out to them, "We'll be right back." We left, shutting the door behind us.

All was quiet in the bivouac. Only where the trucks were assembled were the lamps lit and soldiers milling about. We found our tent, grabbed our gear, and slipped back toward the house. No one noticed us, no one asked us where we were headed. When we went to open the door we found it locked. My hands were full of bags and my rifle was slung over my shoulder. I kicked the door and heard quick steps. The mother opened up and stepped back with a welcoming smile. Ah, why did it have to be so homey? It was sickening.

We spread our wet clothes and blankets on the floor, on the table, the two easy chairs, and on every hook on the wall. I looked over the books once again. During the day the wet had mildewed them, the bindings had come apart, and the colors

225

had run. But I couldn't leave any of them there, not even the math books, because of the Hebrew letters. Our flying letters,* our damn symbols. I wanted to sleep, wanted it to be three days later, wanted not to have taken that night upon myself.

We undressed and lay down in the two clean beds. I don't know what Brodsky was thinking, but as for me, only my embarrassment prevented me from lying down on the floor between my wet blankets.

"We aren't Christians, damn it all," I kept saying to myself, but couldn't fall asleep. I pictured Nehemiah as he looked on our last leave, when we had returned from Egypt, when I had come to say good-by. We sat in his room, Noga and I, and he was talking, as intense and fiery as ever. He discovered the sermon on the mount and began reading it from a Bible, standing, with pathos, in the dim October light.

But I, I was afraid of the New Testament, and as if out to pick a fight, I yelled, "Leave me alone with your Kingdom of Heaven and the other cheek. What's so noble about that sermon? You know they've stuffed that down our throats till we can't breathe. Just let them give us one chance, just once, to be dirty Jews, and we'll grab it, you bet your life. We've got to. How much longer can we go on listening to how we've been booted from one end of the world to the other? 'I sink in deep mire.' † 'Sanctification of the Name.' 'The Three Gifts.' ‡ 'My Sister Ruhama!' § 'The Tale of Nemirov.' || Do I need your sermon? I've heard it since kindergarten and I'm sick of it. Let's be just a little like we are in the Old Testament for once, Nehemiah, and I'll say 'Amen' to you. A little 'eye for an eye,' amen. A little of 'the sins of the fathers on the children,' amen. A little innocent blood under our fingernails so that for once we can have something to be sorry for, to really be ashamed of."

So I yelled then, like a play soldier. But there in that dark

* A reference to the tale of a burning Torah scroll whose letters flew heavenward.

† A chronicle on the pogroms during the Kozak uprisings of the eighteenth century.

‡ A tale of Jewish martyrdom.

§ A poem by Y. L. Gordon on the rape of a Jewish girl.

|| A poem by Bialik on the Kishinev pogrom.

attic I lay silently, listening to the frightened whispers of the women in the kitchen, Nazis. Forget about how lovely the house looks, I told myself, these are a murderer's wife and children, whores who know what's coming to them and what they can expect from the army camping here tonight. Only one thing they don't know: just how tough we really are. A whole day in the granary we had concocted a full pageant of vengeance, the fiery declarations, the ringing words, like my oration before Pinik, like the speech I gave Noga and Nehemiah, like the words Giladi had flung at all of us. Giladi, yes, he more than everyone else—and the most miserable of us all. Why had he stood there arguing with Tamari when he could have just gotten up and done whatever he wanted to? But that was just it. He couldn't have, any more than we could in that Nazi house. What was stopping us, Brodsky and me? Only the fact that we were what we were—impotent, impotent. . . .

4

I raced through a world I had never seen, but as palpable and real as if I had lived there all my life. Our dwelling was at the edge of the village, standing out from all the other black huts with their roofs of pressed straw. I even played by myself, in the puddles of a muddy road, while below, at the foot of a gentle slope, lay a lake of sorts, or a pool, with flocks of white geese waddling around it. The road leading out of the village went around the pond and then crossed the railroad track. It was there that my gaze was directed, for everything came from that direction. A train was creeping slowly out of the forest; there was no one to stop it. It carried open cars full of horses and riders, like out of a painting. The men had blue coats, gaffirs, busbies and long carbines. The train did not stop, but as each car passed the dirt road the horses leaped off gracefully and plunged straight at us. The geese honked in terror, their lordly gait turned into a panicked rout.

I, too, raced for our hut to warn Father and Mother, but the door was locked. With all my might I beat upon the door, but no one would open up. They had forgotten I was outside

227

or were afraid to come near the door. Or maybe they were at work.

The street was long and empty, like after curfew. I raced to the far end of the street, to the large synagogue, but gigantic beetles and tricycles were crawling about there. I slipped through a hole in the fence into one of the courtyards, but there, too, I could not escape unless I could hide in the top branches of one of the trees. If only I could shinny up the smooth white trunk of the eucalyptus they wouldn't be able to catch me. There was no time to lose. The Cossacks were clattering on the cobblestones of the street, women were screaming for help from inside the house. I pressed against the wooden poles supporting the barracks, frantically looking for a hiding place among the foundations. I recognized a voice. It was Hollander's daughter screaming. . . .

Anyone who has not woken up quivering as though he had been shocked, as though an icy sewing machine had stitched his flesh to the bed, cannot imagine how real were those voices, the place, that scene that never happened. Even as I was pursued, digging my nails into the wooden wall, unable to move a muscle, the voices rising from the kitchen, the German women, dull thuds, the hoarse whispering of men, the scraping of furniture—all became starkly real. I lay on the bed of the lily-white girl, struggling to emerge from my nightmare as from a deep lake, but the voices dragged me below the surface like underwater weeds. I cleared a path for myself through the water, but as my breath gave out I still had not reached the air. Something horrible was going on downstairs.

I tore myself loose and sat up.

"Brodsky!" I yelled.

"What do you want?"

Suddenly my head cleared. Brodsky was not sleeping, but was quietly listening to what was going on below us. The women were grappling with men who had broken into the house. Muffled voices and the thudding of bodies met our ears. The girl was screaming helplessly.

"You hear what's going on there!"

I leaped out of bed and in the dark found my pants slung over the chair. Quickly I got dressed.

228

"Where you running to?" His voice cut through the dark like steel lightning, like a polished bayonet. The girl's voice broke into disjointed sobs.

"Are you crazy, Brodsky, or what? You don't hear what they're doing down there?"

I buttoned my pants and my fingers groped for the light switch. My rifle was not loaded and I had to find the bullets.

"Go back to bed, Elisha. They're our boys."

The light filled the room and my eyes closed. Shading them with my palm, I opened them a slit. Brodsky was sitting on the bed in his undershorts, his back against the wall. He was wholly concentrated on the struggle taking place in the kitchen. A smile sealed his lips as if he were guarding some secret scheme. He was taking part in what was going on below and his glazed smile reflected my face.

They're our boys.

The girl's weeping voice crept toward the stairs, struggling to escape, but nailed boots crushed it. I could think of nothing else, nothing else existed at that moment except that stifled weeping. I grabbed a handful of bullets, pulled back the bolt, loaded them, slapped the bolt shut and pulled down the safety with one bullet in the chamber.

"You *schmuck!*" Brodsky leaped from his bed, ready to spring at me. Both of us were barefoot, he in his undershorts and I with the rifle.

"Get away from me, Brodsky!" My back to the door, I grasped the knob. The rifle butt was aimed at Brodsky, ready to strike.

"*Yebyuhamut*, Kruk! Your first bullet in the war you want to put in your buddies!"

I wasn't in control of my thoughts. Only the helpless weeping summoned me from below. I ran down the stairs. The door to the kitchen was open wide and so was the door to the house. The kitchen was all lit up and at the threshold my eyes took in the whole scene: one soldier with bayonet on his gun was pushing the woman and her other daughter back against the wall, between the cupboard and the corner, while the other girl, who had come up to our room, lay on the floor. One soldier was bent over her, his knees pressing down on her spread arms and his hands on her shoulders. Her dress was ripped and she was naked from the waist down. She was crying as though she were struggling to breathe and her fleshy legs fluttered like a slaughtered chicken flung to the ground.

A third soldier, whose face I could see from the doorway, kneeled between her legs. He was flushed with sweat and the blood that had rushed to his head. His cheek was scratched and bleeding and his lips were open wide as if he had to gulp down more air. I recognized the three of them.

"Let the women alone and leave the house. I'm counting to three. Anyone who's still here I shoot without any further warning."

I heard my own voice as though another person had spoken. Never had it been so decisive and calm. The three men were shaken. The one who was shoving the mother and daughter into the corner turned to face me, still holding his rifle.

"Kruk!" he yelled, not able to believe his eyes. "You—"

"Drop the rifle or I shoot."

"You'll shoot? You fucking nurse!" He moved toward me, his bayoneted rifle at the ready. My rifle was steady in my hand. I released the safety, raised the barrel toward the ceiling and squeezed the trigger. In the empty house, in the still of the night, the shot sounded like a grenade going off. The smoke and smell of gunpowder filled the room. The first man dropped his rifle and the two others leaped to their feet, leaving the naked girl on the floor. They all backed to the wall.

"Kruk, you're crazy. What are you shooting in the middle of the night," said the fellow who had pinned the girl down with his knees. His voice was quaking.

"That's all we need, the M.P.'s should come now," said the third.

"Clear out, you bastards." The smoke that had covered me was drifting away. The whole scene seemed unbelievable.

"I'll shoot you down like dogs. *Yalla*, outside."

The three of them moved along the wall toward the door, just like in a movie. The first bent down as he went to pick up his rifle. I lowered my barrel at him and he straightened up, flat against the wall.

"Kruk, you're crazy. They're Nazis. This old whore's husband is an S.S. man. A German told us in the street. He came right over and told us, Kruk. No German ever stood with a rifle to protect a Jewish girl—"

"Get out of here!" Blind rage swept over me. I yelled, not knowing why, yelled to drown out all the voices trying to over-power me. "Take your rifles and clear out. The three of you. I'm counting. One, two—"

They grabbed their weapons and dashed out the open door. I went out after them and saw them running and sliding down toward the bivouac, afraid that the shot would bring other people to the scene. But the street was deathly quiet. Even if their neighbors were being raped or killed, the citizens would not come out of their houses at night.

I turned around and began to climb the stairs to the attic. The woman stood in my path and grasped my hand with her two hands, trying to kiss it. Furiously I shoved her away. The gratitude on her face turned into astonishment as she slipped backward, lost her balance, hit the wall and fell on the bottom step.

I did not stop but raced up the stairs, the rifle in my hand, my bare feet thumping heavily. Brodsky was still sitting on his bed just as he had been when I turned on the light, his eyes glazed, no longer smiling. I went over to the bed, turned to-ward the wall and unloaded the four remaining bullets. I took my rifle kit out of my belt pack and sat down to clean the bar-rel with a well-oiled flannel patch. I did everything crisply, by rote, trying not to lift my head from the rifle. When I saw there was hardly any soot left I oiled the barrel for the last time, wiped my hand on one of the blankets spread out to dry on the floor and went over to the switch to turn out the light.

All at once, as though set off by a spring, Brodsky leaped from his bed, stood before me, shorter than me, his long mus-tache drooping and the sides of his mouth creased sharply. Now he's going to slug me, I thought, and what should I do? I stood by the switch, waiting. Suddenly he spat on the floor between our bare feet.

"Lousy Jew!" he hissed between taut, thin lips. He paused, waiting for my reaction. I was silent. His face twisted in con-tempt. He flung his head down and spat again between our bare feet, went back to his bed, lay down, turned his face to the wall and yanked the cover over his head.

I slapped down the switch so the darkness would conceal me before I burst out in tears. They gushed out with the darkness. I ran to the bed and buried my head in the pillow. It was saturated with the girl's odor. I started, swallowed my tears, got up and began assembling my belongings and packing them. In the process I regained my composure. With automatic movements I gathered my things together in their set order, with no need for a light, stuffing them into the kit bag, the duffel bag and the haversack, all to rid my mind of what had happened, to blot out the memory of my failure. Finally I had acted of my own free will and what had I done?—rushed to save my purity. In an instant all the hymns of hatred had dissolved, leaving me my father's son. Crawling with purity. A man. A misfit.

Now I knew: such were we, condemned to walk the earth with the image of God stamped on our foreheads like the mark of Cain. I couldn't do it, couldn't stand to see a girl raped. Couldn't take it—my delicate Jewish soul. I could hear the sound of armor sprouting on my back. Like a camel's hump, beneath which I and all of us would have to walk forever as beneath the coat of arms of a knight: "How can we beat them if we become like them?"

But didn't we have to, didn't we have to kneel in the muck, just like that fellow had done between the girl's naked legs; wouldn't we go out of our minds going on as we always had, without Tartars, without Huns, without S.S., if we would go on that way to the end of time, groaning beneath the cross of the vengeance we never took, with ravens pecking at us, crying, "In thy blood, live." "Silence the Accuser, silence the Accuser. . . ." *

The silent tears of a weak boy streamed from my eyes and phlegm ran from my nostrils. I filled the kit bag, bundled up the blankets, put on my shoes, buttoned my leggings, put on a fatigue shirt, picked up my gear, grabbed my rifle, and left.

"Elisha!" Brodsky cried after me, but I was already down the stairs. He yelled from above, "Jackass, where you running to in the middle of the night?"

* From the service on the Day of Atonement.

232

I wanted to flee. If I were able, I would have kept on running until I reached the world once again. I swore: the day we reached our permanent camp I would look into getting my discharge as quickly as possible, do anything to escape that continent where I could not live either with our dead or with their living.

Below, in the kitchen, there was light and the woman and her two daughters were walking about. My heavy steps and Brodsky's yelling brought the woman to the door. Again she spouted words whose meaning was so clear, and out of the corner of my eye I saw the other daughter bent over her sister. Once more the woman stretched out her hands, but I passed her by, not to be touched by her cursed gratitude. I opened the door and hurried off to the bivouac, to the remnant of the dark night.

5

Just one more day swathed in that forest as in the night, and the day following—and it would be over. "It all depends," explained Zunenshein, "on the route we take. If we keep heading straight west, we'll cross the Rhine tomorrow, maybe the border even."

I prayed we would. Maybe I was the only one anxious enough to burst until we fled that place. Ever since the night before I was dying to be elsewhere, as though we were traveling through a smoky, pitch-black mountain tunnel starving for light and a breath of air. Maybe it was only I who felt that way because the disaster of the preceding night would not leave my mind.

Like an endless column of black cattle the convoy crept forward, on and on and on. It was enough to drive you crazy. How much land they had! Slowly we rumbled down the Autobahn, heavy trucks stretching out as far as you could see. We had packed our dried-out clothes that day, organized like good soldiers, rechalked the slogans on the trucks' canvases, set the flags flying over the hoods of the trucks, and set our stony faces for the journey. Little Ostreicher kept making calculations excitedly. Even if there were only one hundred meters between one truck and the next, the convoy would stretch from Tel Aviv to Haifa. No, it would be longer. We were traveling in a number of series, each a good distance from the next. "The Germans must be going out of their minds. Didja see 'em this morning?"

We had seen them that morning. We left the field on the outskirts of town and crossed the city on our way to the Auto-bahn. Our M.P.'s, their motorcycles rumbling away, stopped all other traffic. On the steps of half-wrecked houses stood the citizens, looking at us. "What do you think they said when they saw us?" little Ostreicher crowed, "What do you think they said?"

"They should all roast alive," answered Poker.

"After the shots last night and the fire they won't forget us," said little Ostreicher.

After the shots. I lowered my eyes. Brodsky, sitting next to me, didn't react. He had done the same that morning when rumors about the shooting began to fly. Ostreicher had brought the story to Giladi and whispered it into everyone's ear like a terrible secret. During the night, he reported, the boys—those same mysterious "boys"—had broken into German homes and did a bloody job. There was a lot of shooting.

I stood to the side, afraid to look at Brodsky, and listened. The rumor flew back and forth in all directions. "There was a regular massacre last night," the story went. "Some old Ger-man on a bicycle had wandered around the bivouac pointing out Nazi homes." Our men believed the rumor and their eyes lit up with joy. Even I began to have doubts, so anxious was I to forget what had happened. Maybe there were other shots besides my one. After all, everyone else seemed so sure of it. If it were only so.

We stood by the roadside drinking hot tea as we watched the head of the convoy move into the forest, each black, iron beast trotting on the heels of its fellow. At the far end of the field, at the edge of the houses, a black column of smoke rose as though it were the source of the low clouds, black with a foul interior, billowing out like a delicate mushroom. How sweet and melodious the morning cradling the houses and the forest.

234

"Something's on fire over there!" yelled Poker. He, too, had been hoping all the while something would happen. His bleary eyes darted back and forth at every rumor.

"What's on fire?" asked Tamari, looking up from the runningboard of the truck where he was writing in his notebook.

"Look for yourself," said Poker.

We were all able to see. All at once the pillar of smoke had swelled into a conflagration. A large wooden structure, a granary or a rick at the edge of the field, was shooting flames. Pillars of black smoke and streams of sparks flew heavenward like arrows. The low sky was covered with a veil of smoke moving toward the houses. The entire regiment stood by the road in front of the vehicles, hurrahing as though all of us, every one of us, had kindled that rick.

"The bastards, they won't forget us here," exulted little Ostreicher, as though closing the case.

But they would.

The endless convoy crawled forward at a steady pace, heading for its prearranged destination, one day's journey out past the border. We were moving on, but the land was not. The crunching of our tires was as if it had never been; our slogans, flags, our piercing eyes, had already faded with the twilight, with the mist rising from the black forest, with the chill of the night. A two-lane strip of concrete girdled that grassy greenness so it would not burst asunder. Here and there lanes branched off into the forest. In a clearing unravaged by the war stood a fighter plane, as though it had just landed or was about to take off. For an entire day the convoy crept westward while to our right and left black fingers of roadway stretched toward villages and towns whose turrets dotted the hazy horizon; and we were still in the same region. We were crossing enemy territory like a sword cleaves through water. The rear fender of our last jeep would be the end of us and all memories of us.

On we crept. Toward evening we pitched camp between the forest and the road, with Ulm in the distance. Brodsky didn't even hint at what had happened the night before. Early that morning he had returned to the bivouac bringing with him the books I had forgotten in the house. Silently we had folded our tent, prepared for the journey and gone back to being bud-

235

dies as before, traveling and sleeping together. Now the two of us lay down, but even though we did not take off our clothes the wet earth chilled our bodies. Brodsky kindled the stump of a candle and stuck it on a helmet between the two of us, lit a cigarette for himself and offered me one, too. I had begun to smoke on the way to Milan when I stood on the road with a kit bag full of cigarettes, one cigarette after the other. Brodsky always smoked, but only two or three a day, the cigarette carefully cut in half with a razor blade. Now we chain-smoked.

We did not speak to each other. Outside soldiers gathered. I heard Leizi's nasal voice and for a minute thought I heard Bubi, too. No, it wasn't him, but the others were the same ones who always got together whenever we stopped, the same ones who had stretched out by the campfire on the night of the ceasefire, when we returned from Bologna, Brodsky and I. Centuries had passed since that night, it seemed to me. No, not since that night, but since the beginning of the very last week. Felicia's naked body quivered on my fingertips, her smell was in my nostrils. I saw the girl with her dress ripped off in the kitchen and the two soldiers crouching over her. God, how could I ever forget that sight, ever go back to living as though nothing had happened, as though I had not buried men in their uniforms, as though I hadn't met my relative who worked in the ovens, as if I hadn't seen dead, smoking Germans alongside the road, black and eaten away like the beams of a burnt-out house, as though lying with a woman were really simple, simple, simple? . . . I want Noga, I whispered like a little boy closing his eyes not to see the dark, I want our last night in Jerusalem when I touched her body like butterfly's wings, I want everything here not to have happened, I want to be on another continent again, with Europe forgotten. . . .

"So, listen, once we brought a can of shoe polish into the class with a hunk of carbide and water and we stuck them in Chupchik's desk. He went crazy from the stink."

"That's nothing. We wired the door . . ."

"Big deal. Did you ever bring a donkey into class in the middle of a lesson? A real donkey?"

That was them. As always they were locked in their tiny world, cliquish, loud-mouthed, crude, so sure of themselves,

236

not in the least concerned with what was happening all around them. Then again, maybe nothing was really happening, maybe I was just getting worked up over something I should have simply accepted without any upset, like a math exercise. That was all there was to it: they were strong and we were weak, they were where they were and we were elsewhere. It was enough that we were soft weaklings, warped Diaspora Jews. Maybe it was no coincidence I found myself outside that circle once again, with Brodsky again, with the exact opposite of what I had fled to become. I was neither this nor that. . . .

Only a pool of liquid wax remained on the helmet; the wick drooped over and went out. Sergeant Major Isaacson roared in the distance at the band of magpies and they all scattered to their tents. I crushed the cigarette in the wet grass beneath the flap and tried to fall asleep. All that had happened those last few days assailed me, I couldn't push the thoughts away. Pinik, who no longer bore any resemblance to the slender youth who had entered our yard; Hershler, murdered in Vienna; I, who had tried to do what had to be done so we could go on living without our blood forever swimming in our eyes. Impotent, I whispered, picturing Felicia once again, hungry for her body. No, no. They existed, they really did, those high ideals I strove for; it didn't matter what Noga had done. I was still myself, the same as when I enlisted in the army.

I had gone down by myself that day and had met Hershler in the draft office. He had been alone, too. We had enlisted together, his serial number was one digit lower than mine. The war was already far removed from *Aretz*. Everyone was busy making money and me right with the rest. I worked for the war effort and earned more than a pound a day, seven days a week. For the first time there was plenty of money in our home with me the main breadwinner. Suddenly everyone was swamped with prosperity, people began decking themselves out with thick and filigreed gold bracelets, began buying new furniture, went down to the seashore Saturday nights to dance. I had a new suit made with long pants.

Once a week I would get together with Shmeika. Our former classmates were up to their ears in work preparing for matriculation exams, and only Shmeika and I were making money and

putting on the dog studying at nights. He was polishing dia-
monds in Tel Aviv, making more than eighty pounds a month.
My father was earning only seven pounds and Shmeika's father
not even that much. Once a week we would take a walk outside
the *moshava* among the rows of acacias, arguing about God,
the meaning of life or what we had read in the papers. One
day we would wake up and the war would be over. I would only
remember that I had made one pound a day from the war effort,
would have a new suit and would keep dancing at the seashore
Saturday nights. The Africa Corps had been driven out of
Africa for good. The Russians had broken the northern arm
of the pincers and were moving west. Day and night the bomb-
ers roared over us, back and forth, and when the radio would
announce that our planes had bombed a certain place in
southeast Europe, we knew which planes they were.

At that time we heard of the fall of the Warsaw Ghetto. From
Russia, stories began drifting in about what had been done in
reconquered territories. And I—I was barely seventeen . . .
So, at the very moment when dreams were becoming reality, I
was whipped away from my destiny and my visions of being
born a new man. I who had dreamed of rivers, oceans, who had
yearned for glory, found myself in a training camp in Saratand.

"Now?" everyone asked, eyebrows lifted. "You crazy, enlist-
ing now? You got a screw loose or something?"

There in the Black Forest, the day before the end, I could
painfully face the truth; I had fled the stagnant waters of the
moshava, raced off to save my warrior's soul; and on the morrow
I would head back where I had started from, a softie who could
never make it.

"Kruk, you asleep?"

I hesitated, then asked, "Why?"

"Oh, never mind."

"You wanted to say something?"

"No, I thought your cigarette—"

"I put it out."

"Okay."

"Good night," I said.

Brodsky said nothing, but I knew he was still awake. Until
I fell asleep I did not hear him snoring.

238

6

By the last night we had crossed the Rhine and were in a different forest, near Kaiserslautern.

All this I relate from memory, from the scar traced there at the end of July 1945, a nation long.

To the right of the road lay Heidelberg. Zunenshein spoke about the cultural center of Germany and again it seemed as though I could see his longing glow white in the gloom of the truck. He knew the landscape backward and forward and the history of the city for centuries back. "Tschernichovsky," * I said smiling, making a silly gesture toward Zunenshein, "studied in Heidelberg."

"I'll tell you something nicer than that," Zunenshein replied. "The city palace, built more than seven centuries ago, bears the inscription: 'This is the gate of the Lord, the righteous shall enter therein.' In Hebrew."

"The whores!" said Poker.

"They must have smashed the inscription," said Giladi.

"Smashed it?" said Zunenshein. "It's theirs."

"What scenery, what scenery!" Ostreicher whispered almost inaudibly.

Bright sunshine illuminated the turrets against the skyline, far from the road. We traveled on, entering Mannheim. There for the first and last time we saw utter devastation. The convoy glided down the road, but to both sides lay wrecked houses split open their entire length, full of gaping holes without windows or walls. Rubble lay heaped high all around. Our truck sprang to life as though jolted by electricity. Poker and Ostreicher began whistling and jeering at the few passers-by. Ostreicher yelled in German so they should know who we were, the Jews. But there was something pitiful about the whole thing, little Ostreicher standing there shouting in flawless German.

Only when Tamari spoke out did we become fully aware of it: "Why are you yelling in German?"

* Noted Hebrew poet.

239

"They don't believe he blew up the whole city all by himself," said Leizi.

Poker and Ostreicher shut up and returned to their seats. All of us were silent. We went through the city, crossed over the Rhine, rolled through Ludwigshafen beyond the river. All was ruin, but we were passing through like tourists. We were hurrying off with our fists as tightly clenched as ever. All around us lay the rolling countryside, vineyards, a golden glow, stone houses, the peace of twilight. The ruined cities were swallowed up by the broad, teeming stretches of land opening up day after day alongside that one narrow road. We were rolling on toward the border, but the earth was standing still. All we wanted was to be out of there already, to forget it all.

We arrived at Kaiserslautern in a forest at the foot of a rocky hill. Every company set up camp in its allotted area, every tent was set up and pulled taut; within half an hour we were organized. Days were long in those regions; though the sky was bright above us, the shades of night were already spreading out below. The more industrious among us went out to gather twigs, branches, broken wooden crates by the roadside, anything that would serve for a campfire, then brought tins of solar oil. Soon tiny fires were dancing throughout the bivouac.

Poker tried to start up a game with his card crew, who hadn't played for a long time—Brodsky, Giladi, and Mushik the cook. But despite Poker's alacrity the game didn't go off as scheduled. Too many men crowded around. Someone asked Giladi about his trip to the camps—until that night there had been no time for that—and he told about the men he met, the nature of his mission, episodes, in his usual way. "We met a boy," he said, "who reached us after he went back to his town and didn't find a living soul; a Jew, that is. He reached his parents' house and knocked on the door. The new tenants, old acquaintances, were amazed to see him and said, 'You're still alive?' He was afraid to sleep in the city for fear of being killed in the night so he slept in the forests, in hiding, until he crossed the border, just like during the war.

"Catherine the Great once said, 'People are born, earth is not born.' There you can see it. Tomorrow all the ruins will be rebuilt, the orphans will have swarms of kids and twenty years from now they won't know there was a war there. But as for us . . . we have no people. None were left."

Giladi's voice had grown hoarse since that day in the granary. The steel had become a broken pitcher. He, too, knew that our defeat was complete, that we could only escape, flee that continent. Giladi was more wretched than Tamari who stood to the side, outside the circle, listening.

Not wanting to hear, I pushed my way out. I walked off alone, drawn to the small fires beckoning like the forest imps supposed to have led the pure-hearted astray. The earth was carpeted with the intoxicating odor of centuries of decay. Never had I smelled such fragrant air. This was the Rheinland—the congregations of Speyer, Worms and Mainz. Baruch of Mainz* must have lived nearby.

If I ever got to the matriculation exams I would no doubt be asked about Baruch of Mainz. The examiners would ask me to quote, for example, the curses of that crushed man and I, with gallows humor, would tell them some real stories in Zunenshein's language.

Company C was located down the road, and around the bend, where the mountain lay farther away from the road, was Company D. The regimental M.P.'s had set up signs along the road, so making one's way was rather easy.

When I left our circle I had no idea where I was going. But soon I realized I was looking for Bubi. This would be our last chance, we couldn't leave the next day with clean hands. All sorts of rumors were running around the company, as if plans were afoot for striking out at some of the murderers in the dark, anonymously. Maybe, but I didn't believe it. Maybe, but that wasn't the act without which we would never know rest. In my childhood, friends of the family would call me Arabchik, affectionately, because of my dark skin. Often I daydreamed I was a Bedouin who had been adopted by that Jewish couple, Father and Mother. Maybe I was vexed by ancient blood seething within, struggling to break through the Jewish covering. There was no question of what was preferable, worthwhile or possible. There was but one law, even were I to remain the

* Main character in Tschernichovsky's poem of that name, dealing with a pogrom in Mainz.

241

last of the tribe: blood can be avenged only by blood. Afterward—Allah would have mercy. . . .

I would seek out Bubi, take him aside, and give it to him straight from the shoulder, explaining what happened the night before, too. "Come on, Bubi," I'd say, "the two of us, let's go to the first house, the first family, without another word. Forget all the others, but at least the two of us will know we shed blood this side of the border. Everybody's tight-lipped, they all know this night's the last and if we let it slip by, we've lost everything forever. Come on, Bubi."

I didn't find him. Everyone I asked had just seen him—by the chow line, among the tents, at company headquarters. No one knew where he was.

My enthusiasm of the moment before became ludicrous. In my imaginings I had charted out everything to the last detail, but didn't calculate on Bubi's not sitting around waiting for me to show up. Why me all of a sudden? Even when he had been in Company B, before he was transferred, there was nothing between us. And if he had kept his thoughts from Leizi, what would he say were I suddenly to approach him? It was ridiculous, my planning out a murder when it would turn out like the night before, in the kitchen. It was a good thing I didn't find Bubi.

I turned back and slowly walked along the road. A half moon sailed through white clouds. The fires were glimmering softly and flickering out and the men were disappearing into their tents. Such a night always filled me with tender thoughts. Right there, those regions were the background of *Katherine Becomes a Soldier*. I recalled the two heroes, Katherine and her friend—what was his name, Lucienne, I think. I was reminded of Noga, myself, and sadness welled up within me, the same sadness I thought I had gotten over.

It couldn't be possible, I thought, I'll swear on my life Noga couldn't have run after that guy's money or his name, that damn lawyer or whatever the hell he was. That was just small-town gossip that *schmuck* from Jerusalem was spreading and I fell for it. It's just the opposite, Noga always looked on me as a carefree wanderer ready to fly to the end of the world and she didn't want to be a weight around my neck. She wrote me only so I should deny it, so I should write her again and tell her straight out, passionately, "You Noga, only you, no one but you." And I had taken offense. Now I would write. As soon as we reached our destination I would sit down and write. No, I wouldn't just write, I'd submit my request for a discharge for family reasons right away. I had the doctor's certificate. I had to write home to have my parents go to the military authorities in *Aretz* with a real tear-jerker of a story. Noga, I thought, I want you, I'll fight for you, you'll see, you'll understand. I would send Hershler's belongings to his aunt in Beth Israel, but I would keep his books. The next day, as soon as we settled down anywhere, I would begin studying and do nothing else. I wanted to forget all that had taken place in the interim, wanted to go back to Noga, to pure love, to my world, a thousand years back. . . .

"Prick!"

The cry hit me suddenly along with a blow beneath my ear. As I bent over and raised my hand, I was kicked in the rear and fell forward. I recognized the voice; it was one of the three men I had chased away, rifle in hand.

"Fuckin' nurse, gonna protect German girls, huh?"

Again his boot landed on me, but now my head was clear, every muscle tense. I had nothing to protect myself with and I didn't want to expose my face. Pretending I was terrified I shielded my head with my hands, looking all the while at his legs. He made the predictable mistake of circling me, hoping to kick me where it would hurt most. The minute I saw him raise his left boot I sprang for it with all my might. While he struggled to regain his balance with my body wrapped around his right leg, I freed my right hand and with a swift upward thrust slammed my fist into his groin. He screamed in agony. As he doubled over to protect himself, I sprang to my feet and rammed my head into his face the way I learned to do as a kid from the Yemenites at the edge of our neighborhood. I was furious, mad enough to kill, just like years before in school when I had to defend myself against kids bigger than me. My movements were clear cut and murderous; I had only one desire: to drown all my hurt in his body.

"Lemme alone, idiot, I'll kill you, lemme alone—"

243

He was half crying, but that didn't stir up any pity in me. To the contrary, a blind urge to crush him swept over me.

"Fucking nurse, eh?" I whispered as I leaped on top of him, pounding away with short punches, "fucking nurse, eh? . . ."

"Lemme alone, I tell you, lemme alone . . ." His voice creaked like a piece of furniture coming apart. I began to feel my body going empty as if I was suddenly all worn out. The fellow lay on his back covering his face with his forearms and I sat on his belly, my knees pressing against his chest. An open army truck filled with soldiers and girls passed by on the road, leaving a trail of drunken songs behind them. I was sick of the whole thing. It was a good thing there were no witnesses to that shameful fistfight. Why hadn't I let him beat me up for the preceding night, for everything?

I got off him and turned back toward our company. As he lay stretched out on the ground, before he could come to himself, he cried after me, "Wait, you'll be sorry, you'll be sorry . . ."

I was sorry already. I didn't turn around. The dry blows were imprinted on my body and my insides were empty; but at the same time I felt somewhat lighter, happier even at the exhaustion that fell upon me. A few drivers stood at the entrance to our company area fixing one truck by the headlights of another. To the side sat Tamari, who had appropriated a lamp and was writing away in his notebook, as ever. What was he writing, goddamnit? What did he understand?

When the light fell on me, Tamari noticed me, and before I could slip back into the darkness he saw that something had happened.

"Kruk," he called, rising to his feet and hurrying after me, "what happened to you?"

"What happened to me?"

"Somebody hit you, Kruk!"

"Nobody hit me." Tamari and his black notebook and wooden clipboard made me sick. The history he was writing made me sick. I turned my back on him and strode toward the bivouac. He hurried after me and grabbed me.

"Kruk, I insist that you tell me the truth. Who hurt you? You're shaking all over."

244

"I'm shaking because I hit somebody else, if you must know."

I had never spoken to Tamari about anything serious. But now the words came of themselves. "I don't understand—" he began. I cut him off.

"If you don't understand, then what are you writing about all the time?" Tamari released me, taken aback. "You did a terrible thing to us there, Tamari."

"A terrible thing? What are you talking about?"

"About the identification parade, that's what. About Bubi and Hershler. About all of us."

"Kruk, you're—"

"I'm perfectly all right. Didn't you have any nightmares after that parade, Tamari?"

"No, definitely not. Kruk, come here, sit down a minute . . ."

"I want to go to sleep." I strode toward the bivouac with Tamari at my heels. He spoke on and on, but I refused to listen. Only then did my body really begin to ache and my knees tremble.

"You don't want to hear me out?" asked Tamari.

"I have already. Myself, too. Write in that notebook of yours that weaklings have no choice. Write that we remained Jews. Write that the memory of all this will keep coming back at us like a boomerang. We know all the rest."

I got down on all fours and crawled into the tent. Brodsky was snoring already. I crept beneath the blankets fully dressed, sweating, praying I would find myself beyond the few hours separating us from the border. God help my sick heart. I could not shed innocent blood, I would never know peace.

7

The next afternoon we were in France. Everything looked different: a miners' village climbing up a mountain, winding streets, ourselves. A mighty shout swept from one truck to the next. We sang *"Heveinu Shalom Aleichem."* * We found the

* "We brought peace upon you."

245

carton of candy and rained some on every passer-by. We whistled at the legs of the girls. I was nineteen, all in all, with my whole life before me. A girl stood at the crossroads twirling an open parasol. An arrow pointed to Paris: so many kilometers to go. Everything was going back to normal. So it seemed.

If only I could forget that trip, forget how I was stripped naked in my weakness. I will never return there, I whispered to my bleeding memory, but as I spoke, my thoughts turned to pillars of salt. And still I whisper over that memory, over that blood: *Thank God I did not destroy myself in Germany, thank God that was beyond me. I am what I am.*